SUPERNATURAL DETECTIVES

1

SUPERNATURAL DETECTIVES

1

CARNACKI: GHOST FINDER

William Hope Hodgson

JOHN BELL: GHOST EXPOSER

L. T. Meade and Robert Eustace

COACHWHIP PUBLICATIONS

Landisville, Pennsylvania

CARNACKI:
GHOST FINDER

John Bell: Ghost Exposer

CARNACKI:
GHOST FINDER

THE GATEWAY OF THE MONSTER

In response to Carnacki's usual card of invitation to have dinner and listen to a story, I arrived promptly at 427, Cheyne Walk, to find the three others who were always invited to these happy little times, there before me. Five minutes later, Carnacki, Arkright, Jessop, Taylor, and I were all engaged in the "pleasant occupation" of dining.

"You've not been long away, this time," I remarked, as I finished my soup; forgetting momentarily Carnacki's dislike of being asked even to skirt the borders of his story until such time as he was ready. Then he would not stint words.

"That's all," he replied, with brevity; and I changed the subject, remarking that I had been buying a new gun, to which piece of news he gave an intelligent nod, and a smile which I think showed a genuinely good-humored appreciation of my intentional changing of the conversation.

Later, when dinner was finished, Carnacki snugged himself comfortably down in his big chair, along with his pipe, and began his story, with very little circumlocution:—

"As Dodgson was remarking just now, I've only been away a short time, and for a very good reason too—I've only been away a short distance. The exact locality I am afraid I must not tell you; but it is less than twenty miles from here; though, except for changing a name, that won't spoil the story. And it is a story too! One of the most extraordinary things ever I have run against.

"I received a letter a fortnight ago from a man I must call Anderson, asking for an appointment. I arranged a time, and when he came, I found that he wished me to investigate and see whether I could not clear up a long-standing and well—too well—authenticated case of what he termed 'haunting.' He gave me very full particulars, and, finally, as the case seemed to present something unique, I decided to take it up.

"Two days later, I drove to the house late in the afternoon. I found it a very old place, standing quite alone in its own grounds. Anderson had left a letter with the butler, I found, pleading excuses for his absence, and leaving the whole house at my disposal for my investigations. The butler evidently knew the object of my visit, and I questioned him pretty thoroughly during dinner, which I had in rather lonely state. He is an old and privileged servant, and had the history of the Grey Room exact in detail. From him I learned more particulars regarding two things that Anderson had mentioned in but a casual manner. The first was that the door of the Grey Room would be heard in the dead of night to open, and slam heavily, and this even though the butler knew it was locked, and the key on the bunch in his pantry. The second was that the bedclothes would always be found torn off the bed, and hurled in a heap into a corner.

"But it was the door slamming that chiefly bothered the old butler. Many and many a time, he told me, had he lain awake and just got shivering with fright, listening; for sometimes the door would be slammed time after time—thud! thud! thud!—so that sleep was impossible.

"From Anderson, I knew already that the room had a history extending back over a hundred and fifty years. Three people had been strangled in it—an ancestor of his and his wife and child. This is authentic, as I had taken very great pains to discover; so that you can imagine it was with a feeling I had a striking case to investigate that I went upstairs after dinner to have a look at the Grey Room.

"Peter, the old butler, was in rather a state about my going, and assured me with much solemnity that in all the twenty years of his service, no one had ever entered that room after nightfall. He begged me, in quite a fatherly way, to wait till the morning, when there would be no danger, and then he could accompany me himself.

"Of course, I smiled a little at him, and told him not to bother. I explained that I should do no more than look 'round a bit, and, perhaps, affix a few seals. He need not fear; I was used to that sort of thing. But he shook his head when I said that.

"'There isn't many ghosts like ours, sir,' he assured me, with mournful pride. And, by Jove! he was right, as you will see.

"I took a couple of candles, and Peter followed with his bunch of keys. He unlocked the door; but would not come inside with me. He was evidently in a fright, and he renewed his request that I would put off my examination until daylight. Of course, I laughed at him again, and told him he could stand sentry at the door, and catch anything that came out.

"'It never comes outside, sir,' he said, in his funny, old, solemn manner. Somehow, he managed to make me feel as if I were going to have the 'creeps' right away. Anyway, it was one to him, you know.

"I left him there, and examined the room. It is a big apartment, and well furnished in the grand style, with a huge four-poster, which stands with its head to the end wall. There were two candles on the mantelpiece, and two on each of the three tables that were in the room. I lit the lot, and after that, the room felt a little less inhumanly dreary; though, mind you, it was quite fresh, and well kept in every way.

"After I had taken a good look 'round, I sealed lengths of baby ribbon across the windows, along the walls, over the pictures, and over the fireplace and the wall closets. All the time, as I worked, the butler stood just without the door, and I could not persuade him to enter; though I jested him a little, as I stretched the ribbons, and went here and there about my work. Every now and again, he would say:— 'You'll excuse me, I'm sure, sir; but I do wish you would come out, sir. I'm fair in a quake for you.'

"I told him he need not wait; but he was loyal enough in his way to what he considered his duty. He said he could not go away and leave me all alone there. He apologized, but made it very clear that I did not realize the danger of the room; and I could see, generally, that he was in a pretty frightened state. All the same, I had to make the room so that I should know if anything material entered it; so I asked him not to bother me, unless he really heard or saw something. He was beginning to get on my nerves, and the 'feel' of the room was bad enough, without making it any nastier.

"For a time further, I worked, stretching ribbons across the floor, and sealing them, so that the merest touch would have broken them, were anyone to venture into the room in the dark with the intention of playing the fool. All this had taken me far longer than I had anticipated; and, suddenly, I heard a clock strike eleven. I had taken off my coat soon after commencing work; now, however, as I had practically made an end of all that I intended to do, I walked across to the settee, and picked it up. I was in the act of getting into it, when the old butler's voice (he had not said a word for the last hour) came sharp and frightened:— 'Come out, sir, quick! There's something going to happen!' Jove! but I jumped, and then, in the same moment, one of the candles on the table to the left went out. Now whether it was the wind, or what, I do not know; but, just for a moment, I was enough startled to make a run for the door; though I am glad to say that I pulled up, before I reached it. I simply could not bunk out, with the butler standing there, after having, as it were, read him a sort of lesson on 'bein' brave, y'know.' So I just turned right 'round, picked up the two candles off the mantelpiece, and walked across to the table near the bed. Well, I saw nothing. I blew out the candle that was still alight; then I went to those on the two tables, and blew them out. Then, outside of the door, the old man called again:— 'Oh! sir, do be told! Do be told!'

"'All right, Peter,' I said, and by Jove, my voice was not as steady as I should have liked! I made for the door, and had a bit of work not to start running. I took some thundering long strides, as you can imagine. Near the door, I had a sudden feeling that there was a cold wind in the room. It was almost as if the window had been suddenly opened a little. I got to the door, and the old butler gave back a step, in a sort of instinctive way. 'Collar the candles, Peter!' I said, pretty sharply, and shoved them into his hands. I turned, and caught the handle, and slammed the door shut, with a crash. Somehow, do you know, as I did so, I thought I felt something pull back on it; but it must have been only fancy. I turned the key in the lock, and then again, double-locking the door. I felt easier then, and set-to and sealed the door. In addition, I put my card over the keyhole, and sealed it there; after which I pocketed the key, and went downstairs—with Peter; who was nervous and silent, leading the way. Poor old beggar! It had not struck me until that moment that he had been enduring a considerable strain during the last two or three hours.

"About midnight, I went to bed. My room lay at the end of the corridor upon which opens the door of the Grey Room. I counted the doors between it and mine, and found that five rooms lay between. And I am sure you can understand that I was not sorry. Then, just as I was beginning to undress, an idea came to me, and I took my candle and sealing wax, and sealed the doors of all five rooms. If any door slammed in the night, I should know just which one.

"I returned to my room, locked the door, and went to bed. I was waked suddenly from a deep sleep by a loud crash somewhere out in the passage. I sat up in bed, and listened, but heard nothing. Then I lit my candle. I was in the very act of lighting it when there came the bang of a door being violently slammed along the corridor. I jumped out of bed, and got my revolver. I unlocked the door, and went out into the passage, holding my candle high, and keeping the pistol ready. Then a queer thing happened. I could not go a step toward the Grey Room. You all know I am not really a cowardly chap. I've gone into too many cases connected with ghostly things, to be accused of that; but I tell you I funked it, simply funked it, just like any blessed kid. There was something precious unholy in the air that night. I ran back into my bedroom, and shut and locked the door. Then I sat on the bed all night, and listened to the dismal thudding of a door up the corridor. The sound seemed to echo through all the house.

"Daylight came at last, and I washed and dressed. The door had not slammed for about an hour, and I was getting back my nerve again. I felt ashamed of myself; though, in some ways it was silly; for when you're meddling with that sort of thing, your nerve is bound to go, sometimes. And you just have to sit quiet and call yourself a coward until daylight. Sometimes it is more than just cowardice, I fancy. I believe at times it is something warning you, and fighting *for* you. But, all the same, I always feel mean and miserable, after a time like that.

"When the day came properly, I opened my door, and, keeping my revolver handy, went quietly along the passage. I had to pass the head of the stairs on the way, and who should I see coming up, but the old butler, carrying a cup of coffee. He had merely tucked his nightshirt into his trousers, and he had an old pair of carpet slippers on.

"'Hullo, Peter!' I said, feeling suddenly cheerful; for I was as glad as any lost child to have a live human being close to me. 'Where are you off to with the refreshments?'

"The old man gave a start, and slopped some of the coffee. He stared up at me, and I could see that he looked white and done-up. He came on up the stairs, and held out the little tray to me. 'I'm very thankful indeed, sir, to see you safe and well,' he said. 'I feared, one time, you might risk going into the Grey Room, sir. I've lain awake all night, with the sound of the Door. And when it came light, I thought I'd make you a cup of coffee. I knew you would want to look at the seals, and somehow it seems safer if there's two, sir.'

"'Peter,' I said, 'you're a brick. This is very thoughtful of you.' And I drank the coffee. 'Come along,' I told him, and handed him back the tray. 'I'm going to have a look at what the Brutes have been up to. I simply hadn't the pluck to in the night.'

"'I'm very thankful, sir,' he replied. 'Flesh and blood can do nothing, sir, against devils; and that's what's in the Grey Room after dark.'

"I examined the seals on all the doors, as I went along, and found them right; but when I got to the Grey Room, the seal was broken, though the card, over the keyhole, was untouched. I ripped it off, and unlocked the door, and went in, rather cautiously, as you can imagine; but the whole room was empty of anything to frighten one, and there was heaps of light. I examined all my seals, and not a single one was disturbed. The old butler had followed me in, and, suddenly, he called out:— 'The bedclothes, sir!'

"I ran up to the bed, and looked over; and, surely, they were lying in the corner to the left of the bed. Jove! you can imagine how queer I felt. Something *had* been in the room. I stared for a while, from the bed, to the clothes on the floor. I had a feeling that I did not want to touch either. Old Peter, though, did not seem to be affected that way. He went over to the bed coverings, and was going to pick them up, as, doubtless, he had done every day these twenty years back; but I stopped him. I wanted nothing touched, until I had finished my examination. This, I must have spent a full hour over, and then I let Peter straighten up the bed; after which we went out, and I locked the door; for the room was getting on my nerves.

"I had a short walk, and then breakfast; after which I felt more my own man, and so returned to the Grey Room, and, with Peter's help, and one of the maids, I had everything taken out of the room, except the bed—even the very pictures. I examined the walls, floor and ceiling then, with probe, hammer and magnifying glass; but found nothing suspicious. And I can assure you, I began to realize, in very truth, that some incredible thing had been loose in the room during the past night. I sealed up everything again, and went out, locking and sealing the door, as before.

"After dinner, Peter and I unpacked some of my stuff, and I fixed up my camera and flashlight opposite to the door of the Grey Room, with a string from the trigger of the flashlight to the door. Then, you see, if the door were really opened, the flashlight would blare out, and there would be, possibly, a very queer picture to examine in the morning. The last thing I did, before leaving, was to uncap the lens; and after that I went off to my bedroom, and to bed; for I intended to be up at midnight; and to ensure this, I set my little alarm to call me; also I left my candle burning.

"The clock woke me at twelve, and I got up and into my dressing gown and slippers. I shoved my revolver into my right side-pocket, and opened my door. Then, I lit my darkroom lamp, and withdrew the slide, so that it would give a clear light. I carried it up the corridor, about thirty feet, and put it down on the floor, with the open side away from me, so that it would show me anything that might approach along the dark passage. Then I went back, and sat in the doorway of my room, with my revolver handy, staring up the passage toward the place where I knew my camera stood outside the door of the Grey Room.

"I should think I had watched for about an hour and a half, when, suddenly, I heard a faint noise, away up the corridor. I was immediately conscious of a queer prickling sensation about the back of my head, and my hands began to sweat a little. The following instant, the whole end of the passage flicked into sight in the abrupt glare of the flashlight. There came the succeeding darkness, and I peered nervously up the corridor, listening tensely, and trying to find what lay beyond the faint glow of my dark-lamp, which now seemed ridiculously dim by contrast with the tremendous blaze of the flash-power. . . . And then, as I stooped forward, staring and listening, there came the crashing thud of the door of the Grey Room. The sound seemed to fill the whole of the large corridor, and go echoing hollowly through the house. I tell you, I felt horrible—as if my bones were water. Simply beastly. Jove! how I did stare, and how I listened. And then it came again—thud, thud, thud, and then a silence that was almost worse than the noise of the door; for I kept fancying that some awful thing was stealing upon me along the corridor. And then, suddenly, my lamp was put out, and I could not see a yard before me. I realized all at once that I was doing a very silly thing, sitting there, and I jumped up. Even as I did so, I *thought* I heard a sound in the passage, and quite *near* me. I made one backward spring into my room, and slammed and locked the door. I sat on my bed, and stared at the door. I had my revolver in my hand, but it seemed an abominably useless thing. I felt that there was something the other side of that door. For some unknown reason I *knew* it was pressed up against the door, and it was soft. That was just what I thought. Most extraordinary thing to think.

"Presently I got hold of myself a bit, and marked out a pentacle hurriedly with chalk on the polished floor; and there I sat in it almost until dawn. And all the time, away up the corridor, the door of the Grey Room thudded at solemn and horrid intervals. It was a miserable, brutal night.

"When the day began to break, the thudding of the door came gradually to an end, and, at last, I got hold of my courage, and went along the corridor in the half light to cap the lens of my camera. I can tell you, it took some doing; but if I had not done so my photograph would have been spoilt, and I was tremendously keen to save it. I got back to my room, and then set-to and rubbed out the five-pointed star in which I had been sitting.

"Half an hour later there was a tap at my door. It was Peter with my coffee. When I had drunk it, we both went along to the Grey Room. As we went, I had a look at the seals on the other doors; but they were untouched. The seal on the door of the Grey Room was broken, as also was the string from the trigger of the flashlight; but the card over the keyhole was still there. I ripped it off, and opened the door. Nothing unusual was to be seen until we came to the bed; then I saw that, as on the previous day, the bedclothes had been torn off, and hurled into the left-hand corner, exactly where I had seen them before. I felt very queer; but I did not forget to look at all the seals, only to find that not one had been broken.

"Then I turned and looked at old Peter, and he looked at me, nodding his head.

"'Let's get out of here!' I said. 'It's no place for any living human to enter, without proper protection.'

"We went out then, and I locked and sealed the door, again.

"After breakfast, I developed the negative; but it showed only the door of the Grey Room, half opened. Then I left the house, as I wanted to get certain matters and implements that might be necessary to life, perhaps to the spirit, for I intended to spend the coming night in the Grey Room.

"I got back in a cab, about half-past five, with my apparatus, and this, Peter and I carried up to the Grey Room, where I piled it carefully in the center of the floor. When everything was in the room, including a cat which I had brought, I locked and sealed the door, and went toward the bedroom, telling Peter I should not be down for dinner. He said, 'Yes, sir,' and went downstairs, thinking that I was going to turn in, which was what I wanted him to believe, as I knew he would have worried both me and himself, if he had known what I intended.

"But I merely got my camera and flashlight from my bedroom, and hurried back to the Grey Room. I locked and sealed myself in, and set to work, for I had a lot to do before it got dark.

"First, I cleared away all the ribbons across the floor; then I carried the cat—still fastened in its basket—over toward the far wall, and left it. I returned then to the center of the room, and measured out a space twenty-one feet in diameter, which I swept with a 'broom of hyssop.' About this, I drew a circle of chalk, taking care never to step over the circle. Beyond this I smudged, with a bunch of garlic, a broad belt right around the chalked circle, and when this was complete, I took from among my stores in the center a small jar of a certain water. I broke away the parchment, and withdrew the stopper. Then, dipping my left forefinger in the little jar, I went 'round the circle again, making upon the floor, just within the line of chalk, the Second Sign of the Saaamaaa Ritual, and joining each Sign most carefully with the left-handed crescent. I can tell you, I felt easier when this was done, and the 'water circle' complete. Then, I unpacked some more of the stuff that I had brought, and placed a lighted candle in the 'valley' of each Crescent. After that, I drew a Pentacle, so that each of the five points of the defensive star touched the chalk circle. In the five points of the star I placed five portions of the bread, each wrapped in linen, and in the five 'vales,' five opened jars of the water I had used to make the 'water circle.' And now I had my first protective barrier complete.

"Now, anyone, except you who know something of my methods of investigation, might consider all this a piece of useless and foolish superstition; but you all remember the Black Veil case, in which I believe my life was saved by a very similar form of protection, whilst Aster, who sneered at it, and would not come inside, died. I got the idea from the Sigsand MS., written, so far as I can make out, in the 14th century. At first, naturally, I imagined it was just an expression of the superstition of his time; and it was not until a year later that it occurred to me to test his 'Defense,' which I did, as I've just said, in that horrible Black Veil business. You know how *that* turned out. Later, I used it several times, and always I came through safe, until that Moving Fur case. It was only a partial 'defense' therefore, and I nearly died in the pentacle. After that I came across Professor Garder's 'Experiments with a Medium.' When they surrounded the Medium with a current, in vacuum, he lost his power—almost as if it cut him off from the Immaterial. That made me think a lot; and that is how I came to make the Electric Pentacle, which is a most marvelous 'Defense' against certain manifestations. I used the shape of the defensive star for this protection, because I have, personally, no doubt at all but that there is some extraordinary virtue in the old magic figure. Curious thing for a Twentieth Century man to admit, is it not? But, then, as you all know, I never did, and never will, allow myself to be blinded by the little cheap laughter. I ask questions, and keep my eyes open.

"In this last case I had little doubt that I had run up against a supernatural monster, and I meant to take every possible care; for the danger is abominable.

"I turned-to now to fit the Electric Pentacle, setting it so that each of its 'points' and 'vales' coincided exactly with the 'points' and 'vales' of the drawn pentagram upon the floor. Then I connected up the battery, and the next instant the pale blue glare from the intertwining vacuum tubes shone out.

"I glanced about me then, with something of a sigh of relief, and realized suddenly that the dusk was upon me, for the window was grey and unfriendly. Then 'round at the big, empty room, over the double barrier of electric and candle light. I had an abrupt, extraordinary sense of weirdness thrust upon me—in the air, you know; as it were, a sense of something inhuman impending. The room was full of the stench of bruised garlic, a smell I hate.

"I turned now to the camera, and saw that it and the flashlight were in order. Then I tested my revolver, carefully, though I had little thought that it would be needed. Yet, to what extent materialization of an ab-natural creature is possible, given favorable conditions, no one can say; and I had no idea what horrible thing I was going to see, or feel the presence of. I might, in the end, have to fight with a materialized monster. I did not know, and could only be prepared. You see, I never forgot that three other people had been strangled in the bed close to me, and the fierce slamming of the door I had heard myself. I had no doubt that I was investigating a dangerous and ugly case.

"By this time, the night had come; though the room was very light with the burning candles; and I found myself glancing behind me, constantly, and then all 'round the room. It was nervy work waiting for that thing to come. Then, suddenly, I was aware of a little, cold wind sweeping over me, coming from behind. I gave one great nerve-thrill, and a prickly feeling went all over the back of my head. Then I hove myself 'round with a sort of stiff jerk, and stared straight against that queer wind. It seemed to come from the corner of the room to the left of the bed—the place where both times I had found the heap of tossed bedclothes. Yet, I could see nothing unusual; no opening—nothing! . . .

"Abruptly, I was aware that the candles were all a-flicker in that unnatural wind. . . . I believe I just squatted there and stared in a horribly frightened, wooden way for some minutes. I shall never be able to let you know how disgustingly horrible it was sitting in that vile, cold wind! And then, flick! flick! flick! all the candles 'round the outer barrier went out; and there was I, locked and sealed in that room, and with no light beyond the weakish blue glare of the Electric Pentacle.

"A time of abominable tenseness passed, and still that wind blew upon me; and then, suddenly, I knew that something stirred in the corner to the left of the bed. I was made conscious of it, rather by some inward, unused sense than by either sight or sound; for the pale, short-radius glare of the Pentacle gave but a very poor light for seeing by. Yet, as I stared, something began slowly to grow upon my sight—a moving shadow, a little darker than the surrounding shadows. I lost the thing amid the vagueness, and for a moment or two I glanced swiftly from side to side, with a fresh, new sense of impending danger. Then my attention was directed to the bed. All the coverings were being drawn steadily off, with a hateful, stealthy sort of motion. I heard the slow, dragging slither of the clothes; but I could see nothing of the thing that pulled. I was aware in a funny, subconscious, introspective fashion that the 'creep' had come upon me; yet that I was cooler mentally than I had been for some minutes; sufficiently so to feel that my hands were sweating coldly, and to shift my revolver, half-consciously, whilst I rubbed my right hand dry upon my knee; though never, for an instant, taking my gaze or my attention from those moving clothes.

"The faint noises from the bed ceased once, and there was a most intense silence, with only the sound of the blood beating in my head. Yet, immediately afterward, I heard again the slurring of the bedclothes being dragged off the bed. In the midst of my nervous tension I remembered the camera, and reached 'round for it; but without looking away from the bed. And then, you know, all in a moment, the whole of the bed coverings were torn off with extraordinary violence, and I heard the flump they made as they were hurled into the corner.

"There was a time of absolute quietness then for perhaps a couple of minutes; and you can imagine how horrible I felt. The bedclothes had been thrown with such savageness! And, then again, the brutal unnaturalness of the thing that had just been done before me!

"Abruptly, over by the door, I heard a faint noise—a sort of crickling sound, and then a pitter or two upon the floor. A great nervous thrill swept over me, seeming to run up my spine and over the back of my head; for the seal that secured the door had just been broken. Something was there. I could not see the door; at least, I mean to say that it was impossible to say how much I actually saw, and how much my imagination supplied. I made it out, only as a continuation of the grey walls. . . . And then it seemed to me that something dark and indistinct moved and wavered there among the shadows.

"Abruptly, I was aware that the door was opening, and with an effort I reached again for my camera; but before I could aim it the door was slammed with a terrific crash that filled the whole room with a sort of hollow thunder. I jumped, like a frightened child. There seemed such a power behind the noise; as though a vast, wanton Force were 'out.' Can you understand?

"The door was not touched again; but, directly afterward, I heard the basket, in which the cat lay, creak. I tell you, I fairly pringled all along my back. I knew that I was going to learn definitely whether whatever was abroad was dangerous to Life. From the cat there rose suddenly a hideous caterwaul, that ceased abruptly; and then—too late—I snapped off the flashlight. In the great glare, I saw that the basket had been overturned, and the lid was wrenched open, with the cat lying half in, and half out upon the floor. I saw nothing else, but I was full of the knowledge that I was in the presence of some Being or Thing that had power to destroy.

"During the next two or three minutes, there was an odd, noticeable quietness in the room, and you much remember I was half-blinded, for the time, because of the flashlight; so that the whole place seemed to be pitchy dark just beyond the shine of the Pentacle. I tell you it was most horrible. I just knelt there in the star, and whirled 'round, trying to see whether anything was coming at me.

"My power of sight came gradually, and I got a little hold of myself; and abruptly I saw the thing I was looking for, close to the 'water circle.' It was big and indistinct, and wavered curiously, as though the shadow of a vast spider hung suspended in the air, just beyond the barrier. It passed swiftly 'round the circle, and seemed to probe ever toward me; but only to draw back with extraordinary jerky movements, as might a living person if they touched the hot bar of a grate.

"'Round and 'round it moved, and 'round and 'round I turned. Then, just opposite to one of the vales in the pentacles, it seemed to pause, as though preliminary to a tremendous effort. It retired almost beyond the glow of the vacuum light, and then came straight toward me, appearing to gather form and solidity as it came. There seemed a vast, malign determination behind the movement, that must succeed. I was on my knees, and I jerked back, falling on to my left hand and hip, in a wild endeavor to get back from the advancing thing. With my right hand I was grabbing madly for my revolver, which I had let slip. The brutal thing came with one great sweep straight over the garlic and the 'water circle,' almost to the vale of the pentacle. I believe I yelled. Then, just as suddenly as it had swept over, it seemed to be hurled back by some mighty, invisible force.

"It must have been some moments before I realized that I was safe; and then I got myself together in the middle of the pentacles, feeling horribly gone and shaken, and glancing 'round and 'round the barrier; but the thing had vanished. Yet, I had learnt something, for I knew now that the Grey Room was haunted by a monstrous hand.

"Suddenly, as I crouched there, I saw what had so nearly given the monster an opening through the barrier. In my movements within the pentacle I must have touched one of the jars of water; for just where the thing had made its attack the jar that guarded the 'deep' of the vale had been moved to one side, and this had left one of the 'five doorways' unguarded. I put it back, quickly, and felt almost safe again, for I had found the cause, and the defense was still good. And I began to hope again that I should see the morning come in. When I saw that thing so nearly succeed, I had an awful, weak, overwhelming feeling that the barriers could never bring me safe through the night against such a Force. You can understand?

"For a long time I could not see the hand; but, presently, I thought I saw, once or twice, an odd wavering, over among the shadows near the door. A little later, as though in a sudden fit of malignant rage, the dead body of the cat was picked up, and beaten with dull, sickening blows against the solid floor. That made me feel rather queer.

"A minute afterward, the door was opened and slammed twice with tremendous force. The next instant the thing made one swift, vicious dart at me, from out of the shadows. Instinctively, I started sideways from it, and so plucked my hand from upon the Electric

Pentacle, where—for a wickedly careless moment—I had placed it. The monster was hurled off from the neighborhood of the pentacles; though—owing to my inconceivable foolishness—it had been enabled for a second time to pass the outer barriers. I can tell you, I shook for a time, with sheer funk. I moved right to the center of the pentacles again, and knelt there, making myself as small and compact as possible.

"As I knelt, there came to me presently, a vague wonder at the two 'accidents' which had so nearly allowed the brute to get at me. Was I being *influenced* to unconscious voluntary actions that endangered me? The thought took hold of me, and I watched my every movement. Abruptly, I stretched a tired leg, and knocked over one of the jars of water. Some was spilled; but, because of my suspicious watchfulness, I had it upright and back within the vale while yet some of the water remained. Even as I did so, the vast, black, half-materialized hand beat up at me out of the shadows, and seemed to leap almost into my face; so nearly did it approach; but for the third time it was thrown back by some altogether enormous, overmastering force. Yet, apart from the dazed fright in which it left me, I had for a moment that feeling of spiritual sickness, as if some delicate, beautiful, inward grace had suffered, which is felt only upon the too near approach of the ab-human, and is more dreadful, in a strange way, than any physical pain that can be suffered. I knew by this more of the extent and closeness of the danger; and for a long time I was simply cowed by the butt-headed brutality of that Force upon my spirit. I can put it no other way.

"I knelt again in the center of the pentacles, watching myself with more fear, almost, than the monster; for I knew now that, unless I guarded myself from every sudden impulse that came to me, I might simply work my own destruction. Do you see how horrible it all was?

"I spent the rest of the night in a haze of sick fright, and so tense that I could not make a single movement naturally. I was in such fear that any desire for action that came to me might be prompted by the Influence that I knew was at work on me. And outside of the barrier that ghastly thing went 'round and 'round, grabbing and grabbing in the air at me. Twice more was the body of the dead cat molested. The second time, I heard every bone in its body scrunch and crack. And all the time the horrible wind was blowing upon me from the corner of the room to the left of the bed.

"Then, just as the first touch of dawn came into the sky, that unnatural wind ceased, in a single moment; and I could see no sign of the hand. The dawn came slowly, and presently the wan light filled all the room, and made the pale glare of the Electric Pentacle look more unearthly. Yet, it was not until the day had fully come, that I made any attempt to leave the barrier, for I did not know but that there was some method abroad, in the sudden stopping of that wind, to entice me from the pentacles.

"At last, when the dawn was strong and bright, I took one last look 'round, and ran for the door. I got it unlocked, in a nervous and clumsy fashion, then locked it hurriedly, and went to my bedroom, where I lay on the bed, and tried to steady my nerves. Peter came, presently, with the coffee, and when I had drunk it, I told him I meant to have a sleep, as I had been up all night. He took the tray, and went out quietly, and after I had locked my door I turned in properly, and at last got to sleep.

"I woke about midday, and after some lunch, went up to the Grey Room. I switched off the current from the Pentacle, which I had left on in my hurry; also, I removed the body of the cat. You can understand I did not want anyone to see the poor brute. After that, I made a very careful search of the corner where the bedclothes had been thrown. I made several holes, and probed, and found nothing. Then it occurred to me to try with my instrument under the skirting. I did so, and heard my wire ring on metal. I turned the hook end that way, and fished for the thing. At the second go, I got it. It was a small object, and I took it to the window. I found it to be a curious ring, made of some greying material. The curious thing about it was that it was made in the form of a pentagon; that is, the same shape as the inside of the magic pentacle, but without the 'mounts,' which form the points of the defensive star. It was free from all chasing or engraving.

"You will understand that I was excited, when I tell you that I felt sure I held in my hand the famous Luck Ring of the Anderson family; which, indeed, was of all things the one most intimately connected with the history of the haunting. This ring was handed on from father to son through generations, and always—in obedience to some ancient family tradition—each son had to promise never to wear the ring. The ring, I may say, was brought home by one of the Crusaders, under very peculiar circumstances; but the story is too long to go into here.

"It appears that young Sir Hulbert, an ancestor of Anderson's, made a bet, in drink, you know, that he would wear the ring that night. He did so, and in the morning his wife and child were found strangled in the bed, in the very room in which I stood. Many people, it would seem, thought young Sir Hulbert was guilty of having done the thing in drunken anger; and he, in an attempt to prove his innocence, slept a second night in the room. He also was strangled. Since then, as you may imagine, no one has ever spent a night in the Grey Room, until I did so. The ring had been lost so long, that it had become almost a myth; and it was most extraordinary to stand there, with the actual thing in my hand, as you can understand.

"It was whilst I stood there, looking at the ring, that I got an idea. Supposing that it were, in a way, a doorway—you see what I mean? A sort of gap in the world-hedge. It was a queer idea, I know, and probably was not my own, but came to me from the Outside. You see, the wind had come from that part of the room where the ring lay. I thought a lot about it. Then the shape—the inside of a pentacle. It had no 'mounts,' and without mounts, as the Sigsand MS. has it:— 'Thee mownts wych are thee Five Hills of safetie. To lack is to gyve pow'r to thee daemon; and surelie to fayvor the Evill Thynge.' You see, the very shape of the ring was significant; and I determined to test it.

"I unmade the pentacle, for it must be made afresh *and around* the one to be protected. Then I went out and locked the door; after which I left the house, to get certain matters, for neither 'yarbs nor fyre nor water' must be used a second time. I returned about seven thirty, and as soon as the things I had brought had been carried up to the Grey Room, I dismissed Peter for the night, just as I had done the evening before. When he had gone downstairs, I let myself into the room, and locked and sealed the door. I went to the place in the center of the room where all the stuff had been packed, and set to work with all my speed to construct a barrier about me and the ring.

"I do not remember whether I explained it to you. But I had reasoned that, if the ring were in any way a 'medium of admission,' and it were enclosed with me in the Electric Pentacle, it would be, to express it loosely, insulated. Do you see? The Force, which had visible expression as a Hand, would have to stay beyond the Barrier which separates the Ab from the Normal; for the 'gateway' would be removed from accessibility.

"As I was saying, I worked with all my speed to get the barrier completed about me and the ring, for it was already later than I cared to be in that room 'unprotected.' Also, I had a feeling that there would be a vast effort made that night to regain the use of the ring. For I had the strongest conviction that the ring was a necessity to materialization. You will see whether I was right.

"I completed the barriers in about an hour, and you can imagine something of the relief I felt when I felt the pale glare of the Electric Pentacle once more all about me. From then, onward, for about two hours, I sat quietly, facing the corner from which the wind came. About eleven o'clock a queer knowledge came that something was near to me; yet nothing happened for a whole hour after that. Then, suddenly, I felt the cold, queer wind begin to blow upon me. To my astonishment, it seemed now to come from behind me, and I whipped 'round, with a hideous quake of fear. The wind met me in the face. It was blowing up from the floor close to me. I stared down, in a sickening maze of new frights. What on earth had I done now! The ring was there, close beside me, where I had put it. Suddenly, as I stared, bewildered, I was aware that there was something queer about the ring—funny shadowy movements and convolutions. I looked at them, stupidly. And then, abruptly, I knew that the wind was blowing up at me from the ring.

A queer indistinct smoke became visible to me, seeming to pour upward through the ring, and mix with the moving shadows. Suddenly, I realized that I was in more than any mortal danger; for the convoluting shadows about the ring were taking shape, and the death-hand was forming *within* the Pentacle. My Goodness! do you realize it! I had brought the 'gateway' into the pentacles, and the brute was coming through—pouring into the material world, as gas might pour out from the mouth of a pipe.

"I should think that I knelt for a moment in a sort of stunned fright. Then, with a mad, awkward movement, I snatched at the ring, intending to hurl it out of the Pentacle. Yet it eluded me, as though some invisible, living thing jerked it hither and thither. At last, I gripped it; yet, in the same instant, it was torn from my grasp with incredible and brutal force. A great, black shadow covered it, and rose into the air, and came at me. I saw that it was the Hand, vast and nearly perfect in form. I gave one crazy yell, and jumped over the Pentacle and the ring of burning candles, and ran despairingly for the door. I fumbled idiotically and ineffectually with the key, and all the time I stared, with a fear that was like insanity, toward the Barriers. The hand was plunging toward me; yet, even as it had been unable to pass into the Pentacle when the ring was without, so, now that the ring was within, it had no power to pass out. The monster was chained, as surely as any beast would be, were chains riveted upon it.

"Even then, I got a flash of this knowledge; but I was too utterly shaken with fright, to reason; and the instant I managed to get the key turned, I sprang into the passage, and slammed the door with a crash. I locked it, and got to my room somehow; for I was trembling so that I could hardly stand, as you can imagine. I locked myself in, and managed to get the candle lit; then I lay down on my bed, and kept quiet for an hour or two, and so I got steadied.

"I got a little sleep, later; but woke when Peter brought my coffee. When I had drunk it I felt altogether better, and took the old man along with me whilst I had a look into the Grey Room. I opened the door, and peeped in. The candles were still burning, wan against the daylight; and behind them was the pale, glowing star of the

Electric Pentacle. And there, in the middle, was the ring . . . the gateway of the monster, lying demure and ordinary.

"Nothing in the room was touched, and I knew that the brute had never managed to cross the Pentacles. Then I went out, and locked the door.

"After a sleep of some hours, I left the house. I returned in the afternoon in a cab. I had with me an oxy-hydrogen jet, and two cylinders, containing the gases. I carried the things into the Grey Room, and there, in the center of the Electric Pentacle, I erected the little furnace. Five minutes later the Luck Ring, once the 'luck,' but now the 'bane,' of the Anderson family, was no more than a little solid splash of hot metal."

Carnacki felt in his pocket, and pulled out something wrapped in tissue paper. He passed it to me. I opened it, and found a small circle of greyish metal, something like lead, only harder and rather brighter.

"Well?" I asked, at length, after examining it and handing it 'round to the others. "Did that stop the haunting?"

Carnacki nodded. "Yes," he said. "I slept three nights in the Grey Room, before I left. Old Peter nearly fainted when he knew that I meant to; but by the third night he seemed to realise that the house was just safe and ordinary. And, you know, I believe, in his heart, he hardly approved."

Carnacki stood up and began to shake hands. "Out you go!" he said, genially. And presently we went, pondering, to our various homes.

THE HOUSE AMONG THE LAURELS

"This is a curious yarn that I am going to tell you," said Carnacki, as after a quiet little dinner we made ourselves comfortable in his cozy dining room.

"I have just got back from the West of Ireland," he continued. "Wentworth, a friend of mine, has lately had rather an unexpected legacy, in the shape of a large estate and manor, about a mile and a half outside of the village of Korunton. This place is named Gannington Manor, and has been empty a great number of years; as you will find is almost always the case with houses reputed to be haunted, as it is usually termed.

"It seems that when Wentworth went over to take possession, he found the place in very poor repair, and the estate totally uncared for, and, as I know, looking very desolate and lonesome generally. He went through the big house by himself, and he admitted to me that it had an uncomfortable feeling about it; but, of course, that might be nothing more than the natural dismalness of a big, empty house, which has been long uninhabited, and through which you are wandering alone.

"When he had finished his look 'round, he went down to the village, meaning to see the one-time Agent of the Estate, and arrange for someone to go in as caretaker. The Agent, who proved by the way to be a Scotchman, was very willing to take up the management of the Estate once more; but he assured Wentworth that they would get no one to go in as caretaker; and that his—the Agent's—advice was to have the house pulled down, and a new one built.

"This, naturally, astonished my friend, and, as they went down to the village, he managed to get a sort of explanation from the man. It seems that there had been always curious stories told about the place, which in the early days was called Landru Castle, and that within the last seven years there had been two extraordinary deaths there. In each case they had been tramps, who were ignorant of the reputation of the house, and had probably thought the big empty place suitable for a night's free lodging. There had been absolutely no signs of violence to indicate the method by which death was caused, and on each occasion the body had been found in the great entrance hall.

"By this time they had reached the inn where Wentworth had put up, and he told the Agent that he would prove that it was all rubbish about the haunting, by staying a night or two in the Manor himself. The death of the tramps was certainly curious; but did not prove that any supernatural agency had been at work. They were but isolated accidents, spread over a large number of years by the memory of the villagers, which was natural enough in a little place like Korunton. Tramps had to die some time, and in some place, and it proved nothing that two, out of possibly hundreds who had slept in the empty house, had happened to take the opportunity to die under shelter.

"But the Agent took his remark very seriously, and both he and Dennis the landlord of the inn, tried their best to persuade him not to go. For his 'sowl's sake,' Irish Dennis begged him to do no such thing; and because of his 'life's sake,' the Scotchman was equally in earnest.

"It was late afternoon at the time, and as Wentworth told me, it was warm and bright, and it seemed such utter rot to hear those two talking seriously about the impossible. He felt full of pluck, and he made up his mind he would smash the story of the haunting at once by staying that very night in the Manor. He made this quite clear to them, and told them that it would be more to the point and to their credit, if they offered to come up along with him, and keep him company. But poor old Dennis was quite shocked, I believe, at the suggestion; and though Tabbit, the Agent, took it more quietly, he was very solemn about it.

"It seems that Wentworth did go; and though, as he said to me, when the evening began to come on, it seemed a very different sort of thing to tackle.

"A whole crowd of the villagers assembled to see him off; for by this time they all knew of his intention. Wentworth had his gun with him, and a big packet of candles; and he made it clear to them all that it would not be wise for anyone to play any tricks; as he intended to shoot 'at sight.' And then, you know, he got a hint of how serious they considered the whole thing; for one of them came up to him, leading a great bullmastiff, and offered it to him, to take to keep him company. Wentworth patted his gun; but the old man who owned the dog shook his head and explained that the brute might warn him in sufficient time for him to get away from the castle. For it was obvious that he did not consider the gun would prove of any use.

"Wentworth took the dog, and thanked the man. He told me that, already, he was beginning to wish that he had not said definitely that he would go; but, as it was, he was simply forced to. He went through the crowd of men, and found suddenly that they had all turned in a body and were keeping him company. They stayed with him all the way to the Manor, and then went right over the whole place with him.

"It was still daylight when this was finished; though turning to dusk; and, for a while, the men stood about, hesitating, as if they felt ashamed to go away and leave Wentworth there all alone. He told me that, by this time, he would gladly have given fifty pounds to be going back with them. And then, abruptly, an idea came to him. He suggested that they should stay with him, and keep him company through the night. For a time they refused, and tried to persuade him to go back with them; but finally he made a proposition that got home to them all. He planned that they should all go back to the inn, and there get a couple of dozen bottles of whisky, a donkey-load of turf and wood, and some more candles. Then they would come back, and make a great fire in the big fire-place, light all the candles, and put them 'round the place, open the whisky and make a night of it. And, by Jove! he got them to agree.

"They set off back, and were soon at the inn, and here, whilst the donkey was being loaded, and the candles and whisky distributed, Dennis was doing his best to keep Wentworth from going back; but he was a sensible man in his way, for when he found that it was no use, he stopped. You see, he did not want to frighten the others from accompanying Wentworth.

"'I tell ye, sorr,' he told him, ''tis of no use at all, thryin' ter reclaim ther castle. 'Tis curst with innocent blood, an' ye'll be betther pullin' it down, an' buildin' a fine new wan. But if ye be intendin' to shtay this night, kape the big dhoor open whide, an' watch for the bhlood-dhrip. If so much as a single dhrip falls, don't shtay though all the gold in the worrld was offered ye.'

"Wentworth asked him what he meant by the blood-drip.

"'Shure,' he said, ''tis the bhlood av thim as ould Black Mick 'way back in the ould days kilt in their shlape. 'Twas a feud as he pretendid to patch up, an' he invited thim—the O'Haras they was—siventy av thim. An' he fed thim, an' shpoke soft to thim, an' thim thrustin' him, sthayed to shlape with him. Thin, he an' thim with him, stharted in an' mhurdered thim was an' all as they slep'. 'Tis from me father's grandfather ye have the sthory. An' sence thin 'tis death to any, so they say, to pass the night in the castle whin the bhlood-dhrip comes. 'Twill put out candle an' fire, an' thin in the darkness the Virgin Herself would be powerless to protect ye.'

"Wentworth told me he laughed at this; chiefly because, as he put it:— 'One always must laugh at that sort of yarn, however it makes you feel inside.' He asked old Dennis whether he expected him to believe it.

"'Yes, sorr,' said Dennis, 'I do mane ye to b'lieve it; an' please God, if ye'll b'lieve, ye may be back safe befor' mornin'.' The man's serious simplicity took hold of Wentworth, and he held out his hand. But, for all that, he went; and I must admire his pluck.

"There were now about forty men, and when they got back to the Manor—or castle as the villagers always call it—they were not long in getting a big fire going, and lighted candles all 'round the great hall. They had all brought sticks; so that they would have been a pretty formidable lot to tackle by anything simply physical; and, of course, Wentworth had his gun. He kept the whisky in his own charge; for he intended to keep them sober; but he gave them a good strong tot all 'round first, so as to make things seem cheerful; and to get them yearning. If you once let a crowd of men like that grow silent, they begin to think, and then to fancy things.

"The big entrance door had been left wide open, by his orders; which shows that he had taken some notice of Dennis. It was a quiet night, so this did not matter, for the lights kept steady, and all went on in a jolly sort of fashion for about three hours. He had opened a second lot of bottles, and everyone was feeling cheerful; so much so that one of the men called out aloud to the ghosts to come out and show themselves. And then, you know a very extraordinary thing happened; for the ponderous main door swung quietly and steadily to, as though pushed by an invisible hand, and shut with a sharp click.

"Wentworth stared, feeling suddenly rather chilly. Then he remembered the men, and looked 'round at them. Several had ceased their talk, and were staring in a frightened way at the big door; but the great number had never noticed, and were talking and yarning. He reached for his gun, and the following instant the great bullmastiff set up a tremendous barking, which drew the attention of the whole company.

"The hall I should tell you is oblong. The south wall is all windows; but the north and east have rows of doors, leading into the house, whilst the west wall is occupied by the great entrance. The rows of doors leading into the house were all closed, and it was toward one of these in the north wall that the big dog ran; yet he would not go very close; and suddenly the door began to move slowly open, until the blackness of the passage beyond was shown. The dog came back among the men, whimpering, and for a minute there was an absolute silence.

"Then Wentworth went out from the men a little, and aimed his gun at the doorway.

"'Whoever is there, come out, or I shall fire,' he shouted; but nothing came, and he blazed forth both barrels into the dark. As though the report had been a signal, all the doors along the north and east walls moved slowly open, and Wentworth and his men were staring, frightened, into the black shapes of the empty doorways.

"Wentworth loaded his gun quickly, and called to the dog; but the brute was burrowing away in among the men; and this fear on the dog's part frightened Wentworth more, he told me, than anything. Then something else happened. Three of the candles over in the corner of the hall went out; and immediately about half a dozen in different parts of the place. More candles were put out, and the hall had become quite dark in the corners.

"The men were all standing now, holding their clubs, and crowded together. And no one said a word. Wentworth told me he felt positively ill with fright. I know the feeling. Then, suddenly, something splashed on to the back of his left hand. He lifted it, and looked. It was covered with a great splash of red that dripped from his fingers. An old Irishman near to him, saw it, and croaked out in a quavering voice:— 'The bhlood-dhrip!' When the old man called out, they all looked, and in the same instant others felt it upon them. There were frightened cries of:— 'The bhlood-dhrip! The bhlood-dhrip!' And then, about a dozen candles went out simultaneously, and the hall was suddenly dark. The dog let out a great, mournful howl, and there was a horrible little silence, with everyone standing rigid. Then the tension broke, and there was a mad rush for the main door. They wrenched it open, and tumbled out into the dark; but something slammed it with a crash after them, and shut the dog in; for Wentworth heard it howling as they raced down the drive. Yet no one had the pluck to go back to let it out, which does not surprise me.

"Wentworth sent for me the following day. He had heard of me in connection with that Steeple Monster Case. I arrived by the night mail, and put up with Wentworth at the inn. The next day we went up to the old Manor, which certainly lies in rather a wilderness;

though what struck me most was the extraordinary number of laurel bushes about the house. The place was smothered with them; so that the house seemed to be growing up out of a sea of green laurel. These, and the grim, ancient look of the old building, made the place look a bit dank and ghostly, even by daylight.

"The hall was a big place, and well lit by daylight; for which I was not sorry. You see, I had been rather wound-up by Wentworth's yarn. We found one rather funny thing, and that was the great bull-mastiff, lying stiff with its neck broken. This made me feel very serious; for it showed that whether the cause was supernatural or not, there was present in the house some force exceedingly dangerous to life.

"Later, whilst Wentworth stood guard with his shotgun, I made an examination of the hall. The bottles and mugs from which the men had drunk their whisky were scattered about; and all over the place were the candles, stuck upright in their own grease. But in the somewhat brief and general search, I found nothing; and decided to begin my usual exact examination of every square foot of the place—not only of the hall, in this case, but of the whole interior of the castle.

"I spent three uncomfortable weeks, searching; but without result of any kind. And, you know, the care I take at this period is extreme; for I have solved hundreds of cases of so-called 'hauntings' at this early stage, simply by the most minute investigation, and the keeping of a perfectly open mind. But, as I have said, I found nothing. During the whole of the examination, I got Wentworth to stand guard with his loaded shotgun; and I was very particular that we were never caught there after dusk.

"I decided now to make the experiment of staying a night in the great hall, of course 'protected.' I spoke about it to Wentworth; but his own attempt had made him so nervous that he begged me to do no such thing. However, I thought it well worth the risk, and I managed in the end to persuade him to be present.

"With this in view, I went to the neighboring town of Gaunt, and by an arrangement with the Chief Constable I obtained the services of six policemen with their rifles. The arrangement was unofficial, of course, and the men were allowed to volunteer, with a promise of payment.

"When the constables arrived early that evening at the inn, I gave them a good feed; and after that we all set out for the Manor. We had four donkeys with us, loaded with fuel and other matters; also two great boarhounds, which one of the police led. When we reached the house, I set the men to unload the donkeys; whilst Wentworth and I set-to and sealed all the doors, except the main entrance, with tape and wax; for if the doors were really opened, I was going to be sure of the fact. I was going to run no risk of being deceived by ghostly hallucination, or mesmeric influence.

"By the time that this was done, the policemen had unloaded the donkeys, and were waiting, looking about them, curiously. I set two of them to lay a fire in the big grate, and the others I used as I required them. I took one of the boarhounds to the end of the hall furthest from the entrance, and there I drove a staple into the floor, to which I tied the dog with a short tether. Then, 'round him, I drew upon the floor the figure of a Pentacle, in chalk. Outside of the Pentacle, I made a circle with garlic. I did exactly the same thing with the other hound; but over more in the northeast corner of the big hall, where the two rows of doors make the angle.

"When this was done, I cleared the whole center of the hall, and put one of the policemen to sweep it; after which I had all my apparatus carried into the cleared space. Then I went over to the main door and hooked it open, so that the hook would have to be lifted out of the hasp, before the door could be closed. After that, I placed lighted candles before each of the sealed doors, and one in each corner of the big room; and then I lit the fire. When I saw that it was properly alight, I got all the men together, by the pile of things in the center of the room, and took their pipes from them; for, as the Sigsand MS. has it:— 'Theyre must noe lyght come from wythin the barryier.' And I was going to make sure.

"I got my tape measure then, and measured out a circle thirty-three feet in diameter, and immediately chalked it out. The police and Wentworth were tremendously interested, and I took the opportunity to warn them that this was no piece of silly mumming on my part; but done with a definite intention of erecting a barrier between us and any ab-human thing that the night might show to us. I warned them that, as they valued their lives, and more than their lives it might be, no one must on any account whatsoever pass beyond the limits of the barrier that I was making.

"After I had drawn the circle, I took a bunch of the garlic, and smudged it right 'round the chalk circle, a little outside of it. When this was complete, I called for candles from my stock of material. I set the police to lighting them, and as they were lit, I took them, and sealed them down on the floor, just within the chalk circle, five inches apart. As each candle measured approximately one inch in diameter, it took sixty-six candles to complete the circle; and I need hardly say that every number and measurement has a significance.

"Then, from candle to candle I took a 'gayrd' of human hair, entwining it alternately to the left and to the right, until the circle was completed, and the ends of the hair shod with silver, and pressed into the wax of the sixty-sixth candle.

"It had now been dark some time, and I made haste to get the 'defense' complete. To this end, I got the men well together, and began to fit the Electric Pentacle right around us, so that the five points of the Defensive Star came just within the Hair Circle. This did not take me long, and a minute later I had connected up the batteries, and the weak blue glare of the intertwining vacuum tubes shone all around us. I felt happier then; for this Pentacle is, as you all know, a wonderful 'defense.' I have told you before, how the idea came to me, after reading Professor Garder's 'Experiments with a Medium.' He found that a current, of a certain number of vibrations, *in vacuo*, 'insulated' the medium. It is difficult to suggest an explanation non-technically, and if you are really interested you should read Carder's lecture on 'Astral Vibrations Compared with Matero-involuted Vibrations below the Six-Billion Limit.'

"As I stood up from my work, I could hear outside in the night a constant drip from the laurels, which as I have said, come right up around the house, very thick. By the sound, I knew that a 'soft' rain had set in; and there was absolutely no wind, as I could tell by the steady flames of the candles.

"I stood a moment or two, listening, and then one of the men touched my arm, and asked me in a low voice, what they should do. By his tone, I could tell that he was feeling something of the strangeness of it all; and the other men, including Wentworth, were so quiet that I was afraid they were beginning to get shaky.

"I set-to, then, and arranged them with their backs to one common center; so that they were sitting flat upon the floor, with their feet radiating outward. Then, by compass, I laid their legs to the eight chief points, and afterward I drew a circle with chalk around them; and opposite to their feet, I made the Eight Signs of the Saaamaaa Ritual. The eighth place was, of course, empty; but ready for me to occupy at any moment; for I had omitted to make the Sealing Sign to that point, until I had finished all my preparations, and could enter the Inner Star.

"I took a last look 'round the great hall, and saw that the two big hounds were lying quietly, with their noses between their paws. The fire was big and cheerful, and the candles before the two rows of doors, burnt steadily, as well as the solitary ones in the corners. Then I went 'round the little star of men, and warned them not to be frightened whatever happened; but to trust to the 'Defense'; and to let nothing tempt or drive them to cross the Barriers. Also, I told them to watch their movements, and to keep their feet strictly to their places. For the rest, there was to be no shooting, unless I gave the word.

"And now at last, I went to my place, and, sitting down, made the Eighth sign just beyond my feet. Then I arranged my camera and flashlight handy, and examined my revolver.

"Wentworth sat behind the First Sign, and as the numbering went 'round reversed, that put him next to me on my left. I asked him, in a low voice, how he felt; and he told me, rather nervous; but that he felt confidence in my knowledge and was resolved to go through with the matter, whatever happened.

"We settled down to wait. There was no talking, except that, once or twice, the police bent toward one another, and whispered odd remarks concerning the hall, that appeared queerly audible in the intense silence. But in a while there was not even a whisper from anyone, and only the monotonous drip, drip of the quiet rain without the great entrance, and the low, dull sound of the fire in the big fireplace.

"It was a queer group that we made sitting there, back to back, with our legs starred outward; and all around us the strange blue glow of the Pentacle, and beyond that the brilliant shining of the great ring of lighted candles. Outside of the glare of the candles, the large empty hall looked a little gloomy, by contrast, except where the lights shone before the sealed doors, and the blaze of the big fire made a good honest mass of flame. And the feeling of mystery! Can you picture it all?

"It might have been an hour later that it came to me suddenly that I was aware of an extraordinary sense of dreeness, as it were, come into the air of the place. Not the nervous feeling of mystery that had been with us all the time; but a new feeling, as if there were something going to happen any moment.

"Abruptly, there came a slight noise from the east end of the hall, and I felt the star of men move suddenly. 'Steady! Keep steady!' I shouted, and they quietened. I looked up the hall, and saw that the dogs were upon their feet, and staring in an extraordinary fashion toward the great entrance. I turned and stared, also, and felt the men move as they craned their heads to look. Suddenly, the dogs set up a tremendous barking, and I glanced across to them, and found they were still 'pointing' for the big doorway. They ceased their noise just as quickly, and seemed to be listening. In the same instant, I heard a faint chink of metal to my left, that set me staring at the hook which held the great door wide. It moved, even as I looked. Some invisible thing was meddling with it. A queer, sickening thrill went through me, and I felt all the men about me, stiffen and go rigid with intensity. I had a certainty of something impending: as it might be the impression of an invisible, but overwhelming, Presence. The hall was full of a queer silence, and not a sound came from the dogs. *Then I saw the hook slowly raised from out of its hasp, without any visible thing touching it.*

Then a sudden power of movement came to me. I raised my camera, with the flashlight fixed, and snapped it at the door. There came the great blare of the flashlight, and a simultaneous roar of barking from the two dogs.

"The intensity of the flash made all the place seem dark for some moments, and in that time of darkness, I heard a jingle in the direction of the door, and strained to look. The effect of the bright light passed, and I could see clearly again. The great entrance door was being slowly closed. It shut with a sharp snick, and there followed a long silence, broken only by the whimpering of the dogs.

"I turned suddenly, and looked at Wentworth. He was looking at me.

"'Just as it did before,' he whispered.

"'Most extraordinary,' I said, and he nodded and looked 'round, nervously.

"The policemen were pretty quiet, and I judged that they were feeling rather worse than Wentworth; though, for that matter, you must not think that I was altogether natural; yet I have seen so much that is extraordinary, that I daresay I can keep my nerves steady longer than most people.

"I looked over my shoulder at the men, and cautioned them, in a low voice, not to move outside of the Barriers, *whatever happened*; not even though the house should seem to be rocking and about to tumble on to them; for well I knew what some of the great Forces are capable of doing. Yet, unless it should prove to be one of the cases of the more terrible Saiitii Manifestation, we were almost certain of safety, so long as we kept to our order within the Pentacle.

"Perhaps an hour and a half passed, quietly, except when, once in a way, the dogs would whine distressfully. Presently, however, they ceased even from this, and I could see them lying on the floor with their paws over their noses, in a most peculiar fashion, and shivering visibly. The sight made me feel more serious, as you can understand.

"Suddenly, the candle in the corner furthest from the main door went out. An instant later, Wentworth jerked my arm, and I saw that the candle before one of the sealed doors had been put out. I held my camera ready. Then, one after another, every candle about the hall was put out, and with such speed and irregularity, that I could never catch one in the actual act of being extinguished. Yet, for all that, I took a flashlight of the hall in general.

"There was a time in which I sat half-blinded by the great glare of the flash, and I blamed myself for not having remembered to bring a pair of smoked goggles, which I have sometimes used at these times. I had felt the men jump, at the sudden light, and I called out loud to them to sit quiet, and to keep their feet exactly to their proper places. My voice, as you can imagine, sounded rather horrid and frightening in the great room, and altogether it was a beastly moment.

"Then, I was able to see again, and I stared here and there about the hall; but there was nothing showing unusual; only, of course, it was dark now over in the corners.

"Suddenly, I saw that the great fire was blackening. It was going out visibly, as I looked. If I said that some monstrous, invisible, impossible creature sucked the life from it, I could best explain the way the light and flame went out of it. It was most extraordinary to watch. In the time that I watched it, every vestige of fire was gone from it, and there was no light outside of the ring of candles around the Pentacle.

"The deliberateness of the thing troubled me more than I can make clear to you. It conveyed to me such a sense of a calm Deliberate Force present in the hall: The steadfast intention to 'make a darkness' was horrible. The *extent* of the Power to affect the Material was the steadfast intention to 'make a darkness' was horrible. The extent of the Power to affect the Material was now the one constant, anxious questioning in my brain. You can understand?

"Behind me, I heard the policemen moving again, and I knew that they were getting thoroughly frightened. I turned half 'round, and told them, quietly but plainly, that they were safe only so long as they stayed within the Pentacle, in the position in which I had put them. If they once broke, and went outside of the Barrier, no knowledge of mine could state the full extent of the dreadfulness of the danger.

"I steadied them up, by this quiet, straight reminder; but if they had known, as I knew, that there is no certainty in any 'Protection,' they would have suffered a great deal more, and probably have broken the 'Defense,' and made a mad, foolish run for an impossible safety.

"Another hour passed, after this, in an absolute quietness. I had a sense of awful strain and oppression, as though I were a little spirit in the company of some invisible, brooding monster of the unseen world, who, as yet, was scarcely conscious of us. I leant across to Wentworth, and asked him in a whisper whether he had a feeling as if something were in the room. He looked very pale, and his eyes kept always on the move. He glanced just once at me, and nodded; then stared away 'round the hall again. And when I came to think, I was doing the same thing.

"Abruptly, as though a hundred unseen hands had snuffed them, every candle in the Barrier went dead out, and we were left in a darkness that seemed, for a little, absolute; for the light from the Pentacle was too weak and pale to penetrate far across the great hall.

"I tell you, for a moment, I just sat there as though I had been frozen solid. I felt the 'creep' go all over me, and seem to stop in my brain. I felt all at once to be given a power of hearing that was far beyond the normal. I could hear my own heart thudding most given a power of hearing that was far beyond the normal. I could hear my own heart thudding most extraordinarily loud. I began, however, to feel better, after a while; but I simply had not the pluck to move. You can understand?

"Presently, I began to get my courage back. I gripped at my camera and flashlight, and waited. My hands were simply soaked with sweat. I glanced once at Wentworth. I could see him only dimly. His shoulders were hunched a little, his head forward; but though it was motionless, I knew that his eyes were not. It is queer how one knows that sort of thing at times. The police were just as silent. And thus a while passed.

"A sudden sound broke across the silence. From two sides of the room there came faint noises. I recognized them at once, as the breaking of the sealing-wax. *The sealed doors were opening.* I raised the camera and flashlight, and it was a peculiar mixture of fear and courage that helped me to press the button. As the great flare of light lit up the hall I felt the men all about me jump. The darkness fell like a clap of thunder, if you can understand, and seemed tenfold. Yet, in the moment of brightness, I had seen that all the sealed doors were wide open.

"Suddenly, all around us, there sounded a drip, drip, drip, upon the floor of the great hall. I thrilled with a queer, realizing emotion, and a sense of a very real and present danger—*imminent*. The 'blood-drip' had commenced. And the grim question was now whether the Barriers could save us from whatever had come into the huge room.

"Through some awful minutes the 'blood-drip' continued to fall in an increasing rain; and presently some began to fall within the Barriers. I saw several great drops splash and star upon the pale glowing intertwining tubes of the Electric Pentacle; but, strangely enough, I could not trace that any fell among us. Beyond the strange horrible noise of the 'drip,' there was no other sound. And then, abruptly, from the boarhound over in the far corner, there came a terrible yelling howl of agony, followed instantly by a sickening, breaking noise, and an immediate silence. If you have ever, when out shooting, broken a rabbit's neck, you will know the sound—in miniature! Like lightning, the thought sprang into my brain:—*IT has crossed the Pentacle.* For you will remember that I had made one about each of the dogs. I thought instantly, with a sick apprehension, of our own Barriers. There was something in the hall with us that had passed the Barrier of the Pentacle about one of the dogs. In the awful succeeding silence, I positively quivered. And suddenly, one of the men behind me, gave out a scream, like any woman, and bolted for the door. He fumbled, and had it open in a moment. I yelled to the others not to move; but they followed like sheep, and I heard them kick the candles flying, in their panic. One of them stepped on the Electric Pentacle, and smashed it, and there was an utter darkness. In an instant, I realized that I was defenseless against the powers of the Unknown World, and with one savage leap I was out of the useless Barriers, and instantly through the great doorway, and into the night. I believe I yelled with sheer funk.

"The men were a little ahead of me, and I never ceased running, and neither did they. Sometimes, I glanced back over my shoulder; and I kept glancing into the laurels which grew all along the drive. The beastly things kept rustling, rustling in a hollow sort of way, as though something were keeping parallel with me, among them. The rain had stopped, and a dismal little wind kept moaning through the grounds. It was disgusting.

"I caught Wentworth and the police at the lodge gate. We got outside, and ran all the way to the village. We found old Dennis up, waiting for us, and half the villagers to keep him company. He told us that he had known in his 'sowl' that we should come back, that is, if we came back at all; which is not a bad rendering of his remark.

"Fortunately, I had brought my camera away from the house—possibly because the strap had happened to be over my head. Yet, I did not go straight away to develop; but sat with the rest of the bar, where we talked for some hours, trying to be coherent about the whole horrible business.

"Later, however, I went up to my room, and proceeded with my photography. I was steadier now, and it was just possible, so I hoped, that the negatives might show something.

"On two of the plates, I found nothing unusual: but on the third, which was the first one that I snapped, I saw something that made me quite excited. I examined it very carefully with a magnifying glass; then I put it to wash, and slipped a pair of rubber overshoes over my boots.

"The negative had showed me something very extraordinary, and I had made up my mind to test the truth of what it seemed to indicate, without losing another moment. It was no use telling anything to Wentworth and the police, until I was certain; and, also, I believed that I stood a greater chance to succeed by myself;

though, for that matter, I do not suppose anything would have taken them up to the Manor again that night.

"I took my revolver, and went quietly downstairs, and into the dark. The rain had commenced again; but that did not bother me. I walked hard. When I came to the lodge gates, a sudden, queer instinct stopped me from going through, and I climbed the wall into the park. I kept away from the drive, and approached the building through the dismal, dripping laurels. You can imagine how beastly it was. Every time a leaf rustled, I jumped.

"I made my way 'round to the back of the big house, and got in through a little window which I had taken note of during my search; for, of course, I knew the whole place from roof to cellars. I went silently up the kitchen stairs, fairly quivering with funk; and at the top, I went to the left, and then into a long corridor that opened, through one of the doorways we had sealed, into the big hall. I looked up it, and saw a faint flicker of light away at the end; and I tiptoed silently toward it, holding my revolver ready. As I came near to the open door, I heard men's voices, and then a burst of laughing. I went on, until I could see into the hall. There were several men there, all in a group. They were well dressed, and one, at least, I saw was armed. They were examining my 'Barriers' against the Supernatural, with a good deal of unkind laughter. I never felt such a fool in my life.

"It was plain to me that they were a gang of men who had made use of the empty Manor, perhaps for years, for some purpose of their own; and now that Wentworth was attempting to take possession, they were acting up the traditions of the place, with the view of driving him away, and keeping so useful a place still at their disposal. But what they were, I mean whether coiners, thieves, inventors, or what, I could not imagine.

"Presently, they left the Pentacle, and gathered 'round the living boarhound, which seemed curiously quiet, as though it were half-drugged. There was some talk as to whether to let the poor brute live, or not; but finally they decided it would be good policy to kill it. I saw two of them force a twisted loop of rope into its mouth, and the two bights of the loop were brought together at the back of the hound's neck. Then a third man thrust a thick walking-stick through the two loops. The two men with the rope, stooped to hold the dog, so that I could not see what was done; but the poor beast gave a sudden awful howl, and immediately there was a repetition of the uncomfortable breaking sound, I had heard earlier in the night, as you will remember.

"The men stood up, and left the dog lying there, quiet enough now, as you may suppose. For my part, I fully appreciated the calculated remorselessness which had decided upon the animal's death, and the cold determination with which it had been afterward executed so neatly. I guessed that a man who might get into the 'light' of those particular men, would be likely to come to quite as uncomfortable an ending.

"A minute later, one of the men called out to the rest that they should 'shift the wires.' One of the men came toward the doorway of the corridor in which I stood, and I ran quickly back into the darkness of the upper end. I saw the man reach up, and take something from the top of the door, and I heard the slight, ringing jangle of steel wire.

"When he had gone, I ran back again, and saw the men passing, one after another, through an opening in the stairs, formed by one of the marble steps being raised. When the last man had vanished, the slab that made the step was shut down, and there was not a sign of the secret door. It was the seventh step from the bottom, as I took care to count: and a splendid idea; for it was so solid that it did not ring hollow, even to a fairly heavy hammer, as I found later.

"There is little more to tell. I got out of the house as quickly and quietly as possible, and back to the inn. The police came without any coaxing, when they knew the 'ghosts' were normal flesh and blood. We entered the park and the Manor in the same way that I had done. Yet, when we tried to open the step, we failed, and had finally to smash it. This must have warned the haunters; for when we descended to a secret room which we found at the end of a long and narrow passage in the thickness of the walls, we found no one.

"The police were horribly disgusted, as you can imagine; but for my part, I did not care either way. I had 'laid the ghost,' as you might say, and that was what I set out to do. I was not particularly afraid of being laughed at by the others; for they had all been thoroughly 'taken in'; and in the end, I had scored, without their help.

"We searched right through the secret ways, and found that there was an exit, at the end of a long tunnel, which opened in the side of a well, out in the grounds. The ceiling of the hall was hollow, and reached by a little secret stairway inside of the big staircase. The 'blood-drip' was merely colored water, dropped through the minute crevices of the ornamented ceiling. How the candles and the fire were put out, I do not know; for the haunters certainly did not act quite up to tradition, which held that the lights were put out by the 'blood-drip.' Perhaps it was too difficult to direct the fluid, without positively squirting it, which might have given the whole thing away. The candles and the fire may possibly have been extinguished by the agency of carbonic acid gas; but how suspended, I have no idea.

"The secret hiding places were, of course, ancient. There was also, did I tell you? a bell which they had rigged up to ring, when anyone entered the gates at the end of the drive. If I had not climbed the wall, I should have found nothing for my pains; for the bell would have warned them had I gone in through the gateway."

"What was on the negative?" I asked, with much curiosity.

"A picture of the fine wire with which they were grappling for the hook that held the entrance door open. They were doing it from one of the crevices in the ceiling. They had evidently made no preparations for lifting the hook. I suppose they never thought that anyone would make use of it, and so they had to improvise a grapple. The wire was too fine to be seen by the amount of light we had in the hall; but the flashlight picked it out. Do you see?

"The opening of the inner doors was managed by wires, as you will have guessed, which they unshipped after use, or else I should soon have found them, when I made my search.

"I think I have now explained everything. The hound was killed, of course, by the men direct. You see, they made the place as dark as possible, first. Of course, if I had managed to take a flashlight just at that instant, the whole secret of the haunting would have been exposed. But Fate just ordered it the other way."

"And the tramps?" I asked.

"Oh, you mean the two tramps who were found dead in the Manor," said Carnacki. "Well, of course it is impossible to be sure, one way or the other. Perhaps they happened to find out something, and were given a hypodermic. Or it is just as probable that they had come to the time of their dying, and just died naturally. It is conceivable that a great many tramps had slept in the old house, at one time or another."

Carnacki stood up, and knocked out his pipe. We rose also, and went for our coats and hats.

"Out you go!" said Carnacki, genially, using the recognized formula. And we went out on to the Embankment, and presently through the darkness to our various homes.

THE WHISTLING ROOM

Carnacki shook a friendly fist at me as I entered, late. Then he opened the door into the dining room, and ushered the four of us—Jessop, Arkright, Taylor and myself—in to dinner.

We dined well, as usual, and, equally as usual, Carnacki was pretty silent during the meal. At the end, we took our wine and cigars to our usual positions, and Carnacki—having got himself comfortable in his big chair—began without any preliminary:—

"I have just got back from Ireland, again," he said. "And I thought you chaps would be interested to hear my news. Besides, I fancy I shall see the thing clearer, after I have told it all out straight. I must tell you this, though, at the beginning—up to the present moment, I have been utterly and completely 'stumped.' I have tumbled upon one of the most peculiar cases of 'haunting'—or devilment of some sort—that I have come against. Now listen.

"I have been spending the last few weeks at Iastrae Castle, about twenty miles northeast of Galway. I got a letter about a month ago from a Mr. Sid K. Tassoc, who it seemed had bought the place lately, and moved in, only to find that he had bought a very peculiar piece of property.

"When I got there, he met me at the station, driving a jaunting car, and drove me up to the castle, which, by the way, he called a 'house shanty.' I found that he was 'pigging it' there with his boy brother and another American, who seemed to be half-servant and half-companion. It seems that all the servants had left the place, in a body, as you might say, and now they were managing among themselves, assisted by some day-help.

"The three of them got together a scratch feed, and Tassoc told me all about the trouble whilst we were at table. It is most extraordinary, and different from anything that I have had to do with; though that Buzzing Case was very queer, too.

"Tassoc began right in the middle of his story. 'We've got a room in this shanty,' he said, 'which has got a most infernal whistling in it; sort of haunting it. The thing starts any time; you never know when, and it goes on until it frightens you. All the servants have gone, as you know. It's not ordinary whistling, and it isn't the wind. Wait till you hear it.'

"'We're all carrying guns,' said the boy; and slapped his coat pocket.

"'As bad as that?' I said; and the older boy nodded. 'It may be soft,' he replied; 'but wait till you've heard it. Sometimes I think it's some infernal thing, and the next moment, I'm just as sure that someone's playing a trick on me.'

"'Why?' I asked. 'What is to be gained?'

"'You mean,' he said, 'that people usually have some good reason for playing tricks as elaborate as this. Well, I'll tell you. There's a lady in this province, by the name of Miss Donnehue, who's going to be my wife, this day two months. She's more beautiful than they make them, and so far as I can see, I've just stuck my head into an Irish hornet's nest. There's about a score of hot young Irishmen been courting her these two years gone, and now that I'm come along and cut them out, they feel raw against me. Do you begin to understand the possibilities?'

"'Yes,' I said. 'Perhaps I do in a vague sort of way; but I don't see how all this affects the room?'

"'Like this,' he said. 'When I'd fixed it up with Miss Donnehue, I looked out for a place, and bought this little house shanty. Afterward, I told her—one evening during dinner, that I'd decided to tie up here. And then she asked me whether I wasn't afraid of the whistling room. I told her it must have been thrown in gratis, as

I'd heard nothing about it. There were some of her men friends present, and I saw a smile go 'round. I found out, after a bit of questioning, that several people have bought this place during the last twenty-odd years. And it was always on the market again, after a trial.

"'Well, the chaps started to bait me a bit, and offered to take bets after dinner that I'd not stay six months in the place. I looked once or twice to Miss Donnehue, so as to be sure I was "getting the note" of the talkee-talkee; but I could see that she didn't take it as a joke, at all. Partly, I think, because there was a bit of a sneer in the way the men were tackling me, and partly because she really believes there is something in this yarn of the Whistling Room.

"'However, after dinner, I did what I could to even things up with the others. I nailed all their bets, and screwed them down hard and safe. I guess some of them are going to be hard hit, unless I lose; which I don't mean to. Well, there you have practically the whole yarn.'

"'Not quite,' I told him. 'All that I know, is that you have bought a castle with a room in it that is in some way "queer," and that you've been doing some betting. Also, I know that your servants have got frightened and run away. Tell me something about the whistling?'

"'Oh, that!' said Tassoc; 'that started the second night we were in. I'd had a good look 'round the room, in the daytime, as you can understand; for the talk up at Arlestrae—Miss Donnehue's place— had made me wonder a bit. But it seems just as usual as some of the other rooms in the old wing, only perhaps a bit more lonesome. But that may be only because of the talk about it, you know.

"'The whistling started about ten o'clock, on the second night, as I said. Tom and I were in the library, when we heard an awfully queer whistling, coming along the East Corridor—the room is in the East Wing, you know.

"'That's that blessed ghost!' I said to Tom, and we collared the lamps off the table, and went up to have a look. I tell you, even as we dug along the corridor, it took me a bit in the throat, it was so beastly queer. It was a sort of tune, in a way; but more as if a devil or some rotten thing were laughing at you, and going to get 'round at your back. That's how it makes you feel.

"'When we got to the door, we didn't wait; but rushed it open; and then I tell you the sound of the thing fairly hit me in the face. Tom said he got it the same way—sort of felt stunned and bewildered. We looked all 'round, and soon got so nervous, we just cleared out, and I locked the door.

"'We came down here, and had a stiff peg each. Then we got fit again, and began to think we'd been nicely had. So we took sticks, and went out into the grounds, thinking after all it must be some of these confounded Irishmen working the ghost-trick on us. But there was not a leg stirring.

"'We went back into the house, and walked over it, and then paid another visit to the room. But we simply couldn't stand it. We fairly ran out, and locked the door again. I don't know how to put it into words; but I had a feeling of being up against something that was rottenly dangerous. You know! We've carried our guns ever since.

"'Of course, we had a real turn out of the room next day, and the whole house place; and we even hunted 'round the grounds; but there was nothing queer. And now I don't know what to think; except that the sensible part of me tells me that it's some plan of these wild Irishmen to try to take a rise out of me.'

"'Done anything since?' I asked him.

"'Yes,' he said— 'watched outside of the door of the room at nights, and chased 'round the grounds, and sounded the walls and floor of the room. We've done everything we could think of; and it's beginning to get on our nerves, so we sent for you.'

"By this, we had finished eating. As we rose from the table, Tassoc suddenly called out:— 'Ssh! Hark!'

"We were instantly silent, listening. Then I heard it, an extraordinary hooning whistle, monstrous and inhuman, coming from far away through corridors to my right.

"'By G—d!' said Tassoc; 'and it's scarcely dark yet! Collar those candles, both of you, and come along.'

"In a few moments, we were all out of the door and racing up the stairs. Tassoc turned into a long corridor, and we followed, shielding our candles as we ran. The sound seemed to fill all the passage as we drew near, until I had the feeling that the whole air throbbed under the power of some wanton Immense Force—a sense of an actual taint, as you might say, of monstrosity all about us.

"Tassoc unlocked the door; then, giving it a push with his foot, jumped back, and drew his revolver. As the door flew open, the sound beat out at us, with an effect impossible to explain to one who has not heard it—with a certain, horrible personal note in it; as if in there in the darkness you could picture the room rocking and creaking in a mad, vile glee to its own filthy piping and whistling and hooning. To stand there and listen, was to be stunned by Realization. It was as if someone showed you the mouth of a vast pit suddenly, and said:—That's Hell. And you knew that they had spoken the truth. Do you get it, even a little bit?

"I stepped back a pace into the room, and held the candle over my head, and looked quickly 'round. Tassoc and his brother joined me, and the man came up at the back, and we all held our candles high. I was deafened with the shrill, piping hoon of the whistling; and then, clear in my ear, something seemed to be saying to me:— 'Get out of here—quick! Quick! Quick!'

"As you chaps know, I never neglect that sort of thing. Sometimes it may be nothing but nerves; but as you will remember, it was just such a warning that saved me in the 'Grey Dog' Case, and in the 'Yellow Finger' Experiments; as well as other times. Well, I turned sharp 'round to the others: 'Out!' I said. 'For God's sake, *out* quick.' And in an instant I had them into the passage.

"There came an extraordinary yelling scream into the hideous whistling, and then, like a clap of thunder, an utter silence. I slammed the door, and locked it. Then, taking the key, I looked 'round at the others. They were pretty white, and I imagine I must have looked that way too. And there we stood a moment, silent.

"'Come down out of this, and have some whisky,' said Tassoc, at last, in a voice he tried to make ordinary; and he led the way. I was the back man, and I know we all kept looking over our shoulders. When we got downstairs, Tassoc passed the bottle 'round. He took a drink, himself, and slapped his glass down on to the table. Then sat down with a thud.

"'That's a lovely thing to have in the house with you, isn't it!' he said. And directly afterward:— 'What on earth made you hustle us all out like that, Carnacki?'

"'Something seemed to be telling me to get out, quick,' I said. 'Sounds a bit silly, superstitious, I know; but when you are meddling with this sort of thing, you've got to take notice of queer fancies, and risk being laughed at.'

"I told him then about the 'Grey Dog' business, and he nodded a lot to that. 'Of course,' I said, 'this may be nothing more than those would-be rivals of yours playing some funny game; but, personally, though I'm going to keep an open mind, I feel that there is something beastly and dangerous about this thing.'

"We talked for a while longer, and then Tassoc suggested billiards, which we played in a pretty half-hearted fashion, and all the time cocking an ear to the door, as you might say, for sounds; but none came, and later, after coffee, he suggested early bed, and a thorough overhaul of the room on the morrow.

"My bedroom was in the newer part of the castle, and the door opened into the picture gallery. At the East end of the gallery was the entrance to the corridor of the East Wing; this was shut off from the gallery by two old and heavy oak doors, which looked rather odd and quaint beside the more modern doors of the various rooms.

"When I reached my room, I did not go to bed; but began to unpack my instrument trunk, of which I had retained the key. I intended to take one or two preliminary steps at once, in my investigation of the extraordinary whistling.

"Presently, when the castle had settled into quietness, I slipped out of my room, and across to the entrance of the great corridor. I opened one of the low, squat doors, and threw the beam of my pocket searchlight down the passage. It was empty, and I went through the doorway, and pushed-to the oak behind me. Then along the great passageway, throwing my light before and behind, and keeping my revolver handy.

"I had hung a 'protection belt' of garlic 'round my neck, and the smell of it seemed to fill the corridor and give me assurance; for, as you all know, it is a wonderful 'protection' against the more usual Aeiirii forms of semi-materialization, by which I supposed the whistling might be produced; though, at that period of my investigation, I was quite prepared to find it due to some perfectly natural cause; for it is astonishing the enormous number of cases that prove to have nothing abnormal in them.

"In addition to wearing the necklet, I had plugged my ears loosely with garlic, and as I did not intend to stay more than a few minutes in the room, I hoped to be safe.

"When I reached the door, and put my hand into my pocket for the key, I had a sudden feeling of sickening funk. But I was not going to back out, if I could help it. I unlocked the door and turned the handle. Then I gave the door a sharp push with my foot, as Tassoc had done, and drew my revolver, though I did not expect to have any use for it, really.

"I shone the searchlight all 'round the room, and then stepped inside, with a disgustingly horrible feeling of walking slap into a waiting Danger. I stood a few seconds, waiting, and nothing happened, and the empty room showed bare from corner to corner. And then, you know, I realized that the room was full of an abominable silence; can you understand that? A sort of purposeful silence, just as sickening as any of the filthy noises the Things have power to make. Do you remember what I told you about that 'Silent Garden' business? Well, this room had just that same *malevolent* silence—the beastly quietness of a thing that is looking at you and not seeable itself, and thinks that it has got you. Oh, I recognized it instantly, and I whipped the top off my lantern, so as to have light over the *whole* room.

"Then I set-to, working like fury, and keeping my glance all about me. I sealed the two windows with lengths of human hair, right across, and sealed them at every frame. As I worked, a queer, scarcely perceptible tenseness stole into the air of the place, and the silence seemed, if you can understand me, to grow more solid. I knew then that I had no business there without 'full protection'; for I was practically certain that this was no mere Aeiirii development; but one of the worst forms, as the Saiitii; like that 'Grunting Man' case—you know.

"I finished the window, and hurried over to the great fireplace. This is a huge affair, and has a queer gallows-iron, I think they are called, projecting from the back of the arch. I sealed the opening with seven human hairs—the seventh crossing the six others.

"Then, just as I was making an end, a low, mocking whistle grew in the room. A cold, nervous pricking went up my spine, and 'round my forehead from the back. The hideous sound filled all the room with an extraordinary, grotesque parody of human whistling, too gigantic to be human—as if something gargantuan and monstrous made the sounds softly. As I stood there a last moment, pressing down the final seal, I had no doubt but that I had come across one of those rare and horrible cases of the *Inanimate* reproducing the functions of the *Animate*. I made a grab for my lamp, and went quickly to the door, looking over my shoulder, and listening for the thing that I expected. It came, just as I got my hand upon the handle—a squeal of incredible, malevolent anger, piercing through the low hooning of the whistling. I dashed out, slamming the door and locking it. I leant a little against the opposite wall of the corridor, feeling rather funny; for it had been a narrow squeak. . . . 'Theyr be noe sayfetie to be gained bye gayrds of holieness when the monyster hath pow'r to speak throe woode and stoene.' So runs the passage in the Sigsand MS., and I proved it in that 'Nodding Door' business. There is no protection against this particular form of monster, except, possibly, for a fractional period of time; for it can reproduce itself in, or take to its purpose, the very protective material which you may use, and has the power to '*forme* wythine the pentycle'; though not immediately. There is, of course, the possibility of the Unknown Last Line of the Saaamaaa Ritual being uttered; but it is too uncertain to count upon, and the danger is too hideous; and even then it has no power to protect for more than 'maybee fyve beats of the harte,' as the Sigsand has it.

"Inside of the room, there was now a constant, meditative, hooning whistling; but presently this ceased, and the silence seemed worse; for there is such a sense of hidden mischief in a silence.

"After a little, I sealed the door with crossed hairs, and then cleared off down the great passage, and so to bed.

"For a long time I lay awake; but managed eventually to get some sleep. Yet, about two o'clock I was waked by the hooning whistling of the room coming to me, even through the closed doors. The sound was tremendous, and seemed to beat through the whole house with a presiding sense of terror. As if (I remember thinking) some monstrous giant had been holding mad carnival with itself at the end of that great passage.

"I got up and sat on the edge of the bed, wondering whether to go along and have a look at the seal; and suddenly there came a thump on my door, and Tassoc walked in, with his dressing gown over his pajamas.

"'I thought it would have waked you, so I came along to have a talk,' he said. '*I* can't sleep. Beautiful! Isn't it!'

"'Extraordinary!' I said, and tossed him my case.

"He lit a cigarette, and we sat and talked for about an hour; and all the time that noise went on, down at the end of the big corridor.

"Suddenly, Tassoc stood up:—

"'Let's take our guns, and go and examine the brute,' he said, and turned toward the door.

"'No!' I said. 'By Jove—*no!* I can't say anything definite, yet; but I believe that room is about as dangerous as it well can be.'

"'Haunted—*really* haunted?' he asked, keenly and without any of his frequent banter.

"I told him, of course, that I could not say a definite *yes* or *no* to such a question; but that I hoped to be able to make a statement, soon. Then I gave him a little lecture on the False Re-Materialization of the Animate-Force through the Inanimate-Inert. He began then to see the particular way in the room might be dangerous, if it were really the subject of a manifestation.

"About an hour later, the whistling ceased quite suddenly, and Tassoc went off again to bed. I went back to mine, also, and eventually got another spell of sleep.

"In the morning, I went along to the room. I found the seals on the door intact. Then I went in. The window seals and the hair were all right; but the seventh hair across the great fireplace was broken. This set me thinking. I knew that it might, very possibly, have snapped, through my having tensioned it too highly; but then, again, it might have been broken by something else. Yet, it was scarcely possible that a man, for instance, could have passed between the six unbroken hairs; for no one would ever have noticed them, entering the room that way, you see; but just walked through them, ignorant of their very existence.

"I removed the other hairs, and the seals. Then I looked up the chimney. It went up straight, and I could see blue sky at the top. It was a big, open flue, and free from any suggestion of hiding places, or corners. Yet, of course, I did not trust to any such casual examination, and after breakfast, I put on my overalls, and climbed to the very top, sounding all the way; but I found nothing.

"Then I came down, and went over the whole of the room—floor, ceiling, and walls, mapping them out in six-inch squares, and sounding with both hammer and probe. But there was nothing abnormal.

"Afterward, I made a three-weeks search of the whole castle, in the same thorough way; but found nothing. I went even further, then; for at night, when the whistling commenced, I made a microphone test. You see, if the whistling were mechanically produced, this test would have made evident to me the working of the machinery, if there were any such concealed within the walls. It certainly was an up-to-date method of examination, as you must allow.

"Of course, I did not think that any of Tassoc's rivals had fixed up any mechanical contrivance; but I thought it just possible that there had been some such thing for producing the whistling, made away back in the years, perhaps with the intention of giving the room a reputation that would ensure its being free of inquisitive folk. You see what I mean? Well, of course, it was just possible, if this were the case, that someone knew the secret of the machinery, and was utilizing the knowledge to play this devil of a prank on Tassoc. The microphone test of the walls would certainly have made this known to me, as I have said; but there was nothing of the sort in the castle; so that I had practically no doubt at all now, but that it was a genuine case of what is popularly termed 'haunting.'

"All this time, every night, and sometimes most of each night, the hooning whistling of the Room was intolerable. It was as if an intelligence there knew that steps were being taken against it, and piped and hooned in a sort of mad, mocking contempt. I tell you, it was as extraordinary as it was horrible. Time after time, I went along—tiptoeing noiselessly on stockinged feet—to the sealed door (for I always kept the Room sealed). I went at all hours of the night, and often the whistling, inside, would seem to change to a brutally malignant note, as though the half-animate monster saw me plainly through the shut door. And all the time the shrieking, hooning whistling would fill the whole corridor, so that I used to feel a precious lonely chap, messing about there with one of Hell's mysteries.

"And every morning, I would enter the room, and examine the different hairs and seals. You see, after the first week, I had stretched parallel hairs all along the walls of the room, and along the ceiling; but over the floor, which was of polished stone, I had set out little, colourless wafers, tacky-side uppermost. Each wafer was numbered, and they were arranged after a definite plan, so that I should be able to trace the exact movements of any living thing that went across the floor.

"You will see that no material being or creature could possibly have entered that room, without leaving many signs to tell me about it. But nothing was ever disturbed, and I began to think that I should have to risk an attempt to stay the night in the room, in the Electric Pentacle. Yet, mind you, I knew that it would be a crazy thing to do; but I was getting stumped, and ready to do anything.

"Once, about midnight, I did break the seal on the door, and have a quick look in; but, I tell you, the whole Room gave one mad yell, and seemed to come toward me in a great belly of shadows, as if the walls had bellied in toward me. Of course, that must have been fancy. Anyway, the yell was sufficient, and I slammed the door, and locked it, feeling a bit weak down my spine. You know the feeling.

"And then, when I had got to that state of readiness for any-thing, I made something of a discovery. It was about one in the morning, and I was walking slowly 'round the castle, keeping in the soft grass. I had come under the shadow of the East Front, and far above me, I could hear the vile, hooning whistle of the Room, up in the darkness of the unlit wing. Then, suddenly, a little in front of me, I heard a man's voice, speaking low, but evidently in glee:—

"'By George! You chaps, but I wouldn't care to bring a wife home in that!' it said, in the tone of the cultured Irish.

"Someone started to reply; but there came a sharp exclama-tion, and then a rush, and I heard footsteps running in all direc-tions. Evidently, the men had spotted me.

"For a few seconds, I stood there, feeling an awful ass. After all, *they* were at the bottom of the haunting! Do you see what a big fool it made me seem? I had no doubt but that they were some of Tassoc's rivals; and here I had been feeling in every bone that I had hit a real, bad, genuine Case! And then, you know, there came the memory of hundreds of details that made me just as much in doubt again. Anyway, whether it was natural, or ab-natural, there was a great deal yet to be cleared up.

"I told Tassoc, next morning, what I had discovered, and through the whole of every night, for five nights, we kept a close watch 'round the East Wing; but there was never a sign of anyone prowling about; and all the time, almost from evening to dawn, that grotesque whistling would hoon incredibly, far above us in the darkness.

"On the morning after the fifth night, I received a wire from here, which brought me home by the next boat. I explained to

Tassoc that I was simply bound to come away for a few days; but told him to keep up the watch 'round the castle. One thing I was very careful to do, and that was to make him absolutely promise never to go into the Room between sunset and sunrise. I made it clear to him that we knew nothing definite yet, one way or the other; and if the room were what I had first thought it to be, it might be a lot better for him to die first, than enter it after dark.

"When I got here, and had finished my business, I thought you chaps would be interested; and also I wanted to get it all spread out clear in my mind; so I rung you up. I am going over again to-morrow, and when I get back, I ought to have something pretty extraordinary to tell you. By the way, there is a curious thing I forgot to tell you. I tried to get a phonographic record of the whistling; but it simply produced no impression on the wax at all. That is one of the things that has made me feel queer, I can tell you. Another extraordinary thing is that the microphone will not magnify the sound—will not even transmit it; seems to take no account of it, and acts as if it were nonexistent. I am absolutely and utterly stumped, up to the present. I am a wee bit curious to see whether any of your dear clever heads can make daylight of it. *I* cannot—not yet."

He rose to his feet.

"Good night, all," he said, and began to usher us out abruptly, but without offence, into the night.

A fortnight later, he dropped each of us a card, and you can imagine that I was not late this time. When we arrived, Carnacki took us straight into dinner, and when we had finished, and all made ourselves comfortable, he began again, where he had left off:—

"Now just listen quietly; for I have got something pretty queer to tell you. I got back late at night, and I had to walk up to the castle, as I had not warned them that I was coming. It was bright moonlight; so that the walk was rather a pleasure, than otherwise. When I got there, the whole place was in darkness, and I thought I would take a walk 'round outside, to see whether Tassoc or his brother was keeping watch. But I could not find them anywhere, and concluded that they had got tired of it, and gone off to bed.

"As I returned across the front of the East Wing, I caught the hooning whistling of the Room, coming down strangely through the stillness of the night. It had a queer note in it, I remember— low and constant, queerly meditative. I looked up at the window, bright in the moonlight, and got a sudden thought to bring a ladder from the stable yard, and try to get a look into the Room, through the window.

"With this notion, I hunted 'round at the back of the castle, among the straggle of offices, and presently found a long, fairly light ladder; though it was heavy enough for one, goodness knows! And I thought at first that I should never get it reared. I managed at last, and let the ends rest very quietly against the wall, a little below the sill of the larger window. Then, going silently, I went up the ladder. Presently, I had my face above the sill and was looking in alone with the moonlight.

"Of course, the queer whistling sounded louder up there; but it still conveyed that peculiar sense of something whistling quietly to itself—can you understand? Though, for all the meditative low-ness of the note, the horrible, gargantuan quality was distinct—a mighty parody of the human, as if I stood there and listened to the whistling from the lips of a monster with a man's soul.

"And then, you know, I saw something. The floor in the middle of the huge, empty room was puckered upward in the center into a strange soft-looking mound, parted at the top into an ever chang-ing hole, that pulsated to that great, gentle hooning. At times, as I watched, I saw the heaving of the indented mound gap across with a queer, inward suction, as with the drawing of an enormous breath; then the thing would dilate and pout once more to the in-credible melody. And suddenly, as I stared, dumb, it came to me that the thing was living. I was looking at two enormous, black-ened lips, blistered and brutal, there in the pale moonlight. . . .

"Abruptly, they bulged out to a vast, pouting mound of force and sound, stiffened and swollen, and hugely massive and clean-cut in the moon-beams. And a great sweat lay heavy on the vast upper-lip. In the same moment of time, the whistling had burst into a mad screaming note, that seemed to stun me, even where I stood, outside of the window. And then, the following moment, I was staring blankly at the solid, undisturbed floor of the room— smooth, polished stone flooring, from wall to wall; and there was an absolute silence.

"You can picture me staring into the quiet Room, and knowing what I knew. I felt like a sick, frightened kid, and wanted to slide *quietly* down the ladder, and run away. But in that very instant, I heard Tassoc's voice calling to me from within the Room, for help, *help*. My God! but I got such an awful dazed feeling; and I had a vague, bewildered notion that, after all, it was the Irishmen who had got him in there, and were taking it out of him. And then the call came again, and I burst the window, and jumped in to help him. I had a confused idea that the call had come from within the shadow of the great fireplace, and I raced across to it; but there was no one there.

"'Tassoc!' I shouted, and my voice went empty-sounding 'round the great apartment; and then, in a flash, *I knew that Tassoc had never called.* I whirled 'round, sick with fear, toward the window, and as I did so, a frightful, exultant whistling scream burst through the Room. On my left, the end wall had bellied-in toward me, in a pair of gargantuan lips, black and utterly monstrous, to within a yard of my face. I fumbled for a mad instant at my revolver; not for *it*, but myself; for the danger was a thousand times worse than death. And then, suddenly, the Unknown Last Line of the Saaamaaa Ritual was whispered quite audibly in the room. Instantly, the thing happened that I have known once before. There came a sense as of dust falling continually and monotonously, and I knew that my life hung uncertain and suspended for a flash, in a brief, reeling vertigo of unseeable things. Then *that* ended, and I knew that I might live. My soul and body blended again, and life and power came to me. I dashed furiously at the window, and hurled myself out head-foremost; for I can tell you that I had stopped being afraid of death. I crashed down on to the ladder, and slithered, grabbing and grabbing; and so came some way or other alive to the bottom. And there

I sat in the soft, wet grass, with the moonlight all about me; and far above, through the broken window of the Room, there was a low whistling.

"That is the chief of it. I was not hurt, and I went 'round to the front, and knocked Tassoc up. When they let me in, we had a long yarn, over some good whisky—for I was shaken to pieces—and I explained things as much as I could, I told Tassoc that the room would have to come down, and every fragment of it burned in a blast-furnace, erected within a pentacle. He nodded. There was nothing to say. Then I went to bed.

"We turned a small army on to the work, and within ten days, that lovely thing had gone up in smoke, and what was left was calcined, and clean.

"It was when the workmen were stripping the paneling, that I got hold of a sound notion of the beginnings of that beastly development. Over the great fireplace, after the great oak panels had been torn down, I found that there was let into the masonry a scroll-work of stone, with on it an old inscription, in ancient Celtic, that here in this room was burned Dian Tiansay, Jester of King Alzof, who made the Song of Foolishness upon King Ernore of the Seventh Castle.

"When I got the translation clear, I gave it to Tassoc. He was tremendously excited; for he knew the old tale, and took me down to the library to look at an old parchment that gave the story in detail. Afterward, I found that the incident was well-known about the countryside; but always regarded more as a legend than as history. And no one seemed ever to have dreamt that the old East Wing of Iastrae Castle was the remains of the ancient Seventh Castle.

"From the old parchment, I gathered that there had been a pretty dirty job done, away back in the years. It seems that King Alzof and King Ernore had been enemies by birthright, as you might say truly; but that nothing more than a little raiding had occurred on either side for years, until Dian Tiansay made the Song of Foolishness upon King Ernore, and sang it before King Alzof; and so greatly was it appreciated that King Alzof gave the jester one of his ladies, to wife.

"Presently, all the people of the land had come to know the song, and so it came at last to King Ernore, who was so angered that he made war upon his old enemy, and took and burned him and his castle; but Dian Tiansay, the jester, he brought with him to his own place, and having torn his tongue out because of the song which he had made and sung, he imprisoned him in the Room in the East Wing (which was evidently used for unpleasant purposes), and the jester's wife, he kept for himself, having a fancy for her prettiness.

"But one night, Dian Tiansay's wife was not to be found, and in the morning they discovered her lying dead in her husband's arms, and he sitting, whistling the Song of Foolishness, for he had no longer the power to sing it.

"Then they roasted Dian Tiansay, in the great fireplace—probably from that selfsame 'galley-iron' which I have already mentioned. And until he died, Dian Tiansay ceased not to whistle the Song of Foolishness, which he could no longer sing. But afterward, 'in that room' there was often heard at night the sound of something whistling; and there 'grew a power in that room,' so that none dared to sleep in it. And presently, it would seem, the King went to another castle; for the whistling troubled him.

"There you have it all. Of course, that is only a rough rendering of the translation of the parchment. But it sounds extraordinarily quaint. Don't you think so?"

"Yes," I said, answering for the lot. "But how did the thing grow to such a tremendous manifestation?"

"One of those cases of continuity of thought producing a positive action upon the immediate surrounding material," replied Carnacki. "The development must have been going forward through centuries, to have produced such a monstrosity. It was a true instance of Saiitii manifestation, which I can best explain by likening it to a living spiritual fungus, which involves the very structure of the aether-fiber itself, and, of course, in so doing, acquires an essential control over the 'material substance' involved in it. It is impossible to make it plainer in a few words."

"What broke the seventh hair?" asked Taylor.

But Carnacki did not know. He thought it was probably nothing but being too severely tensioned. He also explained that they found out that the men who had run away, had not been up to mischief; but had come over secretly, merely to hear the whistling, which, indeed, had suddenly become the talk of the whole countryside.

"One other thing," said Arkright, "have you any idea what governs the use of the Unknown Last Line of the Saaamaaa Ritual? I know, of course, that it was used by the Ab-human Priests in the Incantation of Raaaee; but what used it on your behalf, and what made it?"

"You had better read Harzan's Monograph, and my Addenda to it, on Astral and Astral Co-ordination and Interference," said Carnacki. "It is an extraordinary subject, and I can only say here that the human vibration may not be insulated from the astral (as is always believed to be the case, in interferences by the Ab-human), without immediate action being taken by those Forces which govern the spinning of the outer circle. In other words, it is being proved, time after time, that there is some inscrutable Protective Force constantly intervening between the human soul (not the body, mind you,) and the Outer Monstrosities. Am I clear?"

"Yes, I think so," I replied. "And you believe that the Room had become the material expression of the ancient Jester—that his soul, rotten with hatred, had bred into a monster—eh?" I asked.

"Yes," said Carnacki, nodding, "I think you've put my thought rather neatly. It is a queer coincidence that Miss Donnehue is supposed to be descended (so I have heard since) from the same King Ernore. It makes one think some curious thoughts, doesn't it? The marriage coming on, and the Room waking to fresh life. If she had gone into that room, ever ... eh? *It* had waited a long time. Sins of the fathers. Yes, I've thought of that. They're to be married next week, and I am to be best man, which is a thing I hate. And he won his bets, rather! Just think, *if* ever she had gone into that room. Pretty horrible, eh?"

He nodded his head, grimly, and we four nodded back. Then he rose and took us collectively to the door, and presently thrust us forth in friendly fashion on the Embankment and into the fresh night air.

"Good night," we all called back, and went to our various homes. If she had, eh? If she had? That is what I kept thinking.

THE HORSE OF THE INVISIBLE

I had that afternoon received an invitation from Carnacki. When I reached his place I found him sitting alone. As I came into the room he rose with a perceptibly stiff movement and extended his left hand. His face seemed to be badly scarred and bruised and his right hand was bandaged. He shook hands and offered me his paper, which I refused. Then he passed me a handful of photographs and returned to his reading.

Now, that is just Carnacki. Not a word had come from him and not a question from me. He would tell us all about it later. I spent about half an hour looking at the photographs which were chiefly "snaps" (some by flashlight) of an extraordinarily pretty girl; though in some of the photographs it was wonderful that her prettiness was so evident for so frightened and startled was her expression that it was difficult not to believe that she had been photographed in the presence of some imminent and overwhelming danger.

The bulk of the photographs were of interiors of different rooms and passages and in every one the girl might be seen, either full length in the distance or closer, with perhaps little more than a hand or arm or portion of the head or dress included in the photograph. All of these had evidently been taken with some definite aim that did not have for its first purpose the picturing of the girl, but obviously of her surroundings and they made me very curious, as you can imagine.

Near the bottom of the pile, however, I came upon something *definitely* extraordinary. It was a photograph of the girl standing abrupt and clear in the great blaze of a flashlight, as was plain to be seen. Her face was turned a little upward as if she had been frightened suddenly by some noise. Directly above her, as though half-formed and coming down out of the shadows, was the shape of a single enormous hoof.

I examined this photograph for a long time without understanding it more than that it had probably to do with some queer case in which Carnacki was interested. When Jessop, Arkright and Taylor came in Carnacki quietly held out his hand for the photographs, which I returned in the same spirit and afterward we all went in to dinner. When we had spent a quiet hour at the table we pulled our chairs 'round and made ourselves snug and Carnacki began:

"I've been North," he said, speaking slowly and painfully between puffs at his pipe. "Up to Hisgins of East Lancashire. It has been a pretty strange business all 'round, as I fancy you chaps will think, when I have finished. I knew before I went, something about the 'horse story,' as I have heard it called; but I never thought of it coming my way, somehow. Also I know *now* that I never considered it seriously—in spite of my rule always to keep an open mind. Funny creatures, we humans!

"Well, I got a wire asking for an appointment, which of course told me that there was some trouble. On the date I fixed old Captain Hisgins himself came up to see me. He told me a great many new details about the horse story; though naturally I had always known the main points and understood that if the first child were a girl, that girl would be haunted by the Horse during her courtship.

"It is, as you can see already, an extraordinary story and though I have always known about it, I have never thought it to be anything more than an old-time legend, as I have already hinted. You see, for seven generations the Hisgins family have had men children for their first-born and even the Hisginses themselves have long considered the tale to be little more than a myth.

"To come to the present, the eldest child of the reigning family is a girl and she has been often teased and warned in jest by her friends and relations that she is the first girl to be the eldest for seven generations and that she would have to keep her men friends at arm's length or go into a nunnery if she hoped to escape the haunting. And this, I think, shows us how thoroughly the tale had grown to be considered as nothing worthy of the least serious thought. Don't you think so?

"Two months ago Miss Hisgins became engaged to Beaumont, a young Naval Officer, and on the evening of the very day of the engagement, before it was even formally announced, a most extraordinary thing happened which resulted in Captain Hisgins making the appointment and my ultimately going down to their place to look into the thing.

"From the old family records and papers that were entrusted to me I found that there could be no possible doubt that prior to something like a hundred and fifty years ago there were some very extraordinary and disagreeable coincidences, to put the thing in the least emotional way. In the whole of the two centuries prior to that date there were five first-born girls out of a total of seven generations of the family. Each of these girls grew up to maidenhood and each became engaged, and each one died during the period of engagement, two by suicide, one by falling from a window, one from a 'broken heart' (presumably heart failure, owing to sudden shock through fright). The fifth girl was killed one evening in the park 'round the house; but just how, there seemed to be no *exact* knowledge; only that there was an impression that she had been kicked by a horse. She was dead when found. Now, you see, all of these deaths might be attributed in a way—even the suicides—to natural causes, I mean as distinct from supernatural. You see? Yet, in every case the maidens had undoubtedly suffered some extraordinary and terrifying experiences during their various courtships for in all of the records there was mention either of the neighing of an unseen horse or of the sounds of an invisible horse galloping, as well as many other peculiar and quite inexplicable manifestations. You begin to understand now, I think, just how extraordinary a business it was that I was asked to look into.

"I gathered from one account that the haunting of the girls was so constant and horrible that two of the girls' lovers fairly ran away from their ladyloves. And I think it was this, more than anything else, that made me feel that there had been something more in it than a mere succession of uncomfortable coincidences.

"I got hold of these facts before I had been many hours in the house and after this I went pretty carefully into the details of the thing that happened on the night of Miss Hisgins' engagement to Beaumont. It seems that as the two of them were going through the big lower corridor, just after dusk and before the lamps had been lighted, there had been a sudden, horrible neighing in the corridor, close to them. Immediately afterward Beaumont received a tremendous blow or kick which broke his right forearm. Then the rest of the family and the servants came running to know what was wrong. Lights were brought and the corridor and, afterward, the whole house searched, but nothing unusual was found.

"You can imagine the excitement in the house and the half incredulous, half believing talk about the old legend. Then, later, in the middle of the night the old Captain was waked by the sound of a great horse galloping 'round and 'round the house.

"Several times after this both Beaumont and the girl said that they had heard the sounds of hoofs near to them after dusk, in several of the rooms and corridors.

"Three nights later Beaumont was waked by a strange neighing in the nighttime seeming to come from the direction of his sweetheart's bedroom. He ran hurriedly for her father and the two of them raced to her room. They found her awake and ill with sheer terror, having been awakened by the neighing, seemingly close to her bed.

"The night before I arrived, there had been a fresh happening and they were all in a frightfully nervy state, as you can imagine.

"I spent most of the first day, as I have hinted, in getting hold of details; but after dinner I slacked off and played billiards all the evening with Beaumont and Miss Hisgins. We stopped about ten o'clock and had coffee and I got Beaumont to give me full particulars about the thing that had happened the evening before.

"He and Miss Hisgins had been sitting quietly in her aunt's boudoir whilst the old lady chaperoned them, behind a book. It was growing dusk and the lamp was at her end of the table. The rest of the house was not yet lit as the evening had come earlier than usual.

"Well, it seems that the door into the hall was open and suddenly the girl said: 'H'sh! what's that?'

"They both listened and then Beaumont heard it—the sound of a horse outside of the front door.

"'Your father?' he suggested, but she reminded him that her father was not riding.

"Of course they were both ready to feel queer, as you can suppose, but Beaumont made an effort to shake this off and went into the hall to see whether anyone was at the entrance. It was pretty dark in the hall and he could see the glass panels of the inner draft door, clear-cut in the darkness of the hall. He walked over to the glass and looked through into the drive beyond, but there nothing in sight.

"He felt nervous and puzzled and opened the inner door and went out on to the carriage-circle. Almost directly afterward the great hall door swung to with a crash behind him. He told me that he had a sudden awful feeling of having been trapped in some way—that is how he put it. He whirled 'round and gripped the door handle, but something seemed to be holding it with a vast grip on the other side. Then, before he could be fixed in his mind that this was so, he was able to turn the handle and open the door.

"He paused a moment in the doorway and peered into the hall, for he had hardly steadied his mind sufficiently to know whether he was really frightened or not. Then he heard his sweetheart blow him a kiss out of the greyness of the big, unlit hall and he knew that she had followed him from the boudoir. He blew her a kiss back and stepped inside the doorway, meaning to go to her. And then, suddenly, in a flash of sickening knowledge he knew that it was not his sweetheart who had blown him that kiss. He knew that something was trying to tempt him alone into the darkness and that the girl had never left the boudoir. He jumped back and in the same instant of time he heard the kiss again, nearer to him. He called out at the top of his voice: 'Mary, stay in the boudoir. Don't move out of the boudoir until I come to you.' He heard her call something in reply from the boudoir and then he had struck a clump of a dozen or so matches and was holding them above his head and looking 'round the hall. There was no one in it, but even as the matches burned out there came the sounds of a great horse galloping down the empty drive.

"Now you see, both he and the girl had heard the sounds of the horse galloping; but when I questioned more closely I found that the aunt had heard nothing, though it is true she is a bit deaf, and she was further back in the room. Of course, both he and Miss Hisgins had been in an extremely nervous state and ready to hear anything. The door might have been slammed by a sudden puff of wind owing to some inner door being opened; and as for the grip on the handle, that may have been nothing more than the snick catching.

"With regard to the kisses and the sounds of the horse galloping, I pointed out that these might have seemed ordinary enough sounds, if they had been only cool enough to reason. As I told him, and as he knew, the sounds of a horse galloping carry a long way on the wind so that what he had heard might have been nothing more than a horse being ridden some distance away. And as for the kiss, plenty of quiet noises—the rustle of a paper or a leaf—have a somewhat similar sound, especially if one is in an overstrung condition and imagining things.

"I finished preaching this little sermon on commonsense versus hysteria as we put out the lights and left the billiard room. But neither Beaumont nor Miss Hisgins would agree that there had been any fancy on their parts.

"We had come out of the billiard room by this time and were going along the passage and I was still doing my best to make both of them see the ordinary, commonplace possibilities of the happening, when what killed my pig, as the saying goes, was the sound of a hoof in the dark billiard room we had just left.

"I felt the 'creep' come on me in a flash, up my spine and over the back of my head. Miss Hisgins whooped like a child with the whooping cough and ran up the passage, giving little gasping screams. Beaumont, however, ripped 'round on his heels and jumped back a couple of yards. I gave back too, a bit, as you can understand.

"'There it is,' he said in a low, breathless voice. 'Perhaps you'll believe now.'

"'There's certainly something,' I whispered, never taking my gaze off the closed door of the billiard room.

"'H'sh!' he muttered. 'There it is again.'

"There was a sound like a great horse pacing 'round and 'round the billiard room with slow, deliberate steps. A horrible cold fright took me so that it seemed impossible to take a full breath, you know the feeling, and then I saw we must have been walking backward for we found ourselves suddenly at the opening of the long passage.

"We stopped there and listened. The sounds went on steadily with a horrible sort of deliberateness, as if the brute were taking a sort of malicious gusto in walking about all over the room which we had just occupied. Do you understand just what I mean?

"Then there was a pause and a long time of absolute quiet except for an excited whispering from some of the people down in the big hall. The sound came plainly up the wide stairway. I fancy they were gathered 'round Miss Hisgins, with some notion of protecting her.

"I should think Beaumont and I stood there, at the end of the passage for about five minutes, listening for any noise in the billiard room. Then I realized what a horrible funk I was in and I said to him: 'I'm going to see what's there.'

"'So'm I,' he answered. He was pretty white, but he had heaps of pluck. I told him to wait one instant and I made a dash into my bedroom and got my camera and flashlight. I slipped my revolver into my right-hand pocket and a knuckle-duster over my left fist, where it was ready and yet would not stop me from being able to work my flashlight.

"Then I ran back to Beaumont. He held out his hand to show me that he had his pistol and I nodded, but whispered to him not to be too quick to shoot, as there might be some silly practical joking at work, after all. He had got a lamp from a bracket in the upper hall which he was holding in the crook of his damaged arm, so that we had a good light. Then we went down the passage toward the billiard room and you can imagine that we were a pretty nervous couple.

"All this time there had not been a sound, but abruptly when we were within perhaps a couple of yards of the door we heard the sudden clumping of a hoof on the solid *parquet* floor of the billiard room. In the instant afterward it seemed to me that the whole place shook beneath the ponderous hoof falls of some huge thing, *coming toward the door.* Both Beaumont and I gave back a pace or two, and then realized and hung on to our courage, as you might say, and waited. The great tread came right up to the door and then stopped and there was an instant of absolute silence, except that so far as I was concerned, the pulsing in my throat and temples almost deafened me.

"I dare say we waited quite half a minute and then came the further restless clumping of a great hoof. Immediately afterward the sounds came right on as if some invisible thing passed through the closed door and the ponderous tread was upon us. We jumped, each of us, to our side of the passage and I know that I spread myself stiff against the wall. The clungk clunck, clungk clunck, of the great hoof falls passed right between us and slowly and with deadly deliberateness, down the passage. I heard them through a haze of blood beats in my ears and temples and my body was extraordinarily rigid and pringling and I was horribly breathless. I stood for a little time like this, my head turned so that I could see up the passage. I was conscious only that there was a hideous danger abroad. Do you understand?

"And then, suddenly, my pluck came back to me. I was aware that the noise of the hoof beats sounded near the other end of the passage. I twisted quickly and got my camera to bear and snapped off the flashlight. Immediately afterward, Beaumont let fly a storm of shots down the passage and began to run, shouting: 'It's after Mary. Run! Run!'

"He rushed down the passage and I after him. We came out on the main landing and heard the sound of a hoof on the stairs and after that, nothing. And from thence onward, nothing.

"Down below us in the big hall I could see a number of the household 'round Miss Hisgins, who seemed to have fainted and there were several of the servants clumped together a little way off, staring up at the main landing and no one saying a single word. And about some twenty steps up the stairs was the old Captain Hisgins with a drawn sword in his hand where he had halted, just below the last hoof sound. I think I never saw anything finer than the old man standing there between his daughter and that infernal thing.

"I daresay you can understand the queer feeling of horror I had at passing that place on the stairs where the sounds had ceased. It was as if the monster were still standing there, invisible. And the peculiar thing was that we never heard another sound of the hoof, either up or down the stairs.

"After they had taken Miss Hisgins to her room I sent word that I should follow, so soon as they were ready for me. And presently, when a message came to tell me that I could come any time, I asked her father to give me a hand with my instrument box and between us we carried it into the girl's bedroom. I had the bed pulled well out into the middle of the room, after which I erected the electric pentacle 'round the bed.

"Then I directed that lamps should be placed 'round the room, but that on no account must any light be made within the pentacle; neither must anyone pass in or out. The girl's mother I had placed within the pentacle and directed that her maid should sit without, ready to carry any message so as to make sure that Mrs. Hisgins did not have to leave the pentacle. I suggested also that the girl's father should stay the night in the room and that he had better be armed.

"When I left the bedroom I found Beaumont waiting outside the door in a miserable state of anxiety. I told him what I had done and explained to him that Miss Hisgins was probably perfectly safe within the 'protection'; but that in addition to her father remaining the night in the room, I intended to stand guard at the door. I told him that I should like him to keep me company, for I knew that he could never sleep, feeling as he did, and I should not be sorry to have a companion. Also, I wanted to have him under my own observation, for there was no doubt but that he was actually in greater danger in some ways than the girl. At least, that was my opinion and is still, as I think you will agree later.

"I asked him whether he would object to my drawing a pentacle 'round him for the night and got him to agree, but I saw that he did not know whether to be superstitious about it or to regard it more as a piece of foolish mumming; but he took it seriously enough when I gave him some particulars about the Black Veil case, when young Aster died. You remember, he said it was a piece of silly superstition and stayed outside. Poor devil!

"The night passed quietly enough until a little while before dawn when we both heard the sounds of a great horse galloping 'round and 'round the house just as old Captain Hisgins had described it. You can imagine how queer it made me feel and directly afterward, I heard someone stir within the bedroom. I knocked at the door, for I was uneasy, and the Captain came. I asked whether everything was right; to which he replied yes, and immediately asked me whether I had heard the galloping, so that I knew he had heard them also. I suggested that it might be well to leave the bedroom door open a little until the dawn came in, as there was certainly something abroad. This was done and he went back into the room, to be near his wife and daughter.

"I had better say here that I was doubtful whether there was any value in the 'Defense' about Miss Hisgins, for what I term the 'personal sounds' of the manifestation were so extraordinarily material that I was inclined to parallel the case with that one of Harford's where the hand of the child kept materializing within the pentacle and patting the floor. As you will remember, that was a hideous business.

"Yet, as it chanced, nothing further happened and so soon as daylight had fully come we all went off to bed.

"Beaumont knocked me up about midday and I went down and made breakfast into lunch. Miss Hisgins was there and seemed in very fair spirits, considering. She told me that I had made her feel almost safe for the first time for days. She told me also that her cousin,

Harry Parsket, was coming down from London and she knew that he would do anything to help fight the ghost. And after that she and Beaumont went out into the grounds to have a little time together.

"I had a walk in the grounds myself and went 'round the house, but saw no traces of hoof marks and after that I spent the rest of the day making an examination of the house, but found nothing.

"I made an end of my search before dark and went to my room to dress for dinner. When I got down the cousin had just arrived and I found him one of the nicest men I have met for a long time. A chap with a tremendous amount of pluck, and the particular kind of man I like to have with me in a bad case like the one I was on. I could see that what puzzled him most was our belief in the genuineness of the haunting and I found myself almost wanting something to happen, just to show him how true it was. As it chanced, something did happen, with a vengeance.

"Beaumont and Miss Hisgins had gone out for a stroll just before the dusk and Captain Hisgins asked me to come into his study for a short chat whilst Parsket went upstairs with his traps, for he had no man with him.

"I had a long conversation with the old Captain in which I pointed out that the 'haunting' had evidently no particular connection with the house, but only with the girl herself and that the sooner she was married, the better as it would give Beaumont a right to be with her at all times and further than this, it might be that the manifestations would cease if the marriage were actually performed.

"The old man nodded agreement to this, especially to the first part and reminded me that three of the girls who were said to have been 'haunted' had been sent away from home and met their deaths whilst away. And then in the midst of our talk there came a pretty frightening interruption, for all at once the old butler rushed into the room, most extraordinarily pale:

"'Miss Mary, sir! Miss Mary, sir!' he gasped. 'She's screaming . . . out in the Park, sir! And they say they can hear the Horse—'

"The Captain made one dive for a rack of arms and snatched down his old sword and ran out, drawing it as he ran. I dashed out and up the stairs, snatched my camera-flashlight and a heavy revolver, gave one yell at Parsket's door: 'The Horse!' and was down and into the grounds.

"Away in the darkness there was a confused shouting and I caught the sounds of shooting, out among the scattered trees. And then, from a patch of blackness to my left, there burst suddenly an infernal gobbling sort of neighing. Instantly I whipped 'round and snapped off the flashlight. The great light blazed out momentarily, showing me the leaves of a big tree close at hand, quivering in the night breeze, but I saw nothing else and then the ten-fold blackness came down upon me and I heard Parsket shouting a little way back to know whether I had seen anything.

"The next instant he was beside me and I felt safer for his company, for there was some incredible thing near to us and I was momentarily blind because of the brightness of the flashlight. 'What was it? What was it?' he kept repeating in an excited voice. And all the time I was staring into the darkness and answering, mechanically, 'I don't know. I don't know.'

"There was a burst of shouting somewhere ahead and then a shot. We ran toward the sounds, yelling to the people not to shoot; for in the darkness and panic there was this danger also. Then there came two of the game-keepers racing hard up the drive with their lanterns and guns; and immediately afterward a row of lights dancing toward us from the house, carried by some of the men-servants.

"As the lights came up I saw we had come close to Beaumont. He was standing over Miss Hisgins and he had his revolver in his hand. Then I saw his face and there was a great wound across his forehead. By him was the Captain, turning his naked sword this way and that, and peering into the darkness; a little behind him stood the old butler, a battle-axe from one of the arm stands in the hall in his hands. Yet there was nothing strange to be seen anywhere.

"We got the girl into the house and left her with her mother and Beaumont, whilst a groom rode for a doctor. And then the rest of us, with four other keepers, all armed with guns and carrying lanterns, searched 'round the home park. But we found nothing.

"When we got back we found that the doctor had been. He had bound up Beaumont's wound, which luckily was not deep, and ordered Miss Hisgins straight to bed. I went upstairs with the Captain and found Beaumont on guard outside of the girl's door. I asked him how he felt and then, so soon as the girl and her mother were ready for us, Captain Hisgins and I went into the bedroom and fixed the pentacle again 'round the bed. They had already got lamps about the room and after I had set the same order of watching as on the previous night, I joined Beaumont outside of the door.

"Parsket had come up while I had been in the bedroom and between us we got some idea from Beaumont as to what had happened out in the Park. It seems that they were coming home after their stroll from the direction of the West Lodge. It had got quite dark and suddenly Miss Hisgins said: 'Hush!' and came to a standstill. He stopped and listened, but heard nothing for a little. Then he caught it—the sound of a horse, seemingly a long way off, galloping toward them over the grass. He told the girl that it was nothing and started to hurry her toward the house, but she was not deceived, of course. In less than a minute they heard it quite close to them in the darkness and they started running. Then Miss Hisgins caught her foot and fell. She began to scream and that is what the butler heard. As Beaumont lifted the girl he heard the hoofs come thudding right at him. He stood over her and fired all five chambers of his revolver right at the sounds. He told us that he was sure he saw something that looked like an enormous horse's head, right upon him in the light of the last flash of his pistol. Immediately afterward he was struck a tremendous blow which knocked him down and then the Captain and the butler came running up, shouting. The rest, of course, we knew.

"About ten o'clock the butler brought us up a tray, for which I was very glad, as the night before I had got rather hungry. I warned Beaumont, however, to be very particular not to drink any spirits and I also made him give me his pipe and matches. At midnight I drew a pentacle 'round him and Parsket and I sat one on each side of him, outside the pentacle, for I had no fear that there would be any manifestation made against anyone except Beaumont or Miss Hisgins.

"After that we kept pretty quiet. The passage was lit by a big lamp at each end so that we had plenty of light and we were all armed, Beaumont and I with revolvers and Parsket with a shotgun. In addition to my weapon I had my camera and flashlight.

"Now and again we talked in whispers and twice the Captain came out of the bedroom to have a word with us. About half-past one we had all grown very silent and suddenly, about twenty minutes later, I held up my hand, silently, for there seemed to be a sound of galloping out in the night. I knocked on the bedroom door for the Captain to open it and when he came I whispered to him that we thought we heard the Horse. For some time we stayed listening, and both Parsket and the Captain thought they heard it; but now I was not so sure, neither was Beaumont. Yet afterward, I thought I heard it again.

"I told Captain Hisgins I thought he had better go into the bedroom and leave the door a little open and this he did. But from that time onward we heard nothing and presently the dawn came in and we all went very thankfully to bed.

"When I was called at lunchtime I had a little surprise, for Captain Hisgins told me that they had held a family council and had decided to take my advice and have the marriage without a day's more delay than possible. Beaumont was already on his way to London to get a special License and they hoped to have the wedding next day.

"This pleased me, for it seemed the sanest thing to be done in the extraordinary circumstances and meanwhile I should continue my investigations; but until the marriage was accomplished, my chief thought was to keep Miss Hisgins near to me.

"After lunch I thought I would take a few experimental photographs of Miss Hisgins and her *surroundings*. Sometimes the camera sees things that would seem very strange to normal human eyesight.

"With this intention and partly to make an excuse to keep her in my company as much as possible, I asked Miss Hisgins to join me in my experiments. She seemed glad to do this and I spent several hours with her, wandering all over the house, from room to room and whenever the impulse came I took a flashlight of her and the room or corridor in which we chanced to be at the moment.

"After we had gone right through the house in this fashion, I asked her whether she felt sufficiently brave to repeat the experiments in the cellars. She said yes, and so I rooted out Captain Hisgins and Parsket, for I was not going to take her even into what you might call artificial darkness without help and companionship at hand.

"When we were ready we went down into the wine cellar, Captain Hisgins carrying a shotgun and Parsket a specially prepared background and a lantern. I got the girl to stand in the middle of the cellar whilst Parsket and the Captain held out the background behind her. Then I fired off the flashlight, and we went into the next cellar where we repeated the experiment.

"Then in the third cellar, a tremendous, pitch-dark place, something extraordinary and horrible manifested itself. I had stationed Miss Hisgins in the center of the place, with her father and Parsket holding the background as before. When all was ready and just as I pressed the trigger of the 'flash,' there came in the cellar that dreadful, gobbling neighing that I had heard out in the Park. It seemed to come from somewhere above the girl and in the glare of the sudden light I saw that she was staring tensely upward, but at no visible thing. And then in the succeeding comparative darkness, I was shouting to the Captain and Parsket to run Miss Hisgins out into the daylight.

"This was done instantly and I shut and locked the door afterward making the First and Eighth signs of the Saaamaaa Ritual opposite to each post and connecting them across the threshold with a triple line.

"In the meanwhile Parsket and Captain Hisgins carried the girl to her mother and left her there, in a half fainting condition whilst I stayed on guard outside of the cellar door, feeling pretty horrible for I knew that there was some disgusting thing inside, and along with this feeling there was a sense of half ashamedness, rather miserable, you know, because I had exposed Miss Hisgins to the danger.

"I had got the Captain's shotgun and when he and Parsket came down again they were each carrying guns and lanterns. I could not possibly tell you the utter relief of spirit and body that came to me when I heard them coming, but just try to imagine what it was like, standing outside of that cellar. Can you?

"I remember noticing, just before I went to unlock the door, how white and ghastly Parsket looked and the old Captain was grey-looking and I wondered whether my face was like theirs. And this, you know, had its own distinct effect upon my nerves, for it seemed to bring the beastliness of the thing crash down on to me in a fresh way. I know it was only sheer will power that carried me up to the door and made me turn the key.

"I paused one little moment and then with a nervy jerk sent the door wide open and held my lantern over my head. Parsket and the Captain came one on each side of me and held up their lanterns, but the place was absolutely empty. Of course, I did not trust to a casual look of this kind, but spent several hours with the help of the two others in sounding every square foot of the floor, ceiling and walls.

"Yet, in the end I had to admit that the place itself was absolutely normal and so we came away. But I sealed the door and outside, opposite each doorpost I made the First and Last signs of the Saaamaaa Ritual, joined them as before, with a triple line. Can you imagine what it was like, searching that cellar?

"When we got upstairs I inquired very anxiously how Miss Hisgins was and the girl came out herself to tell me that she was all right and that I was not to trouble about her, or blame myself, as I told her I had been doing.

"I felt happier then and went off to dress for dinner and after that was done, Parsket and I took one of the bathrooms to develop the negatives that I had been taking. Yet none of the plates had anything to tell us until we came to the one that was taken in the cellar. Parsket was developing and I had taken a batch of the fixed plates out into the lamplight to examine them.

"I had just gone carefully through the lot when I heard a shout from Parsket and when I ran to him he was looking at a partly-developed negative which he was holding up to the red lamp. It showed the girl plainly, looking upward as I had seen her, but the thing that astonished me was the shadow of an enormous hoof, right above her, as if it were coming down upon her out of the shadows. And you know, I had run her bang into that danger. That was the thought that was chief in my mind.

"As soon as the developing was complete I fixed the plate and examined it carefully in a good light. There was no doubt about it at all, the thing above Miss Hisgins was an enormous, shadowy hoof. Yet I was no nearer to coming to any definite knowledge and the only thing I could do was to warn Parsket to say nothing about it to the girl for it would only increase her fright, but I showed the thing to her father for I considered it right that he should know.

"That night we took the same precaution for Miss Hisgins's safety as on the two previous nights and Parsket kept me company; yet the dawn came in without anything unusual having happened and I went off to bed.

"When I got down to lunch I learnt that Beaumont had wired to say that he would be in soon after four; also that a message had been sent to the Rector. And it was generally plain that the ladies of the house were in a tremendous fluster.

"Beaumont's train was late and he did not get home until five, but even then the Rector had not put in an appearance and the butler came in to say that the coachman had returned without him as he had been called away unexpectedly. Twice more during the evening the carriage was sent down, but the clergyman had not returned and we had to delay the marriage until the next day.

"That night I arranged the 'Defense' 'round the girl's bed and the Captain and his wife sat up with her as before. Beaumont, as I expected, insisted on keeping watch with me and he seemed in a curiously frightened mood; not for himself, you know, but for Miss Hisgins. He had a horrible feeling he told me, that there would be a final, dreadful attempt on his sweetheart that night.

"This, of course, I told him was nothing but nerves; yet really, it made me feel very anxious; for I have seen too much not to know that under such circumstances a premonitory *conviction* of impending danger is not necessarily to be put down entirely to nerves. In fact, Beaumont was so simply and earnestly convinced that the night would bring some extraordinary manifestation that I got Parsket to rig up a long cord from the wire of the butler's bell, to come along the passage handy.

"To the butler himself I gave directions not to undress and to give the same order to two of the footmen. If I rang he was to come instantly, with the footmen, carrying lanterns and the lanterns were to be kept ready lit all night. If for any reason the bell did not ring and I blew my whistle, he was to take that as a signal in the place of the bell.

"After I had arranged all these minor details I drew a pentacle about Beaumont and warned him very particularly to stay within it, whatever happened. And when this was done, there was nothing to do but wait and pray that the night would go as quietly as the night before.

"We scarcely talked at all and by about one a.m. we were all very tense and nervous so that at last Parsket got up and began to walk up and down the corridor to steady himself a bit. Presently I slipped off my pumps and joined him and we walked up and down, whispering occasionally for something over an hour, until in turning I caught my foot in the bell cord and went down on my face; but without hurting myself or making a noise.

"When I got up Parsket nudged me.

"'Did you notice that the bell never rang?' he whispered.

"'Jove!' I said, 'you're right.'

"'Wait a minute,' he answered. 'I'll bet it's only a kink somewhere in the cord.' He left his gun and slipped along the passage and taking the top lamp, tiptoed away into the house, carrying Beaumont's revolver ready in his right hand. He was a plucky chap, I remember thinking then, and again, later.

"Just then Beaumont motioned to me for absolute quiet. Directly afterward I heard the thing for which he listened—the sound of a horse galloping, out in the night. I think that I may say I fairly shivered. The sound died away and left a horrible, desolate, eerie feeling in the air, you know. I put my hand out to the bell cord, hoping Parsket had got it clear. Then I waited, glancing before and behind.

"Perhaps two minutes passed, full of what seemed like an almost unearthly quiet. And then, suddenly, down the corridor at the lighted end there sounded the clumping of a great hoof and instantly the lamp was thrown with a tremendous crash and we were in the dark. I tugged hard on the cord and blew the whistle; then I raised my snapshot and fired the flashlight. The corridor blazed into brilliant light, but there was nothing, and then the darkness fell like thunder. I heard the Captain at the bedroom door and shouted to him to bring out a lamp, *quick*; but instead something started to kick the door and I heard the Captain shouting within the bedroom and then the screaming of the women. I had a sudden horrible fear that the monster had got into the bedroom, but in the same instant from up the corridor there came abruptly the vile, gobbling neighing that we had heard in the park and the cellar. I blew the whistle again and groped blindly for the bell cord, shouting to Beaumont to stay in the Pentacle, whatever happened. I yelled again to the Captain to bring out a lamp and there came a smashing sound against the bedroom door. Then I had my matches in my hand, to get some light before that incredible, unseen Monster was upon us.

"The match scraped on the box and flared up dully and in the same instant I heard a faint sound behind me. I whipped 'round in a kind of mad terror and saw something in the light of the match— a monstrous horse-head close to Beaumont.

"'Look out, Beaumont!' I shouted in a sort of scream. 'It's behind you!'

"The match went out abruptly and instantly there came the huge bang of Parsket's double-barrel (both barrels at once), fired evidently single-handed by Beaumont close to my ear, as it seemed. I caught a momentary glimpse of the great head in the flash and of an enormous hoof amid the belch of fire and smoke seeming to be descending upon Beaumont. In the same instant I fired three chambers of my revolver. There was the sound of a dull blow and then that horrible, gobbling neigh broke out close to me. I fired twice at the sound. Immediately afterward something struck me and I was knocked backward. I got on to my knees and shouted for help at the top of my voice. I heard the women screaming behind the closed door of the bedroom and was dully aware that the door was being smashed from the inside, and directly afterward I knew that Beaumont was struggling with some hideous thing near to me. For an instant I held back, stupidly, paralyzed with funk and then, blindly and in a sort of rigid chill of goose flesh I went to help him, shouting his name. I can tell you, I was nearly sick with the naked fear I had on me. There came a little, choking scream out of the darkness, and at that I jumped forward into the dark. I gripped a vast, furry ear. Then something struck me another great blow knocking me sick. I hit back, weak and blind and gripped with my other hand at the incredible thing. Abruptly I was dimly aware of a tremendous crash behind me and a great burst of light. There were other lights in the passage and a noise of feet and shouting. My hand-grips were torn from the thing they held; I shut my eyes stupidly and heard a loud yell above me and then a heavy blow, like a butcher chopping meat and then something fell upon me.

"I was helped to my knees by the Captain and the butler. On the floor lay an enormous horse-head out of which protruded a man's trunk and legs. On the wrists were fixed great hoofs. It was the monster. The Captain cut something with the sword that he held in his hand and stooped and lifted off the mask, for that is what it was. I saw the face then of the man who had worn it. It was Parsket. He had a bad wound across the forehead where the Captain's sword had bit through the mask. I looked bewilderedly from him to Beaumont, who was sitting up, leaning against the wall of the corridor. Then I stared at Parsket again.

"'By Jove!' I said at last, and then I was quiet for I was so ashamed for the man. You can understand, can't you? And he was opening his eyes. And you know, I had grown so to like him.

"And then, you know, just as Parsket was getting back his wits and looking from one to the other of us and beginning to remember, there happened a strange and incredible thing. For from the end of the corridor there sounded suddenly, the clumping of a great hoof. I looked that way and then instantly at Parsket and saw a horrible fear in his face and eyes. He wrenched himself 'round, weakly, and stared in mad terror up the corridor to where the sound had been, and the rest of us stared, in a frozen group. I remember vaguely half sobs and whispers from Miss Hisgins' bedroom, all the while that I stared frightenedly up the corridor.

"The silence lasted several seconds and then, abruptly there came again the clumping of the great hoof, away at the end of the corridor. And immediately afterward the clungk, clunk—clungk, clunk of mighty hoofs coming down the passage toward us.

"Even then, you know, most of us thought it was some mechanism of Parsket's still at work and we were in the queerest mixture of fright and doubt. I think everyone looked at Parsket. And suddenly the Captain shouted out:

"'Stop this damned fooling at once. Haven't you done enough?'

"For my part, I was now frightened for I had a *sense* that there was something horrible and wrong. And then Parsket managed to gasp out:

"'It's not me! My God! It's not me! My God! It's not me.'

"And then, you know, it seemed to come home to everyone in an instant that there was really some dreadful thing coming down the passage. There was a mad rush to get away and even old Captain Hisgins gave back with the butler and the footmen. Beaumont fainted outright, as I found afterward, for he had been badly mauled. I just flattened back against the wall, kneeling as I was, too stupid and dazed even to run. And almost in the same instant the ponderous hoof falls sounded close to me and seeming to shake the solid floor as they passed. Abruptly the great sounds ceased and I knew in a sort of sick fashion that the thing had halted opposite to the door of the girl's bedroom. And then I was aware that Parsket was standing rocking in the doorway with his arms spread across, so as to fill the doorway with his body. Parsket was extraordinarily pale and the blood was running down his face from the wound in his forehead; and then I noticed that he seemed to be looking at something in the passage with a peculiar, desperate, fixed, incredibly masterful gaze. But there was really nothing to be seen. And suddenly the clungk, clunk—clungk, clunk recommenced and passed onward down the passage. In the same moment Parsket pitched forward out of the doorway on to his face.

"There were shouts from the huddle of men down the passage and the two footmen and the butler simply ran, carrying their lanterns, but the Captain went against the side-wall with his back and put the lamp he was carrying over his head. The dull tread of the Horse went past him, and left him unharmed and I heard the monstrous hoof falls going away and away through the quiet house and after that a dead silence.

"Then the Captain moved and came toward us, very slow and shaky and with an extraordinarily grey face.

"I crept toward Parsket and the Captain came to help me. We turned him over and, you know, I knew in a moment that he was dead; but you can imagine what a feeling it sent through me.

"I looked at the Captain and suddenly he said:

"'That—That—That—' and I know that he was trying to tell me that Parsket had stood between his daughter and whatever it was that had gone down the passage. I stood up and steadied him, though I was not very steady myself. And suddenly his face began to work and he went down on to his knees by Parsket and cried like some shaken child. Then the women came out of the doorway of the bedroom and I turned away and left him to them, whilst I over to Beaumont.

"That is practically the whole story and the only thing that is left to me is to try to explain some of the puzzling parts, here and there.

"Perhaps you have seen that Parsket was in love with Miss Hisgins and this fact is the key to a good deal that was extraordinary. He was doubtless responsible for some portions of the 'haunting'; in fact I think for nearly everything, but, you know, I can prove nothing and what I have to tell you is chiefly the result of deduction.

"In the first place, it is obvious that Parsket's intention was to frighten Beaumont away and when he found that he could not do this, I think he grew so desperate that he really intended to kill him. I hate to say this, but the facts force me to think so.

"I am quite certain that it was Parsket who broke Beaumont's arm. He knew all the details of the so-called 'Horse Legend,' and got the idea to work upon the old story for his own end. He evidently had some method of slipping in and out of the house, probably through one of the many French windows, or possibly he had a key to one or two of the garden doors, and when he was supposed to be away, he was really coming down on the quiet and hiding somewhere in the neighborhood.

"The incident of the kiss in the dark hall I put down to sheer nervous imaginings on the part of Beaumont and Miss Hisgins, yet I must say that the sound of the horse outside of the front door is a little difficult to explain away. But I am still inclined to keep to my first idea on this point, that there was nothing really unnatural about it.

"The hoof sounds in the billiard room and down the passage were done by Parsket from the floor below by bumping up against the paneled ceiling with a block of wood tied to one of the window hooks. I proved this by an examination which showed the dents in the woodwork.

"The sounds of the horse galloping 'round the house were possibly made also by Parsket, who must have had a horse tied up in the plantation nearby, unless, indeed, he made the sounds himself, but I do not see how he could have gone fast enough to produce the illusion. In any case, I don't feel perfect certainty on this point. I failed to find any hoof marks, as you remember.

"The gobbling neighing in the park was a ventriloquial achievement on the part of Parsket and the attack out there on Beaumont was also by him, so that when I thought he was in his bedroom, he must have been outside all the time and joined me after I ran out of the front door. This is almost probable. I mean that Parsket was the cause, for if it had been something more serious he would certainly have given up his foolishness, knowing that there was no longer any need for it. I cannot imagine how he escaped being shot, both then and in the last mad action of which I have just told you. He was enormously without fear of any kind for himself as you can see.

"The time when Parsket was with us, when we thought we heard the Horse galloping 'round the house, we must have been deceived. No one was very sure, except, of course, Parsket, who would naturally encourage the belief.

"The neighing in the cellar is where I consider there came the first suspicion into Parsket's mind that there was something more at work than his sham haunting. The neighing was done by him in the same way that he did it in the park; but when I remember how ghastly he looked I feel sure that the sounds must have had some infernal quality added to them which frightened the man himself. Yet, later, he would persuade himself that he had been getting fanciful. Of course, I must not forget that the effect upon Miss Hisgins must have made him feel pretty miserable.

"Then, about the clergyman being called away, we found afterward that it was a bogus errand, or, rather, call and it is apparent that Parsket was at the bottom of this, so as to get a few more hours in which to achieve his end and what that was, a very little imagination will show you; for he had found that Beaumont would not be frightened away. I hate to think this, but I'm bound to. Anyway, it is obvious that the man was temporarily a bit off his normal balance. Love's a queer disease!

"Then, there is no doubt at all but that Parsket left the cord to the butler's bell hitched somewhere so as to give him an excuse to slip away naturally to clear it. This also gave him the opportunity to remove one of the passage lamps. Then he had only to smash the other and the passage was in utter darkness for him to make the attempt on Beaumont.

"In the same way, it was he who locked the door of the bedroom and took the key (it was in his pocket). This prevented the Captain from bringing a light and coming to the rescue. But Captain Hisgins broke down the door with the heavy fender curb and it was his smashing the door that sounded so confusing and frightening in the darkness of the passage.

"The photograph of the monstrous hoof above Miss Hisgins in the cellar is one of the things that I am less sure about. It might have been faked by Parsket, whilst I was out of the room, and this would have been easy enough, to anyone who knew how. But, you know, it does not look like a fake. Yet, there is as much evidence of probability that it was faked, as against; and the thing is too vague for an examination to help to a definite decision so that I will express no opinion, one way or the other. It is certainly a horrible photograph.

"And now I come to that last, dreadful thing. There has been no further manifestation of anything abnormal so that there is an extraordinary uncertainty in my conclusions. If we had not heard those last sounds and if Parsket had not shown that enormous sense of fear the whole of this case could be explained in the way in which I have shown. And, in fact, as you have seen, I am of the opinion that almost all of it can be cleared up, but I see no way of going past the thing we heard at the last and the fear that Parsket showed.

"His death—no, that proves nothing. At the inquest it was described somewhat untechnically as due to heart spasm. That is normal enough and leaves us quite in the dark as to whether he died because he stood between the girl and some incredible thing of monstrosity.

"The look on Parsket's face and the thing he called out when he heard the great hoof sounds coming down the passage seem to show that he had the sudden realization of what before then may have been nothing more than a horrible suspicion. And his fear and appreciation of some tremendous danger approaching was probably more keenly real even than mine. And then he did the one fine, great thing!"

"And the cause?" I said. "What caused it?"

Carnacki shook his head.

"God knows," he answered, with a peculiar, sincere reverence. "If that thing was what it seemed to be one might suggest an explanation which would not offend one's reason, but which may be utterly wrong. Yet I have thought, though it would take a long lecture on Thought Induction to get you to appreciate my reasons, that Parsket had produced what I might term a kind of 'induced haunting,' a kind of induced simulation of his mental conceptions to his desperate thoughts and broodings. It is impossible to make it clearer in a few words."

"But the old story!" I said. "Why may not there have been something in *that*?"

"There may have been something in it," said Carnacki. "But I do not think it had anything to do with this. I have not clearly thought out my reasons, yet; but later I may be able to tell you why I think so."

"And the marriage? And the cellar—was there anything found there?" asked Taylor.

"Yes, the marriage was performed that day in spite of the tragedy," Carnacki told us. "It was the wisest thing to do considering the things that I cannot explain. Yes, I had the floor of that big cellar up, for I had a feeling I might find something there to give me some light. But there was nothing.

"You know, the whole thing is tremendous and extraordinary. I shall never forget the look on Parsket's face. And afterward the disgusting sounds of those great hoofs going away through the quiet house."

Carnacki stood up.

"Out you go!" he said in friendly fashion, using the recognized formula.

And we went presently out into the quiet of the Embankment, and so to our homes.

THE SEARCHER OF THE END HOUSE

It was still evening, as I remember, and the four of us, Jessop, Arkright, Taylor and I, looked disappointedly at Carnacki, where he sat silent in his great chair.

We had come in response to the usual card of invitation, which—as you know—we have come to consider as a sure prelude to a good story; and now, after telling us the short incident of the Three Straw Platters, he had lapsed into a contented silence, and the night not half gone, as I have hinted.

However, as it chanced, some pitying fate jogged Carnacki's elbow, or his memory, and he began again, in his queer level way:—

"The 'Straw Platters' business reminds me of the 'Searcher' Case, which I have sometimes thought might interest you. It was some time ago, in fact a deuce of a long time ago, that the thing happened; and my experience of what I might term 'curious' things was very small at that time.

"I was living with my mother when it occurred, in a small house just outside of Appledorn, on the South Coast. The house was the last of a row of detached cottage villas, each house standing in its own garden; and very dainty little places they were, very old, and most of them smothered in roses; and all with those quaint old leaded windows, and doors of genuine oak. You must try to picture them for the sake of their complete niceness.

"Now I must remind you at the beginning that my mother and I had lived in that little house for two years; and in the whole of that time there had not been a single peculiar happening to worry us.

95

"And then, something happened.

"It was about two o'clock one morning, as I was finishing some letters, that I heard the door of my mother's bedroom open, and she came to the top of the stairs, and knocked on the banisters.

"'All right, dear,' I called; for I suppose she was merely reminding me that I should have been in bed long ago; then I heard her go back to her room, and I hurried my work, for fear she should lie awake, until she heard me safe up to my room.

"When I was finished, I lit my candle, put out the lamp, and went upstairs. As I came opposite the door of my mother's room, I saw that it was open, called good night to her, very softly, and asked whether I should close the door. As there was no answer, I knew that she had dropped off to sleep again, and I closed the door very gently, and turned into my room, just across the passage. As I did so, I experienced a momentary, half-aware sense of a faint, peculiar, disagreeable odor in the passage; but it was not until the following night that I *realized* I had noticed a smell that offended me. You follow me? It is so often like that—one suddenly knows a thing that really recorded itself on one's consciousness, perhaps a year before.

"The next morning at breakfast, I mentioned casually to my mother that she had 'dropped off,' and I had shut the door for her. To my surprise, she assured me she had never been out of her room. I reminded her about the two raps she had given upon the banister; but she still was certain I must be mistaken; and in the end I teased her, saying she had grown so accustomed to my bad habit of sitting up late, that she had come to call me in her sleep. Of course, she denied this, and I let the matter drop; but I was more than a little puzzled, and did not know whether to believe my own explanation, or to take the mater's, which was to put the noises down to the mice, and the open door to the fact that she couldn't have properly latched it, when she went to bed. I suppose, away in the subconscious part of me, I had a stirring of less reasonable thoughts; but certainly, I had no real uneasiness at that time.

"The next night there came a further development. About two thirty a.m., I heard my mother's door open, just as on the previous night, and immediately afterward she rapped sharply, on the banister, as it seemed to me. I stopped my work and called up that I would not be long. As she made no reply, and I did not hear her go back to bed, I had a quick sense of wonder whether she might not be doing it in her sleep, after all, just as I had said.

"With the thought, I stood up, and taking the lamp from the table, began to go toward the door, which was open into the passage. It was then I got a sudden nasty sort of thrill; for it came to me, all at once, that my mother never knocked when I sat up too late; she always called. You will understand I was not really frightened in any way; only vaguely uneasy, and pretty sure she must really be doing the thing in her sleep.

"I went quickly up the stairs, and when I came to the top, my mother was not there; but her door was open. I had a bewildered sense though believing she must have gone quietly back to bed, without my hearing her. I entered her room and found her sleeping quietly and naturally; for the vague sense of trouble in me was sufficiently strong to make me go over to look at her.

"When I was sure that she was perfectly right in every way, I was still a little bothered; but much more inclined to think my suspicion correct and that she had gone quietly back to bed in her sleep, without knowing what she had been doing. This was the most reasonable thing to think, as you must see.

"And then it came to me, suddenly, that vague, queer, mildewy smell in the room; and it was in that instant I became aware I had smelt the same strange, uncertain smell the night before in the passage.

"I was definitely uneasy now, and began to search my mother's room; though with no aim or clear thought of anything, except to assure myself that there was nothing in the room. All the time, you know, I never *expected really* to find anything; only my uneasiness had to be assured.

"In the middle of my search my mother woke up, and of course I had to explain. I told her about her door opening, and the knocks on the banister, and that I had come up and found her asleep. I said nothing about the smell, which was not very distinct; but told her that the thing happening twice had made me a bit nervous, and possibly fanciful, and I thought I would take a look 'round, just to feel satisfied.

"I have thought since that the reason I made no mention of the smell, was not only that I did not want to frighten my mother, for I was scarcely that myself; but because I had only a vague half-knowledge that I associated the smell with fancies too indefinite and peculiar to bear talking about. You will understand that I am able *now* to analyze and put the thing into words; but *then* I did not even know my chief reason for saying nothing; let alone appreciate its possible significance.

"It was my mother, after all, who put part of my vague sensations into words:—

"'What a disagreeable smell!' she exclaimed, and was silent a moment, looking at me. Then:— 'You feel there's something wrong?' still looking at me, very quietly but with a little, nervous note of questioning expectancy.

"'I don't know,' I said. 'I can't understand it, unless you've really been walking about in your sleep.'

"'The smell,' she said.

"'Yes,' I replied. 'That's what puzzles me too. I'll take a walk through the house; but I don't suppose it's anything.'

"I lit her candle, and taking the lamp, I went through the other bedrooms, and afterward all over the house, including the three underground cellars, which was a little trying to the nerves, seeing that I was more nervous than I would admit.

"Then I went back to my mother, and told her there was really nothing to bother about; and, you know, in the end, we talked ourselves into believing it was nothing. My mother would not agree that she might have been sleepwalking; but she was ready to put the door opening down to the fault of the latch, which certainly snicked very lightly. As for the knocks, they might be the old warped woodwork of the house cracking a bit, or a mouse rattling a piece of loose plaster. The smell was more difficult to explain; but finally we agreed that it might easily be the queer night smell of the moist earth, coming in through the open window of my mother's room, from the back garden, or—for that matter—from the little churchyard beyond the big wall at the bottom of the garden.

"And so we quietened down, and finally I went to bed, and to sleep.

"I think this is certainly a lesson on the way we humans can delude ourselves; for there was not one of these explanations that my reason could really accept. Try to imagine yourself in the same circumstances, and you will see how absurd our attempts to explain the happenings really were.

"In the morning, when I came down to breakfast, we talked it all over again, and whilst we agreed that it was strange, we also agreed that we had begun to imagine funny things in the backs of our minds, which now we felt half ashamed to admit. This is very strange when you come to look into it; but very human.

"And then that night again my mother's door was slammed once more just after midnight. I caught up the lamp, and when I reached her door, I found it shut. I opened it quickly, and went in, to find my mother lying with her eyes open, and rather nervous; having been waked by the bang of the door. But what upset me more than anything, was the fact that there was a disgusting smell in the passage and in her room.

"Whilst I was asking her whether she was all right, a door slammed twice downstairs; and you can imagine how it made me feel. My mother and I looked at one another; and then I lit her candle, and taking the poker from the fender, went downstairs with the lamp, beginning to feel really nervous. The cumulative effect of so many queer happenings was getting hold of me; and all the *apparently* reasonable explanations seemed futile.

"The horrible smell seemed to be very strong in the downstairs passage; also in the front room and the cellars; but chiefly in the passage. I made a very thorough search of the house, and when I had finished, I knew that all the lower windows and doors were properly shut and fastened, and that there was no living thing in the house, beyond our two selves. Then I went up to my mother's room again, and we talked the thing over for an hour or more, and in the end came to the conclusion that we might, after all, be reading too much into a number of little things; but, you know, inside of us, we did not believe this.

"Later, when we had talked ourselves into a more comfortable state of mind, I said good night, and went off to bed; and presently managed to get to sleep.

"In the early hours of the morning, whilst it was still dark, I was waked by a loud noise. I sat up in bed, and listened. And from downstairs, I heard:—bang, bang, bang, one door after another being slammed; at least, that is the impression the sounds gave to me.

"I jumped out of bed, with the tingle and shiver of sudden fright on me; and at the same moment, as I lit my candle, my door was pushed slowly open; I had left it unlatched, so as not to feel that my mother was quite shut off from me.

"'Who's there?' I shouted out, in a voice twice as deep as my natural one, and with a queer breathlessness, that sudden fright so often gives one. 'Who's there?'

"Then I heard my mother saying:—

"'It's me, Thomas. Whatever is happening downstairs?'

"She was in the room by this, and I saw she had her bedroom poker in one hand, and her candle in the other. I could have smiled at her, had it not been for the extraordinary sounds downstairs.

"I got into my slippers, and reached down an old sword bayonet from the wall; then I picked up my candle, and begged my mother not to come; but I knew it would be little use, if she had made up her mind; and she had, with the result that she acted as a sort of rearguard for me, during our search. I know, in some ways, I was very glad to have her with me, as you will understand.

"By this time, the door slamming had ceased, and there seemed, probably because of the contrast, to be an appalling silence in the house. However, I led the way, holding my candle high, and keeping the sword bayonet very handy. Downstairs we found all the doors wide open; although the outer doors and the windows were closed all right. I began to wonder whether the noises had been made by the doors after all. Of one thing only were we sure, and that was, there was no living thing in the house, beside ourselves, while everywhere throughout the house, there was the taint of that disgusting odor.

"Of course it was absurd to try to make believe any longer. There was something strange about the house; and as soon as it was daylight, I set my mother to packing; and soon after breakfast, I saw her off by train.

"Then I set to work to try to clear up the mystery. I went first to the landlord, and told him all the circumstances. From him, I found that twelve or fifteen years back, the house had got rather a curious name from three or four tenants; with the result that it had remained empty a long while; in the end he had let it at a low rent to a Captain Tobias, on the one condition that he should hold his tongue, if he saw anything peculiar. The landlord's idea—as he told me frankly—was to free the house from these tales of 'something queer,' by keeping a tenant in it, and then to sell it for the best price he could get.

"However, when Captain Tobias left, after a ten years' tenancy, there was no longer any talk about the house; so when I offered to take it on a five years' lease, he had jumped at the offer. This was the whole story; so he gave me to understand. When I pressed him for details of the supposed peculiar happenings in the house, all those years back, he said the tenants had talked about a woman who always moved about the house at night. Some tenants never saw anything; but others would not stay out the first month's tenancy.

"One thing the landlord was particular to point out, that no tenant had ever complained about knockings, or door slamming. As for the smell, he seemed positively indignant about it; but why, I don't suppose he knew himself, except that he probably had some vague feeling that it was an indirect accusation on my part that the drains were not right.

"In the end, I suggested that he should come down and spend the night with me. He agreed at once, especially as I told him I intended to keep the whole business quiet, and try to get to the bottom of the curious affair; for he was anxious to keep the rumor of the haunting from getting about.

"About three o'clock that afternoon, he came down, and we made a thorough search of the house, which, however, revealed nothing unusual. Afterward, the landlord made one or two tests, which showed him the drainage was in perfect order; after that we made our preparations for sitting up all night.

"First, we borrowed two policemen's dark lanterns from the station nearby, and where the superintendent and I were friendly, and as soon as it was really dusk, the landlord went up to his house for his gun. I had the sword bayonet I have told you about; and when the landlord got back, we sat talking in my study until nearly midnight.

"Then we lit the lanterns and went upstairs. We placed the lanterns, gun and bayonet handy on the table; then I shut and sealed the bedroom doors; afterward we took our seats, and turned off the lights.

"From then until two o'clock, nothing happened; but a little after two, as I found by holding my watch near the faint glow of the closed lanterns, I had a time of extraordinary nervousness; and I bent toward the landlord, and whispered to him that I had a queer feeling something was about to happen, and to be ready with his lantern; at the same time I reached out toward mine. In the very instant I made this movement, the darkness which filled the passage seemed to become suddenly of a dull violet color; not, as if a light had been shone; but as if the natural blackness of the night had changed color. And then, coming through this violet night, through this violet-colored gloom, came a little naked Child, running. In an extraordinary way, the Child seemed not to be distinct from the surrounding gloom; but almost as if it were a concentration of that extraordinary atmosphere; as if that gloomy color which had changed the night, came from the Child. It seems impossible to make clear to you; but try to understand it.

"The Child went past me, running, with the natural movement of the legs of a chubby human child, but in an absolute and inconceivable silence. It was a very small Child, and must have passed under the table; but I saw the Child through the table, as if it had been only a slightly darker shadow than the colored gloom. In the

same instant, I saw that a fluctuating glimmer of violet light outlined the metal of the gun-barrels and the blade of the sword bayonet, making them seem like faint shapes of glimmering light, floating unsupported where the tabletop should have shown solid.

"Now, curiously, as I saw these things, I was subconsciously
aware that I heard the anxious breathing of the landlord, quite clear
and labored, close to my elbow, where he waited nervously with
his hands on the lantern. I realized in that moment that he saw
nothing; but waited in the darkness, for my warning to come true.

"Even as I took heed of these minor things, I saw the Child jump
to one side, and hide behind some half-seen object that was certainly nothing belonging to the passage. I stared, intently, with a
most extraordinary thrill of expectant wonder, with fright making
goose flesh of my back. And even as I stared, I solved for myself
the less important problem of what the two black clouds were that
hung over a part of the table. I think it very curious and interesting,
the double working of the mind, often so much more apparent during
times of stress. The two clouds came from two faintly shining
shapes, which I knew must be the metal of the lanterns; and the
things that looked black to the sight with which I was then seeing,
could be nothing else but what to normal human sight is known as
light. This phenomenon I have always remembered. I have twice
seen a somewhat similar thing; in the Dark Light Case and in that
trouble of Maetheson's, which you know about.

"Even as I understood this matter of the lights, I was looking
to my left, to understand why the Child was hiding. And suddenly,
I heard the landlord shout out:— 'The Woman!' But I saw nothing.
I had a disagreeable sense that something repugnant was near to
me, and I was aware in the same moment that the landlord was
gripping my arm in a hard, frightened grip. Then I was looking
back to where the Child had hidden. I saw the Child peeping out
from behind its hiding place, seeming to be looking up the passage; but whether in fear I could not tell. Then it came out, and
ran headlong away, through the place where should have been the
wall of my mother's bedroom; but the Sense with which I was seeing these things, showed me the wall only as a vague, upright

shadow, unsubstantial. And immediately the child was lost to me, in the dull violet gloom. At the same time, I felt the landlord press back against me, as if something had passed close to him; and he called out again, a hoarse sort of cry:— 'The Woman! The Woman!' and turned the shade clumsily from off his lantern. But I had seen no Woman; and the passage showed empty, as he shone the beam of his light jerkily to and fro; but chiefly in the direction of the doorway of my mother's room.

"He was still clutching my arm, and had risen to his feet; and now, mechanically and almost slowly, I picked up my lantern and turned on the light. I shone it, a little dazedly, at the seals upon the doors; but none were broken; then I sent the light to and fro, up and down the passage; but there was nothing; and I turned to the landlord, who was saying something in a rather incoherent fashion. As my light passed over his face, I noted, in a dull sort of way, that he was drenched with sweat.

"Then my wits became more handleable, and I began to catch the drift of his words:— 'Did you see her? Did you see her?' he was saying, over and over again; and then I found myself telling him, in quite a level voice, that I had not seen any Woman. He became more coherent then, and I found that he had seen a Woman come from the end of the passage, and go past us; but he could not describe her, except that she kept stopping and looking about her, and had even peered at the wall, close beside him, as if looking for something. But what seemed to trouble him most, was that she had not seemed to see him at all. He repeated this so often, that in the end I told him, in an absurd sort of way, that he ought to be very glad she had not. What did it all mean? was the question; somehow I was not so frightened, as utterly bewildered. I had seen less then, than since; but what I had seen, had made me feel adrift from my anchorage of Reason.

"What did it mean? He had seen a Woman, searching for something. *I* had not seen this Woman. *I* had seen a Child, running away, and hiding from Something or Someone. *He* had not seen the Child, or the other things—only the Woman. And *I* had not seen her. What did it all mean?

"I had said nothing to the landlord about the Child. I had been too bewildered, and I realized that it would be futile to attempt an explanation. He was already stupid with the thing he had seen; and not the kind of man to understand. All this went through my mind as we stood there, shining the lanterns to and fro. All the time, intermingled with a streak of practical reasoning, I was questioning myself, what did it all mean? What was the Woman searching for; what was the Child running from?

"Suddenly, as I stood there, bewildered and nervous, making random answers to the landlord, a door below was violently slammed, and directly I caught the horrible reek of which I have told you.

"'There!' I said to the landlord, and caught his arm, in my turn. 'The Smell! Do *you* smell it?'

"He looked at me so stupidly that in a sort of nervous anger, I shook him.

"'Yes,' he said, in a queer voice, trying to shine the light from his shaking lantern at the stair head.

"'Come on!' I said, and picked up my bayonet; and he came, carrying his gun awkwardly. I think he came, more because he was afraid to be left alone, than because he had any pluck left, poor beggar. I never sneer at that kind of funk, at least very seldom; for when it takes hold of you, it makes rags of your courage.

"I led the way downstairs, shining my light into the lower passage, and afterward at the doors to see whether they were shut; for I had closed and latched them, placing a corner of a mat against each door, so I should know which had been opened.

"I saw at once that none of the doors had been opened; then I threw the beam of my light down alongside the stairway, in order to see the mat I had placed against the door at the top of the cellar stairs. I got a horrid thrill; for the mat was flat! I paused a couple of seconds, shining my light to and fro in the passage, and holding fast to my courage, I went down the stairs.

"As I came to the bottom step, I saw patches of wet all up and down the passage. I shone my lantern on them. It was the imprint of a wet foot on the oilcloth of the passage; not an ordinary footprint, but a queer, soft, flabby, spreading imprint, that gave me a feeling of extraordinary horror.

"Backward and forward I flashed the light over the impossible marks and saw them everywhere. Suddenly I noticed that they led to each of the closed doors. I felt something touch my back, and glanced 'round swiftly, to find the landlord had come close to me, almost pressing against me, in his fear.

"'It's all right,' I said, but in a rather breathless whisper, meaning to put a little courage into him; for I could feel that he was shaking through all his body. Even then as I tried to get him steadied enough to be of some use, his gun went off with a tremendous bang. He jumped, and yelled with sheer terror; and I swore because of the shock.

"'Give it to me, for God's sake!' I said, and slipped the gun from his hand; and in the same instant there was a sound of running steps up the garden path, and immediately the flash of a bull's-eye lantern upon the fan light over the front door. Then the door was tried, and directly afterward there came a thunderous knocking, which told me a policeman had heard the shot.

"I went to the door, and opened it. Fortunately the constable knew me, and when I had beckoned him in, I was able to explain matters in a very short time. While doing this, Inspector Johnstone came up the path, having missed the officer, and seeing lights and the open door. I told him as briefly as possible what had occurred, and did not mention the Child or the Woman; for it would have seem too fantastic for him to notice. I showed him the queer, wet footprints and how they went toward the closed doors. I explained quickly about the mats, and how that the one against the cellar door was flat, which showed the door had been opened.

"The inspector nodded, and told the constable to guard the door at the top of the cellar stairs. He then asked the hall lamp to be lit, after which he took the policeman's lantern, and led the way into the front room. He paused with the door wide open, and threw the light all 'round; then he jumped into the room, and looked behind the door; there was no one there; but all over the polished oak floor, between the scattered rugs, went the marks of those horrible spreading footprints; and the room permeated with the horrible odor.

"The inspector searched the room carefully, and then went into the middle room, using the same precautions. There was nothing in the middle room, or in the kitchen or pantry; but everywhere went the wet footmarks through all the rooms, showing plainly wherever there were woodwork or oilcloth; and always there was the smell.

"The inspector ceased from his search of the rooms, and spent a minute in trying whether the mats would really fall flat when the doors were open, or merely ruckle up in a way as to appear they had been untouched; but in each case, the mats fell flat, and remained so.

"'Extraordinary!' I heard Johnstone mutter to himself. And then he went toward the cellar door. He had inquired at first whether there were windows to the cellar, and when he learned there was no way out, except by the door, he had left this part of the search to the last.

"As Johnstone came up to the door, the policeman made a motion of salute, and said something in a low voice; and something in the tone made me flick my light across him. I saw then that the man was very white, and he looked strange and bewildered.

"'What?' said Johnstone impatiently. 'Speak up!'

"'A woman come along 'ere, sir, and went through this 'ere door,' said the constable, clearly, but with a curious monotonous intonation that is sometimes heard from an unintelligent man.

"'Speak up!' shouted the inspector.

"'A woman come along and went through this 'ere door,' repeated the man, monotonously.

"The inspector caught the man by the shoulder, and deliberately sniffed his breath.

"'No!' he said. And then sarcastically:— 'I hope you held the door open politely for the lady.'

"'The door weren't opened, sir,' said the man, simply.

"'Are you mad—' began Johnstone.

"'No,' broke in the landlord's voice from the back. Speaking steadily enough. 'I saw the Woman upstairs.' It was evident that he had got back his control again.

"'I'm afraid, Inspector Johnstone,' I said, 'that there's more in this than you think. I certainly saw some very extraordinary things upstairs.'

"The inspector seemed about to say something; but instead, he turned again to the door, and flashed his light down and 'round about the mat. I saw then that the strange, horrible footmarks came straight up to the cellar door; and the last print showed *under* the door; yet the policeman said the door had not been opened.

"And suddenly, without any intention, or realization of what I was saying, I asked the landlord:—

"'What were the feet like?'

"I received no answer; for the inspector was ordering the constable to open the cellar door, and the man was not obeying. Johnstone repeated the order, and at last, in a queer automatic way, the man obeyed, and pushed the door open. The loathsome smell beat up at us, in a great wave of horror, and the inspector came backward a step.

"'My God!' he said, and went forward again, and shone his light down the steps; but there was nothing visible, only that on each step showed the unnatural footprints.

"The inspector brought the beam of the light vividly on the top step; and there, clear in the light, there was something small, moving. The inspector bent to look, and the policeman and I with him. I don't want to disgust you; but the thing we looked at was a maggot. The policeman backed suddenly out of the doorway:

"'The churchyard,' he said, '. . . at the back of the 'ouse.'

"'Silence!' said Johnstone, with a queer break in the word, and I knew that at last he was frightened. He put his lantern into the doorway, and shone it from step to step, following the footprints down into the darkness; then he stepped back from the open doorway, and we all gave back with him. He looked 'round, and I had a feeling that he was looking for a weapon of some kind.

"'Your gun,' I said to the landlord, and he brought it from the front hall, and passed it over to the inspector, who took it and ejected the empty shell from the right barrel. He held out his hand for a live cartridge, which the landlord brought from his pocket. He loaded the gun and snapped the breech. He turned to the constable:—

"'Come on,' he said, and moved toward the cellar doorway.

"'I ain't comin', sir,' said the policeman, very white in the face.

"With a sudden blaze of passion, the inspector took the man by the scruff and hove him bodily down into the darkness, and he went downward, screaming. The inspector followed him instantly, with his lantern and the gun; and I after the inspector, with the bayonet ready. Behind me, I heard the landlord.

"At the bottom of the stairs, the inspector was helping the policeman to his feet, where he stood swaying a moment, in a bewildered fashion; then the inspector went into the front cellar, and his man followed him in stupid fashion; but evidently no longer with any thought of running away from the horror.

"We all crowded into the front cellar, flashing our lights to and fro. Inspector Johnstone was examining the floor, and I saw that the footmarks went all 'round the cellar, into all the corners, and across the floor. I thought suddenly of the Child that was running away from Something. Do you see the thing that I was seeing vaguely?

"We went out of the cellar in a body, for there was nothing to be found. In the next cellar, the footprints went everywhere in that queer erratic fashion, as of someone searching for something, or following some blind scent.

"In the third cellar the prints ended at the shallow well that had been the old water supply of the house. The well was full to the brim, and the water so clear that the pebbly bottom was plainly to be seen, as we shone the lights into the water. The search came to an abrupt end, and we stood about the well, looking at one another, in an absolute, horrible silence.

"Johnstone made another examination of the footprints; then he shone his light again into the clear shallow water, searching each inch of the plainly seen bottom; but there was nothing there. The cellar was full of the dreadful smell; and everyone stood silent, except for the constant turning of the lamps to and fro around the cellar.

"The inspector looked up from his search of the well, and nodded quietly across at me, with his sudden acknowledgment that our belief was now his belief, the smell in the cellar seemed to grow more dreadful, and to be, as it were, a menace—the material expression that some monstrous thing was there with us, invisible.

"'I think—' began the inspector, and shone his light toward the stairway; and at this the constable's restraint went utterly, and he ran for the stairs, making a queer sound in his throat.

"The landlord followed, at a quick walk, and then the inspector and I. He waited a single instant for me, and we went up together, treading on the same steps, and with our lights held backward. At the top, I slammed and locked the stair door, and wiped my forehead, and my hands were shaking.

"The inspector asked me to give his man a glass of whisky, and then he sent him on his beat. He stayed a short while with the landlord and me, and it was arranged that he would join us again the following night and watch the well with us from midnight until daylight. Then he left us, just as the dawn was coming in. The landlord and I locked up the house, and went over to his place for a sleep.

"In the afternoon, the landlord and I returned to the house, to make arrangements for the night. He was very quiet, and I felt he was to be relied on, now that he had been 'salted,' as it were, with his fright of the previous night.

"We opened all the doors and windows, and blew the house through very thoroughly; and in the meanwhile, we lit the lamps in the house, and took them into the cellars, where we set them all about, so as to have light everywhere. Then we carried down three chairs and a table, and set them in the cellar where the well was sunk. After that, we stretched thin piano wire across the cellar, about nine inches from the floor, at such a height that it should catch anything moving about in the dark.

"When this was done, I went through the house with the landlord, and sealed every window and door in the place, excepting only the front door and the door at the top of the cellar stairs.

"Meanwhile, a local wire-smith was making something to my order; and when the landlord and I had finished tea at his house, we went down to see how the smith was getting on. We found the thing complete. It looked rather like a huge parrot's cage, without any bottom, of very heavy gage wire, and stood about seven feet high and was four feet in diameter. Fortunately, I remembered to have it made longitudinally in two halves, or else we should never have got it through the doorways and down the cellar stairs.

"I told the wire-smith to bring the cage up to the house so he could fit the two halves rigidly together. As we returned, I called in at an ironmonger's, where I bought some thin hemp rope and an iron rack pulley, like those used in Lancashire for hauling up the ceiling clothes racks, which you will find in every cottage. I bought also a couple of pitchforks.

"'We shan't want to touch it,' I said to the landlord; and he nodded, rather white all at once.

"As soon as the cage arrived and had been fitted together in the cellar, I sent away the smith; and the landlord and I suspended it over the well, into which it fitted easily. After a lot of trouble, we managed to hang it so perfectly central from the rope over the iron pulley, that when hoisted to the ceiling and dropped, it went every time plunk into the well, like a candle-extinguisher. When we had it finally arranged, I hoisted it up once more, to the ready position, and made the rope fast to a heavy wooden pillar, which stood in the middle of the cellar.

"By ten o'clock, I had everything arranged, with the two pitchforks and the two police lanterns; also some whisky and sandwiches. Underneath the table I had several buckets full of disinfectant.

"A little after eleven o'clock, there was a knock at the front door, and when I went, I found Inspector Johnstone had arrived, and brought with him one of his plainclothes men. You will understand how pleased I was to see there would be this addition to our watch;

for he looked a tough, nerveless man, brainy and collected; and one I should have picked to help us with the horrible job I felt pretty sure we should have to do that night.

"When the inspector and the detective had entered, I shut and locked the front door; then, while the inspector held the light, I sealed the door carefully, with tape and wax. At the head of the cellar stairs, I shut and locked that door also, and sealed it in the same way.

"As we entered the cellar, I warned Johnstone and his man to be careful not to fall over the wires; and then, as I saw his surprise at my arrangements, I began to explain my ideas and intentions, to all of which he listened with strong approval. I was pleased to see also that the detective was nodding his head, as I talked, in a way that showed he appreciated all my precautions.

"As he put his lantern down, the inspector picked up one of the pitchforks, and balanced it in his hand; he looked at me, and nodded.

"'The best thing,' he said. 'I only wish you'd got two more.'

"Then we all took our seats, the detective getting a washing stool from the corner of the cellar. From then, until a quarter to twelve, we talked quietly, whilst we made a light supper of whisky and sandwiches; after which, we cleared everything off the table, excepting the lanterns and the pitchforks. One of the latter, I handed to the inspector; the other I took myself, and then, having set my chair so as to be handy to the rope which lowered the cage into the well, I went 'round the cellar and put out every lamp.

"I groped my way to my chair, and arranged the pitchfork and the dark lantern ready to my hand; after which I suggested that everyone should keep an absolute silence throughout the watch. I asked, also, that no lantern should be turned on, until I gave the word.

"I put my watch on the table, where a faint glow from my lantern made me able to see the time. For an hour nothing happened, and everyone kept an absolute silence, except for an occasional uneasy movement.

"About half-past one, however, I was conscious again of the same extraordinary and peculiar nervousness, which I had felt on the previous night. I put my hand out quickly, and eased the hitched rope from around the pillar. The inspector seemed aware of the movement; for I saw the faint light from his lantern, move a little, as if he had suddenly taken hold of it, in readiness.

"A minute later, I noticed there was a change in the color of the night in the cellar, and it grew slowly violet tinted upon my eyes. I glanced to and fro, quickly, in the new darkness, and even as I looked, I was conscious that the violet color deepened. In the direction of the well, but seeming to be at a great distance, there was, as it were, a nucleus to the change; and the nucleus came swiftly toward us, appearing to come from a great space, almost in a single moment. It came near, and I saw again that it was a little naked Child, running, and seeming to be of the violet night in which it ran.

"The Child came with a natural running movement, exactly as I described it before; but in a silence so peculiarly intense, that it was as if it brought the silence with it. About half-way between the well and the table, the Child turned swiftly, and looked back at something invisible to me; and suddenly it went down into a crouching attitude, and seemed to be hiding behind something that showed vaguely; but there was nothing there, except the bare floor of the cellar; nothing, I mean, of our world.

"I could hear the breathing of the three other men, with a wonderful distinctness; and also the tick of my watch upon the table seemed to sound as loud and as slow as the tick of an old grandfather's clock. Someway I knew that none of the others saw what I was seeing.

"Abruptly, the landlord, who was next to me, let out his breath with a little hissing sound; I knew then that something was visible to him. There came a creak from the table, and I had a feeling that the inspector was leaning forward, looking at something that I could not see. The landlord reached out his hand through the darkness, and fumbled a moment to catch my arm:—

"'The Woman!' he whispered, close to my ear. 'Over by the well.'

"I stared hard in that direction; but saw nothing, except that the violet color of the cellar seemed a little duller just there.

"I looked back quickly to the vague place where the Child was hiding. I saw it was peering back from its hiding place. Suddenly it rose and ran straight for the middle of the table, which showed only as vague shadow half-way between my eyes and the unseen floor. As the Child ran under the table, the steel prongs of my pitch-fork glimmered with a violet, fluctuating light. A little way off, there showed high up in the gloom, the vaguely shining outline of the other fork, so I knew the inspector had it raised in his hand, ready. There was no doubt but that he saw something. On the table, the metal of the five lanterns shone with the same strange glow; and about each lantern there was a little cloud of absolute blackness, where the phenomenon that is light to our natural eyes, came through the fittings; and in this complete darkness, the metal of each lantern showed plain, as might a cat's-eye in a nest of black cotton wool.

"Just beyond the table, the Child paused again, and stood, seeming to oscillate a little upon its feet, which gave the impression that it was lighter and vaguer than a thistle-down; and yet, in the same moment, another part of me seemed to know that it was to me, as something that might be beyond thick, invisible glass, and subject to conditions and forces that I was unable to compre-hend.

"The Child was looking back again, and my gaze went the same way. I stared across the cellar, and saw the cage hanging clear in the violet light, every wire and tie outlined with its glimmering; above it there was a little space of gloom, and then the dull shining of the iron pulley which I had screwed into the ceiling.

"I stared in a bewildered way 'round the cellar; there were thin lines of vague fire crossing the floor in all directions; and suddenly I remembered the piano wire that the landlord and I had stretched. But there was nothing else to be seen, except that near the table there were indistinct glimmerings of light, and at the far end the outline of a dull glowing revolver, evidently in the detective's pocket. I remember a sort of subconscious satisfaction, as I settled the point in a queer automatic fashion. On the table, near to me, there was a little shapeless collection of the light; and this I knew, after an instant's consideration, to be the steel portions of my watch.

"I had looked several times at the Child, and 'round at the cellar, whilst I was decided these trifles; and had found it still in that attitude of hiding from something. But now, suddenly, it ran clear away into the distance, and was nothing more than a slightly deeper colored nucleus far away in the strange colored atmosphere.

"The landlord gave out a queer little cry, and twisted over against me, as if to avoid something. From the inspector there came a sharp breathing sound, as if he had been suddenly drenched with cold water. Then suddenly the violet color went out of the night, and I was conscious of the nearness of something monstrous and repugnant.

"There was a tense silence, and the blackness of the cellar seemed absolute, with only the faint glow about each of the lanterns on the table. Then, in the darkness and the silence, there came a faint tinkle of water from the well, as if something were rising noiselessly out of it, and the water running back with a gentle tinkling. In the same instant, there came to me a sudden waft of the awful smell.

"I gave a sharp cry of warning to the inspector, and loosed the rope. There came instantly the sharp splash of the cage entering the water; and then, with a stiff, frightened movement, I opened the shutter of my lantern, and shone the light at the cage, shouting to the others to do the same.

"As my light struck the cage, I saw that about two feet of it projected from the top of the well, and there was something protruding up out of the water, into the cage. I stared, with a feeling that I recognized the thing; and then, as the other lanterns were opened, I saw that it was a leg of mutton. The thing was held by a brawny fist and arm, that rose out of the water. I stood utterly bewildered, watching to see what was coming. In a moment there rose into view a great bearded face, that I felt for one quick instant was the face of a drowned man, long dead. Then the face opened at the mouth part, and spluttered and coughed. Another big hand came into view, and wiped the water from the eyes, which blinked rapidly, and then fixed themselves into a stare at the lights.

"From the detective there came a sudden shout:—

"'Captain Tobias!' he shouted, and the inspector echoed him; and instantly burst into loud roars of laughter.

"The inspector and the detective ran across the cellar to the cage; and I followed, still bewildered. The man in the cage was holding the leg of mutton as far away from him, as possible, and holding his nose.

"'Lift thig dam trap, quig!' he shouted in a stifled voice; but the inspector and the detective simply doubled before him, and tried to hold their noses, whilst they laughed, and the light from their lanterns went dancing all over the place.

"'Quig! quig!' said the man in the cage, still holding his nose, and trying to speak plainly.

"Then Johnstone and the detective stopped laughing, and lifted the cage. The man in the well threw the leg across the cellar, and turned swiftly to go down into the well; but the officers were too quick for him, and had him out in a twinkling. Whilst they held him, dripping upon the floor, the inspector jerked his thumb in the direction of the offending leg, and the landlord, having harpooned it with one of the pitchforks, ran with it upstairs and so into the open air.

"Meanwhile, I had given the man from the well a stiff tot of whisky; for which he thanked me with a cheerful nod, and having emptied the glass at a draft, held his hand for the bottle, which he finished, as if it had been so much water.

"As you will remember, it was a Captain Tobias who had been the previous tenant; and this was the very man who had appeared from the well. In the course of the talk that followed, I learned the reason for Captain Tobias leaving the house; he had been wanted by the police for smuggling. He had undergone imprisonment; and had been released only a couple of weeks earlier.

"He had returned to find new tenants in his old home. He had entered the house through the well, the walls of which were not continued to the bottom (this I will deal with later); and gone up by a little stairway in the cellar wall, which opened at the top through a panel beside my mother's bedroom. This panel was opened, by revolving the left doorpost of the bedroom door, with the result that the bedroom door always became unlatched, in the process of opening the panel.

"The captain complained, without any bitterness, that the panel had warped, and that each time he opened it, it made a cracking noise. This had been evidently what I mistook for raps. He would not give his reason for entering the house; but it was pretty obvious that he had hidden something, which he wanted to get. However, as he found it impossible to get into the house without the risk of being caught, he decided to try to drive us out, relying on the bad reputation of the house, and his own artistic efforts as a ghost. I must say he succeeded. He intended then to rent the house again, as before; and would then, of course have plenty of time to get whatever he had hidden. The house suited him admirably; for there was a passage—as he showed me afterward—connecting the dummy well with the crypt of the church beyond the garden wall; and these, in turn, were connected with certain caves in the cliffs, which went down to the beach beyond the church.

"In the course of his talk, Captain Tobias offered to take the house off my hands; and as this suited me perfectly, for I was about stalled with it, and the plan also suited the landlord, it was decided that no steps should be taken against him; and that the whole business should be hushed up.

"I asked the captain whether there was really anything queer about the house; whether he had ever seen anything. He said yes, that he had twice seen a Woman going about the house. We all looked at one another, when the captain said that. He told us she never bothered him, and that he had only seen her twice, and on each occasion it had followed a narrow escape from the Revenue people.

"Captain Tobias was an observant man; he had seen how I had placed the mats against the doors; and after entering the rooms, and walking all about them, so as to leave the foot-marks of an old pair of wet woollen slippers everywhere, he had deliberately put the mats back as he found them.

"The maggot which had dropped from his disgusting leg of mutton had been an accident, and beyond even his horrible planning. He was hugely delighted to learn how it had affected us.

"The moldy smell I had noticed was from the little closed stairway, when the captain opened the panel. The door slamming was also another of his contributions.

"I come now to the end of the captain's ghost play; and to the difficulty of trying to explain the other peculiar things. In the first place, it was obvious there was something genuinely strange in the house; which made itself manifest as a Woman. Many different people had seen this Woman, under differing circumstances, so it is impossible to put the thing down to fancy; at the same time it must seem extraordinary that I should have lived two years in the house, and seen nothing; whilst the policeman saw the Woman, before he had been there twenty minutes; the landlord, the detective, and the inspector all saw her.

"I can only surmise that *fear* was in every case the key, as I might say, which opened the senses to the presence of the Woman. The policeman was a highly-strung man, and when he became frightened, was able to see the Woman. The same reasoning applies all 'round. *I* saw nothing, until I became really frightened; then I saw, not the Woman; but a Child, running away from Something or Someone. However, I will touch on that later. In short, until a very strong degree of fear was present, no one was affected by the Force which made Itself evident, as a Woman. My theory explains why some tenants were never aware of anything strange in the house, whilst others left immediately. The more sensitive they were, the less would be the degree of fear necessary to make them aware of the Force present in the house.

"The peculiar shining of all the metal objects in the cellar had been visible only to me. The cause, naturally I do not know; neither do I know why I, alone, was able to see the shining."

"The Child," I asked. "Can you explain that part at all? Why *you* didn't see the Woman, and why *they* didn't see the Child. Was it merely the same Force, appearing differently to different people?"

"No," said Carnacki, "I can't explain that. But I am quite sure that the Woman and the Child were not only two complete and different entities; but even they were each not in quite the same planes of existence.

"To give you a root idea, however, it is held in the Sigsand MS. that a child '*still* born' is 'Snatyched back bye thee Haggs.' This is crude; but may yet contain an elemental truth. Yet, before I make this clearer, let me tell you a thought that has often been made. It may be that physical birth is but a secondary process; and that prior to the possibility, the Mother Spirit searches for, until it finds, the small Element—the primal Ego or child's soul. It may be that a certain waywardness would cause such to strive to evade capture by the Mother Spirit. It may have been such a thing as this that I saw. I have always tried to think so; but it is impossible to ignore the sense of repulsion that I felt when the unseen Woman went past me. This repulsion carries forward the idea suggested in the Sigsand MS., that a stillborn child is thus, because its ego or spirit has been snatched back by the 'Hags.' In other words, by certain of the Monstrosities of the Outer Circle. The thought is inconceivably terrible, and probably the more so because it is so fragmentary. It leaves us with the conception of a child's soul adrift halfway between two lives, and running through Eternity from Something incredible and inconceivable (because not understood) to our senses.

"The thing is beyond further discussion; for it is futile to attempt to discuss a thing, to any purpose, of which one has a knowledge so fragmentary as this. There is one thought, which is often mine. Perhaps there is a Mother Spirit—"

"And the well?" said Arkright. "How did the captain get in from the other side?"

"As I said before," answered Carnacki. "The side walls of the well did not reach to the bottom; so that you had only to dip down into the water, and come up again on the other side of the wall, under the cellar floor, and so climb into the passage. Of course, the water was the same height on both sides of the walls. Don't ask me who made the well entrance or the little stairway; for I don't know. The house was very old, as I have told you; and that sort of thing was useful in the old days."

"And the Child," I said, coming back to the thing which chiefly interested me. "You would say that the birth must have occurred in that house; and in this way, one might suppose that the house to have become *en rapport*, if I can use the word in that way, with the Forces that produced the tragedy?"

"Yes," replied Carnacki. "This is, supposing we take the suggestion of the Sigsand MS., to account for the phenomenon."

"There may be other houses—" I began.

"There are," said Carnacki; and stood up.

"Out you go," he said, genially, using the recognized formula. And in five minutes we were on the Embankment, going thoughtfully to our various homes.

THE THING INVISIBLE

Carnacki had just returned to Cheyne Walk, Chelsea. I was aware of this interesting fact by reason of the curt and quaintly worded postcard which I was rereading, and by which I was requested to present myself at his house not later than seven o'clock on that evening. Mr. Carnacki had, as I and the others of his strictly limited circle of friends knew, been away in Kent for the past three weeks; but beyond that, we had no knowledge. Carnacki was genially secretive and curt, and spoke only when he was ready to speak. When this stage arrived, I and his three other friends—Jessop, Arkright, and Taylor—would receive a card or a wire, asking us to call. Not one of us ever willingly missed, for after a thoroughly sensible little dinner Carnacki would snuggle down into his big armchair, light his pipe, and wait whilst we arranged ourselves comfortably in our accustomed seats and nooks. Then he would begin to talk.

Upon this particular night I was the first to arrive and found Carnacki sitting, quietly smoking over a paper. He stood up, shook me firmly by the hand, pointed to a chair, and sat down again, never having uttered a word.

For my part, I said nothing either. I knew the man too well to bother him with questions or the weather, and so took a seat and a cigarette. Presently the three others turned up and after that we spent a comfortable and busy hour at dinner.

Dinner over, Carnacki snugged himself down into his great chair, as I have said was his habit, filled his pipe and puffed for awhile, his gaze directed thoughtfully at the fire. The rest of us, if I may so express it, made ourselves cozy, each after his own particular manner. A minute or so later Carnacki began to speak, ignoring any preliminary remarks, and going straight to the subject of the story we knew he had to tell:

"I have just come back from Sir Alfred Jarnock's place at Burtontree, in South Kent," he began, without removing his gaze from the fire. "Most extraordinary things have been happening down there lately and Mr. George Jarnock, the eldest son, wired to ask me to run over and see whether I could help to clear matters up a bit. I went.

"When I got there, I found that they have an old Chapel attached to the castle which has had quite a distinguished reputation for being what is popularly termed 'haunted.' They have been rather proud of this, as I managed to discover, until quite lately when something very disagreeable occurred, which served to remind them that family ghosts are not always content, as I might say, to remain purely ornamental.

"It sounds almost laughable, I know, to hear of a long-respected supernatural phenomenon growing unexpectedly dangerous; and in this case, the tale of the haunting was considered as little more than an old myth, except after nightfall, when possibly it became more plausible seeming.

"But however this may be, there is no doubt at all but that what I might term the Haunting Essence which lived in the place, had become suddenly dangerous—deadly dangerous too, the old butler being nearly stabbed to death one night in the Chapel, with a peculiar old dagger.

"It is, in fact, this dagger which is popularly supposed to 'haunt' the Chapel. At least, there has been always a story handed down in the family that this dagger would attack any enemy who should dare to venture into the Chapel, after nightfall. But, of course, this had been taken with just about the same amount of seriousness that people take most ghost tales, and that is not usually of a worryingly *real* nature. I mean that most people never quite know how much or how little they believe of matters ab-human or ab-normal, and generally they never have an opportunity to learn. And, indeed, as you are all aware, I am as big a skeptic concerning the truth of ghost tales as any man you are likely to meet; only I am what I might term an unprejudiced skeptic. I am not given to either believing or disbelieving things 'on principle,' as I have found many idiots prone to be, and what is more, some of them not ashamed to boast of the insane fact. I view all reported 'hauntings' as unproven until I have examined into them, and I am bound to admit that ninety-nine cases in a hundred turn out to be sheer bosh and fancy. But the hundredth! Well, if it were not for the hundredth, I should have few stories to tell you—eh?

"Of course, after the attack on the butler, it became evident that there was at least 'something' in the old story concerning the dagger, and I found everyone in a half belief that the queer old weapon did really strike the butler, either by the aid of some inherent force, which I found them peculiarly unable to explain, or else in the hand of some invisible thing or monster of the Outer World!

"From considerable experience, I knew that it was much more likely that the butler had been 'knifed' by some vicious and quite material human!

"Naturally, the first thing to do, was to test this probability of human agency, and I set to work to make a pretty drastic examination of the people who knew most about the tragedy.

"The result of this examination, both pleased and surprised me, for it left me with very good reasons for belief that I had come upon one of those extraordinary rare 'true manifestations' of the extrusion of a Force from the Outside. In more popular phraseology—a genuine case of haunting.

"These are the facts: On the previous Sunday evening but one, Sir Alfred Jarnock's household had attended family service, as usual, in the Chapel. You see, the Rector goes over to officiate twice each Sunday, after concluding his duties at the public Church about three miles away.

"At the end of the service in the Chapel, Sir Alfred Jarnock, his son Mr. George Jarnock, and the Rector had stood for a couple of minutes, talking, whilst old Bellett the butler went 'round, putting out the candles.

"Suddenly, the Rector remembered that he had left his small prayer book on the Communion table in the morning; he turned, and asked the butler to get it for him before he blew out the chancel candles.

"Now I have particularly called your attention to this because it is important in that it provides witnesses in a most fortunate manner at an extraordinary moment. You see, the Rector's turning to speak to Bellett had naturally caused both Sir Alfred Jarnock and his son to glance in the direction of the butler, and it was at this identical instant and whilst all three were looking at him, that the old butler was stabbed—there, full in the candlelight, before their eyes.

"I took the opportunity to call early upon the Rector, after I had questioned Mr. George Jarnock, who replied to my queries in place of Sir Alfred Jarnock, for the older man was in a nervous and shaken condition as a result of the happening, and his son wished him to avoid dwelling upon the scene as much as possible.

"The Rector's version was clear and vivid, and he had evidently received the astonishment of his life. He pictured to me the whole affair—Bellett, up at the chancel gate, going for the prayer book, and absolutely alone; and then the *blow*, out of the Void, he described it; and the *force* prodigious—the old man being driven headlong into the body of the Chapel. Like the kick of a great horse, the Rector said, his benevolent old eyes bright and intense with the effort he had actually witnessed, in defiance of all that he had hitherto believed.

"When I left him, he went back to the writing which he had put aside when I appeared. I feel sure that he was developing the first unorthodox sermon that he had ever evolved. He was a dear old chap, and I should certainly like to have heard it.

"The last man I visited was the butler. He was, of course, in a frightfully weak and shaken condition, but he could tell me nothing that did not point to there being a Power abroad in the Chapel. He told the same tale, in every minute particle, that I had learned from the others. He had been just going up to put out the altar candles and fetch the Rector's book, when something struck him an enormous blow high up on the left breast and he was driven headlong into the aisle.

"Examination had shown that he had been stabbed by the dagger—of which I will tell you more in a moment—that hung always above the altar. The weapon had entered, fortunately, some inches above the heart, just under the collarbone, which had been broken by the stupendous force of the blow, the dagger itself being driven clean through the body, and out through the scapula behind.

"The poor old fellow could not talk much, and I soon left him; but what he had told me was sufficient to make it unmistakable that no living person had been within yards of him when he was attacked; and, as I knew, this fact was verified by three capable and responsible witnesses, independent of Bellett himself.

"The thing now was to search the Chapel, which is small and extremely old. It is very massively built, and entered through only one door, which leads out of the castle itself, and the key of which is kept by Sir Alfred Jarnock, the butler having no duplicate.

"The shape of the Chapel is oblong, and the altar is railed off after the usual fashion. There are two tombs in the body of the place; but none in the chancel, which is bare, except for the tall candlesticks, and the chancel rail, beyond which is the undraped altar of solid marble, upon which stand four small candlesticks, two at each end.

"Above the altar hangs the 'waeful dagger,' as I had learned it was named. I fancy the term has been taken from an old vellum, which describes the dagger and its supposed abnormal properties. I took the dagger down, and examined it minutely and with method. The blade is ten inches long, two inches broad at the base, and tapering to a rounded but sharp point, rather peculiar. It is double-edged.

"The metal sheath is curious for having a crosspiece, which, taken with the fact that the sheath itself is continued three parts up the hilt of the dagger (in a most inconvenient fashion), gives it the appearance of a cross. That this is not unintentional is shown by an engraving of the Christ crucified upon one side, whilst upon the other, in Latin, is the inscription: 'Vengeance is Mine, I will Repay.' A quaint and rather terrible conjunction of ideas. Upon the blade of the dagger is graven in old English capitals: I WATCH. I STRIKE. On the butt of the hilt there is carved deeply a Pentacle.

"This is a pretty accurate description of the peculiar old weapon that has had the curious and uncomfortable reputation of being able (either of its own accord or in the hand of something invisible) to strike murderously any enemy of the Jarnock family who may chance to enter the Chapel after nightfall. I may tell you here and now, that before I left, I had very good reason to put certain doubts behind me; for I tested the deadliness of the thing myself.

"As you know, however, at this point of my investigation, I was still at that stage where I considered the existence of a supernatural Force unproven. In the meanwhile, I treated the Chapel drastically, sounding and scrutinizing the walls and floor, dealing with them almost foot by foot, and particularly examining the two tombs.

"At the end of this search, I had in a ladder, and made a close survey of the groined roof. I passed three days in this fashion, and by the evening of the third day I had proved to my entire satisfaction that there is no place in the whole of that Chapel where any living being could have hidden, and also that the only way of ingress and egress to and from the Chapel is through the doorway which leads into the castle, the door of which was always kept locked, and the key kept by Sir Alfred Jarnock himself, as I have told you. I mean, of course, that this doorway is the only entrance practicable to material people.

"Yes, as you will see, even had I discovered some other opening, secret or otherwise, it would not have helped at all to explain the mystery of the incredible attack, in a normal fashion. For the butler, as you know, was struck in full sight of the Rector, Sir Jarnock and his son. And old Bellett himself knew that no living person had touched him. . . . 'Out of the Void,' the Rector had described the inhumanly brutal attack. 'Out of the Void!' A strange feeling it gives one—eh?

"And this is the thing that I had been called in to bottom!

"After considerable thought, I decided on a plan of action. I proposed to Sir Alfred Jarnock that I should spend a night in the Chapel, and keep a constant watch upon the dagger. But to this, the old knight—a little, wizened, nervous man—would not listen for a moment. He, at least, I felt assured had no doubt of the reality of some dangerous supernatural Force a-roam at night in the Chapel. He informed me that it had been his habit every evening to lock the Chapel door, so that no one might foolishly or heedlessly run the risk of any peril that it might hold at night, and that he could not allow me to attempt such a thing after what had happened to the butler.

"I could see that Sir Alfred Jarnock was very much in earnest, and would evidently have held himself to blame had he allowed me to make the experiment and any harm come to me; so I said nothing in argument; and presently, pleading the fatigue of his years and health, he said goodnight, and left me; having given me the impression of being a polite but rather superstitious, old gentleman.

"That night, however, whilst I was undressing, I saw how I might achieve the thing I wished, and be able to enter the Chapel after dark, without making Sir Alfred Jarnock nervous. On the morrow, when I borrowed the key, I would take an impression, and have a duplicate made. Then, with my private key, I could do just what I liked.

"In the morning I carried out my idea. I borrowed the key, as I wanted to take a photograph of the chancel by daylight. When I had done this I locked up the Chapel and handed the key to Sir Alfred Jarnock, having first taken an impression in soap. I had brought out the exposed plate—in its slide—with me; but the camera I had left exactly as it was, as I wanted to take a second photograph of the chancel that night, from the same position.

"I took the dark slide into Burtontree, also the cake of soap with the impress. The soap I left with the local ironmonger, who was something of a locksmith and promised to let me have my duplicate, finished, if I would call in two hours. This I did, having in the meanwhile found out a photographer where I developed the plate, and left it to dry, telling him I would call next day. At the end of the two hours I went for my key and found it ready, much to my satisfaction. Then I returned to the castle.

"After dinner that evening, I played billiards with young Jarnock for a couple of hours. Then I had a cup of coffee and went off to my room, telling him I was feeling awfully tired. He nodded and told me he felt the same way. I was glad, for I wanted the house to settle as soon as possible.

"I locked the door of my room, then from under the bed—where I had hidden them earlier in the evening—I drew out several fine pieces of plate armor, which I had removed from the armory. There was also a shirt of chain mail, with a sort of quilted hood of mail to go over the head.

"I buckled on the plate armor, and found it extraordinarily uncomfortable, and over all I drew on the chain mail. I know nothing about armor, but from what I have learned since, I must have put on parts of two suits. Anyway, I felt beastly, clamped and clumsy and unable to move my arms and legs naturally. But I knew that the thing I was thinking of doing called for some sort of protection for my body. Over the armor I pulled on my dressing gown and shoved my revolver into one of the side pockets—and my repeating flash-light into the other. My dark lantern I carried in my hand.

"As soon as I was ready I went out into the passage and listened. I had been some considerable time making my preparations and I found that now the big hall and staircase were in darkness and all the house seemed quiet. I stepped back and closed and locked my door. Then, very slowly and silently I went downstairs to the hall and turned into the passage that led to the Chapel.

"I reached the door and tried my key. It fitted perfectly and a moment later I was in the Chapel, with the door locked behind me, and all about me the utter dree silence of the place, with just the faint showings of the outlines of the stained, leaded windows, making the darkness and lonesomeness almost the more apparent.

"Now it would be silly to say I did not feel queer. I felt very queer indeed. You just try, any of you, to imagine yourself standing there in the dark silence and remembering not only the legend that was attached to the place, but what had really happened to the old butler only a little while gone. I can tell you, as I stood there, I could believe that something invisible was coming toward me in the air of the Chapel. Yet, I had got to go through with the business, and I just took hold of my little bit of courage and set to work.

"First of all I switched on my light, then I began a careful tour of the place; examining every corner and nook. I found nothing unusual. At the chancel gate I held up my lamp and flashed the light at the dagger. It hung there, right enough, above the altar, but I remember thinking of the word 'demure,' as I looked at it. However, I pushed the thought away, for what I was doing needed no addition of uncomfortable thoughts.

"I completed the tour of the place, with a constantly growing awareness of its utter chill and unkind desolation—an atmosphere of cold dismalness seemed to be everywhere, and the quiet was abominable.

"At the conclusion of my search I walked across to where I had left my camera focused upon the chancel. From the satchel that I had put beneath the tripod I took out a dark slide and inserted it in the camera, drawing the shutter. After that I uncapped the lens, pulled out my flashlight apparatus, and pressed the trigger. There was an intense, brilliant flash that made the whole of the interior of the Chapel jump into sight, and disappear as quickly. Then, in the light from my lantern, I inserted the shutter into the slide, and reversed the slide, so as to have a fresh plate ready to expose at any time.

"After I had done this I shut off my lantern and sat down in one of the pews near to my camera. I cannot say what I expected to happen, but I had an extraordinary feeling, almost a conviction, that something peculiar or horrible would soon occur. It was, you know, as if I knew.

"An hour passed, of absolute silence. The time I knew by the far-off, faint chime of a clock that had been erected over the stables. I was beastly cold, for the whole place is without any kind of heating pipes or furnace, as I had noticed during my search, so that the temperature was sufficiently uncomfortable to suit my frame of mind. I felt like a kind of human periwinkle encased in boilerplate and frozen with cold and funk. And, you know, somehow the dark about me seemed to press coldly against my face. I cannot say whether any of you have ever had the feeling, but if you have, you will know just how disgustingly unnerving it is. And then, all at once, I had a horrible sense that something was moving in the place. It was not that I could hear anything but I had a kind of intuitive knowledge that something had stirred in the darkness. Can you imagine how I felt?

"Suddenly my courage went. I put up my mailed arms over my face. I wanted to protect it. I had got a sudden sickening feeling that something was hovering over me in the dark. Talk about fright! I could have shouted if I had not been afraid of the noise. . . . And then, abruptly, I heard something. Away up the aisle, there sounded a dull clang of metal, as it might be the tread of a mailed heel upon the stone of the aisle. I sat immovable. I was fighting with all my strength to get back my courage. I could not take my arms down from over my face, but I knew that I was getting hold of the gritty part of me again. And suddenly I made a mighty effort and lowered my arms. I held my face up in the darkness. And, I tell you, I respect myself for the act, because I thought truly at that moment that I was going to die. But I think, just then, by the slow revulsion of feeling which had assisted my effort, I was less sick, in that instant, at the thought of having to die, than at the knowledge of the utter weak cowardice that had so unexpectedly shaken me all to bits, for a time.

"Do I make myself clear? You understand, I feel sure, that the sense of respect, which I spoke of, is not really unhealthy egotism; because, you see, I am not blind to the state of mind which helped me. I mean that if I had uncovered my face by a sheer effort of will, unhelped by any revulsion of feeling, I should have done a thing much more worthy of mention. But, even as it was, there were elements in the act, worthy of respect. You follow me, don't you?

"And, you know, nothing touched me, after all! So that, in a little while, I had got back a bit to my normal, and felt steady enough to go through with the business without any more funking.

"I daresay a couple of minutes passed, and then, away up near the chancel, there came again that clang, as though an armored foot stepped cautiously. By Jove! but it made me stiffen. And suddenly the thought came that the sound I heard might be the rattle of the dagger above the altar. It was not a particularly sensible notion, for the sound was far too heavy and resonant for such a cause. Yet, as can be easily understood, my reason was bound to submit somewhat to my fancy at such a time. I remember now, that the idea of that insensate thing becoming animate, and attacking me, did not occur to me with any sense of possibility or reality. I thought rather, in a vague way, of some invisible monster of outer space fumbling at the dagger. I remembered the old Rector's description of the attack on the butler . . . *out of the void*. And he had described the stupendous force of the blow as being 'like the kick of a great horse.' You can see how uncomfortably my thoughts were running.

"I felt 'round swiftly and cautiously for my lantern. I found it close to me, on the pew seat, and with a sudden, jerky movement, I switched on the light. I flashed it up the aisle, to and fro across the chancel, but I could see nothing to frighten me. I turned quickly, and sent the jet of light darting across and across the rear end of the Chapel; then on each side of me, before and behind, up at the roof and down at the marble floor, but nowhere was there any visible thing to put me in fear, not a thing that need have set my flesh thrilling; just the quiet Chapel, cold, and eternally silent. You know the feeling.

"I had been standing, whilst I sent the light about the Chapel, but now I pulled out my revolver, and then, with a tremendous effort of will, switched off the light, and sat down again in the darkness, to continue my constant watch.

"It seemed to me that quite half an hour, or even more, must have passed, after this, during which no sound had broken the intense stillness. I had grown less nervously tense, for the flashing of the light 'round the place had made me feel less out of all bounds of the normal—it had given me something of that unreasoned sense of safety that a nervous child obtains at night, by covering its head up with the bedclothes. This just about illustrates the completely human illogicalness of the workings of my feelings; for, as you know, whatever Creature, Thing, or Being it was that had made that extraordinary and horrible attack on the old butler, it had certainly not been visible.

"And so you must picture me sitting there in the dark; clumsy with armor, and with my revolver in one hand, and nursing my lantern, ready, with the other. And then it was, after this little time of partial relief from intense nervousness, that there came a fresh strain on me; for somewhere in the utter quiet of the Chapel, I thought I heard something. I listened, tense and rigid, my heart booming just a little in my ears for a moment; then I thought I heard it again. I felt sure that something had moved at the top of the aisle. I strained in the darkness, to hark; and my eyes showed me blackness within blackness, wherever I glanced, so that I took no heed of what they told me; for even if I looked at the dim loom of the stained window at the top of the chancel, my sight gave me the shapes of vague shadows passing noiseless and ghostly across, constantly. There was a time of almost peculiar silence, horrible to me, as I felt just then. And suddenly I seemed to hear a sound again, nearer to me, and repeated, infinitely stealthy. It was as if a vast, soft tread were coming slowly down the aisle.

"Can you imagine how I felt? I do not think you can. I did not move, any more than the stone effigies on the two tombs; but sat there, *stiffened*. I fancied now, that I heard the tread all about the Chapel. And then, you know, I was just as sure in a moment that I could not hear it—that I had never heard it.

"Some particularly long minutes passed, about this time; but I think my nerves must have quieted a bit; for I remember being sufficiently aware of my feelings, to realize that the muscles of my shoulders *ached*, with the way that they must have been contracted, as I sat there, hunching myself, rigid. Mind you, I was still in a disgusting funk; but what I might call the 'imminent sense of danger' seemed to have eased from around me; at any rate, I felt, in some curious fashion, that there was a respite—a temporary cessation of malignity from about me. It is impossible to word my feelings more clearly to you, for I cannot see them more clearly than this, myself.

"Yet, you must not picture me as sitting there, free from strain; for the nerve tension was so great that my heart action was a little out of normal control, the blood beat making a dull booming at times in my ears, with the result that I had the sensation that I could not hear acutely. This is a simply beastly feeling, especially under such circumstances.

"I was sitting like this, listening, as I might say with body and soul, when suddenly I got that hideous conviction again that something was moving in the air of the place. The feeling seemed to stiffen me, as I sat, and my head appeared to tighten, as if all the scalp had grown *tense*. This was so real, that I suffered an actual pain, most peculiar and at the same time intense; the whole head pained. I had a fierce desire to cover my face again with my mailed arms, but I fought it off. If I had given way then to that, I should simply have bunked straight out of the place. I sat and sweated coldly (that's the bald truth), with the 'creep' busy at my spine. . . .

"And then, abruptly, once more I thought I heard the sound of that huge, soft tread on the aisle, and this time closer to me. There was an awful little silence, during which I had the feeling that something enormous was bending over toward me, from the aisle. . . . And then, through the booming of the blood in my ears, there came a slight sound from the place where my camera stood—a disagreeable sort of slithering sound, and then a sharp tap. I had the lantern ready in my left hand, and now I snapped it on, desperately, and shone it straight above me, for I had a conviction that there was something there. But I saw nothing. Immediately I flashed the light at the camera, and along the aisle, but again there was nothing visible. I wheeled 'round, shooting the beam of light in a great circle about the place; to and fro I shone it, jerking it here and there, but it showed me nothing.

"I had stood up the instant that I had seen that there was nothing in sight over me, and now I determined to visit the chancel, and see whether the dagger had been touched. I stepped out of the pew into the aisle, and here I came to an abrupt pause, for an almost invincible, sick repugnance was fighting me back from the upper part of the Chapel. A constant, queer prickling went up and down my spine, and a dull ache took me in the small of the back, as I fought with myself to conquer this sudden new feeling of terror and horror. I tell you, that no one who has not been through these kinds of experiences, has any idea of the sheer, actual physical pain attendant upon, and resulting from, the intense nerve strain that ghostly fright sets up in the human system. I stood there feeling positively ill. But I got myself in hand, as it were, in about half a minute, and then I went, walking, I expect, as jerky as a mechanical tin man, and switching the light from side to side, before and behind, and over my head continually. And the hand that held my revolver sweated so much, that the thing fairly slipped in my fist. Does not sound very heroic, does it?

"I passed through the short chancel, and reached the step that led up to the small gate in the chancel rail. I threw the beam from my lantern upon the dagger. Yes, I thought, it's all right. Abruptly, it seemed to me that there was something wanting, and I leaned forward over the chancel gate to peer, holding the light high. My suspicion was hideously correct. *The dagger had gone.* Only the cross-shaped sheath hung there above the altar.

"In a sudden, frightened flash of imagination, I pictured the thing adrift in the Chapel, moving here and there, as though of its own volition; for whatever Force wielded it, was certainly beyond visibility. I turned my head stiffly over to the left, glancing frightenedly behind me, and flashing the light to help my eyes. In the same instant I was struck a tremendous blow over the left breast, and hurled backward from the chancel rail, into the aisle, my armor clanging loudly in the horrible silence. I landed on my back, and slithered along on the polished marble. My shoulder struck the corner of a pew front, and brought me up, half stunned. I scrambled to my feet, horribly sick and shaken; but the fear that was on me, making little of that at the moment. I was minus both revolver and lantern, and utterly bewildered as to just where I was standing. I bowed my head, and made a scrambling run in the complete darkness and dashed into a pew. I jumped back, staggering, got my bearings a little, and raced down the center of the aisle, putting my mailed arms over my face. I plunged into my camera, hurling it among the pews. I crashed into the font, and reeled back. Then I was at the exit. I fumbled madly in my dressing gown pocket for the key. I found it and scraped at the door, feverishly, for the keyhole. I found the keyhole, turned the key, burst the door open, and was into the passage. I slammed the door and leant hard against it, gasping, whilst I felt crazily again for the keyhole, this time to lock the door upon what was in the Chapel. I succeeded, and began to feel my way stupidly along the wall of the corridor. Presently I had come to the big hall, and so in a little to my room.

"In my room, I sat for a while, until I had steadied down something to the normal. After a time I commenced to strip off the armor. I saw then that both the chain mail and the plate armor had been pierced over the breast. And, suddenly, it came home to me that the Thing had struck for my heart.

"Stripping rapidly, I found that the skin of the breast over the heart had just been cut sufficiently to allow a little blood to stain my shirt, nothing more. Only, the whole breast was badly bruised and intensely painful. You can imagine what would have happened if I had not worn the armor. In any case, it is a marvel that I was not knocked senseless.

"I did not go to bed at all that night, but sat upon the edge, thinking, and waiting for the dawn; for I had to remove my litter before Sir Alfred Jarnock should enter, if I were to hide from him the fact that I had managed a duplicate key.

"So soon as the pale light of the morning had strengthened sufficiently to show me the various details of my room, I made my way quietly down to the Chapel. Very silently, and with tense nerves, I opened the door. The chill light of the dawn made distinct the whole place—everything seeming instinct with a ghostly, unearthly quiet. Can you get the feeling? I waited several minutes at the door, allowing the morning to grow, and likewise my courage, I suppose. Presently the rising sun threw an odd beam right in through the big, East window, making colored sunshine all the length of the Chapel. And then, with a tremendous effort, I forced myself to enter.

"I went up the aisle to where I had overthrown my camera in the darkness. The legs of the tripod were sticking up from the interior of a pew, and I expected to find the machine smashed to pieces; yet, beyond that the ground glass was broken, there was no real damage done.

"I replaced the camera in the position from which I had taken the previous photography; but the slide containing the plate I had exposed by flashlight I removed and put into one of my side pockets, regretting that I had not taken a second flash picture at the instant when I heard those strange sounds up in the chancel.

"Having tidied my photographic apparatus, I went to the chancel to recover my lantern and revolver, which had both—as you know—been knocked from my hands when I was stabbed. I found the lantern lying, hopelessly bent, with smashed lens, just under the pulpit. My revolver I must have held until my shoulder struck the pew, for it was lying there in the aisle, just about where I believe I cannoned into the pew corner. It was quite undamaged.

"Having secured these two articles, I walked up to the chancel rail to see whether the dagger had returned, or been returned, to its sheath above the altar. Before, however, I reached the chancel rail, I had a slight shock; for there on the floor of the chancel, about a yard away from where I had been struck, lay the dagger, quiet and demure upon the polished marble pavement. I wonder whether you will, any of you, understand the nervousness that took me at the sight of the thing. With a sudden, unreasoned action, I jumped forward and put my foot on it, to hold it there. Can you understand? Do you? And, you know, I could not stoop down and pick it up with my hands for quite a minute, I should think. Afterward, when I had done so, however, and handled it a little, this feeling passed away and my Reason (and also, I expect, the daylight) made me feel that I had been a little bit of an ass. Quite natural, though, I assure you! Yet it was a new kind of fear to me. I'm taking no notice of the cheap joke about the ass! I am talking about the curiousness of learning in that moment a new shade or quality of fear that had hitherto been outside of my knowledge or imagination. Does it interest you?

"I examined the dagger, minutely, turning it over and over in my hands and never—as I suddenly discovered—holding it loosely. It was as if I were subconsciously surprised that it lay quiet in my hands. Yet even this feeling passed, largely, after a short while. The curious weapon showed no signs of the blow, except that the dull color of the blade was slightly brighter on the rounded point that had cut through the armor.

"Presently, when I had made an end of staring at the dagger, I went up the chancel step and in through the little gate. Then, kneeling upon the altar, I replaced the dagger in its sheath, and came outside of the rail again, closing the gate after me and feeling awarely uncomfortable because the horrible old weapon was back again in its accustomed place. I suppose, without analyzing my feelings very deeply, I had an unreasoned and only half-conscious belief that there was a greater probability of danger when the dagger hung in its five century resting place than when it was out of it! Yet, somehow I don't think this is a very good explanation, when I remember the *demure* look the thing seemed to have when I saw it lying on the floor of the chancel. Only I know this, that when I had replaced the dagger I had quite a touch of nerves and I stopped only to pick up my lantern from where I had placed it whilst I examined the weapon, after which I went down the quiet aisle at a pretty quick walk, and so got out of the place.

"That the nerve tension had been considerable, I realized, when I had locked the door behind me. I felt no inclination now to think of old Sir Alfred as a hypochondriac because he had taken such hyper-seeming precautions regarding the Chapel. I had a sudden wonder as to whether he might not have some knowledge of a long prior tragedy in which the dagger had been concerned.

"I returned to my room, washed, shaved and dressed, after which I read awhile. Then I went downstairs and got the acting butler to give me some sandwiches and a cup of coffee.

"Half an hour later I was heading for Burtontree, as hard as I could walk; for a sudden idea had come to me, which I was anxious to test. I reached the town a little before eight thirty, and found the local photographer with his shutters still up. I did not wait, but knocked until he appeared with his coat off, evidently in the act of dealing with his breakfast. In a few words I made clear that I wanted the use of his dark room immediately, and this he at once placed at my disposal.

"I had brought with me the slide which contained the plate that I had used with the flashlight, and as soon as I was ready I set to work to develop. Yet, it was not the plate which I had exposed, that I first put into the solution, but the second plate, which had been ready in the camera during all the time of my waiting in the darkness. You see, the lens had been uncapped all that while, so that the whole chancel had been, as it were, under observation.

"You all know something of my experiments in 'Lightless Photography,' that is, appreciating light. It was X-ray work that started me in that direction. Yet, you must understand, though I was attempting to develop this 'unexposed' plate, I had no definite idea of results—nothing more than a vague hope that it might show me something.

"Yet, because of the possibilities, it was with the most intense and absorbing interest that I watched the plate under the action of the developer. Presently I saw a faint smudge of black appear in the upper part, and after that others, indistinct and wavering of outline. I held the negative up to the light. The marks were rather small, and were almost entirely confined to one end of the plate, but as I have said, lacked definiteness. Yet, such as they were, they were sufficient to make me very excited and I shoved the thing quickly back into the solution.

"For some minutes further I watched it, lifting it out once or twice to make a more exact scrutiny, but could not imagine what the markings might represent, until suddenly it occurred to me that in one of two places they certainly had shapes suggestive of a cross hilted dagger. Yet, the shapes were sufficiently indefinite to make me careful not to let myself be over-impressed by the uncomfortable resemblance, though I must confess, the very thought was sufficient to set some odd thrills adrift in me.

"I carried development a little further, then put the negative into the hypo, and commenced work upon the other plate. This came up nicely, and very soon I had a really decent negative that appeared similar in every respect (except for the difference of lighting) to the negative I had taken during the previous day. I fixed the plate, then having washed both it and the 'unexposed' one for a few minutes under the tap, I put them into methylated spirits for fifteen minutes, after which I carried them into the photographer's kitchen and dried them in the oven.

"Whilst the two plates were drying the photographer and I made an enlargement from the negative I had taken by daylight. Then we did the same with the two that I had just developed, washing them as quickly as possible, for I was not troubling about the permanency of the prints, and drying them with spirits.

"When this was done I took them to the window and made a thorough examination, commencing with the one that appeared to show shadowy daggers in several places. Yet, though it was now enlarged, I was still unable to feel convinced that the marks truly represented anything abnormal; and because of this, I put it on one side, determined not to let my imagination play too large a part in constructing weapons out of the indefinite outlines.

"I took up the two other enlargements, both of the chancel, as you will remember, and commenced to compare them. For some minutes I examined them without being able to distinguish any difference in the scene they portrayed, and then abruptly, I saw something in which they varied. In the second enlargement—the one made from the flashlight negative—the dagger was not in its sheath. Yet, I had felt sure it was there but a few minutes before I took the photograph.

"After this discovery I began to compare the two enlargements in a very different manner from my previous scrutiny. I borrowed a pair of calipers from the photographer and with these I carried out a most methodical and exact comparison of the details shown in the two photographs.

"Suddenly I came upon something that set me all tingling with excitement. I threw the calipers down, paid the photographer, and walked out through the shop into the street. The three enlargements I took with me, making them into a roll as I went. At the corner of the street I had the luck to get a cab and was soon back at the castle.

"I hurried up to my room and put the photographs way; then I went down to see whether I could find Sir Alfred Jarnock; but Mr. George Jarnock, who met me, told me that his father was too unwell to rise and would prefer that no one entered the Chapel unless he were about.

"Young Jarnock made a half apologetic excuse for his father; remarking that Sir Alfred Jarnock was perhaps inclined to be a little over careful; but that, considering what had happened, we must agree that the need for his carefulness had been justified. He added, also, that even before the horrible attack on the butler his father had been just as particular, always keeping the key and never allowing the door to be unlocked except when the place was in use for Divine Service, and for an hour each forenoon when the cleaners were in.

"To all this I nodded understandingly; but when, presently, the young man left me I took my duplicate key and made for the door of the Chapel. I went in and locked it behind me, after which I carried out some intensely interesting and rather weird experiments. These proved successful to such an extent that I came out of the place in a perfect fever of excitement. I inquired for Mr. George Jarnock and was told that he was in the morning room.

"'Come along,' I said, when I had found him. 'Please give me a lift. I've something exceedingly strange to show you.'

"He was palpably very much puzzled, but came quickly. As we strode along he asked me a score of questions, to all of which I just shook my head, asking him to wait a little.

"I led the way to the Armory. Here I suggested that he should take one side of a dummy, dressed in half plate armor, whilst I took the other. He nodded, though obviously vastly bewildered, and together we carried the thing to the Chapel door. When he saw me take out my key and open the way for us he appeared even more astonished, but held himself in, evidently waiting for me to explain. We entered the Chapel and I locked the door behind us, after which we carted the armored dummy up the aisle to the gate of the chancel rail where we put it down upon its round, wooden stand.

"'Stand back!' I shouted suddenly as young Jarnock made a movement to open the gate. 'My God, man! you mustn't do that!'

"'Do what?' he asked, half-startled and half-irritated by my words and manner.

"'One minute,' I said. 'Just stand to the side a moment, and watch.'

"He stepped to the left whilst I took the dummy in my arms and turned it to face the altar, so that it stood close to the gate. Then, standing well away on the right side, I pressed the back of the thing so that it leant forward a little upon the gate, which flew open. In the same instant, the dummy was struck a tremendous blow that hurled it into the aisle, the armor rattling and clanging upon the polished marble floor.

"'Good God!' shouted young Jarnock, and ran back from the chancel rail, his face very white.

"'Come and look at the thing,' I said, and led the way to where the dummy lay, its armored upper limbs all splayed adrift in queer contortions. I stooped over it and pointed. There, driven right through the thick steel breastplate, was the 'waeful dagger.'

"'Good God!' said young Jarnock again. 'Good God! It's the dagger! The thing's been stabbed, same as Bellett!'

"'Yes,' I replied, and saw him glance swiftly toward the entrance of the Chapel. But I will do him the justice to say that he never budged an inch.

"'Come and see how it was done,' I said, and led the way back to the chancel rail. From the wall to the left of the altar I took down a long, curiously ornamented, iron instrument, not unlike a short spear. The sharp end of this I inserted in a hole in the left-hand gatepost of the chancel gateway. I lifted hard, and a section of the post, from the floor upward, bent inward toward the altar, as though hinged at the bottom. Down it went, leaving the remaining part of the post standing. As I bent the movable portion lower there came a quick click and a section of the floor slid to one side, showing a long, shallow cavity, sufficient to enclose the post. I put my weight to the lever and hove the post down into the niche. Immediately there was a sharp clang, as some catch snicked in, and held it against the powerful operating spring.

"I went over now to the dummy, and after a few minute's work managed to wrench the dagger loose out of the armor. I brought the old weapon and placed its hilt in a hole near the top of the post where it fitted loosely, the point upward. After that I went again to the lever and gave another strong heave, and the post descended about a foot, to the bottom of the cavity, catching there with another clang. I withdrew the lever and the narrow strip of floor slid back, covering post and dagger, and looking no different from the surrounding surface.

"Then I shut the chancel gate, and we both stood well to one side. I took the spear-like lever, and gave the gate a little push, so that it opened. Instantly there was a loud thud, and something sang through the air, striking the bottom wall of the Chapel. It was the dagger. I showed Jarnock then that the other half of the post had sprung back into place, making the whole post as thick as the one upon the right-hand side of the gate.

"'There!' I said, turning to the young man and tapping the divided post. 'There's the "invisible" thing that used the dagger, but who the deuce is the person who sets the trap?' I looked at him keenly as I spoke.

"'My father is the only one who has a key,' he said. 'So it's practically impossible for anyone to get in and meddle.'

"I looked at him again, but it was obvious that he had not yet reached out to any conclusion.

"'See here, Mr. Jarnock,' I said, perhaps rather curter than I should have done, considering what I had to say. 'Are you quite sure that Sir Alfred is quite balanced—mentally?'

"He looked at me, half frightenedly and flushing a little. I realized then how badly I put it.

"'I—I don't know,' he replied, after a slight pause and was then silent, except for one or two incoherent half remarks.

"'Tell the truth,' I said. 'Haven't you suspected something, now and again? You needn't be afraid to tell me.'

"'Well,' he answered slowly, 'I'll admit I've thought Father a little—a little strange, perhaps, at times. But I've always tried to think I was mistaken. I've always hoped no one else would see it. You see, I'm very fond of the old guvnor.'

"I nodded.

"'Quite right, too,' I said. 'There's not the least need to make any kind of scandal about this. We must do something, though, but in a quiet way. No fuss, you know. I should go and have a chat with your father, and tell him we've found out about this thing.' I touched the divided post.

"Young Jarnock seemed very grateful for my advice and after shaking my hand pretty hard, took my key, and let himself out of the Chapel. He came back in about an hour, looking rather upset. He told me that my conclusions were perfectly correct. It was Sir Alfred Jarnock who had set the trap, both on the night that the butler was nearly killed, and on the past night. Indeed, it seemed that the old gentleman had set it every night for many years. He had learnt of its existence from an old manuscript book in the Castle library. It had been planned and used in an earlier age as a protection for the gold vessels of the ritual, which were, it seemed, kept in a hidden recess at the back of the altar.

"This recess Sir Alfred Jarnock had utilized, secretly, to store his wife's jewelry. She had died some twelve years back, and the young man told me that his father had never seemed quite himself since.

"I mentioned to young Jarnock how puzzled I was that the trap had been set *before* the service, on the night that the butler was struck; for, if I understood him aright, his father had been in the habit of setting the trap late every night and unsetting it each morning before anyone entered the Chapel. He replied that his father, in a fit of temporary forgetfulness (natural enough in his neurotic condition), must have set it too early and hence what had so nearly proved a tragedy.

"That is about all there is to tell. The old man is not (so far as I could learn), really insane in the popularly accepted sense of the word. He is extremely neurotic and has developed into a hypochondriac, the whole condition probably brought about by the shock and sorrow resultant on the death of his wife, leading to years of sad broodings and to overmuch of his own company and thoughts. Indeed, young Jarnock told me that his father would sometimes pray for hours together, alone in the Chapel." Carnacki made an end of speaking and leant forward for a spill.

"But you've never told us just *how* you discovered the secret of the divided post and all that," I said, speaking for the four of us.

"Oh, that!" replied Carnacki, puffing vigorously at his pipe. "I found—on comparing the—photos, that the one—taken in the—daytime, showed a thicker left-hand gatepost, than the one taken at night by the flashlight. That put me on to the track. I saw at once that there might be some mechanical dodge at the back of the whole queer business and nothing at all of an abnormal nature. I examined the post and the rest was simple enough, you know.

"By the way," he continued, rising and going to the mantelpiece, "you may be interested to have a look at the so-called 'waeful dagger.' Young Jarnock was kind enough to present it to me, as a little memento of my adventure."

He handed it 'round to us and whilst we examined it, stood silent before the fire, puffing meditatively at his pipe.

"Jarnock and I made the trap so that it won't work," he remarked after a few moments. "I've got the dagger, as you see, and old Bellett's getting about again, so that the whole business can be hushed up, decently. All the same I fancy the Chapel will never lose its reputation as a dangerous place. Should be pretty safe now to keep valuables in."

"There's two things you haven't explained yet," I said. "What do you think caused the two clangey sounds when you were in the Chapel in the dark? And do you believe the soft tready sounds were real, or only a fancy, with your being so worked up and tense?"

"Don't know for certain about the clangs," replied Carnacki. "I've puzzled quite a bit about them. I can only think that the spring which worked the post must have 'given' a trifle, slipped you know, in the catch. If it did, under such a tension, it would make a bit of a ringing noise. And a little sound goes a long way in the middle of the night when you're thinking of 'ghostesses.' You can understand that—eh?"

"Yes," I agreed. "And the other sounds?"

"Well, the same thing—I mean the extraordinary quietness— may help to explain these a bit. They may have been some usual enough sound that would never have been noticed under ordinary conditions, or they may have been only fancy. It is just impossible to say. They were disgustingly real to me. As for the slithery noise, I am pretty sure that one of the tripod legs of my camera must have slipped a few inches: if it did so, it may easily have jolted the lens cap off the baseboard, which would account for that queer little tap which I heard directly after."

"How do you account for the dagger being in its place above the altar when you first examined it that night?" I asked. "How could it be there, when at that very moment it was set in the trap?"

"That was my mistake," replied Carnacki. "The dagger could not possibly have been in its sheath at the time, though I thought it was. You see, the curious cross-hilted sheath gave the appearance of the complete weapon, as you can understand. The hilt of the dagger protrudes very little above the continued portion of the sheath—a most inconvenient arrangement for drawing quickly!" He nodded sagely at the lot of us and yawned, then glanced at the clock.

"Out you go!" he said, in friendly fashion, using the recognized formula. "I want a sleep."

We rose, shook him by the hand, and went out presently into the night and the quiet of the Embankment, and so to our homes.

THE HAUNTED *JARVEE*

"Seen anything of Carnacki lately?" I asked Arkright when we met in the City.

"No," he replied. "He's probably off on one of his jaunts. We'll be having a card one of these days inviting us to No. 472, Cheyne Walk, and then we'll hear all about it. Queer chap that."

He nodded, and went on his way. It was some months now since we four—Jessop, Arkright, Taylor and myself—had received the usual summons to drop in at No. 472 and hear Carnacki's story of his latest case. What talks they were! Stories of all kinds and true in every word, yet full of weird and extraordinary incidents that held one silent and awed until he had finished.

Strangely enough, the following morning brought me a curtly worded card telling me to be at No. 472 at seven o'clock promptly. I was the first to arrive, Jessop and Taylor soon followed and just before dinner was announced Arkright came in.

Dinner over, Carnacki as usual passed round his smokes, snuggled himself down luxuriously in his favourite armchair and went straight to the story we knew he had invited us to hear.

"I've been on a trip in one of the real old-time sailing ships," he said without any preliminary remarks. "The *Jarvee*, owned by my old friend Captain Thompson. I went on the voyage primarily for my health, but I picked on the old *Jarvee* because Captain Thompson had often told me there was something queer about her. I used to ask him up here whenever he came ashore and try to get him to tell me more about it, you know; but the funny thing was he never could tell me anything definite concerning her queerness. He seemed always to know but when it came to putting his knowledge into words it was as if he found that the reality melted out of it. He would end up usually by saying that you saw things and then he would wave his hands vaguely, but further than that he never seemed able to pass on the knowledge of something strange which he had noticed about the ship, except odd outside details.

"'Can't keep men in her no-how,' he often told me. 'They get frightened and they see things and they feel things. An' I've lost a power o' men out of her. Fallen from aloft, you know. She's getting a bad name.' And then he'd shake his head very solemnly.

"Old Thompson was a brick in every way. When I got aboard I found that he had given me the use of a whole empty cabin opening off my own as my laboratory and workshop. He gave the carpenter orders to fit up the empty cabin with shelves and other conveniences according to my directions and in a couple of days I had all the apparatus, both mechanical and electric with which I had conducted my other ghost-hunts, neatly and safely stowed away, for I took a great deal of gear with me as I intended to interest myself by examining thoroughly into the mystery about which the captain was at once so positive and so vague.

"During the first fortnight out I followed my usual methods of making a thorough and exhaustive search. This I did with the most scrupulous care, but found nothing abnormal of any kind in the whole vessel. She was an old wooden ship and I took care to sound and measure every casement and bulkhead, to examine every exit from the holds and to seal all the hatches. These and many other precautions I took, but at the end of the fortnight I had neither seen anything nor found anything.

"The old barque was just, to all seeming, a healthy, average old-timer jogging along comfortably from one port to another. And save for an indefinable sense of what I could now describe as 'abnormal peace' about the ship I could find nothing to justify the old captain's solemn and frequent assurances that I would see soon enough for myself. This he would say often as we walked the poop together; afterwards stopping to take a long, expectant, half-fearful look at the immensity of the sea around.

"Then on the eighteenth day something truly happened. I had been pacing the poop as usual with old Thompson when suddenly he stopped and looked up at the mizzen royal which had just begun to flap against the mast. He glanced at the wind-vane near him, then ruffled his hat back and stared at the sea.

"'Wind's droppin', mister. There'll be trouble tonight,' he said. 'D'you see yon?' And he pointed away to windward.

"'What?' I asked, staring with a curious little thrill that was due to more than curiosity. 'Where?'

"'Right off the beam,' he said. 'Comin' from under the sun.'

"'I don't see anything,' I explained after a long stare at the wide-spreading silence of the sea that was already glassing into a dead calm surface now that the wind had died.

"'Yon shadow fixin',' said the old man, reaching for his glasses.

"He focussed them and took a long look, then passed them across to me and pointed with his finger. 'Just under the sun,' he repeated. 'Comin' towards us at the rate o' knots.' He was curiously calm and matter-of-fact and yet I felt that a certain excitement had him in the throat; so that I took the glasses eagerly and stared according to his directions.

"After a minute I saw it—a vague shadow upon the still surface of the sea that seemed to move towards us as I stared. For a moment I gazed fascinated, yet ready every moment to swear that I saw nothing and in the same instant to be assured that there was truly *something* out there upon the water, apparently coming towards the ship.

"'It's only a shadow, captain,' I said at length.

"'Just so, mister,' he replied simply. 'Have a look over the stern to the norrard.' He spoke in the quietest way, as a man speaks who is sure of all his facts and who is facing an experience he has faced before, yet who salts his natural matter-of-factness with a deep and constant excitement.

"At the captain's hint I turned about and directed the glasses to the northward. For a while I searched, sweeping my aided vision to and fro over the greying arc of the sea.

"Then I saw the thing plain in the field of the glass—a vague something, a shadow upon the water and the shadow seemed to be moving towards the ship.

"'That's queer,' I muttered with a funny little stirring at the back of my throat.

"'Now to the west'ard, mister,' said the captain, still speaking in his peculiar level way.

"I looked to the westward and in a minute I picked up the thing—a third shadow that seemed to move across the sea as I watched it.

"'My God, captain,' I exclaimed, 'what does it mean?'

"'That's just what I want to know, mister,' said the captain. 'I've seen 'em before and thought sometimes I must be going mad. Sometimes they're plain an' sometimes they're scarce to be seen, an' sometimes they're like livin' things, an' sometimes they're like nought at all but silly fancies. D' you wonder I couldn't name 'em proper to you?'

"I did not answer for I was staring now expectantly towards the south along the length of the barque. Afar off on the horizon my glasses picked up something dark and vague upon the surface of the sea, a shadow it seemed which grew plainer.

"'My God!' I muttered again. 'This is real. This—' I turned again to the eastward.

"'Comin' in from the four points, ain't they,' said Captain Thompson and he blew his whistle.

"'Take them three r'yals off her,' he told the mate, 'an' tell one of the boys to shove lanterns up on the sherpoles. Get the men down smart before dark,' he concluded as the mate moved off to see the orders carried out.

"'I'm sendin' no men aloft to-night,' he said to me. 'I've lost enough that way.'

"'They may be only shadows, captain, after all,' I said, still look-ing earnestly at that far-off grey vagueness on the eastward sea.

'Bit of mist or cloud floating low.' Yet though I said this I had no belief that it was so. And as for old Captain Thompson, he never took the trouble to answer, but reached for his glasses which I passed to him.

"'Gettin' thin an' disappearin' as they come near,' he said presently. 'I know, I've seen 'em do that oft an' plenty before. They'll be close round the ship soon but you nor me won't see them, nor no one else, but they'll be there. I wish 'twas mornin'. I do that!'

"He had handed the glasses back to me and I had been staring at each of the oncoming shadows in turn. It was as Captain Thompson had said. As they drew nearer they seemed to spread and thin out and presently to become dissipated into the grey of the gloaming so that I could easily have imagined that I watched merely four little portions of grey cloud, expanding naturally into impalpableness and invisibility.

"'Wish I'd took them t'gallants off her while I was about it,' remarked the old man presently. 'Can't think to send no one off the decks to-night, not unless there's real need.' He slipped away from me and peered at the aneroid in the skylight. 'Glass steady, anyhow,' he muttered as he came away, seeming more satisfied.

"By this time the men had all returned to the decks and the night was down upon us so that I could watch the queer, dissolving shadows which approached the ship.

"Yet as I walked the poop with old Captain Thompson, you can imagine how I grew to feel. Often I found myself looking over my shoulder with quick, jerky glances; for it seemed to me that in the curtains of gloom that hung just beyond the rails there must be a vague, incredible thing looking inboard.

"I questioned the captain in a thousand ways, but could get little out of him beyond what I knew. It was as if he had no power to convey to another the knowledge which he possessed and I could ask no one else, for every other man in the ship was newly signed on, including the mates, which was in itself a significant fact.

"'You'll see for yourself, mister,' was the refrain with which the captain parried my questions, so that it began to seem as if he almost *feared* to put anything he knew into words. Yet once, when I had jerked round with a nervous feeling that something was at my back he said calmly enough: 'Naught to fear, mister, whilst you're in the light and on the decks.' His attitude was extraordinary in the way in which he *accepted* the situation. He appeared to have no personal fear.

"The night passed quietly until about eleven o'clock when suddenly and without one atom of warning a furious squall burst on the vessel. There was something monstrous and abnormal in the wind; it was as if some power were using the elements to an infernal purpose. Yet the captain met the situation calmly. The helm was put down and the sails shaken while the three t'gallants were lowered. Then the three upper topsails. Yet still the breeze roared over us, almost drowning the thunder which the sails were making in the night.

"'Split 'em to ribbons!' the captain yelled in my ear above the noise of the wind. 'Can't help it. I ain't sendin' no men aloft tonight unless she seems like to shake the sticks out of her. That's what bothers me.'

"For nearly an hour after that, until eight bells went at midnight, the wind showed no signs of easing but breezed up harder than ever. And all the while the skipper and I walked the poop, he ever and again peering up anxiously through the darkness at the banging and thrashing sails.

"For my part I could do nothing except stare round and round at the extraordinarily dark night in which the ship seemed to be embedded solidly. The very feel and sound of the wind gave me a sort of constant horror, for there seemed to be an unnaturalness rampant in the atmosphere. But how much this was the effect of my over-strung nerves and excited imagination, I cannot say. Certainly, in all my experience I had never come across anything just like what I felt and endured through that peculiar squall.

"At eight bells when the other watch came on deck the captain was forced to send all hands aloft to make the canvas fast, as he had begun to fear that he would actually lose his masts if he delayed longer. This was done and the barque snugged right down.

"Yet, though the work was done successfully, the captain's fears were justified in a sufficiently horrible way, for as the men were beginning to make their way in off the wards there was a loud crying and shouting aloft and immediately afterwards a crash down on the main deck, followed instantly by a second crash.

"'My God! Two of 'em!' shouted the skipper as he snatched a lamp from the forrard binnacle. Then down on to the main deck. It was as he had said. Two of the men had fallen, or—as the thought came to me—been thrown from aloft and were lying silent on the deck. Above us in the darkness I heard a few vague shouts followed by a curious quiet, save for the constant blast of the wind whose whistling and howling in the rigging seemed but to accentuate the complete and frightened silence of the men aloft. Then I was aware that the men were coming down swiftly and presently one after the other came with a quick leap out of the rigging and stood about the two fallen men with odd exclamations and questions which always merged off instantly into new silence.

"And all the time I was conscious of a most extraordinary sense of oppression and frightened distress and fearful expectation, for it seemed to me, standing there near the dead in that unnatural wind that a power of evil filled all the night about the ship and that some fresh horror was imminent.

"The following morning there was a solemn little service, very rough and crude, but undertaken with a nice reverence and the two men who had fallen were tilted off from a hatch-cover and plunged suddenly out of sight. As I watched them vanish in the deep blue of the water an idea came to me and I spent part of the afternoon talking it over with the captain, after which I passed the rest of the time until sunset was upon us in arranging and fitting up a part of my electrical apparatus. Then I went on deck and had a good look round. The evening was beautifully calm and ideal for the experiment which I had in mind, for the wind had died away with a peculiar suddenness after the death of the two men and all that day the sea had been like glass.

"To a certain extent I believed that I comprehended the primary cause of the vague but peculiar manifestations which I had witnessed the previous evening and which Captain Thompson believed implicitly to be intimately connected with the death of the two sailormen.

"I believed the origin of the happenings to lie in a strange but perfectly understandable cause, *i.e.*, in that phenomenon known technically as 'attractive vibrations.' Harzam, in his monograph on 'Induced Hauntings,' points out that such are invariably produced by 'induced vibrations,' that is, by temporary vibrations set up by some outside cause.

"This is somewhat abstruse to follow out in a story of this kind, but it was on a long consideration of these points that I had resolved to make experiments to see whether I could not produce a counter or 'repellent' vibration, a thing which Harzam had succeeded in producing on three occasions and in which I have had a partial success once, failing only because of the imperfectness of the apparatus I had aboard.

"As I have said, I can scarcely follow the reasoning further in a brief record such as this, neither do I think it would be of interest to you who are interested only in the startling and weird side of my investigations. Yet I have told you sufficient to show you the germ of my reasonings and to enable you to follow intelligently my hopes and expectations in sending out what I hoped would prove 'repellent' vibrations.

"Therefore it was that when the sun had descended to within ten degrees of the visible horizon the captain and I began to watch for the appearance of the shadows. Presently, under the sun, I discovered the same peculiar appearance of a moving greyness which I had seen on the preceding night and almost immediately Captain Thompson told me that he saw the same to the south.

"To the north and east we perceived the same extraordinary thing and I at once set my electric apparatus at work, sending out the strange repelling force to the dim, far shadows of mystery which moved steadily out of the distance towards the vessel.

"Earlier in the evening the captain had snugged the barque right down to her topsails, for as he said, until the calm went he would risk nothing. According to him it was always during calm weather that the extraordinary manifestations occurred. In this case he was certainly justified, for a most tremendous squall struck the ship in the middle watch, taking the fore upper topsail right out of the ropes.

"At the time when it came I was lying down on a locker in the saloon, but I ran up on to the poop as the vessel canted under the enormous force of the wind. Here I found the air pressure tremendous and the noise of the squall stunning. And over it all and through it all I was conscious of something abnormal and threatening that set my nerves uncomfortably acute. The thing was not natural.

"Yet, despite the carrying away of the topsail, not a man was sent aloft.

"'Let 'em all go!' said old Captain Thompson. 'I'd have shortened her down to the bare sticks if I'd done all I wanted!'

"About two a.m. the squall passed with astonishing suddenness and the night showed clear above the vessel. From then onward I paced the poop with the skipper, often pausing at the break to look along the lighted main deck. It was on one of these occasions that I saw something peculiar. It was like a vague flitting of an impossible shadow between me and the whiteness of the well-scrubbed decks. Yet, even as I stared, the thing was gone and I could not say with surety that I had seen anything.

"'Pretty plain to see, mister,' said the captain's voice at my elbow. 'I've only seen that once before an' we lost half of the hands that trip. We'd better be at 'ome, I'm thinkin'. It'll end in scrappin' her, sure.'

"The old man's calmness bewildered me almost as much as the confirmation his remark gave that I had really seen something abnormal floating between me and the deck eight feet below us.

"'Good lord, Captain Thompson,' I exclaimed, 'this is simply infernal!'

"'Just that,' he agreed. 'I said, mister, you'd see if you'd wait. And this ain't the half. You wait till you sees 'em looking like little black clouds all over the sea round the ship and movin' steady with the ship. All the same, I ain't seen 'em aboard but the once. Guess we're in for it.'

"'How do you mean?' I asked. But though I questioned him in every way I could get nothing satisfactory out of him.

"'You'll see, mister. You wait an' see. She's a queer un.' And that was about the extent of his further efforts and methods of enlightening me.

"From then on through the rest of the watch I leaned over the break of the poop, staring down at the maindeck and odd whiles taking quick glances to the rear. The skipper had resumed his steady pacing of the poop, but now and again he would come to a pause beside me and ask calmly enough whether I had seen any more of 'them there.'

"Several times I saw the vagueness of something drifting in the lights of the lanterns and a sort of wavering in the air in this place and that, as if it might be an attenuated something having movement, that was half-seen for a moment and then gone before my brain could record anything definite.

"Towards the end of the watch, however, both the captain and I saw something very extraordinary. He had just come beside me and was leaning over the rail across the break. 'Another of 'em there,' he remarked in his calm way, giving me a gentle nudge and nodding his head towards the port side of the maindeck, a yard or two to our left.

"In the place he had indicated there was a faint, dull shadowy spot seeming suspended about a foot above the deck. This grew more visible and there was movement in it and a constant, oily-seeming whirling from the centre outwards. The thing expanded to several feet across, with the lighted planks of the deck showing vaguely through. The movement from the centre outwards was now becoming very distinct, till the whole strange shape blackened and grew more dense, so that the deck below was hidden.

"Then as I stared with the most intense interest there went a thinning movement over the thing and almost directly it had dissolved so that there was nothing more to be seen than a vague rounded shape of shadow, hovering and convoluting dimly between us and the deck below. This gradually thinned out and vanished and we were both of us left staring down at a piece of the deck where the planking and pitched seams showed plain and distinct in the light from the lamps that were now hung nightly on the sherpoles.

"'Mighty queer that, mister,' said the captain meditatively as he fumbled for his pipe. 'Mighty queer.' Then he lit his pipe and began again his pacing of the poop.

"The calm lasted for a week with the sea like glass and every night without warning there was a repetition of the extraordinary squall, so that the captain had everything made fast at dusk and waited patiently for a trade wind.

"Each evening I experimented further with my attempts to set up 'repellent' vibrations, but without result. I am not sure whether I ought to say that my meddling produced no result; for the calm gradually assumed a more unnatural permanent aspect whilst the sea looked more than ever like a plain of glass, bulged anon with the low oily roll of some deep swell. For the rest, there was by day a silence so profound as to give a sense of unrealness, for never a sea-bird hove in sight whilst the movement of the vessel was so slight as scarce to keep up the constant creak, creak of spars and gear, which is the ordinary accompaniment of a calm.

"The sea appeared to have become an emblem of desolation and freeness, so that it seemed to me at last that there was no more any known world, but just one great ocean going on for ever into the far distances in every direction. At night the strange squalls assumed a far greater violence so that sometimes it seemed as if the very spars would be ripped and twisted out of the vessel, yet fortunately no harm came in that wise.

"As the days passed I became convinced at last that my experiments were producing very distinct results, though the opposite to those which I hoped to produce, for now at each sunset a sort of grey cloud resembling light smoke would appear far away in every quarter almost immediately upon the commencement of the vibrations, with the effect that I desisted from any prolonged attempt and became more tentative in my experiments.

"At last, however, when we had endured this condition of affairs for a week, I had a long talk with old Captain Thompson and he agreed to let me carry out a bold experiment to its conclusion. It was to keep the vibrations going steadily at full power from a little before sunset until the dawn and to take careful notes of the results.

"With this in view, all was made ready. The royal and t'gallant yards were sent down, all the sails stowed and everything about the decks made fast. A sea anchor was rigged out over the bows and a long line of cable veered away. This was to ensure the vessel coming head to wind should one of those strange squalls strike us from any quarter during the night.

"Late in the afternoon the men were sent into the fo'c'sle and told that they might please themselves and turn in or do anything they liked, but that they were not to come on deck during the night whatever happened. To ensure this the port and starboard doors were padlocked. Afterwards I made the first and the eighth signs of the Saaamaaa Ritual opposite each door-post, connecting them with triple lines crossed at every seventh inch. You've dipped deeper into the science of magic than I have, Arkright, and you will know what that means. Following this I ran a wire entirely around the outside of the fo'c'sle and connected it up with my machinery, which I had erected in the sail-locker aft.

"'In any case,' I explained to the captain, 'they run practically no risk other than the general risk which we may expect in the form of a terrific storm-burst. The real danger will be to those who are "meddling." The "path of the vibrations" will make a kind of "halo" round the apparatus. I shall have to be there to control and I'm willing to risk it, but you'd better get into your cabin and the three mates must do the same.'

"This the old captain refused to do and the three mates begged to be allowed to stay and 'see the fun.' I warned them very seriously that there might be a very disagreeable and unavoidable danger, but they agreed to risk it and I can tell you I was not sorry to have their companionship.

"I set to work then, making them help where I needed help, and so presently I had all my gear in order. Then I led my wires up through the skylight from the cabin and set the vibrator dial and trembler-box level, screwing them solidly down to the poop-deck, in the clear space that lay between the foreside of the skylight and the lid of the sail locker.

"I got the three mates and the captain to take their places close together and I warned them not to move whatever happened. I set to work then, alone, and chalked a temporary pentacle about the whole lot of us, including the apparatus. Afterwards I made haste to get the tubes of my electric pentacle fitted all about us, for it was getting on to dusk. As soon as this was done I switched on the current into the vacuum tubes and immediately the pale sickly glare shone dull all about us, seeming cold and unreal in the last light of the evening.

"Immediately afterwards I set the vibrations beating out into all space and then I took my seat beside the control board. Here I had a few words with the others, warning them again whatever they might hear or see not to leave the pentacle, if they valued their lives. They nodded to this and I knew that they were fully impressed with the possibility of the unknown danger that we were meddling with.

"Then we settled down to watch. We were all in our oilskins, for I expected the experiment to include some very peculiar behaviour on the part of the elements and so we were ready to face the night. One other thing I was careful to do and that was to con-fiscate all matches so that no one should forgetfully light his pipe, for the light rays are 'paths' to certain of the Forces.

"With a pair of marine glasses I was staring round at the hori-zon. All around, but miles away in the greying of the evening, there seemed to be a strange, vague darkening of the surface of the sea. This became more distinct and it seemed to me presently that it might be a slight, low-lying mist far away about the ship. I watched it very intently and the captain and the three mates were doing likewise through their glasses.

"'Coming in on us at the rate o' knots, mister,' said the old man in a low voice. 'This is what I call playin' with 'ell. I only hope it'll all come right.' That was all he said and afterwards there was absolute silence from him and the others through the strange hours that followed.

"As the night stole down upon the sea we lost sight of the peculiar incoming circle of mist and there was a period of the most intense and oppressive silence to the five of us, sitting there watchful and quiet within the pale glow of the electric pentacle.

"A while later there came a sort of strange, noiseless lightning. By noiseless I mean that while the flashes appeared to be near at hand and lit up all the vague sea around, yet there was no thunder; neither, so it appeared to me, did there seem to be any *reality* in the flashes. This is a queer thing to say but it describes my impressions. It was as if I saw a representation of lightning rather than the physical electricity itself. No, of course, I am not pretending to use the word in its technical sense.

"Abruptly a strange quivering went through the vessel from end to end and died away. I looked fore and aft and then glanced at the four men who stared back at me with a sort of dumb and half-frightened wonder, but no one said anything. About five minutes passed with no sound anywhere except the faint buzz of the apparatus and nothing visible anywhere except the noiseless lightning which came down, flash after flash, lighting the sea all around the vessel.

"Then a most extraordinary thing happened. The peculiar quivering passed again through the ship and died away. It was followed immediately by a kind of undulation of the vessel, first fore and aft and then from side to side. I can give you no better illustration of the strangeness of the movement on that glass-like sea than to say that it was just such a movement as might have been given her had an invisible giant hand lifted her and toyed with her, canting her this way and that with a certain curious and rather sickening rhythm of movement. This appeared to last about two minutes, so far as I can guess, and ended with the ship being shaken up and down several times, after which there came again the quivering and then quietness.

"A full hour must have passed during which I observed nothing except that twice the vessel was faintly shaken and the second time this was followed by a slight repetition of the curious undulations. This, however, lasted but a few seconds and afterwards there was only the abnormal and oppressive silence of the night, punctured time after time by these noiseless flashes of lightning. All the time I did my best to study the appearance of the sea and atmosphere around the ship.

"One thing was apparent, that the surrounding wall of vagueness had drawn in more upon the ship, so that the brightest flashes now showed me no more than about a clear quarter of a mile of ocean around us, after which the sight was just lost in trying to penetrate a kind of shadowy distance that yet had no depth in it, but which still lacked any power to arrest the vision at any particular point so that one could not know definitely whether there was anything there or not, but only that one's sight was limited by some phenomenon which hid all the distant sea. Do I make this clear?

"The strange, noiseless lightning increased in vividness and the flashes began to come more frequently. This went on till they were almost continuous, so that all the near sea could be watched with scarce an intermission. Yet the brightness of the flashes seemed to have no power to dull the pale light of the curious detached glows that circled in silent multitudes about us.

"About this time I became aware of a strange sense of breathlessness. Each breath seemed to be drawn with difficulty and presently with a sense of positive distress. The three mates and the captain were breathing with curious little gasps and the faint buzz of the vibrator seemed to come from a great distance away. For the rest there was such a silence as made itself known like a dull, numbing ache upon the brain.

"The minutes passed slowly and then, abruptly, I saw something new. There were grey things floating in the air about the ship which were so vague and attenuated that at first I could not be sure that I saw anything, but in a while there could be no doubt that they were there.

"They began to show plainer in the constant glare of the quiet lightning and growing darker and darker they increased visibly in size. They appeared to be but a few feet above the level of the sea and they began to assume humped shapes.

"For quite half an hour, which seemed indefinitely longer, I watched those strange humps like little hills of blackness floating just above the surface of the water and moving round and round the vessel with a slow, everlasting circling that produced on my eyes the feeling that it was all a dream.

"It was later still that I discovered still another thing. Each of those great vague mounds had begun to oscillate as it circled round about us. I was conscious at the same time that there was communicated to the vessel the beginning of a similar oscillating movement, so very slight at first that I could scarcely be sure she so much as moved.

"The movement of the ship grew with a steady oscillation, the bows lifting first and then the stern, as if she were pivoted amidships. This ceased and she settled down on to a level keel with a series of queer jerks as if her weight were being slowly lowered again to the buoying of the water.

"Suddenly there came a cessation of the extraordinary lightning and we were in an absolute blackness with only the pale sickly glow of the electric pentacle above us and the faint buzz of the apparatus seeming far away in the night. Can you picture it all? The five of us there, tense and watchful and wondering what was going to happen.

"The thing began gently—a little jerk upward of the starboard side of the vessel, then a second jerk, then a third and the whole ship was canted distinctly to port. It continued in a kind of slow rhythmic tilting with curious timed pauses between the jerks and suddenly, you know, I saw that we were in absolute danger, for the vessel was being capsized by some enormous Force in the utter silence and blackness of that night.

"'My God, mister, stop it!' came the captain's voice, quick and very hoarse. 'She'll be gone in a moment! She'll be gone!'

"He had got on to his knees and was staring round and gripping at the deck. The three mates were also gripping at the deck with their palms to stop them from sliding down the violent slope. In that moment came a final tilting of the side of the vessel and the deck rose up almost like a wall. I snatched at the lever of the vibrator and switched it over.

"Instantly the angle of the deck decreased as the vessel righted several feet with a jerk. The righting movement continued with little rhythmic jerks until the ship was once more on an even keel.

"And even as she righted I was aware of an alteration in the tenseness of the atmosphere and a great noise far off to starboard. It was the roaring of wind. A huge flash of lightning was followed by others and the thunder crashed continually overhead. The noise of the wind to starboard rose to a loud screaming and drove towards us through the night. Then the lightning ceased and the deep roll of the thunder was lost in the nearer sound of the wind which was now within a mile of us and making a most hideous, bellowing scream. The shrill howling came at us out of the dark and covered every other sound. It was as if all the night on that side were a vast cliff, sending down high and monstrous echoes upon us. This is a queer thing to say, I know, but it may help you to get the feeling of the thing; for that just describes exactly how it felt to me at the time—that queer, echoing, empty sense above us in the night, yet all the emptiness filled with sound on high. Do you get it? It was most extraordinary and there was a grand something about it all as if one had come suddenly upon the steeps of some monstrous lost world.

"Then the wind rushed out at us and stunned us wit its sound and force and fury. We were smothered and half-stunned. The vessel went over on to her port side merely from pressure of the wind on her naked spars and side. The whole night seemed one yell and the foam roared and snowed over us in countless tons. I have never known anything like it. We were all splayed about the poop, holding on to anything we could, while the pentacle was smashed to atoms so that we were in complete darkness. The storm-burst had come down on us.

"Towards morning the storm calmed and by evening we were running before a fine breeze; yet the pumps had to be kept going steadily for we had sprung a pretty bad leak, which proved so serious that we had to take to the boats two days later. However, we were picked up that night so that we had only a short time of it. As for the *Jarvee*, she is now safely at the bottom of the Atlantic, where she had better remain for ever."

Carnacki came to an end and tapped out his pipe.

"But you haven't explained," I remonstrated. "What made her like that? What made her different from other ships? Why did those shadows and things come to her? What's your idea?"

"Well," replied Carnacki, "in my opinion she was a focus. That is a technical term which I can best explain by saying that she possessed the 'attractive vibration' that is the power to draw to her any psychic waves in the vicinity, much in the way of a medium. The way in which the 'vibration' is acquired—to use a technical term again—is, of course, purely a matter for supposition. She may have developed it during the years, owing to a suitability of conditions or it may have been in her ('of her' is a better term) from the very day her keel was laid. I mean the direction in which she lay the condition of the atmosphere, the state of the 'electric tensions,' the very blows of the hammers and the accidental combining of materials suited to such an end—all might tend to such a thing. And this is only to speak of the *known*. The vast *unknown* it is vain to speculate upon in a brief chatter like this.

"I would like to remind you here of that idea of mine that certain forms of so-called 'hauntings' may have their cause in the 'attractive vibrations.' A building or a ship—just as I have indicated—may develop 'vibrations,' even as certain materials in combination under the proper conditions will certainly develop an electric current.

"To say more in a talk of this scope is useless. I am more inclined to remind you of the glass which will vibrate to a certain note struck upon a piano and to silence all your worrying questions with that simple little unanswered one: What is electricity? When we've got that clear it will be time to take the next step in a more dogmatic fashion. We are but speculating on the coasts of a strange country of mystery. In this case, I think the next best step for you all will be home and bed."

And with this terse ending, in the most genial way possible, Carnacki ushered us out presently on to the quiet chill of the Embankment, replying heartily to our various good-nights.

THE HOG

We had finished dinner and Carnacki had drawn his big chair up to the fire, and started his pipe.

Jessop, Arkright, Taylor and I had each of us taken up our favourite positions, and waited for Carnacki to begin.

"What I'm going to tell you about happened in the next room," he said, after drawing at his pipe for a while. "It has been a terrible experience. Doctor Witton first brought the case to my notice. We'd been chatting over a pipe at the Club one night about an article in the *Lancet*, and Witton mentioned having just such a similar case in a man called Bains. I was interested at once. It was one of those cases of a gap or flaw in a man's protection barrier, I call it. A failure to be what I might term efficiently insulated—spiritually—from the outer monstrosities.

"From what I knew of Witton, I knew he'd be no use. You all know Witton. A decent sort, hard-headed, practical, stand-no-kind-of-nonsense sort of man, all right at his own job when that job's a fractured leg or a broken collarbone; but he'd never have made anything of the Bains case."

For a space Carnacki puffed meditatively at his pipe, and we waited for him to go on with his tale.

"I told Witton to send Bains to me," he resumed, "and the following Saturday he came up. A little sensitive man. I liked him as soon as I set eyes on him. After a bit, I got him to explain what was troubling him, and questioned him about what Doctor Witton had called his 'dreams.'

"'They're more than dreams,' he said, 'they're so real that they're actual experiences to me. They're simply horrible. And yet there's nothing very definite in them to tell you about. They generally come just as I am going off to sleep. I'm hardly over before suddenly I seem to have got down into some deep, vague place with some inexplicable and frightful horror all about me. I can never understand what it is, for I never see anything, only I always get a sudden knowledge like a warning that I have got down into some terrible place—a sort of hell-place I might call it, where I've no business ever to have wandered; and the warning is always insistent—even imperative—that I must get out, get out, or some enormous horror will come at me.'

"'Can't you pull yourself back?' I asked him. 'Can't you wake up?'

"'No,' he told me. 'That's just what I can't do, try as I will. I can't stop going along this labyrinth-of-hell as I call it to myself, towards some dreadful unknown Horror. The warning is repeated, ever so strongly—almost as if the live me of my waking moments was awake and aware. Something seems to warn me to wake up, that whatever I do I must wake, wake, and then my consciousness comes suddenly alive and I know that my body is there in the bed, but my essence or spirit is still down there in that hell, wherever it is, in a danger that is both unknown and inexpressible; but so overwhelming that my whole spirit seems sick with terror.

"'I keep saying to myself all the time that I must wake up,' he continued, 'but it is as if my spirit is still down there, and as if my consciousness knows that some tremendous invisible Power is fighting against me. I know that if I do not wake then, I shall never wake up again, but go down deeper and deeper into some stupendous horror of soul destruction. So then I fight. My body lies in the bed there, and *pulls*. And the power down there in that labyrinth exerts itself too so that a feeling of despair, greater than any I have ever known on this earth, comes on me. I know that if I give way and cease to fight, and do not wake, then I shall pass out—out to that monstrous Horror which seems to be silently calling my soul to destruction.

"'Then I make a final stupendous effort,' he continued, 'and my brain seems to fill my body like the ghost of my soul. I can even open my eyes and see with my brain, or consciousness, out of my own eyes. I can see the bedclothes, and I know just how I am lying in the bed; yet the real me is down in that hell in terrible danger. Can you get me?' he asked.

"'Perfectly,' I replied.

"'Well, you know,' he went on, 'I fight and fight. Down there in that great pit my very soul seems to shrink back from the call of some brooding horror that impels it silently a little further, always a little further round a visible corner, which if I once pass I know I shall never return again to this world. Desperately I fight brain and consciousness fighting together to help it. The agony is so great that I could scream were it not that I am rigid and frozen in the bed with fear.

"'Then, just when my strength seems almost gone, soul and body win, and blend slowly. And I lie there worn out with this terrible extraordinary fight. I have still a sense of a dreadful horror all about me, as if out of that horrible place some brooding monstrosity had followed me up, and hangs still and silent and invisible over me, threatening me there in my bed. Do I make it clear to you?' he asked. 'It's like some monstrous Presence.'

"'Yes,' I said. 'I follow you.'

"The man's forehead was actually covered with sweat, so keenly did he live again through the horrors he had experienced.

"After a while he continued:

"'Now comes the most curious part of the dream or whatever it is,' he said. 'There's always a sound I hear as I lie there exhausted in the bed. It comes while the bedroom is still full of the sort of atmosphere of monstrosity that seems to come up with me when I get out of that place. I hear the sound coming up out of that enormous depth, and it is always the noise of pigs—pigs grunting, you know. It's just simply dreadful. The dream is always the same. Sometimes I've had it every single night for a week, until I fight not to go to sleep; but, of course, I have to sleep sometimes. I think that's how a person might go mad, don't you?' he finished.

"I nodded, and looked at his sensitive face. Poor beggar! He had been through it, and no mistake.

"'Tell me some more,' I said. 'The grunting—what does it sound like exactly?'

"'It's just like pigs grunting,' he told me again. 'Only much more awful. There are grunts, and squeals and pig-howls, like you hear when their food is being brought to them at a pig farm. You know those large pig farms where they keep hundreds of pigs. All the grunts, squeals and howls blend into one brutal chaos of sound— only it isn't a chaos. It all blends in a queer horrible way. I've heard it. A sort of swinish clamouring melody that grunts and roars and shrieks in chunks of grunting sounds, all tied together with squealings and shot through with pig howls. I've sometimes thought there was a definite beat in it; for every now and again there comes a gargantuan GRUNT, breaking through the million pig-voiced roaring—a stupendous GRUNT that comes in with a beat. Can you understand me? It seems to shake everything. . . . It's like a spiritual earthquake. The howling, squealing, grunting, rolling clamour of swinish noise coming up out of that place, and then the monstrous GRUNT rising up through it all, an ever-re-curring beat out of the depth—the voice of the swine-mother of monstrosity beating up from below through that chorus of mad swine-hunger. . . . It's no use! I can't explain it. No one ever could. It's just terrible! And I'm afraid you're saying to yourself that I'm in a bad way; that I want a change or a tonic; that I must buck up or I'll land myself in a madhouse. If only you could understand! Doctor Witton seemed to half understand, I thought; but I know he's only sent me to you as a sort of last hope. He thinks I'm booked for the asylum. I could tell it.'

"'Nonsense!' I said. 'Don't talk such rubbish. You're as sane as I am. Your ability to think clearly what you want to tell me, and then to transmit it to me so well that you compel my mental retina to see something of what you have seen, stands sponsor for your mental balance.

"'I am going to investigate your case, and if it is what I suspect, one of those rare instances of a "flaw" or "gap" in your protective barrier (what I might call your spiritual insulation from the Outer Monstrosities) I've no doubt we can end the trouble. But we've got to go properly into the matter first, and there will certainly be danger in doing so.'

"'I'll risk it,' replied Bains. 'I can't go on like this any longer.'

"'Very well,' I told him. 'Go out now, and come back at five o'clock. I shall be ready for you then. And don't worry about your sanity. You're all right, and we'll soon make things safe for you again. Just keep cheerful and don't brood about it.'

"I put in the whole afternoon preparing my experimenting room, across the landing there, for his case. When he returned at five o'clock I was ready for him and took him straight into the room.

"It gets dark now about six-thirty, as you know, and I had just nice time before it grew dusk to finish my arrangements. I prefer always to be ready before the dark comes.

"Bains touched my elbow as we walked into the room.

"'There's something I ought to have told you,' he said, looking rather sheepish. 'I've somehow felt a bit ashamed of it.'

"'Out with it,' I replied.

"He hesitated a moment, then it came out with a jerk.

"'I told you about the grunting of the pigs,' he said. 'Well, I grunt too. I know it's horrible. When I lie there in bed and hear those sounds after I've come up, I just grunt back as if in reply. I can't stop myself. I just do it. Something makes me. I never told Doctor Witton that. I couldn't. I'm sure now you think me mad,' he concluded.

"He looked into my face, anxious and queerly ashamed.

"'It's only the natural sequence of the abnormal events, and I'm glad you told me,' I said, slapping him on the back. 'It follows logically on what you had already told me. I have had two cases that in some way resembled yours.'

"'What happened?' he asked me. 'Did they get better?'

"'One of them is alive and well today, Mr. Bains,' I replied. 'The other man lost his nerve, and fortunately for all concerned, he is dead.'

"I shut the door and locked it as I spoke, and Bains stared round, rather alarmed, I fancy, at my apparatus.

"'What are you going to do?' he asked. 'Will it be a dangerous experiment?'

"'Dangerous enough,' I answered, 'if you fail to follow my instructions absolutely in everything. We both run the risk of never leaving this room alive. Have I your word that I can depend on you to obey me whatever happens?'

"He stared round the room and then back at me.

"'Yes,' he replied. And, you know, I felt he would prove the right kind of stuff when the moment came.

"I began now to get things finally in train for the night's work. I told Bains to take off his coat and his boots. Then I dressed him entirely from head to foot in a single thick rubber combination-overall, with rubber gloves, and a helmet with ear-flaps of the same material attached.

"I dressed myself in a similar suit. Then I began on the next stage of the night's preparations.

"First I must tell you that the room measures thirty-nine feet by thirty-seven, and has a plain board floor over which is fitted a heavy, half-inch rubber covering.

"I had cleared the floor entirely, all but the exact centre where I had placed a glass-legged, upholstered table, a pile of vacuum tubes and batteries, and three pieces of special apparatus which my experiment required.

"'Now Bains,' I called, 'come and stand over here by this table. Don't move about. I've got to erect a protective "barrier" round us, and on no account must either of us cross over it by even so much as a hand or foot, once it is built.'

"We went over to the middle of the room, and he stood by the glass-legged table while I began to fit the vacuum tubing together round us.

"I intended to use the new spectrum 'defense' which I have been perfecting lately. This, I must tell you, consists of seven glass vacuum circles with the red on the outside, and the colour circles lying inside it, in the order of orange, yellow, green, blue, indigo and violet.

"The room was still fairly light, but a slight quantity of dusk seemed to be already in the atmosphere, and I worked quickly.

"Suddenly, as I fitted the glass tubes together I was aware of some vague sense of nerve-strain, and glancing round at Bains who was standing there by the table I noticed him staring fixedly before him. He looked absolutely drowned in uncomfortable memories.

"'For goodness' sake stop thinking of those horrors,' I called out to him. 'I shall want you to think hard enough about them later; but in this specially constructed room it is better not to dwell on things of that kind till the barriers are up. Keep your mind on anything normal or superficial—the theatre will do—think about that last piece you saw at the Gaiety. I'll talk to you in a moment.'

"Twenty minutes later the 'barrier' was completed all round us, and I connected up the batteries. The room by this time was greying with the coming dusk, and the seven differently coloured circles shone out with extraordinary effect, sending out a cold glare.

"'By Jove!' cried Bains, 'that's very wonderful—very wonderful!'

"My other apparatus which I now began to arrange consisted of a specially made camera, a modified form of phonograph with ear-pieces instead of a horn, and a glass disk composed of many fathoms of glass vacuum tubes arranged in a special way. It had two wires leading to an electrode constructed to fit round the head.

"By the time I had looked over and fixed up these three things, night had practically come, and the darkened room shone most strangely in the curious upward glare of the seven vacuum tubes.

"'Now, Bains,' I said, 'I want you to lie on this table. Now put your hands down by your sides and lie quiet and think. You've just got two things to do,' I told him. 'One is to lie there and concentrate your thoughts on the details of the dream you are always having, and the other is not to move off this table whatever you see or hear, or whatever happens, unless I tell you. You understand, don't you?'

"'Yes,' he answered, 'I think you may rely on me not to make a fool of myself. I feel curiously safe with you somehow.'

"'I'm glad of that,' I replied. 'But I don't want you to minimise the possible danger too much. There may be horrible danger. Now, just let me fix this band on your head,' I added, as I adjusted the electrode. I gave him a few more instructions, telling him to concentrate his thoughts particularly upon the noises he heard just as he was waking, and I warned him again not to let himself fall asleep. 'Don't talk,' I said, 'and don't take any notice of me. If you find I disturb your concentration keep your eyes closed.'

"He lay back and I walked over to the glass disk arranging the camera in front of it on its stand in such a way that the lens was opposite the centre of the disk.

"I had scarcely done this when a ripple of greenish light ran across the vacuum tubes of the disk. This vanished, and for maybe a minute there was complete darkness. Then the green light rippled once more across it—rippled and swung round, and began to dance in varying shades from a deep heavy green to a rank ugly shade; back and forward, back and forward.

"Every half second or so there shot across the varying greens a flicker of yellow, an ugly, heavy repulsive yellow, and then abruptly there came sweeping across the disk a great beat of muddy red. This died as quickly as it came, and gave place to the changing greens shot through by the unpleasant and ugly yellow hues. About every seventh second the disk was submerged, and the other colours momentarily blotted out by the great beat of heavy, muddy red which swept over everything.

"'He's concentrating on those sounds,' I said to myself, and I felt queerly excited as I hurried on with my operations. I threw a word over my shoulder to Bains.

"'Don't get scared, whatever happens,' I said. 'You're all right!'

"I proceeded now to operate my camera. It had a long roll of specially prepared paper ribbon in place of a film or plates. By turning the handle the roll passed through the machine exposing the ribbon.

"It took about five minutes to finish the roll, and during all that time the green lights predominated; but the dull heavy beat of muddy red never ceased to flow across the vacuum tubes of the disk at every seventh second. It was like a recurrent beat in some unheard and somehow displeasing melody.

"Lifting the exposed spool of paper ribbon out of the camera I laid it horizontally in the two 'rests' that I had arranged for it on my modified gramophone. Where the paper had been acted upon by the varying coloured lights which had appeared on the disk, the prepared surface had risen in curious, irregular little waves.

"I unrolled about a foot of the ribbon and attached the loose end to an empty spool-roller (on the opposite side of the machine) which I had geared to the driving clockwork mechanism of the gramophone. Then I took the diaphragm and lowered it gently into place above the ribbon. Instead of the usual needle the diaphragm was fitted with a beautifully made metal-filament brush, about an inch broad, which just covered the whole breadth of the ribbon. This fine and fragile brush rested lightly on the prepared surface of the paper, and when I started the machine the ribbon began to pass under the brush, and as it passed, the delicate metal-filament 'bristles' followed every minute inequality of those tiny, irregular wave-like excrescences on the surface.

"I put the ear-pieces to my ears, and instantly I knew that I had succeeded in actually recording what Bains had heard in his sleep. In fact, I was even then hearing 'mentally' by means of his effort of memory. I was listening to what appeared to be the faint, far-off squealing and grunting of countless swine. It was extraordinary, and at the same time exquisitely horrible and vile. It frightened me, with a sense of my having come suddenly and unexpectedly too near to something foul and most abominably dangerous.

"So strong and imperative was this feeling that I twitched the ear-pieces out of my ears, and sat a while staring round the room trying to steady my sensations back to normality.

"The room looked strange and vague in the dull glow of light from the circles, and I had a feeling that a taint of monstrosity was all about me in the air. I remembered what Bains had told me of the feeling he'd always had after coming up out of 'that place'—as if some horrible atmosphere had followed him up and filled his bedroom. I understood him perfectly now—so much so that I had mentally used almost his exact phrase in explaining to myself what I felt.

"Turning round to speak to him I saw there was something curious about the centre of the 'defense.'

"Now, before I tell you fellows any more I must explain that there are certain, what I call 'focussing,' qualities about this new 'defense' I've been trying.

"The Sigsand manuscript puts it something like this: 'Avoid diversities of colour; nor stand ye within the barrier of the colour lights; for in colour hath Satan a delight. Nor can he abide in the Deep if ye adventure against him armed with red purple. So be warned. Neither forget that in blue, which is God's colour in the Heavens, ye have safety.'

"You see, from that statement in the Sigsand manuscript I got my first notion for this new 'defense' of mine. I have aimed to make it a 'defense' and yet have 'focussing' or 'drawing' qualities such as the Sigsand hints at. I have experimented enormously, and I've proved that reds and purples—the two extreme colours of the spectrum—are fairly dangerous; so much so that I suspect they actually 'draw' or 'focus' the outside forces. Any action or 'meddling' on the part of the experimentalist is tremendously enhanced in its effect if the action is taken within barriers composed of these colours, in certain proportions and tints.

"In the same way blue is distinctly a 'general defense.' Yellow appears to be neutral, and green a wonderful protection within limits. Orange, as far as I can tell, is slightly attractive and indigo is dangerous by itself in a limited way, but in certain combinations with the other colours it becomes a very powerful 'defense.' I've not yet discovered a tenth of the possibilities of these circles of mine. It's a kind of colour organ upon which I seem to play a tune of colour combinations that can be either safe or infernal in its effects. You know I have a keyboard with a separate switch to each of the colour circles.

"Well, you fellows will understand now what I felt when I saw the curious appearance of the floor in the middle of the 'defense.' It looked exactly as if a circular shadow lay, not just on the floor, but a few inches above it. The shadow seemed to deepen and blacken at the centre even while I watched it. It appeared to be spreading from the centre outwardly, and all the time it grew darker.

"I was watchful, and not a little puzzled; for the combination of lights that I had switched on approximated a moderately safe 'general defense.' Understand, I had no intention of making a focus until I had learnt more. In fact, I meant that first investigation not to go beyond a tentative inquiry into the kind of thing I had got to deal with.

"I knelt down quickly and felt the floor with the palm of my hand, but it was quite normal to the feel, and that reassured me that there was no Saaitii mischief abroad; for that is a form of danger which can involve, and make use of, the very material of the 'defense' itself. It can materialise out of everything except fire.

"As I knelt there I realised all at once that the legs of the table on which Bains lay were partly hidden in the ever blackening shadow, and my hands seemed to grow vague as I felt at the floor.

"I got up and stood away a couple of feet so as to see the phenomenon from a little distance. It struck me then that there was something different about the table itself. It seemed unaccountably lower.

"'It's the shadow hiding the legs,' I thought to myself. 'This promises to be interesting; but I'd better not let things go too far.'

"I called out to Bains to stop thinking so hard. 'Stop concentrating for a bit,' I said; but he never answered, and it occurred to me suddenly that the table appeared to be still lower.

"'Bains,' I shouted, 'stop thinking a moment.' Then in a flash I realised it. 'Wake up, man! Wake up!' I cried.

"He had fallen over asleep—the very last thing he should have done; for it increased the danger twofold. No wonder I had been getting such good results! The poor beggar was worn out with his sleepless nights. He neither moved nor spoke as I strode across to him.

"'Wake up!' I shouted again, shaking him by the shoulder.

"My voice echoed uncomfortably round the big empty room; and Bains lay like a dead man.

"As I shook him again I noticed that I appeared to be standing up to my knees in the circular shadow. It looked like the mouth of a pit. My legs, from the knees downwards, were vague. The floor under my feet felt solid and firm when I stamped on it; but all the same I had a feeling that things were going a bit too far, so striding across to the switchboard I switched on the 'full defense.'

"Stepping back quickly to the table I had a horrible and sickening shock. The table had sunk quite unmistakably. Its top was within a couple of feet of the floor, and the legs had that fore-shortened appearance that one sees when a stick is thrust into water. They looked vague and shadowy in the peculiar circle of dark shadows which had such an extraordinary resemblance to the black mouth of a pit. I could see only the top of the table plainly with Bains lying motionless on it; and the whole thing was going down, as I stared, into that black circle.

"There was not a moment to lose, and like a flash I caught Bains round his neck and body and lifted him clean up into my arms off the table. And as I lifted him he grunted like a great swine in my ear.

"The sound sent a thrill of horrible funk through me. It was just as though I held a hog in my arms instead of a human. I nearly dropped him. Then I held his face to the light and stared down at him. His eyes were half opened, and he was looking at me apparently as if he saw me perfectly.

"Then he grunted again. I could feel his small body quiver with the sound.

"I called out to him. 'Bains,' I said, 'can you hear me?'

"His eyes still gazed at me; and then, as we looked at each other, he grunted like a swine again.

"I let go one hand, and hit him across the cheek, a stinging slap.

"'Wake up, Bains!' I shouted. 'Wake up!' But I might have hit a corpse. He just stared up at me. And. suddenly I bent lower and looked into his eyes more closely. I never saw such a fixed, intelligent, mad horror as I saw there. It knocked out all my sudden disgust. Can you understand?

"I glanced round quickly at the table. It stood there at its normal height; and, indeed, it was in every way normal. The curious shadow that had somehow suggested to me the black mouth of the pit had vanished. I felt relieved; for it seemed to me that I had entirely broken up any possibility of a partial 'focus' by means of the full 'defense' which I had switched on.

"I laid Bains on the floor, and stood up to look round and consider what was best to do. I dared not step outside of the barriers, until any 'dangerous tensions' there might be in the room had been dissipated. Nor was it wise, even inside the full 'defense,' to have him sleeping the kind of sleep he was in; not without certain preparations having been made first, which I had not made.

"I can tell you, I felt beastly anxious. I glanced down at Bains, and had a sudden fresh shock; for the peculiar circular shadow was forming all round him again, where he lay on the floor. His hands and face showed curiously vague, and distorted, as they might have looked through a few inches of faintly stained water. But his eyes were somehow clear to see. They were staring up, mute and terrible, at me, through that horrible darkening shadow.

"I stopped, and with one quick lift, tore him up off the floor into my arms, and for the third time he grunted like a swine, there in my arms. It was damnable.

"I stood up, in the barrier, holding Bains, and looked about the room again; then back at the floor. The shadow was still thick round about my feet, and I stepped quickly across to the other side of the table. I stared at the shadow, and saw that it had vanished; then I glanced down again at my feet, and had another shock; for the shadow was showing faintly again, all round where I stood.

"I moved a pace, and watched the shadow become invisible; and then, once more, like a slow stain, it began to grow about my feet.

"I moved again, a pace, and stared round the room, meditating a break for the door. And then, in that instant, I saw that this would be certainly impossible; for there was something indefinite in the atmosphere of the room—something that moved, circling slowly about the barrier.

"I glanced down at my feet, and saw that the shadow had grown thick about them. I stepped a pace to the right, and as it disappeared, I stared again round the big room and somehow it seemed tremendously big and unfamiliar. I wonder whether you can understand.

"As I stared I saw again the indefinite something that floated in the air of the room. I watched it steadily for maybe a minute. It went twice completely round the barrier in that time. And, suddenly, I saw it more distinctly. It looked like a small puff of black smoke.

"And then I had something else to think about; for all at once I was aware of an extraordinary feeling of vertigo, and in the same moment, a sense of sinking—I was sinking bodily. I literally sickened as I glanced down, for I saw in that moment that I had gone down, almost up to my thighs into what appeared to be actually the shadowy, but quite unmistakable, mouth of a pit. Do you understand? I was sinking down into this thing, with Bains in my arms.

"A feeling of furious anger came over me, and I swung my right boot forward with a fierce kick. I kicked nothing tangible, for I went clean through the side of the shadowy thing, and fetched up against the table, with a crash. I had come through something that made all my skin creep and tingle—an invisible, vague something which resembled an electric tension. I felt that if it had been stronger, I might not have been able to charge through as I had. I wonder if I make it clear to you?

"I whirled round, but the beastly thing had gone; yet even as I stood there by the table, the slow greying of a circular shadow began to form again about my feet.

"I stepped to the other side of the table, and leaned against it for a moment: for I was shaking from head to foot with a feeling of extraordinary horror upon me, that was in some way, different from any kind of horror I have ever felt. It was as if I had in that one moment been near something no human has any right to be near, for his soul's sake. And abruptly, I wondered whether I had not felt just one brief touch of the horror that the rigid Bains was even then enduring as I held him in my arms.

"Outside of the barrier there were now several of the curious little clouds. Each one looked exactly like a little puff of black smoke. They increased as I watched them, which I did for several minutes; but all the time as I watched, I kept moving from one part to another of the 'defense,' so as to prevent the shadow forming round my feet again.

"Presently, I found that my constant changing of position had resolved into a slow monotonous walk round and round, inside the 'defense'; and all the time I had to carry the unnaturally rigid body of poor Bains.

"It began to tire me; for though he was small, his rigidity made him dreadfully awkward and tiring to hold, as you can understand; yet I could not think what else to do; for I had stopped shaking him, or trying to wake him, for the simple reason that he was as wide awake as I was mentally; though but physically inanimate, through one of those partial spiritual disassociations which he had tried to explain to me.

"Now I had previously switched out the red, orange, yellow and green circles, and had on the full defense of the blue end of the spectrum—I knew that one of the repelling vibrations of each of the three colours: blue, indigo and violet were beating out protectingly into space; yet they were proving insufficient, and I was in the position of having either to take some desperate action to stimulate Bains to an even greater effort of will than I judged him to be making, or else to risk experimenting with fresh combinations of the defensive colours.

"You see, as things were at that moment, the danger was increasing steadily; for plainly, from the appearance of the air of the room outside the barrier, there were some mighty dangerous tensions generating. While inside the danger was also increasing; the steady recurrence of the shadow proving that the 'defense' was insufficient.

"In short, I feared that Bains in his peculiar condition was literally a 'doorway' into the 'defense'; and unless I could wake him or find out the correct combinations of circles necessary to set up stronger repelling vibrations against that particular danger, there were very ugly possibilities ahead. I felt I had been incredibly rash not to have foreseen the possibility of Bains falling asleep under the hypnotic effect of deliberately paralleling the associations of sleep.

"Unless I could increase the repulsion of the barriers or wake him there was every likelihood of having to chose between a rush for the door—which the condition of the atmosphere outside the barrier showed to be practically impossible—or of throwing him outside the barrier, which, of course, was equally not possible.

"All this time I was walking round and round inside the barrier, when suddenly I saw a new development of the danger which threatened us. Right in the centre of the 'defense' the shadow had formed into an intensely black circle, about a foot wide.

"This increased as I looked at it. It was horrible to see it grow. It crept out in an ever widening circle till it was quite a yard across.

"Quickly I put Bains on the floor. A tremendous attempt was evidently going to be made by some outside force to enter the 'defense,' and it was up to me to make a final effort to help Bains to 'wake up.' I took out my lancet, and pushed up his left coat sleeve.

"What I was going to do was a terrible risk, I knew, for there is no doubt that in some extraordinary fashion blood attracts.

"The Sigsand mentions it particularly in one passage which runs something like this: 'In blood there is the Voice which calleth through all space. Ye Monsters in ye Deep hear, and hearing, they lust. Likewise hath it a greater power to reclaim backward ye soul that doth wander foolish adrift from ye body in which it doth have natural abiding. But woe unto him that doth spill ye blood in ye deadly hour; for there will be surely Monsters that shall hear ye Blood Cry.'

"That risk I had to run. I knew that the blood would call to the outer forces; but equally I knew that it should call even more loudly to that portion of Bains' 'Essence' that was adrift from him, down in those depths.

"Before lancing him, I glanced at the shadow. It had spread out until the nearest edge was not more than two feet away from Bains' right shoulder; and the edge was creeping nearer, like the blackening edge of burning paper, even while I stared. The whole thing had a less shadowy, less ghostly appearance than at any time before. And it looked simply and literally like the black mouth of a pit.

"'Now, Bains,' I said, 'pull yourself together, man. Wake up!' And at the same time as I spoke to him, I used my lancet quickly but superficially.

"I watched the little red spot of blood well up, then trickle round his wrist and fall to the floor of the 'defense.' And in the moment that it fell the thing that I had feared happened. There was a sound like a low peal of thunder in the room, and curious deadly-looking flashes of light rippled here and there along the floor outside the barrier.

"Once more I called to him, trying to speak firmly and steadily as I saw that the horrible shadowy circle had spread across every inch of the floor space of the centre of the 'defense,' making it appear as if both Bains and I were suspended above an unutterable black void—the black void that stared up at me out of the throat of that shadowy pit. And yet, all the time I could feel the floor solid under my knees as I knelt beside Bains holding his wrist.

"'Bains!' I called once more, trying not to shout madly at him. 'Bains, wake up! Wake up, man! Wake up!'

"But he never moved, only stared up at me with eyes of quiet horror that seemed to be looking at me out of some dreadful eternity.

"By this time the shadow had blackened all around us, and I felt that strangely terrible vertigo coming over me again. Jumping to my feet I caught up Bains in my arms and stepped over the first of the protective circles—the violet, and stood between it and the indigo circle, holding Bains as close to me as possible so as to prevent any portion of his helpless body from protruding outside the indigo and blue circles.

"From the black shadowy mouth which now filled the whole of the centre of the 'defense' there came a faint sound—not near but seeming to come up at me out of unknown abysses. Very, very faint and lost it sounded, but I recognised it as unmistakably the infinitely remote murmur of countless swine.

"And that same moment Bains, as if answering the sound, grunted like a swine in my arms.

"There I stood between the glass vacuum tubes of the circles, gazing dizzily into that black shadowy pit-mouth, which seemed to drop sheer into hell from below my left elbow.

"Things had gone so utterly beyond all that I had thought of, and it had all somehow come about so gradually and yet so suddenly, that I was really a bit below my natural self. I felt mentally paralysed, and could think of nothing except that not twenty feet away was the door and the outer natural world; and here was I face to face with some unthought-of danger, and all adrift, what to do to avoid it.

"You fellows will understand this better when I tell you that the bluish glare from the three circles showed me that there were now hundreds and hundreds of those small smoke-like puffs of black cloud circling round and round outside the barrier in an unvarying, unending procession.

"And all the time I was holding the rigid body of Bains in my arms, trying not to give way to the loathing that got me each time he grunted. Every twenty or thirty seconds he grunted, as if in answer to the sounds which were almost too faint for my normal hearing. I can tell you, it was like holding something worse than a corpse in my arms, standing there balanced between physical death on the one side and soul destruction on the other.

"Abruptly, from out of the deep that lay so close that my elbow and shoulder overhung it, there came again a hint, marvellously faint murmur of swine, so utterly far away that the sound was as remote as a lost echo.

"Bains answered it with a pig-like squeal that set every fibre in me protesting in sheer human revolt, and I sweated coldly from head to foot. Pulling myself together I tried to pierce down into the mouth of the great shadow when, for the second time, a low peel of thunder sounded in the room, and every joint in my body seemed to jolt and burn.

"In turning to look down the pit I had allowed one of Bains' heels to protrude for a moment slightly beyond the blue circle, and a fraction of the 'tension' outside the barrier had evidently discharged through Bains and me. Had I been standing directly inside the 'defense' instead of being 'insulated' from it by the violet circle, then no doubt things might have been much more serious. As it was, I had, psychically, that dreadful *soiled* feeling which the healthy human always experiences when he comes too closely in contact with certain Outer Monstrosities. Do you fellows remember how I had just the same feeling when the Hand came too near me in the 'Gateway' case?

"The physical effects were sufficiently interesting to mention; for Bains' left boot had been ripped open, and the leg of his trousers was charred to the knee, while all around the leg were numbers of bluish marks in the form of irregular spirals.

"I stood there holding Bains, and shaking from head to foot. My head ached and each joint had a queer numbish feeling; but my physical pains were nothing compared with my mental distress. I felt that we were done! I had no room to turn or move for the space between the violet circle which was the innermost, and the blue circle which was the outermost of those in use was thirty-one inches, including the one inch of the indigo circle. So you see I was forced to stand there like an image, fearing each moment lest I should get another shock, and quite unable to think what to do.

"I daresay five minutes passed in this fashion. Bains had not grunted once since the 'tension' caught him, and for this I was just simply thankful; though at first I must confess I had feared for a moment that he was dead.

"No further sounds had come up out of the black mouth to my left, and I grew steady enough again to begin to look about me, and think a bit. I leant again so as to look directly down into the shadowy pit. The edge of the circular mouth was now quite defined, and had a curious solid look, as if it were formed out of some substance like black glass.

"Below the edge, I could trace the appearance of solidity for a considerable distance, though in a vague sort of way. The centre of this extraordinary phenomenon was simple and unmitigated blackness—an utter velvety blackness that seemed to soak the very light out of the room down into it. I could see nothing else, and if anything else came out of it except a complete silence, it was the atmosphere of frightening suggestion that was affecting me more and more every minute.

"I turned away slowly and carefully, so as not to run any risks of allowing either Bains or myself to expose any part of us over the blue circle. Then I saw that things outside of the blue circle had developed considerably; for the odd, black puffs of smoke-like cloud had increased enormously and blent into a great, gloomy, circular wall of tufted cloud, going round and round and round eternally, and hiding the rest of the room entirely from me.

"Perhaps a minute passed, while I stared at this thing; and then, you know, the room was shaken slightly. This shaking lasted for three or four seconds, and then passed; but it came again in about half a minute, and was repeated from time to time. There was a queer oscillating quality in the shaking that made me think suddenly of that *Jarvee* Haunting case. You remember it?

"There came again the shaking, and a ripple of deadly light seemed to play round the outside of the barrier; and then, abruptly, the room was full of a strange roaring—a brutish enormous yelling, grunting storm of swine-sounds.

"They fell away into a complete silence, and the rigid Bains grunted twice in my arms, as if answering. Then the storm of swine noise came again, beating up in a gigantic riot of brute sound that roared through the room, piping, squealing, grunting, and howling. And as it sank with a steady declination, there came a single gargantuan grunt out of some dreadful throat of monstrousness, and in one beat, the crashing chorus of unknown millions of swine came thundering and raging through the room again.

"There was more in that sound than mere chaos—there was a mighty devilish rhythm in it. Suddenly, it swept down again into a multitudinous swinish whispering and minor gruntings of unthinkable millions; and then with a rolling deafening bellow of sound came the single vast grunt. And, as if lifted upon it the swine roar of the millions of the beasts beat up through the room again; and

at every seventh second, as I knew well enough without the need
of the watch on my wrist, came the single storm beat of the great
grunt out of the throat of unknowable monstrosity—and in my
arms, Bains, the human, grunted in time to the swine melody—a
rigid grunting monster there in my two arms.

"I tell you from head to foot I shook and sweated. I believe I
prayed; but if I did I don't know what I prayed. I have never before
felt or endured just what I felt, standing there in that thirty-one-
inch space, with that grunting thing in my arms, and the hell
melody beating up out of the great Deeps: and to my right, 'tensions' that would have torn me into a bundle of blazing tattered
flesh, if I had jumped out over the barriers.

"And then, with an effect like a clap of unexpected thunder,
the vast storm of sound ceased; and the room was full of silence
and an unimaginable horror.

"This silence continued. I want to say something which may
sound a bit silly; but the silence seemed to *trickle* round the room.
I don't know why I felt it like that; but my words give you just what
I seemed to feel, as I stood there holding the softly grunting body
of Bains.

"The circular, gloomy wall of dense black cloud enclosed the
barrier as completely as ever, and moved round and round and
round, with a slow, 'eternal' movement. And at the back of that
black wall of circling cloud, a dead silence went *trickling* round
the room, out of my sight. Do you understand at all? . . .

"It seemed to me to show very clearly the state of almost insane mental and psychic tension I was enduring. . . . The way in
which my brain insisted that the silence was trickling round the
room, interests me enormously; for I was either in a state approxi-
mating a phase of madness, or else I was, psychically, tuned to
some abnormal pitch of awaredness and sensitiveness in which
silence had ceased to be an abstract quality, and had become to
me a definite concrete element, much as (to use a stupidly crude
illustration), the invisible moisture of the atmosphere becomes a
visible and concrete element when it becomes deposited as water.
I wonder whether this thought attracts you as it does me?

"And then, you know, a slow awaredness grew in me of some further horror to come. This sensation or knowledge or whatever it should be named, was so strong that I had a sudden feeling of suffocation. . . . I felt that I could bear no more; and that if anything else happened, I should just pull out my revolver and shoot Bains through the head, and then myself, and so end the whole dreadful business.

"This feeling, however, soon passed; and I felt stronger and more ready to face things again. Also, I had the first, though still indefinite, idea of a way in which to make things a bit safer; but I was too dazed to see how to 'shape' to help myself efficiently.

"And then a low, far-off whining stole up into the room, and I knew that the danger was coming. I leant slowly to my left, taking care not to let Bains' feet stick over the blue circle, and stared down into the blackness of the pit that dropped sheer into some Unknown, from under my left elbow.

"The whining died; but far down in the blackness, there was something—just a remote luminous spot. I stood in a grim silence for maybe ten long minutes, and looked down at the thing. It was increasing in size all the time, and had become much plainer to see; yet it was still lost in the far, tremendous Deep.

"Then, as I stood and looked, the low whining sound crept up to me again, and Bains, who had lain like a log in my arms all the time, answered it with a long animal-like whine, that was somehow newly abominable.

"A very curious thing happened then; for all around the edge of the pit, that looked so peculiarly like black glass, there came a sudden, luminous glowing. It came and went oddly, smouldering queerly round and round the edge in an opposite direction to the circling of the wall of black, tufted cloud on the outside of the barrier.

"This peculiar glowing finally disappeared, and, abruptly, out of the tremendous Deep, I was conscious of a dreadful quality or 'atmosphere' of monstrousness that was coming up out of the pit. If I said there had been a sudden *waft* of it, this would very well describe the actuality of it; but the spiritual sickness of distress that it caused me to feel, I am simply stumped to explain to you. It was something that made me feel I should be soiled to the very core of me, if I did not beat it off from me with my will.

"I leant sharply away from the pit towards the outer of the burning circles. I meant to see that no part of my body should overhang the pit whilst that disgusting power was beating up out of the unknown depths.

"And thus it was, facing so rigidly away from the centre of the 'defense,' I saw presently a fresh thing; for there was something, many things, I began to think, on the other side of the gloomy wall that moved everlastingly around the outside of the barrier.

"The first thing I noticed was a queer disturbance of the ever circling cloud-wall. This disturbance was within eighteen inches of the floor, and directly before me. There was a curious, 'puddling' action in the misty wall; as if something were meddling with it. The area of this peculiar little disturbance could not have been more than a foot across, and it did not remain opposite to me; but was taken round by the circling of the wall.

"When it came past me again, I noticed that it was bulging slightly inwards towards me: and as it moved away from me once more, I saw another similar disturbance, and then a third and a fourth, all in different parts of the slowly whirling black wall; and all of them were no more than about eighteen inches from the floor.

"When the first one came opposite me again, I saw that the slight bulge had grown into a very distinct protuberance towards me.

"All around the moving wall, there had now come these curious swellings. They continued to reach inwards, and to elongate; and all the time they kept in a constant movement.

"Suddenly, one of them broke, or opened, at the apex, and there protruded through, for an instant, the tip of a pallid, but unmistakable *snout*. It was gone at once, but I had seen the thing distinctly; and within a minute, I saw another one poke suddenly through the wall, to my right, and withdraw as quickly. I could not look at the base of the strange, black, moving circle about the barrier without seeing a swinish snout peep through momentarily, in this place or that.

"I stared at these things in a very peculiar state of mind. There was so great a weight of the abnormal about me, before and behind and every way, that to a certain extent it bred in me a sort of antidote to fear. Can you understand? It produced in me a temporary dazedness in which things and the horror of things became less real. I stared at them, as a child stares out from a fast train at a quickly passing night-landscape, oddly hit by the furnaces of unknown industries. I *want* you to try to understand.

"In my arms Bains lay quiet and rigid; and my arms and back ached until I was one dull ache in all my body; but I was only partly conscious of this when I roused momentarily from my psychic to my physical awaredness, to shift him to another position, less intolerable temporarily to my tired arms and back.

"There was suddenly a fresh thing—a low but enormous, solitary grunt came rolling, vast and brutal into the room. It made the still body of Bains quiver against me, and he grunted thrice in return, with the voice of a young pig.

"High up in the moving wall of the barrier, I saw a fluffing out of the black tufted clouds; and a pig's hoof and leg, as far as the knuckle, came through and pawed a moment. This was about nine or ten feet above the floor. As it gradually disappeared I heard a low grunting from the other side of the veil of clouds which broke out suddenly into a diafaeon of brute-sound, grunting, squealing and swine-howling; all formed into a sound that was the essential melody of the brute—a grunting, squealing howling roar that rose, roar by roar, howl by howl and squeal by squeal to a crescendo of horrors—the bestial growths, longings, zests and acts of some grotto of hell. . . . It is no use, I can't give it to you. I get dumb with the failure of my command over speech to tell you what that grunting, howling, roaring melody conveyed to me. It had in it something so inexplicably *below* the horizons of the soul in its monstrousness and fearfulness that the ordinary simple fear of death itself, with all its attendant agonies and terrors and sorrows, seemed like a thought of something peaceful and infinitely holy compared with the fear of those unknown elements in that dreadful roaring melody. And the sound was with me *inside* the room—

there right in the room with me. Yet I seemed not to be aware of confining walls, but of echoing spaces of gargantuan corridors. Curious! I had in my mind those two words—gargantuan corridors.

As the rolling chaos of swine melody beat itself away on every side, there came booming through it a single grunt, the single recurring grunt of the HOG; for I knew now that I was actually and without any doubt hearing the beat of monstrosity, the HOG.

"In the Sigsand the thing is described something like this: 'Ye Hogge which ye Almighty alone hath power upon. If in sleep or in ye hour of danger ye hear the voice of ye Hogge, cease ye to meddle. For ye Hogge doth be of ye outer Monstrous Ones, nor shall any human come nigh him nor continue meddling when ye hear his voice, for in ye earlier life upon the world did the Hogge have power, and shall again in ye end. And in that ye Hogge had once a power upon ye earth, so doth he crave sore to come again. And dreadful shall be ye harm to ye soul if ye continue to meddle, and to let ye beast come nigh. And I say unto all, if ye have brought this dire danger upon ye, have memory of ye cross, for of all sign hath ye Hogge a horror.'

"There's a lot more, but I can't remember it all and that is about the substance of it.

"There was I holding Bains who was all the time howling that dreadful grunt out with the voice of a swine. I wonder I didn't go mad. It was, I believe, the antidote of dazedness produced by the strain which helped me through each moment.

"A minute later, or perhaps five minutes, I had a sudden new sensation, like a warning cutting through my dulled feelings. I turned my head; but there was nothing behind me, and bending over to my left I seemed to be looking down into that black depth which fell away sheer under my left elbow. At that moment the roaring bellow of swine-noise ceased and I seemed to be staring down into miles of black aether at something that hung there—a pallid face floating far down and remote—a great swine face.

"And as I gazed I saw it grow bigger. A seemingly motionless, pallid swine-face rising upward out of the depth. And suddenly I realised that I was actually looking at the Hog.

"For perhaps a full minute I stared down through the darkness at that thing swimming like some far-off, dead-white planet in the stupendous void. And then I simply woke up bang, as you might say, to the possession of my faculties. For just a certain over-degree of strain had brought about the dumbly helpful anaesthesia of dazedness, so this sudden overwhelming supreme fact of horror produced, in turn, its reaction from inertness to action. I passed in one moment from listlessness to a fierce efficiency.

"I knew that I had, through some accident, penetrated beyond all previous 'bounds,' and that I stood where no human soul had any right to be, and that in but a few of the puny minutes of earth's time I might be dead.

"Whether Bains had passed beyond the 'lines of retraction' or not, I could not tell. I put him down carefully but quickly on his side, between the inner circles—that is, the violet circle and the indigo circle—where he lay grunting slowly. Feeling that the dreadful moment had come I drew out my automatic. It seemed best to make sure of our end before that thing in the depth came any nearer: for once Bains in his present condition came within what I might term the 'inductive forces' of the monster, he would cease to be human. There would happen, as in that case of Aster who stayed outside the pentacles in the Black Veil Case, what can only be described as a pathological, spiritual change—literally in other words, soul destruction.

"And then something seemed to be telling me not to shoot. This sounds perhaps a bit superstitious; but I meant to kill Bains in that moment, and what stopped me was a distinct message from the outside.

"I tell you, it sent a great thrill of hope through me, for I knew that the forces which govern the spinning of the outer circle were intervening. But the very fact of the intervention proved to me afresh the enormous spiritual peril into which we had stumbled; for that inscrutable Protective Force only intervenes between the human *soul* and the Outer Monstrosities.

"The moment I received that message I stood up like a flash and turned towards the pit, stepping over the violet circle slap into the mouth of darkness. I had to take the risk in order to get at the switch board which lay on the glass shelf under the table top in the centre. I could not shake free from the horror of the idea that I might fall down through that awful blackness. The floor felt solid enough under me; but I seemed to be walking on nothing above a black void, like an inverted starless night, with the face of the approaching Hog rising up from far down under my feet—a silent, incredible thing out of the abyss—a pallid, floating swine-face, framed in enormous blackness.

"Two quick, nervous strides took me to the table standing there in the centre with its glass legs apparently resting on nothing. I grabbed out the switch board, sliding out the vulcanite plate which carried the switch-control of the blue circle. The battery which fed this circle was the right-hand one of the row of seven, and each battery was marked with the letter of its circle painted on it, so that in an emergency I could select any particular battery in a moment.

"As I snatched up the B switch I had a grim enough warning of the unknown dangers that I was risking in that short journey of two steps; for that dreadful sense of vertigo returned suddenly and for one horrible moment I saw everything through a blurred medium as if I were trying to look through water.

"Below me, far away down between my feet I could see the Hog which, in some peculiar way, looked different—clearer and much nearer, and enormous. I felt it had got nearer to me all in a moment. And suddenly I had the impression I was descending bodily.

"I had a sense of a tremendous force being used to push me over the side of that pit, but with every shred of will power I had in me I hurled myself into the smoky appearance that hid everything and reached the violet circle where Bains lay in front of me.

"Here I crouched down on my heels, and with my two arms out before me I slipped the nails of each forefinger under the vulcanite base of the blue circle, which I lifted very gently so that when the base was far enough from the floor I could push the tips of my fingers underneath. I took care to keep from reaching farther under than the inner edge of the glowing tube which rested on the two-inch-broad foundation of vulcanite.

"Very slowly I stood upright, lifting the side of the blue circle with me. My feet were between the indigo and the violet circles, and only the blue circle between me and sudden death; for if it had snapped with the unusual strain I was putting upon it by lifting it like that, I knew that I should in all probability go west pretty quickly.

"So you fellows can imagine what I felt like. I was conscious of a disagreeable faint prickling that was strongest in the tips of my fingers and wrists, and the blue circle seemed to vibrate strangely as if minute particles of something were impinging upon it in countless millions. Along the shining glass tubes for a couple of feet on each side of my hands a queer haze of tiny sparks boiled and whirled in the form of an extraordinary halo.

"Stepping forward over the indigo circle I pushed the blue circle out against the slowly moving wall of black cloud causing a ripple of tiny pale flashes to curl in over the circle. These flashes ran along the vacuum tube until they came to the place where the blue circle crossed the indigo, and there they flicked off into space with sharp cracks of sound.

"As I advanced slowly and carefully with the blue circle a most extraordinary thing happened, for the moving wall of cloud gave from it in a great belly of shadow, and appeared to thin away from before it. Lowering my edge of the circle to the floor I stepped over Bains and right into the mouth of the pit, lifting the other side of the circle over the table. It creaked as if it were about to break in half as I lifted it, but eventually it came over safely.

"When I looked again into the depth of that shadow I saw below me the dreadful pallid head of the Hog floating in a circle of night. It struck me that it glowed very slightly—just a vague luminosity. And quite near—comparatively. No one could have judged distances in that black void.

"Picking up the edge of the blue circle again as I had done before, I took it out further till it was half clear of the indigo circle. Then I picked up Bains and carried him to that portion of the floor guarded by the part of the blue circle which was clear of the 'defense.' Then I lifted the circle and started to move it forward as quickly as I dared, shivering each time the joints squeaked as the whole fabric of it groaned with the strain I was putting upon it. And all the time the moving wall of tufted clouds gave from the edge of the blue circle, bellying away from it in a marvellous fashion as if blown by an unheard wind.

"From time to time little flashes of light had begun to flick in over the blue circle, and I began to wonder whether it would be able to hold out the 'tension' until I had dragged it clear of the defense.

"Once it was clear I hoped the abnormal stress would cease from about us, and concentrate chiefly around the 'defense' again, and the attractions of the negative 'tension.'

"Just then I heard a sharp tap behind me, and the blue circle jarred somewhat, having now ridden completely over the violet and indigo circles, and dropped clear on to the floor. The same instant there came a low rolling noise as of thunder, and a curious roaring. The black circling wall had thinned away from around us and the room showed clearly once more, yet nothing was to be seen except that now and then a peculiar bluish flicker of light would ripple across the floor.

"Turning to look at the 'defense' I noticed it was surrounded by the circling wall of black cloud, and looked strangely extraordinary seen from the outside. It resembled a slightly swaying squat funnel of whirling black mist reaching from the floor to the ceiling, and through it I could see glowing, sometimes vague and sometimes plain, the indigo and violet circles. And then as I watched, the whole room seemed suddenly filled with an awful presence which pressed upon me with a weight of horror that was the very essence of spiritual deathliness.

"Kneeling there in the blue circle by Bains, my initiative faculties stupefied and temporarily paralysed, I could form no further plan of escape, and indeed I seemed to care for nothing at the moment. I felt I had already escaped from immediate destruction and I was strung up to an amazing pitch of indifference to any minor horrors.

"Bains all this while had been quietly lying on his side. I rolled him over and looked closely at his eyes, taking care on account of his condition not to gaze *into* them; for if he had passed beyond the 'line of retraction' he would be dangerous. I mean, if the 'wandering' part of his essence had been assimilated by the Hog, then Bains would be spiritually accessible and might be even then no more than the outer form of the man, charged with radiation of the monstrous ego of the Hog, and therefore capable of what I might term for want of a more exact phrase, a psychically *infective* force; such force being more readily transmitted through the eyes than any other way, and capable of producing a brain storm of an extremely dangerous character.

"I found Bains, however, with both eyes with an extraordinary distressed interned quality; not the eyeballs, remember, but a reflex action transmitted from the 'mental eye' to the physical eye, and giving to the physical eye an expression of thought instead of sight. I wonder whether I make this clear to you?

"Abruptly, from every part of the room there broke out the noise of those hoofs again, making the place echo with the sound as if a thousand swine had started suddenly from an absolute immobility into a mad charge. The whole riot of animal sound seemed to heave itself in one wave towards the oddly swaying and circling funnel of black cloud which rose from floor to ceiling around the violet and indigo circles.

"As the sounds ceased I saw something was rising up through the middle of the 'defense.' It rose with a slow steady movement. I saw it pale and huge through the swaying, whirling funnel of cloud—a monstrous pallid snout rising out of that unknowable abyss. . . . It rose higher like a huge pale mound. Through a thinning of the cloud curtain I saw one small eye. . . . I shall never see a pig's eye again without feeling something of what I felt then. A pig's eye with a sort of hell-light of vile understanding shining at the back of it.

"And then suddenly a dreadful terror came over me, for I saw the beginning of the end that I had been dreading all along—I saw through the slow whirl of the cloud curtains that the violet circle had begun to leave the floor. It was being taken up on the spread of the vast snout.

"Straining my eyes to see through the swaying funnel of clouds I saw that the violet circle had melted and was running down the pale sides of the snout in streams of violet-coloured fire. And as it melted there came a change in the atmosphere of the room. The black funnel shone with a dull gloomy red, and a heavy red glow filled the room.

"The change was such as one might experience if one had been looking through a protective glass at some light and the glass had been suddenly removed. But there was a further change that I realised directly through my feelings. It was as if the horrible presence in the room had come closer to my own soul. I wonder if I am making it at all clear to you. Before, it had oppressed me somewhat as a death on a very gloomy and dreary day beats down upon one's spirit. But now there was a savage menace, and the actual feeling of a foul thing *close up against me*. It was horrible, simply horrible.

"And then Bains moved. For the first time since he went to sleep the rigidity went out of him, and rolling suddenly over on to his stomach he fumbled up in a curious animal-like fashion, on to his hands and feet. Then he charged straight across the blue circle towards the thing in the 'defense.'

"With a shriek I jumped to pull him back; but it was not my voice that stopped him. It was the blue circle. It made him give back from it as though some invisible hand had jerked him backwards. He threw up his head like a hog, squealing with the voice of a swine, and started off round the inside of the blue circle. Round and round it he went, twice attempting to bolt across it to the horror in that swaying funnel of cloud. Each time he was thrown back, and each time he squealed like a great swine, the sounds echoing round the room in a horrible fashion as though they came from somewhere a long way off.

"By this time I was fairly sure that Bains had indeed passed the 'line of retraction,' and the knowledge brought a fresh and more hopeless horror and pity to me, and a grimmer fear for myself. I knew that if it were so, it was not Bains I had with me in the circle but a monster, and that for my own last chance of safety I should have to get him outside of the circle.

"He had ceased his tireless running round and round, and now lay on his side grunting continually and softly in a dismal kind of way. As the slowly whirling clouds thinned a little I saw again that pallid face with some clearness. It was still rising, but slowly, very slowly, and again a hope grew in me that it might be checked by the 'defense.' Quite plainly I saw that the horror was looking at Bains, and at that moment I saved my own life and soul by looking down. There, close to me on the floor was the thing that looked like Bains, its hands stretched out to grip my ankles. Another second, and I should have been tripped *outwards*. Do you realise what that would have meant?

"It was no time to hesitate. I simply jumped and came down crash with my knees on top of Bains. He lay quiet enough after a short struggle; but I took off my braces and lashed his hands up behind him. And I shivered with the very touch of him, as though I was touching something monstrous.

"By the time I had finished I noticed that the reddish glow in the room had deepened quite considerably, and the whole room was darker. The destruction of the violet circle had reduced the light perceptibly; but the darkness that I am speaking of was something more than that. It seemed as if something now had come into the atmosphere of the room—a sort of gloom, and in spite of the shining of the blue circle and the indigo circle inside the funnel of cloud, there was now more red light than anything else.

"Opposite me the huge, cloud-shrouded monster in the indigo circle appeared to be motionless. I could see its outline vaguely all the time, and only when the cloud funnel thinned could I see it plainly—a vast, snouted mound, faintly and whitely luminous, one gargantuan side turned towards me, and near the base of the slope a minute slit out of which shone one whitish eye.

"Presently through the thin gloomy red vapour I saw something that killed the hope in me, and gave me a horrible despair; for the indigo circle, the final barrier of the defense, was being slowly lifted into the air—the Hog had begun to rise higher. I could see its dreadful snout rising upwards out of the cloud. Slowly, very slowly, the snout rose up, and the indigo circle went up with it.

"In the dead stillness of that room I got a strange sense that all eternity was tense and utterly still as if certain powers knew of this horror I had brought into the world. . . . And then I had an awareness of something coming . . . something from far, far away. It was as if some hidden unknown part of my brain knew it. Can you understand? There was somewhere in the heights of space a light that was coming near. I seemed to *hear* it coming. I could just see the body of Bains on the floor, huddled and shapeless and inert. Within the swaying veil of cloud the monster showed as a vast pale, faintly luminous mound, hugely snouted—an infernal hillock of monstrosity, pallid and deadly amid the redness that hung in the atmosphere of the room.

"Something told me that it was making a final effort against the help that was coming. I saw the indigo circle was now some inches from the floor, and every moment I expected to see it flash into streams of indigo fire running down the pale slopes of the snout. I could see the circle beginning to move upward at a perceptible speed. The monster was triumphing.

"Out in some realm of space a low continuous thunder sounded. The thing in the great heights was coming fast, but it could never come in time. The thunder grew from a low, far mutter into a deep steady rolling of sound. . . . It grew louder and louder, and as it grew I saw the indigo circle, now shining through the red gloom of the room, was a whole foot off the floor. I thought I saw a faint splutter of indigo light. . . . The final circle of the barrier was beginning to melt.

"That instant the thunder of the thing in flight which my brain heard so plainly, rose into a crashing, a world-shaking bellow of speed, making the room rock and vibrate to an immensity of sound. A strange flash of blue flame ripped open the funnel of cloud momentarily from top to base, and I saw for one brief instant the pallid monstrosity of the Hog, stark and pale and dreadful.

"Then the sides of the funnel joined again hiding the thing from me as the funnel became submerged quickly into a dome of silent blue light—God's own colour! All at once it seemed the cloud had gone, and from floor to ceiling of the room, in awful majesty, like a living Presence, there appeared that dome of blue fire banded with three rings of green light at equal distances. There was no sound or movement, not even a flicker, nor could I see anything in the light: for looking into it was like looking into the cold blue of the skies. But I felt sure that there had come to our aid one of those inscrutable forces which govern the spinning of the outer circle, for the dome of blue light, banded with three green bands of silent fire, was the outward or visible sign of an enormous force, undoubtedly of a defensive nature.

"Through ten minutes of absolute silence I stood there in the blue circle watching the phenomenon. Minute by minute I saw the heavy repellent red driven out of the room as the place lightened quite noticeably. And as it lightened, the body of Bains began to resolve out of a shapeless length of shadow, detail by detail, until I could see the braces with which I had lashed his wrists together.

"And as I looked at him his body moved slightly, and in a weak but perfectly sane voice he said:

"'I've had it again! My God! I've had it again!'

"I knelt down quickly by his side and loosened the braces from his wrists, helping him to turn over and sit up. He gripped my arm a little crazily with both hands.

"'I went to sleep after all,' he said. 'And I've been down there again. My God! It nearly had me. I was down in that awful place and it seemed to be just round a great corner, and I was stopped from coming back. I seemed to have been fighting for ages and ages. I felt I was going mad. Mad! I've been nearly down into a hell. I could hear you calling down to me from some awful height. I could hear your voice echoing along yellow passages. They *were* yellow. I know they were. And I tried to come and I couldn't.'

"'Did you see me?' I asked him when he stopped, gasping.

"'No,' he answered, leaning his head against my shoulder. 'I tell you it nearly got me that time. I shall never dare go to sleep again as long as I live. Why didn't you wake me?'

"'I did,' I told him. 'I had you in my arms most of the time. You kept looking up into my eyes as if you knew I was there.'

"'I know,' he said. 'I remember now; but you seemed to be up at the top of a frightful hole, miles and miles up from me, and those horrors were grunting and squealing and howling, and trying to catch me and keep me down there. But I couldn't see anything— only the yellow walls of those passages. And all the time there was something round the corner.'

"'Anyway, you're safe enough now,' I told him. 'And I'll guarantee you shall be safe in the future.'

"The room had grown dark save for the light from the blue circle. The dome had disappeared, the whirling funnel of black cloud had gone, the Hog had gone, and the light had died out of the indigo circle. And the atmosphere of the room was safe and normal again as I proved by moving the switch, which was near me, so as to lessen the defensive power of the blue circle and enable me to 'feel' the outside tension. Then I turned to Bains.

"'Come along,' I said. 'We'll go and get something to eat, and have a rest.'

"But Bains was already sleeping like a tired child, his head pillowed on his hand. 'Poor little devil!' I said as I picked him up in my arms. 'Poor little devil!'

"I walked across to the main switchboard and threw over the current so as to throw the 'V' protective pulse out of the four walls and the door; then I carried Bains out into the sweet wholesome normality of everything. It seemed wonderful, coming out of that chamber of horrors, and it seemed wonderful still to see my bedroom door opposite, wide open, with the bed looking so soft and white as usual—so ordinary and human. Can you chaps understand?

"I carried Bains into the room and put him on the couch; and then it was I realised how much I'd been up against, for when I was getting myself a drink I dropped the bottle and had to get another.

"After I had made Bains drink a glass I laid him on the bed.

"'Now,' I said, 'look into my eyes fixedly. Do you hear me? You are going off to sleep safely and soundly, and if anything troubles you, obey me and *wake up*. Now, sleep—sleep—sleep!'

"I swept my hands down over his eyes half a dozen times, and he fell over like a child. I knew that if the danger came again he would obey my will and wake up. I intend to cure him, partly by hypnotic suggestion, partly by a certain electrical treatment which I am getting Doctor Witton to give him.

"That night I slept on the couch, and when I went to look at Bains in the morning I found him still sleeping, so leaving him there I went into the test room to examine results. I found them very surprising.

"Inside the room I had a queer feeling, as you can imagine. It was extraordinary to stand there in that curious bluish light from the 'treated' windows, and see the blue circle lying, still glowing, where I had left it; and further on, the 'defense,' lying circle within circle, all 'out'; and in the centre the glass-legged table standing where a few hours before it had been submerged in the horrible monstrosity of the Hog. I tell you, it all seemed like a wild and horrible dream as I stood there and looked. I have carried out some curious tests in there before now, as you know, but I've never come nearer to a catastrophe.

"I left the door open so as not to feel shut in, and then I walked over to the 'defense.' I was intensely curious to see what had happened physically under the action of such a force as the Hog. I found unmistakable signs that proved the thing had been indeed a Saaitii manifestation, for there had been no psychic or physical illusion about the melting of the violet circle. There remained nothing of it except a ring of patches of melted glass. The gutta base had been fused entirely, but the floor and everything was intact. You see, the Saaitii forms can often attack and destroy, or even make use of, the very defensive material used against them.

"Stepping over the outer circle and looking closely at the indigo circle I saw that it was melted clean through in several places. Another fraction of time and the Hog would have been free to expand as an invisible mist of horror and destruction into the atmosphere of the world. And then, in that very moment of time, salvation had come. I wonder if you can get my feelings as I stood there staring down at the destroyed barrier."

Carnacki began to knock out his pipe which is always a sign that he has ended his tale, and is ready to answer any questions we may want to ask.

Taylor was first in. "Why didn't you use the Electric Pentacle as well as your new spectrum circles?" he asked.

"Because," replied Carnacki, "the pentacle is simply 'defensive' and I wished to have the power to make a 'focus' during the early part of the experiment, and then, at the critical moment, to change the combination of the colours so as to have a 'defense' against the results of the 'focus.' You follow me.

"You see," he went on, seeing we hadn't grasped his meaning, "there can be no 'focus' within a pentacle. It is just of a 'defensive' nature. Even if I had switched the current out of the electric pentacle I should still have had to contend with the peculiar and undoubtedly 'defensive' power that its form seems to exert, and this would have been sufficient to 'blur' the focus.

"In this new research work I'm doing, I'm bound to use a 'focus' and so the pentacle is barred. But I'm not sure it matters. I'm convinced this new spectrum 'defense' of mine will prove absolutely invulnerable when I've learnt how to use it; but it will take me some time. This last case has taught me something new. I had never thought of combining green with blue; but the three bands of green in the blue of that dome has set me thinking. If only I knew the right combinations! It's the combinations I've got to learn. You'll understand better the importance of these combinations when I remind you that green by itself is, in a very limited way, more deadly than red itself—and red is the danger colour of all."

"Tell us, Carnacki," I said, "what is the Hog? Can you? I mean what kind of monstrosity is it? Did you *really* see it, or was it all some horrible, dangerous kind of dream? How do you know it was one of the outer monsters? And what is the difference between that sort of danger and the sort of thing you saw in the Gateway of the Monster case? And what. . . . ?"

"Steady!" laughed Carnacki. "One at a time! I'll answer all your questions; but I don't think I'll take them quite in your order. For instance, speaking about actually seeing the Hog, I might say that, speaking generally, things seen of a 'ghostly' nature are not seen with the eyes; they are seen with the mental eye which has this psychic quality, not always developed to a useable state, in addition to its 'normal' duty of revealing to the brain what our physical eyes record.

"You will understand that when we see 'ghostly' things it is often the 'mental' eye performing simultaneously the duty of revealing to the brain what the physical eye sees as well as what it sees itself. The two sights blending their functions in such a fashion gives us the impression that we are actually seeing through our physical eyes the whole of the 'sight' that is being revealed to the brain.

"In this way we get an impression of seeing with our physical eyes both the material and the immaterial parts of an 'abnormal' scene; for each part being received and revealed to the brain by machinery suitable to the particular purpose appears to have equal value of reality that is, it appears to be equally material. Do you follow me?"

We nodded our assent, and Carnacki continued:

"In the same way, were anything to threaten our psychic body we should have the impression, generally speaking, that it was our physical body that had been threatened, because our psychic sensations and impressions would be super-imposed upon our physical, in the same way that our psychic and our physical sight are super-imposed.

"Our sensations would blend in such a way that it would be impossible to differentiate between what we felt physically and what we felt psychically. To explain better what I mean. A man may seem to himself, in a 'ghostly' adventure, to fall *actually*. That is, to be falling in a physical sense; but all the while it may be his psychic entity, or being—call it what you will—that is falling. But to his brain there is presented the sensation of falling all together. Do you get me?

"At the same time, please remember that the danger is none the less because it is his psychic body that falls. I am referring to the sensation I had of falling during the time of stepping across the mouth of that pit. My physical body could walk over it easily and feel the floor solid under me; but my psychic body was in very real danger of falling. Indeed, I may be said to have literally *carried* my psychic body over, held within me by the pull of my life-force. You see, to my psychic body the pit was as real and as actual as a coal pit would have been to my physical body. It was merely the pull of my life-force which prevented my psychic body from falling out of me, rather like a plummet, down through the everlasting depths in obedience to the giant pull of the monster.

"As you will remember, the pull of the Hog was too great for my life-force to withstand, and, psychically, I began to fall. Immediately on my brain was recorded a sensation identical with that which would have been recorded on it had my actual physical body been falling. It was a mad risk I took, but as you know, I had to take it to get to the switch and the battery. When I had that physical sense of falling and seemed to see the black misty sides of the pit all around me, it was my mental eye recording upon the brain what it was seeing. My psychic body had actually begun to fall and was really below the edge of the pit but still in contact with me. In other words my physical magnetic and psychic 'haloes' were still mingled. My physical body was still standing firmly upon the floor of the room, but if I had not each time by effort or will forced my physical body across to the side, my psychic body would have fallen completely out of 'contact' with me, and gone like some ghostly meteorite, obedient to the pull of the Hog.

"The curious sensation I had of forcing myself through an obstructing medium was not a physical sensation at all, as we understand that word, but rather the psychic sensation of forcing my entity to re-cross the 'gap' that had already formed between my falling psychic body now below the edge of the pit and my physical body standing on the floor of the room. And that 'gap' was full of a force that strove to prevent my body and soul from rejoining. It was a terrible experience. Do you remember how I could still see with my brain through the eyes of my psychic body, though it had already fallen some distance out of me? That is an extraordinary thing to remember.

"However, to get ahead, all 'ghostly' phenomena are extremely diffuse in a normal state. They become actively physically dangerous in all cases where they are concentrated. The best off-hand illustration I can think of is the all-familiar electricity—a force which, by the way, we are too prone to imagine we understand because we've named and harnessed it, to use a popular phrase. But we don't understand it at all! It is still a complete fundamental mystery. Well, electricity when diffused is an 'imagined and unpictured something,' but when concentrated it is sudden death. Have you got me in that?

"Take, for instance, that explanation, as a very, very crude sort of illustration of what the Hog is. The Hog is one of those million-mile-long clouds of 'nebulosity' lying in the Outer Circle. It is because of this that I term those clouds of force the Outer Monsters.

"What they are exactly is a tremendous question to answer. I sometimes wonder whether Dodgson there realises just how impossible it is to answer some of his questions," and Carnacki laughed.

"But to make a brief attempt at it. There is around this planet, and presumably others, of course, circles of what I might call 'emanations.' This is an extremely light gas, or shall I say aether. Poor aether, it's been hard worked in its time!

"Go back one moment to your school-days, and bear in mind that at one time the earth was just a sphere of extremely hot gases. These gases condensed in the form of materials and other 'solid' matters; but there are some that are not yet solidified—air, for instance. Well, we have an earth-sphere of solid matter on which to stamp as solidly as we like; and round about that sphere there lies a ring of gases the constituents of which enter largely into all life, as we understand life—that is, air.

"But this is not the only circle of gas which is floating round us. There are, as I have been forced to conclude, larger and more attenuated 'gas' belts lying, zone on zone, far up and around us. These compose what I have called the inner circles. They are surrounded in turn by a circle or belt of what I have called, for want of a better word, 'emanations.'

"This circle which I have named the Outer Circle can not lie less than a hundred thousand miles off the earth, and has a thickness which I have presumed to be anything between five and ten million miles. I believe, but I cannot prove, that it does not spin with the earth but in the opposite direction, for which a plausible cause might be found in the study of the theory upon which a certain electrical machine is constructed.

"I have reason to believe that the spinning of this, the Outer Circle, is disturbed from time to time through causes which are quite unknown to me, but which I believe are based in physical phenomena. Now, the Outer Circle is the psychic circle, yet it is also physical. To illustrate what I mean I must again instance electricity, and say that just as electricity discovered itself to us as something quite different from any of our previous conceptions of matter, so is the Psychic or Outer Circle different from any of our previous conceptions of matter. Yet it is none the less physical in its origin, and in the sense that electricity is physical, the Outer or Psychic Circle is physical in its constituents. Speaking pictorially it is, physically, to the Inner Circle what the Inner Circle is to the upper strata of the air, and what the air—as we know that intimate gas—is to the waters and the waters to the solid world. You get my line of suggestion?"

We all nodded, and Carnacki resumed.

"Well, now let me apply all this to what I am leading up to. I suggest that these million-mile-long clouds of monstrosity with float in the Psychic or Outer Circle, are bred of the elements of that circle. They are tremendous psychic forces, bred out of its elements just as an octopus or shark is bred out of the sea, or a tiger or any other physical force is bred out of the elements of its earth-and-air surroundings.

"To go further, a physical man is composed entirely from the constituents of earth and air, by which terms I include sunlight and water and 'condiments'! In other words without earth and air he could not *be!* Or to put it another way, earth and air breed within themselves the materials of the body and the brain, and therefore, presumably, the machine of intelligence.

"Now apply this line of thought to the Psychic or Outer Circle which though so attenuated that I may crudely presume it to be approximate to our conception of aether, yet contains all the elements for the production of certain phases of force and intelligence. But these elements are in a form as little like matter as the emanations of scent are like the scent itself. Equally, the force-and-intelligence-producing capacity of the Outer Circle no more approximates to the life-and-intelligence-producing capacity of the earth and air than the results of the Outer Circle constituents resemble the results of earth and air. I wonder whether I make it clear.

"And so it seems to me we have the conception of a huge psychic world, bred out of the physical, lying far outside of this world and completely encompassing it, except for the doorways about which I hope to tell you some other evening. This enormous psychic world of the Outer Circle 'breeds'—if I may use the term, its own psychic forces and intelligences, monstrous and otherwise, just as this world produces its own physical forces and intelligences—beings, animals, insects, etc., monstrous and otherwise.

"The monstrosities of the Outer Circle are malignant towards all that we consider most desirable, just in the same way a shark or a tiger may be considered malignant, in a physical way, to all that we consider desirable. They are predatory—as all positive force is predatory. They have desires regarding us which are incredibly more dreadful to our minds when comprehended than an intelligent sheep would consider our desires towards its own carcass. They plunder and destroy to satisfy lusts and hungers exactly as other forms of existence plunder and destroy to satisfy their lusts and hungers. And the desire of these monsters is chiefly, if not always, for the psychic entity of the human.

"But that's as much as I can tell you tonight. Some evening I want to tell you about the tremendous mystery of the Psychic Doorways. In the meantime, have I made things a bit clearer to you, Dodgson?"

"Yes, and no," I answered. "You've been a brick to make the attempt, but there are still about ten thousand other things I want to know."

Carnacki stood up. "Out you go!" he said using the recognised formula in friendly fashion. "Out you go! I want a sleep."

And shaking him by the hand we strolled out on to the quiet Embankment.

THE FIND

In response to Carnacki's usual card of invitation to dinner I arrived in good time at Cheyne Walk to find Arkright, Taylor and Jessop already there, and a few minutes later we were seated round the dining table.

We dined well as usual, and as nearly always happened at these gatherings Carnacki talked on every subject under the sun but the one on which we had all expectations. It was not until we were all seated comfortably in our respective armchairs that he began.

"A very simple case," he told us, puffing at his pipe. "Quite a simple bit of mental analysis. I had been talking one day to Jones of Malbrey and Jones, the editors of the *Bibliophile and Book Table*, and he mentioned having come across a book called the *Dumpley's Acrostics*. Now the only known copy of this book is in the Caylen Museum. This second copy which had been picked up by a Mr. Ludwig appeared to be genuine. Both Malbrey and Jones pronounced it to be so, and that, to anyone knowing their reputation, would pretty well settle it.

"I heard all about the book from my old friend Van Dyll, the Dutchman who happened to be at the Club for lunch.

"'What do you know about a book called *Dumpley's Acrostics*?' I asked him.

"'You might as well ask me what I know of your city of London, my friend,' he replied. 'I know all there is to know which is very little. There was but one copy of that extraordinary book printed, and that copy is now in the Caylen Museum.'

"'Exactly what I had thought,' I told him.

"'The book was written by John Dumpley,' he continued, 'and presented to Queen Elizabeth on her fortieth birthday. She had a passion for word-play of that kind—which is merely literary gymnastics but was raised by Dumpley to an extraordinary height of involved and scandalous punning in which those unsavoury tales of those at Court are told with a wit and pretended innocence that is incredible in its malicious skill.

"'The type was distributed and the manuscript burnt immediately after printing that one copy which was for the Queen. The book was presented to her by Lord Welbeck who paid John Dumpley twenty English guineas and twelve sheep each year with twelve firkins of Miller Abbott's ale to hold his tongue. Lord Welbeck wished to be thought the author of the book, and undoubtedly he had supplied Dumpley with the very scandalous and intimate details of famous Court personages about whom the book is written.

"'He had his own name put in the place of Dumpley's; for though it was not a matter for much pride for a well born man to write well in those days, still a good wit such as the *Acrostics* was deemed to be was a thing for high praise at the Court.'

"'I'd no idea it was as famous as you say,' I told him.

"'It has a great fame among a few,' replied Van Dyll, 'because it is at the same time unique and of a value both historic and intrinsic. There are collectors today who would give their souls if a second copy might be discovered. But that's impossible.'

"'The impossible seems to have been achieved,' I said. 'A second copy is being offered for sale by a Mr. Ludwig. I have been asked to make a few investigations. Hence my inquiries.'

"Van Dyll almost exploded.

"'Impossible!' he roared. 'It's another fraud!'

"Then I fired my shell.

"'Messrs. Malbrey and Jones have pronounced it unmistakably genuine,' I said, 'and they are, as you know, above suspicion. Also Mr. Ludwig's account of how he bought the book at a "dump" sale in the Charing Cross Road seems quite straight and above-board.

He got it at Bentloes, and I've just been up there. Mr. Bentloes says it is quite possible though not probable. And anyway, he's mighty sick about it. I don't wonder, either!'

"Van Dyll got to his feet.

"'Come on round to Malbrey and Jones,' he said excitedly, and we went straight off to the offices of the bibliophile where Dyll is well-known.

"'What's all this about?' he called out almost before he got into the Editors' private room. 'What's all this about the *Dumpley's Acrostics*, eh? Show it to me. Where is it?'

"'It's that newly discovered copy of the *Acrostics* the Professor is asking for,' I explained to Mr. Malbrey who was at his desk. 'He's somewhat upset at the news I've just given him.'

"Probably to no other men in England, except its lawful owner, would Malbrey have handed the discovered volume on so brief a notice. But Van Dyll is among the great ones when it comes to bibliology, and Malbrey merely wheeled round in his office chair and opened a large safe. From this he took a volume wrapped about with tissue paper, and standing up he handed it ceremoniously to Professor Dyll.

"Van Dyll literally snatched it from him, tore off the paper and ran to the window to have a better light. There for nearly an hour, while we watched in silence, he examined the book, using a magnifying glass as he studied type, paper, and binding.

"At last he sat back and brushed his hand across his forehead.

"'Well?' we all asked.

"'It appears to be genuine,' he said. 'Before pronouncing finally upon it, however, I should like to have the opportunity of comparing it with the authentic copy in the Caylen Museum.'

"Mr. Malbrey rose from his seat and closed his desk.

"'I shall be delighted to come with you now, Professor,' he said. 'We shall be only too pleased to have your opinion in the next issue of the *Bibliophile* which we are making a special Dumpley number, for the interest aroused by this find will be enormous among collectors.'

"When we all arrived at the Museum, Van Dyll sent in his name to the chief librarian and we were all invited into his private room. Here the Professor stated the facts and showed him the book he had brought along with him.

"The librarian was tremendously interested, and after a brief examination of the copy expressed his opinion that it was apparently genuine, but he would like to compare it with the authentic copy.

"This he did and the three experts compared the book with the Museum copy for considerably over an hour, during which time I listened keenly and jotted down from time to time in my notebook my own conclusions.

"The verdict of all three was finally unanimous that the newly found copy of the *Acrostics* was undoubtedly genuine and printed at the same time and from the same type as the Museum copy.

"'Gentlemen,' I said, 'as I am working in the interests of Messrs. Malbrey and Jones, may I ask two questions? First, I should like to ask the librarian whether the Museum copy has ever been lent out of the Museum.'

"'Certainly not,' replied the librarian. 'Rare editions are never loaned, and are rarely even handled except in the presence of an attendant.'

"'Thanks,' I said. 'That ought to settle things pretty well. The other question I wish to ask is why were you all so convinced before that there was but one copy in existence?'

"'Because,' said the librarian, 'as both Mr. Malbrey and Professor Dyll could tell you, Lord Welbeck states in his private *Memoirs* that only one copy was printed. He appears to have been determined upon this, apparently to enhance the value of his gift to the Queen. He states clearly that he had the one copy printed, and that the printing was done entirely in his presence at the House of Pennywell, Printers of Lamprey Court. You can see the name at the beginning of the book. He also personally superintended the distribution of the type and burnt the manuscript and even the proof-pulls, as he says. Indeed, so precise and unmistakable are his statements on these points that I should always refuse to consider the authenticity of any "found" copy unless it could stand such a drastic test as this one has been put through. But here is the copy,' he went on, 'unmistakably genuine, and we have to take the evidence of our senses rather than the evidence of Lord Welbeck's statement. The finding of this book is a kind of literary thunderbolt. It will make some commotion in the collecting dovecotes if I'm not mistaken!'

"'What should you estimate its possible value at?' I asked him.

"He shrugged his shoulders.

"'Impossible to say,' he answered. 'If I were a rich man I would gladly give a thousand pounds to possess it. Professor Dyll there, being more fortunately endowed with worldly wealth, would probably outbid me unmercifully! I expect if Messrs. Malbrey and Jones do not buy it soon it will go across to America in the wake of half the treasures of the earth.'

"We separated then and went our various ways. I returned here, had a cup of tea and sat down for a good long think, for I wasn't at all satisfied in my mind that everything was as plain and aboveboard as it seemed.

"'Now,' I said to myself, 'let's have a little plain and unbiased reasoning applied, and see what comes of the test.'

"'First of all there is the apparently incontrovertible statement in Lord Welbeck's *Memoirs* that there was only one copy of the *Acrostics* printed. That titled gentleman evidently took extraordinary pains to see that no second copy of the book was printed, and the very proofs he burned. Also this copy is no conglomeration of collected printer's proofs, for the examination the three experts have given it quite preclude that idea. All this points then to what I might term "Certainty Number One," that only one copy was printed.

"'But now—come to the next step, a second copy has been proved today to exist. That is Certainty Number Two. And the two make that impossibility—a paradox. Therefore, though of the two certainties I may be bound in the end to accept the second, yet equally I cannot accept the complete smashing of the plain statement made in Lord Welbeck's private *Memoirs*. There seems to be more in this than meets the eye.'"

Carnacki puffed thoughtfully at his pipe for a few minutes before he resumed his story.

"In the next few days," he continued, "by simple methods of deduction and a matter-of-fact following of the dues that were thereby indicated, I had laid bare as cunningly planned a little drama of clever crime as I have ever met with.

"I got into communication with Scotland Yard, my clients Messrs. Malbrey and Jones, Ralph Ludwig the owner of the find, and Mr. Notts the librarian. I arranged for a detective from the Yard to meet us all at the offices of the *Bibliophile and Book Table*, and I managed to persuade Notts to bring along with him the Museum copy of the *Acrostics*.

"In this way I had my stage set, with all the characters involved, in that little bookish office of the hundred-year-old *Collectors' Weekly*.

"The meeting was for three in the afternoon, and when they had all arrived I asked them to listen to me for a few minutes.

"'Gentlemen,' I said, 'I should like you to follow me a little in a line of reasoning which I wish to indicate to you. Two days ago Mr. Ludwig brought to this office a copy of a book of which only one copy was supposed to be extant. An examination of his find by three experts, perhaps the three greatest experts in England, proved it to be undoubtedly genuine. That is fact number one. Fact number two is that there were the very best reasons for supposing there could *not* be two original copies of this particular book in existence.

"'Now we were forced, by the experts' opinion, into accepting the first fact as indubitable. But there still remained to explain away the second fact, that is, the good reason for supposing that only one copy of this book was originally printed.

"'I found that although I was forced to accept the fact of the finding of the second copy, yet I could not see how to explain away the good reason I have mentioned. Therefore, not feeling that my reason was satisfied I followed the line of investigation which un-satisfied reason indicated. I went to the Caylen Museum and asked questions.

"'I had already learned from Mr. Notts that rare editions were never loaned. And an examination of the registers showed that the *Acrostics* had been referred to only three times by three different people in the last two years, and then, as I knew, always in the presence of an attendant. This seemed proof enough that I was hunting a mare's nest; but reason still asserted that there were more things not explained. So I went home and thought it all out again.

"'One deduction remained from all my hours of thinking. That was that the three different men who had examined the book within the last two years could be the only line of explanation left to me. I had found out their names—Charles, Noble and Waterfield. My meditations suggested a handwriting expert, and the two of us vis-ited the Museum register with the result that I found my reason had not led me astray. The expert pronounced the handwriting of the three men to be the handwriting of one and the same person.

"'My next step was simple. I came here to the office with the expert and asked if I could be shown any handwriting of Mr. Ralph Ludwig. I could, and the expert assured me that Mr. Ludwig was the man who had written the three different signatures in the reg-ister of the Museum.

"'The next step is deduction on my part and is indicated by rea-soning as the only possible lines on which Mr. Ludwig could have worked. I can only suppose that he must have come across a dummy copy of the *Acrostics* in some way or other, possibly in the bundle of books he says he picked up at Bentloes' sale. This blank-paper dummy of the book would be made up by the printers and book-binders so as to enable Lord Welbeck to see how the *Acrostics* would bind up and bulk. The method is common in the publishing trade, as you know. The binding may be exactly a duplicate of what the finished article will be, but the inside is nothing but blank pa-per of the same thickness and quality as that on which the book will be printed. In this way a publisher can see beforehand just how the book will look.

"'I am quite convinced that I have described the first step in Mr. Ludwig's ingenious little plot. He made only three visits to the Museum and as you will see in a minute, if he had not been provided with a facsimile in binding of the *Acrostics* on his first visit, he could not have carried out his plot under four. Moreover, unless I am mistaken in my psychology of the incident it was through becoming possessed of this particular dummy copy that he thought out this scheme. Is that not so, Mr. Ludwig?' I asked him. But he refused to reply to my question, and sat there looking very crestfallen.

"'Well, gentlemen,' I went on, 'the rest is plain sailing. He went the first time to the Museum to study their copy, after which he deftly replaced it with the dummy one he had brought in with him. The attendant took the copy—which was externally identical with the original and replaced it in its case. This was, of course, the one big risk in Mr. Ludwig's little adventure. A smaller risk was that someone should call and ask for the *Acrostics* before he could replace it with the original, for this was what he meant to do, and which he did after he had photographed each page. Isn't that so, Mr. Ludwig?' I asked him; but he still refused to open his mouth.

"'This,' I resumed, 'accounts for his second visit when he returned the original and started to print on a handpress the photographic blocks which he had prepared. Once the pages were bound up in the dummy he went back to the Museum and exchanged the copies, this time taking away for keeps the Museum copy and leaving the very excellently printed dummy in its place. Each time, as you know, he used a new name and a new handwriting, and probably disguises of some kind; for he had no wish to be connected with the Museum copy. That is all I have to tell you; but I hardly think Mr. Ludwig will care to deny my story, eh, Mr. Ludwig?'"

Carnacki knocked out the ashes of his, pipe as he finished.

"I can't imagine what he stole it for," said Arkright. "He could surely never have hoped to sell it."

"No, that's true," Carnacki replied. "Certainly not in the open market. He would have to sell it to some unscrupulous collector who would, of course, knowing it was stolen, give him next to nothing for it, and might in the end hand him over to the police. But don't you see if he could so arrange that the Museum still had its copy he might sell his own without fear in the open market to the highest bidder, as an authentic second copy which had come to light. He had sense to know that *his* copy would be mercilessly challenged and examined, and that is why he made his third exchange, and finally left his dummy, printed as exactly like the original as was possible, and took away with him the authentic copy."

"But the two books were bound to be compared," I argued.

"Quite true, but the copy at the Museum would not be so suspiciously examined. Everyone considered that book beyond suspicion. If the three experts had given the same attention to the false copy in the Museum which they thought all the time was the original, I don't suppose for a moment this little story would have been told. It's a very good example of the way people take things for granted. Out you go!" he said, genially, which was his usual method of dismissing us. And a few minutes later we were out on the Embankment.

JOHN BELL:
GHOST EXPOSER

INTRODUCTION

It so happened that the circumstances of fate allowed me to follow my own bent in the choice of a profession. From my earliest youth the weird, the mysterious had an irresistible fascination for me. Having private means, I resolved to follow my unique inclinations, and I am now well known to all my friends as a professional exposer of ghosts, and one who can clear away the mysteries of most haunted houses. Up to the present I have never had cause to regret my choice, but at the same time I cannot too strongly advise any one who thinks of following my example to hesitate before engaging himself in tasks that entail time, expense, thankless labour, often ridicule, and not seldom great personal danger. To explain, by the application of science, phenomena attributed to spiritual agencies has been the work of my life. I have, naturally, gone through strange difficulties in accomplishing my mission. I propose in these pages to relate the histories of certain queer events, enveloped at first in mystery, and apparently dark with portent, but, nevertheless, when grappled with in the true spirit of science, capable of explanation.

THE MYSTERY OF THE CIRCULAR CHAMBER

One day in late September I received the following letter from my lawyer:—

"My Dear Bell,—

"I shall esteem it a favour if you can make it convenient to call upon me at ten o'clock to-morrow morning on a matter of extreme privacy."

At the appointed hour I was shown into Mr. Edgcombe's private room. I had known him for years—we were, in fact, old friends—and I was startled now by the look of worry, not to say anxiety, on his usually serene features.

"You are the very man I want, Bell," he cried. "Sit down; I have a great deal to say to you. There is a mystery of a very grave nature which I hope you may solve for me. It is in connection with a house said to be haunted."

He fixed his bright eyes on my face as he spoke. I sat perfectly silent, waiting for him to continue.

"In the first place," he resumed, "I must ask you to regard the matter as confidential."

"Certainly," I answered.

"You know," he went on, "that I have often laughed at your special hobby, but it occurred to me yesterday that the experiences you have lived through may enable you to give me valuable assistance in this difficulty."

"I will do my best for you, Edgcombe," I replied.

He lay back in his chair, folding his hands.

"The case is briefly as follows," he began. "It is connected with the family of the Wentworths. The only son, Archibald, the artist, has just died under most extraordinary circumstances. He was, as you probably know, one of the most promising water-colour painters of the younger school, and his pictures in this year's Academy met with universal praise. He was the heir to the Wentworth estates, and his death has caused a complication of claims from a member of a collateral branch of the family, who, when the present squire dies, is entitled to the money. This man has spent the greater part of his life in Australia, is badly off, and evidently belongs to a rowdy set. He has been to see me two or three times, and I must say frankly that I am not taken with his appearance."

"Had he anything to do with the death?" I interrupted.

"Nothing whatever, as you will quickly perceive. Wentworth has been accustomed from time to time to go alone on sketching tours to different parts of the country. He has tramped about on foot, and visited odd, out-of-the-way nooks searching for subjects. He never took much money with him, and always travelled as an apparently poor man. A month ago he started off alone on one of these tours. He had a handsome commission from Barlow & Co., picture-dealers in the Strand. He was to paint certain parts of the river Merran; and although he certainly did not need money, he seemed glad of an object for a good ramble. He parted with his family in the best of health and spirits, and wrote to them from time to time; but a week ago they heard the news that he had died suddenly at an inn on the Merran. There was, of course, an inquest and an autopsy. Dr. Miles Gordon, the Wentworths' consulting physician, was telegraphed for, and was present at the post-mortem examination. He is absolutely puzzled to account for the death. The medical examination showed Wentworth to be in apparently perfect health at the time. There was no lesion to be discovered upon which to base a different opinion, all the organs being healthy. Neither was there any trace of poison, nor marks of violence. The coroner's verdict was that Wentworth died of syncope, which, as you know perhaps, is a synonym for an unknown cause. The inn where he died is a very lonely one, and has the reputation of being haunted. The landlord seems to bear a bad character, although nothing has ever been proved against him. But a young girl who lives at the inn gave evidence which at first startled every one. She said at the inquest that she had earnestly warned Wentworth not to sleep in the haunted room. She had scarcely told the coroner so before she fell to the floor in an epileptic fit. When she came to herself she was sullen and silent, and nothing more could be extracted from her. The old man, the innkeeper, explained that the girl was half-witted, but he did not attempt to deny that the house had the reputation of being haunted, and said that he had himself begged Wentworth not to put up there. Well, that is about the whole of the story. The coroner's inquest seems to deny the evidence of foul play, but I have my very strong suspicions. What I want you to do is to ascertain if they are correct. Will you undertake the case?"

"I will certainly do so," I replied. "Please let me have any further particulars, and a written document to show, in case of need, that I am acting under your directions."

Edgcombe agreed to this, and I soon afterwards took my leave. The case had the features of an interesting problem, and I hoped that I should prove successful in solving it.

That evening I made my plans carefully. I would go into —shire early on the following morning, assuming for my purpose the character of an amateur photographer. Having got all necessary particulars from Edgcombe, I made a careful mental map of my operations. First of all I would visit a little village of the name of Harkhurst, and put up at the inn, the Crown and Thistle. Here Wentworth had spent a fortnight when he first started on his commission to make drawings of the river Merran. I thought it likely that I should obtain some information there. Circumstances must guide me as to my further steps, but my intention was to proceed from Harkhurst to the Castle Inn, which was situated about six miles further up the river. This was the inn where the tragedy had occurred.

Towards evening on the following day I arrived at Harkhurst. When my carriage drew up at the Crown and Thistle, the landlady was standing in the doorway. She was a buxom-looking dame, with a kindly face. I asked for a bed.

"Certainly, sir," she answered. She turned with me into the little inn, and taking me upstairs, showed me a small room, quite clean and comfortable, looking out on the yard. I said it would do capitally, and she hurried downstairs to prepare my supper. After this meal, which proved to be excellent, I determined to visit the landlord in the bar. I found him chatty and communicative.

"This is a lonely place," he said; "we don't often have a soul staying with us for a month at a time." As he spoke he walked to the door, and I followed him. The shades of night were beginning to fall, but the picturesqueness of the little hamlet could not but commend itself to me.

"And yet it is a lovely spot," I said. "I should have thought tourists would have thronged to it. It is at least an ideal place for photographers."

"You are right there, sir," replied the man; "and although we don't often have company to stay in the inn, now and then we have a stray artist. It's not three weeks back," he continued, "that we had a gentleman like you, sir, only a bit younger, to stay with us for a week or two. He was an artist, and drew from morning till night—ah, poor fellow!"

"Why do you say that?" I asked.

"I have good cause, sir. Here, wife," continued the landlord, looking over his shoulder at Mrs. Johnson, the landlady, who now appeared on the scene, "this gentleman has been asking me questions about our visitor, Mr. Wentworth, but perhaps we ought not to inflict such a dismal story upon him to-night."

"Pray do," I said; "what you have already hinted at arouses my curiosity. Why should you pity Mr. Wentworth?"

"He is dead, sir," said the landlady, in a solemn voice. I gave a pretended start, and she continued,—

"And it was all his own fault. Ah, dear! it makes me almost cry to think of it. He was as nice a gentleman as I ever set eyes on, and so strong, hearty, and pleasant. Well, sir, everything went well until one day he said to me, 'I am about to leave you, Mrs. Johnson. I am going to a little place called the Castle Inn, further up the Merran.'

"'The Castle Inn!' I cried. 'No, Mr. Wentworth, that you won't, not if you value your life.'

"'And why not?' he said, looking at me with as merry blue eyes as you ever saw in anybody's head. 'Why should I not visit the Castle Inn? I have a commission to make some drawings of that special bend of the river.'

"'Well, then, sir,' I answered, 'if that is the case, you'll just have a horse and trap from here and drive over as often as you want to. For the Castle Inn ain't a fit place for a Christian to put up at.'

"'What do you mean?' he asked of me.

"'It is said to be haunted, sir, and what does happen in that house the Lord only knows, but there's not been a visitor at the inn for some years, not since Bailiff Holt came by his death.'

"'Came by his death?' he asked. 'And how was that?'

"'God knows, but I don't,' I answered. 'At the coroner's inquest it was said that he died from syncope, whatever that means, but the folks round here said it was fright.' Mr. Wentworth just laughed at me. He didn't mind a word I said, and the next day, sir, he was off, carrying his belongings with him."

"Well, and what happened?" I asked, seeing that she paused.

"What happened, sir? Just what I expected. Two days afterwards came the news of his death. Poor young gentleman! He died in the very room where Holt had breathed his last; and, oh, if there wasn't a fuss and to-do, for it turned out that, although he seemed quite poor to us, with little or no money, he was no end of a swell, and had rich relations, and big estates coming to him; and, of course, there was a coroner's inquest and all the rest, and great doctors came down from London, and our Dr. Stanmore, who lives down the street, was sent for, and though they did all they could, and examined him, as it were, with a microscope, they could find no cause for death, and so they give it out that it was syncope, just as they did in the case of poor Holt. But, sir, it wasn't; it was fright, sheer fright. The place is haunted. It's a mysterious, dreadful house, and I only hope you won't have nothing to do with it."

She added a few more words and presently left us.

"That's a strange story," I said, turning to Johnson; "your wife has excited my curiosity. I should much like to get further particulars."

"There don't seem to be anything more to tell, sir," replied Johnson. "It's true what the wife says, that the Castle Inn has a bad name. It's not the first, no, nor the second, death that has occurred there."

"You mentioned your village doctor; do you think he could enlighten me on the subject?"

"I am sure he would do his best, sir. He lives only six doors away, in a red house. Maybe you wouldn't mind stepping down the street and speaking to him?"

"You are sure he would not think it a liberty?"

"Not he, sir; he'll be only too pleased to exchange a word with some one outside this sleepy little place."

"Then I'll call on him," I answered, and taking up my hat I strolled down the street. I was lucky in finding Dr. Stanmore at home, and the moment I saw his face I determined to take him into my confidence.

"The fact is this," I said, when he had shaken hands with me, "I should not dream of taking this liberty did I not feel certain that you could help me."

"And in what way?" he asked, not stiffly, but with a keen, inquiring, interested glance.

"I have been sent down from London to inquire into the Wentworth mystery," I said.

"Is that so?" he said, with a start. Then he continued gravely: "I fear you have come on a wild-goose chase. There was nothing discovered at the autopsy to account for the death. There were no marks on the body, and all the organs were healthy. I met Wentworth often while he was staying here, and he was as hearty and strong-looking a young man as I have ever come across."

"But the Castle Inn has a bad reputation," I said.

"That is true; the people here are afraid of it. It is said to be haunted. But really, sir, you and I need not trouble ourselves about stupid reports of that sort. Old Bindloss, the landlord, has lived there for years, and there has never been anything proved against him."

"Is he alone?"

"No; his wife and a grandchild live there also."

"A grandchild?" I said. "Did not this girl give some startling evidence at the inquest?"

"Nothing of any consequence," replied Dr. Stanmore; "she only repeated what Bindloss had already said himself—that the house was haunted, and that she had asked Wentworth not to sleep in the room."

"Has anything ever been done to explain the reason why this room is said to be haunted?" I continued.

"Not that I know of. Rats are probably at the bottom of it."

"But have not there been other deaths in the house?"

"That is true."

"How many?"

"Well, I have myself attended no less than three similar inquests."

"And what was the verdict of the jury?"

"In each case the verdict was death from syncope."

"Which means, cause unknown," I said, jumping impatiently to my feet. "I wonder, Dr. Stanmore, that you are satisfied to leave the matter in such a state."

"And, pray, what can I do?" he inquired. "I am asked to examine a body. I find all the organs in perfect health; I cannot trace the least appearance of violence, nor can I detect poison. What other evidence can I honestly give?"

"I can only say that I should not be satisfied," I replied. "I now wish to add that I have come down from London determined to solve this mystery. I shall myself put up at the Castle Inn."

"Well?" said Dr. Stanmore.

"And sleep in the haunted room."

"Of course you don't believe in the ghost."

"No; but I believe in foul play. Now, Dr. Stanmore, will you help me?"

"Most certainly, if I can. What do you wish me to do?"

"This—I shall go to the Castle Inn to-morrow. If at the end of three days I do not return here, will you go in search of me, and at the same time post this letter to Mr. Edgcombe, my London lawyer?"

"If you do not appear in three days I'll kick up no end of a row," said Dr. Stanmore, "and, of course, post your letter."

Soon afterwards I shook hands with the doctor and left him.

After an early dinner on the following day, I parted with my good-natured landlord and his wife, and with my knapsack and kodak strapped over my shoulders, started on my way. I took care to tell no one that I was going to the Castle Inn, and for this purpose doubled back through a wood, and so found the right road. The sun was nearly setting when at last I approached a broken-down signpost, on which, in half-obliterated characters, I could read the words, "To the Castle Inn." I found myself now at the entrance of a small lane, which was evidently little frequented, as it was considerably grass-grown. From where I stood I could catch no sight of any habitation, but just at that moment a low, somewhat inconsequent laugh fell upon my ears. I turned quickly and saw a pretty girl, with bright eyes and a childish face, gazing at me with interest. I had little doubt that she was old Bindloss's granddaughter.

"Will you kindly tell me," I asked, "if this is the way to the Castle Inn?"

My remark evidently startled her. She made a bound forward, seized me by my hand, and tried to push me away from the entrance to the lane into the high road.

"Go away!" she cried; "we have no beds fit for gentlemen at the Castle Inn. Go! go!" she continued, and she pointed up the winding road. Her eyes were now blazing in her head, but I noticed that her lips trembled, and that very little would cause her to burst into tears.

"But I am tired and footsore," I answered. "I should like to put up at the inn for the night."

"Don't!" she repeated; "they'll put you into a room with a ghost. Don't go; 'tain't a place for gentlemen." Here she burst not into tears, but into a fit of high, shrill, almost idiotic laughter. She suddenly clapped one of her hands to her forehead, and, turning, flew almost as fast as the wind down the narrow lane and out of sight.

I followed her quickly. I did not believe that the girl was quite as mad as she seemed, but I had little doubt that she had something extraordinary weighing on her mind.

At the next turn I came in view of the inn. It was a queer-looking old place, and I stopped for a moment to look at it.

The house was entirely built of stone. There were two storeys to the centre part, which was square, and at the four corners stood four round towers. The house was built right on the river, just below a large mill-pond. I walked up to the door and pounded on it with my stick. It was shut, and looked as inhospitable as the rest of the place. After a moment's delay it was opened two or three inches, and the surly face of an old woman peeped out.

"And what may you be wanting?" she asked.

"A bed for the night," I replied; "can you accommodate me?"

She glanced suspiciously first at me and then at my camera.

"You are an artist, I make no doubt," she said, "and we don't want no more of them here."

She was about to slam the door in my face, but I pushed my foot between it and the lintel.

"I am easily pleased," I said; "can you not give me some sort of bed for the night?"

"You had best have nothing to do with us," she answered. "You go off to Harkhurst; they can put you up at the Crown and Thistle."

"I have just come from there," I answered. "As a matter of fact, I could not walk another mile."

"We don't want visitors at the Castle Inn," she continued. Here she peered forward and looked into my face. "You had best be off," she repeated; "they say the place is haunted."

I uttered a laugh.

"You don't expect me to believe that?" I said. She glanced at me from head to foot. Her face was ominously grave.

"You had best know all, sir," she said, after a pause. "Something happens in this house, and no living soul knows what it is, for they who have seen it have never yet survived to tell the tale. It's not more than a week back that a young gentleman came here. He was like you, bold as brass, and he too wanted a bed, and would take no denial. I told him plain, and so did my man, that the place was haunted. He didn't mind no more than you mind. Well, he slept in the only room we have got for guests, and he—he died there."

"What did he die of?" I asked.

"Fright," was the answer, brief and laconic. "Now do you want to come or not?"

"Yes; I don't believe in ghosts. I want the bed, and I am determined to have it."

The woman flung the door wide open.

"Don't say as I ain't warned you," she cried. "Come in, if you must." She led me into the kitchen, where a fire burned sullenly on the hearth.

"Sit you down, and I'll send for Bindloss," she said. "I can only promise to give you a bed if Bindloss agrees. Liz, come along here this minute."

A quick young step was heard in the passage, and the pretty girl whom I had seen at the top of the lane entered. Her eyes sought my face, her lips moved as if to say something, but no sound issued from them.

"Go and find your grandad," said the old woman. "Tell him there is a gentleman here that wants a bed. Ask him what's to be done."

The girl favoured me with a long and peculiar glance, then turning on her heel she left the room. As soon as she did so the old woman peered forward and looked curiously at me.

"I'm sorry you are staying," she said; "don't forget as I warned you. Remember, this ain't a proper inn at all. Once it was a mill, but that was afore Bindloss's day and mine. Gents would come in the summer and put up for the fishing, but then the story of the ghost got abroad, and lately we have no visitors to speak of, only an odd one now and then who ain't wanted—no, he ain't wanted. You see, there was three deaths here. Yes"—she held up one of her skinny hands and began to count on her fingers— "yes, three up to the present; three, that's it. Ah, here comes Bindloss."

A shuffling step was heard in the passage, and an old man, bent with age, and wearing a long white beard, entered the room.

"We has no beds for strangers," he said, speaking in an aggressive and loud tone. "Hasn't the wife said so? We don't let out beds here."

"As that is the case, you have no right to have that signpost at the end of the lane," I retorted. "I am not in a mood to walk eight miles for a shelter in a country I know nothing about. Cannot you put me up somehow?"

"I have told the gentleman everything, Sam," said the wife. "He is just for all the world like young Mr. Wentworth, and not a bit frightened."

The old landlord came up and faced me.

"Look you here," he said, "you stay on at your peril. I don't want you, nor do the wife. Now is it 'yes' or 'no'?"

"It is 'yes,'" I said.

"There's only one room you can sleep in."

"One room is sufficient."

"It's the one Mr. Wentworth died in. Hadn't you best take up your traps and be off?"

"No, I shall stay."

"Then there's no more to be said."

"Run, Liz," said the woman, "and light the fire in the parlour."

The girl left the room, and the woman, taking up a candle, said she would take me to the chamber where I was to sleep. She led me down a long and narrow passage, and then, opening a door, down two steps into the most extraordinary-looking room I had ever seen. The walls were completely circular, covered with a paper of a staring grotesque pattern. A small iron bedstead projected into the middle of the floor, which was uncarpeted except for a slip of matting beside it. A cheap deal wash-hand-stand, a couple of chairs, and a small table with a blurred looking-glass stood against the wall beneath a deep embrasure, in which there was a window. This was evidently a room in one of the circular towers. I had never seen less inviting quarters.

"Your supper will be ready directly, sir," said the woman, and placing the candle on the little table, she left me.

The place felt damp and draughty, and the flame of the candle flickered about, causing the tallow to gutter to one side. There was no fireplace in the room, and above, the walls converged to a point, giving the whole place the appearance of an enormous extinguisher. I made a hurried and necessarily limited toilet, and went into the parlour. I was standing by the fire, which was burning badly, when the door opened, and the girl Liz came in, bearing a tray in her hand. She laid the tray on the table and came up softly to me.

"Fools come to this house," she said, "and you are one."

"Pray let me have my supper, and don't talk," I replied. "I am tired and hungry, and want to go to bed."

Liz stood perfectly still for a moment.

"'Tain't worth it," she said; then, in a meditative voice, "no, 'tain't worth it. But I'll say no more. Folks will never be warned!"

Her grandmother's voice calling her caused her to bound from the room.

My supper proved better than I had expected, and, having finished it, I strolled into the kitchen, anxious to have a further talk with the old man. He was seated alone by the fire, a great mastiff lying at his feet.

"Can you tell me why the house is supposed to be haunted?" I asked suddenly, stooping down to speak to him.

"How should I know?" he cried hoarsely. "The wife and me have been here twenty years, and never seen nor heard anything, but for certain folks do die in the house. It's mortal unpleasant for me, for the doctors come along, and the coroner, and there's an inquest and no end of fuss. The folks die, although no one has ever laid a finger on 'em; the doctors can't prove why they are dead, but dead they be. Well, there ain't no use saying more. You are here, and maybe you'll pass the one night all right."

"I shall go to bed at once," I said, "but I should like some candles. Can you supply me?"

The man turned and looked at his wife, who at that moment entered the kitchen. She went to the dresser, opened a wooden box, and taking out three or four tallow candles, put them into my hand.

I rose, simulating a yawn.

"Good-night, sir," said the old man; "good-night; I wish you well."

A moment later I had entered my bedroom, and having shut the door, proceeded to give it a careful examination. As far as I could make out, there was no entrance to the room except by the door, which was shaped to fit the circular walls. I noticed, however, that there was an unaccountable draught, and this I at last discovered came from below the oak wainscoting of the wall. I could not in any way account for the draught, but it existed to an unpleasant extent. The bed, I further saw, was somewhat peculiar; it had no castors on the four legs, which were let down about half an inch into sockets provided for them in the wooden floor. This discovery excited my suspicions still further. It was evident that the bed was intended to remain in a particular position. I saw that it directly faced the little window sunk deep into the thick wall, so that any one in bed would look directly at the window. I examined my watch, found that it was past eleven, and placing both the candles on a tiny table near the bed, I lay down without undressing. I was on the alert to catch the slightest noise, but the hours dragged on and nothing occurred. In the house all was silence, and outside the splashing and churning of the water falling over the wheel came distinctly to my ears.

I lay awake all night, but as morning dawned fell into an uneasy sleep. I awoke to see the broad daylight streaming in at the small window.

Making a hasty toilet, I went out for a walk, and presently came in to breakfast. It had been laid for me in the big kitchen, and the old man was seated by the hearth.

"Well," said the woman, "I hope you slept comfortable, sir."

I answered in the affirmative, and now perceived that old Bindloss and his wife were in the humour to be agreeable. They said that if I was satisfied with the room I might spend another night at the inn. I told them that I had a great many photographs to take, and would be much obliged for the permission. As I spoke I looked round for the girl, Liz. She was nowhere to be seen.

"Where is your grand-daughter?" I asked of the old woman.

"She has gone away for the day," was the reply. "It's too much for Liz to see strangers. She gets excited, and then the fits come on."

"What sort of fits?"

"I can't tell what they are called, but they're bad, and weaken her, poor thing! Liz ought never to be excited." Here Bindloss gave his wife a warning glance; she lowered her eyes, and going across to the range, began to stir the contents of something in a saucepan.

That afternoon I borrowed some lines from Bindloss, and, taking an old boat which was moored to the bank of the mill-pond, set off under the pretence of fishing for pike. The weather was perfect for the time of year.

Waiting my opportunity, I brought the boat up to land on the bank that dammed up the stream, and getting out walked along it in the direction of the mill-wheel, over which the water was now rushing.

As I observed it from this side of the bank, I saw that the tower in which my room was placed must at one time have been part of the mill itself, and I further noticed that the masonry was comparatively new, showing that alterations must have taken place when the house was abandoned as a mill and was turned into an inn. I clambered down the side of the wheel, holding on to the beams, which were green and slippery, and peered through the paddles.

As I was making my examination, a voice suddenly startled me.

"What are you doing down there?"

I looked up; old Bindloss was standing on the bank looking down at me. He was alone, and his face was contorted with a queer mixture of fear and passion. I hastily hoisted myself up, and stood beside him.

"What are you poking about down there for?" he said, pushing his ugly old face into mine as he spoke. "You fool! if you had fallen you would have been drowned. No one could swim a stroke in that mill-race. And then there would have been another death, and all the old fuss over again! Look here, sir, will you have the goodness to get out of the place? I don't want you here any more."

"I intend to leave to-morrow morning," I answered in a pacifying voice, "and I am really very much obliged to you for warning me about the mill."

"You had best not go near it again," he said in a menacing voice, and then he turned hastily away. I watched him as he climbed up a steep bank and disappeared from view. He was going in the opposite direction from the house. Seizing the opportunity of his absence, I once more approached the mill. Was it possible that Wentworth had been hurled into it? But had this been the case there would have been signs and marks on the body. Having reached the wheel, I clambered boldly down. It was now getting dusk, but I could see that a prolongation of the axle entered the wall of the tower. The fittings were also in wonderfully good order, and the bolt that held the great wheel only required to be drawn out to set it in motion.

That evening during supper I thought very hard. I perceived that Bindloss was angry, also that he was suspicious and alarmed. I saw plainly that the only way to really discover what had been done to Wentworth was to cause the old ruffian to try similar means to get rid of me. This was a dangerous expedient, but I felt desperate, and my curiosity as well as interest were keenly aroused. Having finished my supper, I went into the passage preparatory to going into the kitchen. I had on felt slippers, and my footfall made no noise. As I approached the door I heard Bindloss saying to his wife,—

"He's been poking about the mill-wheel; I wish he would make himself scarce."

"Oh, he can't find out anything," was the reply. "You keep quiet, Bindloss; he'll be off in the morning."

"That's as may be," was the answer, and then there came a harsh and very disagreeable laugh. I waited for a moment, and then entered the kitchen. Bindloss was alone now; he was bending over the fire, smoking.

"I shall leave early in the morning," I said, "so please have my bill ready for me." I then seated myself near him, drawing up my chair close to the blaze. He looked as if he resented this, but said nothing.

"I am very curious about the deaths which occur in this house," I said, after a pause. "How many did you say there were?"

"That is nothing to you," he answered. "We never wanted you here; you can go when you please."

"I shall go to-morrow morning, but I wish to say something now."

"And what may that be?"

"I don't believe in that story about the place being haunted."

"Oh, you don't, don't you?" He dropped his pipe, and his glittering eyes gazed at me with a mixture of anger and ill-concealed alarm.

"No," I paused, then I said slowly and emphatically, "I went back to the mill even after your warning, and—"

"What?" he cried, starting to his feet.

"Nothing," I answered; "only I don't believe in the ghost."

His face turned not only white but livid. I left him without another word. I saw that his suspicions had been much strengthened by my words. This I intended. To induce the ruffian to do his worst was the only way to wring his secret from him.

My hideous room looked exactly as it had done on the previous evening. The grotesque pattern on the walls seemed to start out in bold relief. Some of the ugly lines seemed at that moment, to my imagination, almost to take human shape, to convert themselves into ogre-like faces, and to grin at me. Was I too daring? Was it wrong of me to risk my life in this manner? I was terribly tired, and, curious as it may seem, my greatest fear at that crucial moment was the dread that I might fall asleep. I had spent two nights with scarcely any repose, and felt that at any moment, notwithstanding all my efforts, slumber might visit me. In order to give Bindloss full opportunity for carrying out his scheme, it was necessary for me to get into bed, and even to feign sleep. In my present exhausted condition the pretence of slumber would easily lapse into the reality. This risk, however, which really was a very grave one, must be run. Without undressing I got into bed, pulling the bed-clothes well over me. In my hand I held my revolver. I deliberately put out the candles, and then lay motionless, waiting for events. The house was quiet as the grave—there was not a stir, and gradually my nerves, excited as they were, began to calm down. As I had fully expected, overpowering sleepiness seized me, and, notwithstanding every effort, I found myself drifting away into the land of dreams. I began to wish that whatever apparition was to appear would do so at once and get it over. Gradually but surely I seemed to pass from all memory of my present world, and to live in a strange and terrible phantasmagoria. In that state I slept, in that state also I dreamt, and dreamt horribly.

I thought that I was dancing a waltz with an enormously tall woman. She towered above me, clasping me in her arms, and began to whirl me round and round at a giddy speed. I could hear the crashing music of a distant band. Faster and faster, round and round some great empty hall was I whirled. I knew that I was losing my senses, and screamed to her to stop and let me go. Suddenly there was a terrible crash close to me. Good God! I found myself awake, but—I was still moving. Where was I? Where was I going? I leapt up on the bed, only to reel and fall heavily backwards upon the floor. What was the matter? Why was I sliding, sliding? Had I suddenly gone mad, or was I still suffering from some hideous nightmare? I tried to move, to stagger to my feet. Then by slow degrees my senses began to return, and I knew where I was. I was in the circular room, the room where Wentworth had died; but what was happening to me I could not divine. I only knew that I was being whirled round and round at a velocity that was every moment increasing. By the moonlight that struggled in through the window I saw that the floor and the bed upon it was revolving, but the table was lying on its side, and its fall must have awakened me.

I could not see any other furniture in the room. By what mysterious manner had it been removed? Making a great effort, I crawled to the centre of this awful chamber, and, seizing the foot of the bed, struggled to my feet. Here I knew there would be less motion, and I could just manage to see the outline of the door. I had taken the precaution to slip the revolver into my pocket, and I still felt that if human agency appeared, I had a chance of selling my life dearly; but surely the horror I was passing through was invented by no living man! As the floor of the room revolved in the direction of the door I made a dash for it, but was carried swiftly past, and again fell heavily. When I came round again I made a frantic effort to cling to one of the steps, but in vain; the head of the bedstead caught me as it flew round, and tore my arms away. In another moment I believe I should have gone raving mad with terror. My head felt as if it would burst; I found it impossible to think consecutively. The only idea which really possessed me was a mad wish to escape from this hideous place. I struggled to the bedstead, and dragging the legs from their sockets, pulled it into the middle of the room away from the wall. With this out of the way, I managed at last to reach the door in safety.

The moment my hand grasped the handle I leapt upon the little step and tried to wrench the door open. It was locked, locked from without; it defied my every effort. I had only just standing room for my feet. Below me the floor of the room was still racing round with terrible speed. I dared scarcely look at it, for the giddiness in my head increased each moment. The next instant a soft footstep was distinctly audible, and I saw a gleam of light through a chink of the door. I heard a hand fumbling at the lock, the door was slowly opened outwards, and I saw the face of Bindloss.

For a moment he did not perceive me, for I was crouching down on the step, and the next instant with all my force I flung myself upon him. He uttered a yell of terror. The lantern he carried dropped and went out, but I had gripped him round the neck with my fingers, driving them deep down into his lean, sinewy throat. With frantic speed I pulled him along the passage up to a window, through which the moonlight was shining. Here I released my hold of his throat, but immediately covered him with my revolver.

"Down on your knees, or you are a dead man!" I cried. "Confess everything, or I shoot you through the heart."

His courage had evidently forsaken him; he began to whimper and cry bitterly.

"Spare my life," he screamed. "I will tell everything, only spare my life."

"Be quick about it," I said; "I am in no humour to be merciful. Out with the truth."

I was listening anxiously for the wife's step, but except for the low hum of machinery and the splashing of the water I heard nothing.

"Speak," I said, giving the old man a shake. His lips trembled, his words came out falteringly.

"It was Wentworth's doing," he panted.

"Wentworth? Not the murdered man?" I cried.

"No, no, his cousin. The ruffian who has been the curse of my life. Owing to that last death he inherits the property. He is the real owner of the mill, and he invented the revolving floor. There were deaths—oh yes, oh yes. It was so easy, and I wanted the money. The police never suspected, nor did the doctors. Wentworth was bitter hard on me, and I got into his power." Here he choked and sobbed. "I am a miserable old man, sir," he gasped.

"So you killed your victims for the sake of money?" I said, grasping him by the shoulder.

"Yes," he said, "yes. The bailiff had twenty pounds all in gold; no one ever knew. I took it and was able to satisfy Wentworth for a bit."

"And what about Archibald Wentworth?"

"That was his doing, and I was to be paid."

"And now finally you wanted to get rid of me?"

"Yes; for you suspected."

As I spoke I perceived by the ghastly light of the moon another door near. I opened it and saw that it was the entrance to a small dark lumber room. I pushed the old man in, turned the key in the lock, and ran downstairs. The wife was still unaccountably absent. I opened the front door, and trembling, exhausted, drenched in perspiration, found myself in the open air. Every nerve was shaken. At that terrible moment I was not in the least master of myself. My one desire was to fly from the hideous place. I had just reached the little gate when a hand, light as a feather, touched my arm. I looked up; the girl Liz stood before me.

"You are saved," she said; "thank God! I tried all I could to stop the wheel. See, I am drenched to the skin; I could not manage it. But at least I locked Grannie up. She's in the kitchen, sound asleep. She drank a lot of gin."

"Where were you all day yesterday?" I asked.

"Locked up in a room in the further tower, but I managed to squeeze through the window, although it half killed me. I knew if you stayed that they would try it on to-night. Thank God you are saved."

"Well, don't keep me now," I said; "I have been saved as by a miracle. You are a good girl; I am much obliged to you. You must tell me another time how you manage to live through all these horrors."

"Ain't I all but mad?" was her pathetic reply. "Oh, my God, what I suffer!" She pressed her hand to her face; the look in her eyes was terrible. But I could not wait now to talk to her further. I hastily left the place.

How I reached Harkhurst I can never tell, but early in the morning I found myself there. I went straight to Dr. Stanmore's house, and having got him up, I communicated my story. He and I together immediately visited the superintendent of police. Having told my exciting tale, we took a trap and all three returned to the Castle Inn. We were back there before eight o'clock on the following morning. But as the police officer expected, the place was empty. Bindloss had been rescued from the dark closet, and he and his wife and the girl Liz had all flown. The doctor, the police officer, and I, all went up to the circular room. We then descended to the basement, and after a careful examination we discovered a low door, through which we crept; we then found ourselves in a dark vault, which was full of machinery. By the light of a lantern we examined it. Here we saw an explanation of the whole trick. The shaft of the mill-wheel which was let through the wall of the tower was continuous as the axle of a vertical cogged wheel, and by a multiplication action turned a large horizontal wheel into which a vertical shaft descended. This shaft was let into the centre of four crossbeams, supporting the floor of the room in which I had slept. All round the circular edge of the floor was a steel rim which turned in a circular socket. It needed but a touch to set this hideous apparatus in motion.

The police immediately started in pursuit of Bindloss, and I returned to London. That evening Edgcombe and I visited Dr. Miles Gordon. Hard-headed old physician that he was, he was literally aghast when I told him my story. He explained to me that a man placed in the position in which I was when the floor began to move would by means of centrifugal force suffer from enormous congestion of the brain. In fact, the revolving floor would induce an artificial condition of apoplexy. If the victim were drugged or even only sleeping heavily, and the floor began to move slowly, insensibility would almost immediately be induced, which would soon pass into coma and death, and a post-mortem examination some hours afterwards would show no cause for death, as the brain would appear perfectly healthy, the blood having again left it.

From the presence of Dr. Miles Gordon, Edgcombe and I went to Scotland Yard, and the whole affair was put into the hands of the London detective force. With the clue which I had almost sacrificed my life to furnish, they quickly did the rest. Wentworth was arrested, and under pressure was induced to make a full confession, but old Bindloss had already told me the gist of the story. Wentworth's father had owned the mill, had got into trouble with the law, and changed his name. In fact, he had spent five years in penal servitude. He then went to Australia and made money. He died when his son was a young man. This youth inherited all the father's vices. He came home, visited the mill, and, being of a mechanical turn of mind, invented the revolving floor. He changed the mill into an inn, put Bindloss, one of his "pals," into possession with the full intention of murdering unwary travellers from time to time for their money.

The police, however, wanted him for a forged bill, and he thought it best to fly. Bindloss was left in full possession. Worried by Wentworth, who had him in his power for a grave crime committed years ago, he himself on two occasions murdered a victim in the circular room. Meanwhile several unexpected deaths had taken place in the older branch of the Wentworth family, and Archibald Wentworth alone stood between his cousin and the great estates. Wentworth came home, and with the aid of Bindloss got Archibald into his power. The young artist slept in the fatal room, and his death was the result. At this moment Wentworth and Bindloss are committed for trial at the Old Bailey, and there is no doubt what the result will be.

The ghost mystery in connection with the Castle Inn has, of course, been explained away for ever.

THE WARDER OF THE DOOR

"If you don't believe it, you can read it for yourself," said Allen Clinton, climbing up the steps and searching among the volumes on the top shelf.

I lay back in my chair. The beams from the sinking sun shone through the stained glass of the windows of the old library, and dyed the rows of black leather volumes with bands of red and yellow.

"Here, Bell!"

I took a musty volume from Allen Clinton, which he had unearthed from its resting-place.

"It is about the middle of the book," he continued eagerly. "You will see it in big, black, old English letters."

I turned over the pages containing the family tree and other archives of the Clintons till I came to the one I was seeking. It contained the curse which had rested on the family since 1400. Slowly and with difficulty I deciphered the words of this terrible denunciation.

"And in this cell its coffin lieth, the coffin which hath not human shape, for which reason no holy ground receiveth it. Here shall it rest to curse the family of ye Clyntons from generation to generation. And for this reason, as soon as the soul shall pass from the body of each first-born, which is the heir, it shall become the warder of the door by day and by night. Day and night shall his spirit stand by the door, to keep the door closed till the son shall release the spirit of the father from the watch and take his place, till his son in turn shall die. And whoso entereth into the cell shall be the prisoner of the soul that guardeth the door till it shall let him go."

"What a ghastly idea!" I said, glancing up at the young man who was watching me as I read. "But you say this cell has never been found. I should say its existence was a myth, and, of course, the curse on the soul of the first-born to keep the door shut as warder is absurd. Matter does not obey witchcraft."

"The odd part of it is," replied Allen, "that every other detail of the Abbey referred to in this record has been identified; but this cell with its horrible contents has never been found."

It certainly was a curious legend, and I allow it made some impression on me. I fancied, too, that somewhere I had heard something similar, but my memory failed to trace it.

I had come down to Clinton Abbey three days before for some pheasant shooting.

It was now Sunday afternoon. The family, with the exception of old Sir Henry, Allen, and myself, were at church. Sir Henry, now nearly eighty years of age and a chronic invalid, had retired to his room for his afternoon sleep. The younger Clinton and I had gone out for a stroll round the grounds, and since we returned our conversation had run upon the family history till it arrived at the legend of the family curse. Presently, the door of the library was slowly opened, and Sir Henry, in his black velvet coat, which formed such a striking contrast to his snowy white beard and hair, entered the room. I rose from my chair, and, giving him my arm, assisted him to his favourite couch. He sank down into its luxurious depths with a sigh, but as he did so his eyes caught the old volume which I had laid on the table beside it. He started forward, took the book in his hand, and looked across at his son.

"Did you take this book down?" he said sharply.

"Yes, father; I got it out to show it to Bell. He is interested in the history of the Abbey, and—"

"Then return it to its place at once," interrupted the old man, his black eyes blazing with sudden passion. "You know how I dislike having my books disarranged, and this one above all. Stay, give it to me."

He struggled up from the couch, and, taking the volume, locked it up in one of the drawers of his writing-table, and then sat back again on the sofa. His hands were trembling, as if some sudden fear had taken possession of him.

"Did you say that Phyllis Curzon is coming to-morrow?" asked the old man presently of his son in an irritable voice.

"Yes, father, of course; don't you remember? Mrs. Curzon and Phyllis are coming to stay for a fortnight; and, by the way," he added, starting to his feet as he spoke, "that reminds me I must go and tell Grace—"

The rest of the sentence was lost in the closing of the door. As soon as we were alone, Sir Henry looked across at me for a few moments without speaking. Then he said,—

"I am sorry I was so short just now. I am not myself. I do not know what is the matter with me. I feel all to pieces. I cannot sleep. I do not think my time is very long now, and I am worried about Allen. The fact is, I would give anything to stop this engagement. I wish he would not marry."

"I am sorry to hear you say that, sir," I answered. "I should have thought you would have been anxious to see your son happily married."

"Most men would," was the reply; "but I have my reasons for wishing things otherwise."

"What do you mean?" I could not help asking.

"I cannot explain myself; I wish I could. It would be best for Allen to let the old family die out. There, perhaps I am foolish about it, and of course I cannot really stop the marriage, but I am worried and troubled about many things."

"I wish I could help you, sir," I said impulsively. "If there is anything I can possibly do, you know you have only to ask me."

"Thank you, Bell, I know you would; but I cannot tell you. Some day I may. But there, I am afraid—horribly afraid."

The trembling again seized him, and he put his hands over his eyes as if to shut out some terrible sight.

"Don't repeat a word of what I have told you to Allen or any one else," he said suddenly. "It is possible that some day I may ask you to help me; and remember, Bell, I trust you."

He held out his hand, which I took. In another moment the butler entered with the lamps, and I took advantage of the interruption to make my way to the drawing-room.

The next day the Curzons arrived, and a hasty glance showed me that Phyllis was a charming girl. She was tall, slightly built, with a figure both upright and graceful, and a handsome, somewhat proud face. When in perfect repose her expression was somewhat haughty; but the moment she spoke her face became vivacious, kindly, charming to an extraordinary degree; she had a gay laugh, a sweet smile, a sympathetic manner. I was certain she had the kindest of hearts, and was sure that Allen had made an admirable choice.

A few days went by, and at last the evening before the day when I was to return to London arrived. Phyllis's mother had gone to bed a short time before, as she had complained of headache, and Allen suddenly proposed, as the night was a perfect one, that we should go out and enjoy a moonlight stroll.

Phyllis laughed with glee at the suggestion, and ran at once into the hall to take a wrap from one of the pegs.

"Allen," she said to her lover, who was following her, "you and I will go first."

"No, young lady, on this occasion you and I will have that privilege," said Sir Henry. He had also come into the hall, and, to our astonishment, announced his intention of accompanying us in our walk.

Phyllis bestowed upon him a startled glance, then she laid her hand lightly on his arm, nodded back at Allen with a smile, and walked on in front somewhat rapidly. Allen and I followed in the rear.

"Now, what does my father mean by this?" said Allen to me. "He never goes out at night; but he has not been well lately. I sometimes think he grows queerer every day."

"He is very far from well, I am certain," I answered.

We stayed out for about half an hour and returned home by a path which led into the house through a side entrance. Phyllis was waiting for us in the hall.

"Where is my father?" asked Allen, going up to her.

"He is tired and has gone to bed," she answered. "Good-night, Allen."

"Won't you come into the drawing-room?" he asked in some astonishment.

"No, I am tired."

She nodded to him without touching his hand; her eyes, I could not help noticing, had a queer expression. She ran upstairs.

I saw that Allen was startled by her manner; but as he did not say anything, neither did I.

The next day at breakfast I was told that the Curzons had already left the Abbey. Allen was full of astonishment and, I could see, a good deal annoyed. He and I breakfasted alone in the old library. His father was too ill to come downstairs.

An hour later I was on my way back to London. Many things there engaged my immediate attention, and Allen, his engagement, Sir Henry, and the old family curse, sank more or less into the background of my mind.

Three months afterwards, on the 7th of January, I saw to my sorrow in the *Times* the announcement of Sir Henry Clinton's death.

From time to time in the interim I had heard from the son, saying that his father was failing fast. He further mentioned that his own wedding was fixed for the twenty-first of the present month. Now, of course, it must be postponed. I felt truly sorry for Allen, and wrote immediately a long letter of condolence.

On the following day I received a wire from him, imploring me to go down to the Abbey as soon as possible, saying that he was in great difficulty.

I packed a few things hastily, and arrived at Clinton Abbey at six in the evening. The house was silent and subdued—the funeral was to take place the next day. Clinton came into the hall and gripped me warmly by the hand. I noticed at once how worn and worried he looked.

"This is good of you, Bell," he said. "I cannot tell you how grateful I am to you for coming. You are the one man who can help me, for I know you have had much experience in matters of this sort.

Come into the library and I will tell you everything. We shall dine alone this evening, as my mother and the girls are keeping to their own apartments for to-night."

As soon as we were seated, he plunged at once into his story.

"I must give you a sort of prelude to what has just occurred," he began. "You remember, when you were last here, how abruptly Phyllis and her mother left the Abbey?"

I nodded. I remembered well.

"On the morning after you had left us I had a long letter from Phyllis," continued Allen. "In it she told me of an extraordinary request my father had made to her during that moonlight walk—nothing more nor less than an earnest wish that she would herself terminate our engagement. She spoke quite frankly, as she always does, assuring me of her unalterable love and devotion, but saying that under the circumstances it was absolutely necessary to have an explanation. Frantic with almost ungovernable rage, I sought my father in his study. I laid Phyllis's letter before him and asked him what it meant. He looked at me with the most unutterable expression of weariness and pathos.

"'Yes, my boy, I did it,' he said. 'Phyllis is quite right. I did ask of her, as earnestly as a very old man could plead, that she would bring the engagement to an end.'

"'But why?' I asked. 'Why?'

"'That I am unable to tell you,' he replied.

"I lost my temper and said some words to him which I now regret. He made no sort of reply. When I had done speaking he said slowly,—

"'I make all allowance for your emotion, Allen; your feelings are no more than natural.'

"'You have done me a very sore injury,' I retorted. 'What can Phyllis think of this? She will never be the same again. I am going to see her to-day.'

"He did not utter another word, and I left him. I was absent from home for about a week. It took me nearly that time to induce Phyllis to overlook my father's extraordinary request, and to let matters go on exactly as they had done before.

"After fixing our engagement, if possible, more firmly than ever, and also arranging the date of our wedding, I returned home. When I did so I told my father what I had done.

"'As you will,' he replied, and then he sank into great gloom. From that moment, although I watched him day and night, and did everything that love and tenderness could suggest, he never seemed to rally. He scarcely spoke, and remained, whenever we were together, bowed in deep and painful reverie. A week ago he took to his bed."

Here Allen paused.

"I now come to events up to date," he said. "Of course, as you may suppose, I was with my father to the last. A few hours before he passed away he called me to his bedside, and to my astonishment began once more talking about my engagement. He implored me with the utmost earnestness even now at the eleventh hour to break it off. It was not too late, he said, and added further that nothing would give him ease in dying but the knowledge that I would promise him to remain single. Of course I tried to humour him. He took my hand, looked me in the eyes with an expression which I shall never forget, and said,—

"'Allen, make me a solemn promise that you will never marry.'

"This I naturally had to refuse, and then he told me that, expecting my obstinacy, he had written me a letter which I should find in his safe, but I was not to open it till after his death. I found it this morning. Bell, it is the most extraordinary communication, and either it is entirely a figment of his imagination, for his brain powers were failing very much at the last, or else it is the most awful thing I ever heard of. Here is the letter; read it for yourself."

I took the paper from his hand and read the following matter in shaky, almost illegible writing:—

"My dear Boy,—When you read this I shall have passed away. For the last six months my life has been a living death. The horror began in the following way. You know what a deep interest I have always taken in the family history of our house. I have spent the latter years of my life in verifying each detail, and my intention was, had health been given me, to publish a great deal of it in a suitable volume.

"On the special night to which I am about to allude, I sat up late in my study reading the book which I saw you show to Bell a short time ago. In particular, I was much attracted by the terrible curse which the old abbot in the fourteenth century had bestowed upon the family. I read the awful words again and again. I knew that all the other details in the volume had been verified, but that the vault with the coffin had never yet been found. Presently I grew drowsy, and I suppose I must have fallen asleep. In my sleep I had a dream; I thought that some one came into the room, touched me on the shoulder, and said 'Come.' I looked up; a tall figure beckoned to me. The voice and the figure belonged to my late father. In my dream I rose immediately, although I did not know why I went nor where I was going. The figure went on in front, it entered the hall. I took one of the candles from the table and the key of the chapel, unbolted the door and went out. Still the voice kept saying 'Come, come,' and the figure of my father walked in front of me. I went across the quadrangle, unlocked the chapel door, and entered.

"A death-like silence was around me. I crossed the nave to the north aisle; the figure still went in front of me; it entered the great pew which is said to be haunted, and walked straight up to the effigy of the old abbot who had pronounced the curse. This, as you know, is built into the opposite wall. Bending forward, the figure pressed the eyes of the old monk, and immediately a stone started out of its place, revealing a staircase behind. I was about to hurry forward, when I must have knocked against something. I felt a sensation of pain, and suddenly awoke. What was my amazement to find that I had acted on my dream, had crossed the quadrangle, and was in the chapel; in fact, was standing in the old pew! Of course there was no figure of any sort visible, but the moonlight shed a cold radiance over all the place. I felt very much startled and impressed, but was just about to return to the house in some wonder at the curious vision which I had experienced, when, raising my startled eyes, I saw that part of it at least was real. The old monk seemed to grin at me from his marble effigy, and beside him was a blank open space. I hurried to it and saw a narrow flight of stairs. I cannot explain what my emotions were, but my keenest feeling at that moment was a strong and horrible curiosity. Holding the candle in my hand, I went down the steps. They terminated at the beginning of a long passage. This I quickly traversed, and at last found myself beside an iron door. It was not locked, but hasped, and was very hard to open; in fact, it required nearly all my strength; at last I pulled it open towards me, and there in a small cell lay the coffin, as the words of the curse said. I gazed at it in horror. I did not dare to enter. It was a wedged-shaped coffin studded with great nails. But as I looked my blood froze within me, for slowly, very slowly, as if pushed by some unseen hand, the great heavy door began to close, quicker and quicker, until with a crash that echoed and re-echoed through the empty vault, it shut.

"Terror-stricken, I rushed from the vault and reached my room once more.

"Now I know that this great curse is true; that my father's spirit is there to guard the door and close it, for I saw it with my own eyes, and while you read this know that I am there. I charge you, therefore, not to marry—bring no child into the world to perpetuate this terrible curse. Let the family die out if you have the courage. It is much, I know, to ask; but whether you do or not, come to me there, and if by sign or word I can communicate with you I will do so, but hold the secret safe. Meet me there before my body is laid to rest, when body and soul are still not far from each other. Farewell.

—Your loving father,
"Henry Clinton."

I read this strange letter over carefully twice, and laid it down. For a moment I hardly knew what to say. It was certainly the most uncanny thing I had ever come across.

"What do you think of it?" asked Allen at last.

"Well, of course there are only two possible solutions," I answered. "One is that your father not only dreamt the beginning of this story—which, remember, he allows himself—but the whole of it."

"And the other?" asked Allen, seeing that I paused.

"The other," I continued, "I hardly know what to say yet. Of course we will investigate the whole thing, that is our only chance of arriving at a solution. It is absurd to let matters rest as they are. We had better try to-night."

Clinton winced and hesitated.

"Something must be done, of course," he answered; "but the worst of it is Phyllis and her mother are coming here early to-morrow in time for the funeral, and I cannot meet her—no, I cannot, poor girl!—while I feel as I do."

"We will go to the vault to-night," I said.

Clinton rose from his chair and looked at me.

"I don't like this thing at all, Bell," he continued. "I am not by nature in any sense of the word a superstitious man, but I tell you frankly nothing would induce me to go alone into that chapel to-night; if you come with me, that, of course, alters matters. I know the pew my father refers to well; it is beneath the window of St. Sebastian."

Soon afterwards I went to my room and dressed; and Allen and I dined tête-à-tête in the great dining-room. The old butler waited on us with funereal solemnity, and I did all I could to lure Clinton's thoughts into a more cheerful and healthier channel.

I cannot say that I was very successful. I further noticed that he scarcely ate anything, and seemed altogether to be in a state of nervous tension painful to witness.

After dinner we went into the smoking-room, and at eleven o'clock I proposed that we should make a start.

Clinton braced himself together and we went out. He got the chapel keys, and then going to the stables we borrowed a lantern, and a moment afterwards found ourselves in the sacred edifice. The moon was at her full, and by the pale light which was diffused through the south windows the architecture of the interior could be faintly seen. The Gothic arches that flanked the centre aisle with their quaint pillars, each with a carved figure of one of the saints, were quite visible, and further in the darkness of the chancel the dim outlines of the choir and altar-table with its white marble reredos could be just discerned.

We closed the door softly and, Clinton leading the way with the lantern, we walked up the centre aisle paved with the brasses of his dead ancestors. We trod gently on tiptoe as one instinctively does at night. Turning beneath the little pulpit we reached the north transept, and here Clinton stopped and turned round. He was very white, but his voice was quiet.

"This is the pew," he whispered. "It has always been called the haunted pew of Sir Hugh Clinton."

I took the lantern from him and we entered. I crossed the pew immediately and went up to the effigy of the old abbot.

"Let us examine him closely," I said. I held up the lantern, getting it to shine on each part of the face, the vestments, and the figure. The eyes, although vacant, as in all statuary, seemed to me at that moment to be uncanny and peculiar. Giving Allen the lantern to hold, I placed a finger firmly on each. The next moment I could not refrain from an exclamation; a stone at the side immediately rolled back, revealing the steps which were spoken of by the old man in his narrative.

"It is true! It is true!" cried Clinton excitedly.

"It certainly looks like it," I remarked: "but never mind, we have the chance now of investigating this matter thoroughly."

"Are you going down?" asked Clinton.

"Certainly I am," I replied. "Let us go together."

Immediately afterwards we crept through the opening and began to descend. There was only just room to do so in single file, and I went first with the lantern. In another moment we were in the long passage, and soon we were confronted by a door in an arched stone framework. Up till now Clinton had shown little sign of alarm, but here, at the trysting-place to which his father's soul had summoned him, he seemed suddenly to lose his nerve. He leant against the wall and for a moment I thought he would have fallen. I held up the lantern and examined the door and walls carefully. Then approaching I lifted the iron latch of the heavy door. It was very hard to move, but at last by seizing the edge I dragged it open to its full against the wall of the passage. Having done so I peered inside, holding the lantern above my head. As I did so I heard Clinton cry out,—

"Look, look," he said, and turning I saw that the great door had swung back against me, almost shutting me within the cell.

Telling Clinton to hold it back by force, I stepped inside and saw at my feet the ghastly coffin. The legend then so far was true. I bent down and examined the queer, misshapen thing with great care. Its shape was that of an enormous wedge, and it was apparently made of some dark old wood, and was bound with iron at the corners. Having looked at it all round, I went out and, flinging back the door which Clinton had been holding open, stood aside to watch. Slowly, very slowly, as we both stood in the passage—slowly, as if pushed by some invisible hand, the door commenced to swing round, and, increasing in velocity, shut with a noisy clang.

Seizing it once again, I dragged it open and, while Clinton held it in that position, made a careful examination. Up to the present I saw nothing to be much alarmed about. There were fifty ways in which a door might shut of its own accord. There might be a hidden spring or tilted hinges; draught, of course, was out of the question. I looked at the hinges, they were of iron and set in the solid masonry. Nor could I discover any spring or hidden contrivance, as when the door was wide open there was an interval of several inches between it and the wall. We tried it again and again with the same result, and at last, as it was closing, I seized it to prevent it.

I now experienced a very odd sensation; I certainly felt as if I were resisting an unseen person who was pressing hard against the door at the other side. Directly it was released it continued its course. I allow I was quite unable to understand the mystery. Suddenly an idea struck me.

"What does the legend say?" I asked, turning to Clinton. "'That the soul is to guard the door, to close it upon the coffin?'"

"Those are the words," answered Allen, speaking with some difficulty.

"Now if that is true," I continued, "and we take the coffin out, the spirit won't shut the door; if it does shut it, it disproves the whole thing at once, and shows it to be merely a clever mechanical contrivance. Come, Clinton, help me to get the coffin out."

"I dare not, Bell," he whispered hoarsely. "I daren't go inside."

"Nonsense, man," I said, feeling now a little annoyed at the whole thing. "Here, put the lantern down and hold the door back." I stepped in and, getting behind the coffin, put out all my strength and shoved it into the passage.

"Now, then," I cried, "I'll bet you fifty pounds to five the door will shut just the same." I dragged the coffin clear of the door and told him to let go. Clinton had scarcely done so before, stepping back, he clutched my arm.

"Look," he whispered; "do you see that it will not shut now? My father is waiting for the coffin to be put back. This is awful!"

I gazed at the door in horror; it was perfectly true, it remained wide open, and quite still. I sprang forward, seized it, and now endeavoured to close it. It was as if some one was trying to hold it open; it required considerable force to stir it, and it was only with difficulty I could move it at all. At last I managed to shut it, but the moment I let go it swung back open of its own accord and struck against the wall, where it remained just as before. In the dead silence that followed I could hear Clinton breathing quickly behind me, and I knew he was holding himself for all he was worth.

At that moment there suddenly came over me a sensation which I had once experienced before, and which I was twice destined to experience again. It is impossible to describe it, but it seized me, laying siege to my brain till I felt like a child in its power. It was as if I were slowly drowning in the great ocean of silence that enveloped us. Time itself seemed to have disappeared. At my feet lay the misshapen thing, and the lantern behind it cast a fantastic shadow of its distorted outline on the cell wall before me.

"Speak; say something," I cried to Clinton. The sharp sound of my voice broke the spell. I felt myself again, and smiled at the trick my nerves had played on me. I bent down and once more laid my hands on the coffin, but before I had time to push it back into its place Clinton had gone up the passage like a man who is flying to escape a hurled javelin.

Exerting all my force to prevent the door from swinging back by keeping my leg against it, I had just got the coffin into the cell and was going out, when I heard a shrill cry, and Clinton came tearing back down the passage.

"I can't get out! The stone has sunk into its place! We are locked in!" he screamed, and, wild with fear, he plunged headlong into the cell, upsetting me in his career before I could check him. I sprang back to the door as it was closing. I was too late. Before I could reach it, it had shut with a loud clang in obedience to the infernal witchcraft.

"You have done it now," I cried angrily. "Do you see? Why, man, we are buried alive in this ghastly hole!"

The lantern I had placed just inside the door, and by its dim light, as I looked at him, I saw the terror of a madman creep into Clinton's eyes.

"Buried alive!" he shouted, with a peal of hysterical laughter. "Yes, and, Bell, it's your doing; you are a devil in human shape!" With a wild paroxysm of fury he flung himself upon me. There was the ferocity of a wild beast in his spring. He upset the lantern and left us in total darkness.

The struggle was short. We might be buried alive, but I was not going to die by his hand, and seizing him by the throat I pinned him against the wall.

"Keep quiet," I shouted. "It is your thundering stupidity that has caused all this. Stay where you are until I strike a match."

I luckily had some vestas in the little silver box which I always carry on my watch-chain, and striking one I relit the lantern. Clinton's paroxysm was over, and sinking to the floor he lay there shivering and cowering.

It was a terrible situation, and I knew that our only hope was for me to keep my presence of mind. With a great effort I forced myself to think calmly over what could be done. To shout for help would have been but a useless waste of breath.

Suddenly an idea struck me. "Have you got your father's letter?" I cried eagerly.

"I have," he answered; "it is in my pocket."

My last ray of hope vanished. Our only chance was that if he had left it at the house some one might discover the letter and come to our rescue by its instructions. It had been a faint hope, and it disappeared almost as quickly as it had come to me. Without it no one would ever find the way to the vault that had remained a secret for ages. I was determined, however, not to die without a struggle for freedom. Taking the lantern, I examined every nook and cranny of the cell for some other exit. It was a fruitless search. No sign of any way out could I find, and we had absolutely no means to unfasten the door from the inner side. Taking a few short steps, I flung myself again and again at the heavy door. It never budged an inch, and, bruised and sweating at every pore, I sat down on the coffin and tried to collect all my faculties.

Clinton was silent, and seemed utterly stunned. He sat still, gazing with a vacant stare at the door.

The time dragged heavily, and there was nothing to do but to wait for a horrible death from starvation. It was more than likely, too, that Clinton would go mad; already his nerves were strained to the utmost. Altogether I had never found myself in a worse plight.

It seemed like an eternity that we sat there, neither of us speaking a word. Over and over again I repeated to myself the words of the terrible curse: "And whoso entereth into the cell shall be the prisoner of the soul that guardeth the door till it shall let him go." When would the shapeless form that was inside the coffin let us go? Doubtless when our bones were dry.

I looked at my watch. It was half-past eleven o'clock. Surely we had been more than ten minutes in this awful place! We had left the house at eleven, and I knew that must have been many hours ago. I glanced at the second hand. The watch had stopped.

"What is the time, Clinton?" I asked. "My watch has stopped."

"What does it matter?" he murmured. "What is time to us now? The sooner we die the better."

He pulled out his watch as he spoke, and held it to the lantern.

"Twenty-five minutes past eleven," he murmured dreamily.

"Good heavens!" I cried, starting up. "Has your watch stopped, too?"

Then, like the leap of a lightning flash, an idea struck me.

"I have got it; I have got it! My God! I believe I have got it!" I cried, seizing him by the arm.

"Got what?" he replied, staring wildly at me.

"Why, the secret—the curse—the door. Don't you see?"

I pulled out the large knife I always carry by a chain and swivel in my trouser pocket, and telling Clinton to hold the lantern, opened the little blade-saw and attacked the coffin with it.

"I believe the secret of our deliverance lies in this," I panted, working away furiously.

In ten minutes I had sawn half through the wooden edge, then, handing my tool to Clinton, I told him to continue the work while I rested. After a few minutes I took the knife again, and at last, after nearly half an hour had gone by, succeeded in making a small hole in the lid. Inserting my two fingers, I felt some rough, uneven masses. I was now fearfully excited. Tearing at the opening like a madman, I enlarged it and extracted what looked like a large piece of coal. I knew in an instant what it was. It was magnetic iron-ore. Holding it down to my knife, the blade flew to it.

"Here is the mystery of the soul," I cried; "now we can use it to open the door."

I had known a great conjurer once, who had deceived and puzzled his audience with a box trick on similar lines: the man opening the box from the inside by drawing down the lock with a magnet. Would this do the same? I felt that our lives hung on the next moment. Taking the mass, I pressed it against the door just opposite the hasp, and slid it up against the wood. My heart leapt as I heard the hasp fly up outside, and with a push the door opened.

"We are saved," I shouted. "We are saved by a miracle!"

"Bell, you are a genius," gasped poor Clinton; "but now, how about the stone at the end of the passage?"

"We will soon see about that," I cried, taking the lantern. "Half the danger is over, at any rate; and the worst half, too."

We rushed along the passage and up the stair until we reached the top.

"Why, Clinton," I cried, holding up the lantern, "the place was not shut at all."

Nor was it. In his terror he had imagined it.

"I could not see in the dark, and I was nearly dead with fright," he said. "Oh, Bell, let us get out of this as quickly as we can!"

We crushed through the aperture and once more stood in the chapel. I then pushed the stone back into its place.

Dawn was just breaking when we escaped from the chapel. We hastened across to the house. In the hall the clock pointed to five.

"Well, we have had an awful time," I said, as we stood in the hall together; "but at least, Clinton, the end was worth the ghastly terror. I have knocked the bottom out of your family legend for ever."

"I don't even now quite understand," he said.

"Don't you?—but it is so easy. That coffin never contained a body at all, but was filled, as you perceive, with fragments of magnetic iron-ore. For what diabolical purposes the cell was intended, it is, of course, impossible to say; but that it must have been meant as a human trap there is little doubt. The inventor certainly exercised no small ingenuity when he devised his diabolical plot, for it was obvious that the door, which was made of iron, would swing towards the coffin wherever it happened to be placed. Thus the door would shut if the coffin were inside the cell, and would remain open if the coffin were brought out. A cleverer method for simulating a spiritual agency it would be hard to find. Of course, the monk must have known well that magnetic iron-ore never loses its quality and would ensure the deception remaining potent for ages."

"But how did you discover by means of our watches?" asked Clinton.

"Any one who understands magnetism can reply to that," I said. "It is a well-known fact that a strong magnet plays havoc with watches. The fact of both our watches going wrong first gave me a clue to the mystery."

Later in the day the whole of this strange affair was explained to Miss Curzon, and not long afterwards the passage and entrance to the chapel were bricked up.

It is needless to add that six months later the pair were married, and, I believe, are as happy as they deserve.

THE MYSTERY OF THE FELWYN TUNNEL

I was making experiments of some interest at South Kensington, and hoped that I had perfected a small but not unimportant discovery, when, on returning home one evening in late October in the year 1893, I found a visiting card on my table. On it were inscribed the words, "Mr. Geoffrey Bainbridge." This name was quite unknown to me, so I rang the bell and inquired of my servant who the visitor had been. He described him as a gentleman who wished to see me on most urgent business, and said further that Mr. Bainbridge intended to call again later in the evening. It was with both curiosity and vexation that I awaited the return of the stranger. Urgent business with me generally meant a hurried rush to one part of the country or the other. I did not want to leave London just then; and when at half-past nine Mr. Geoffrey Bainbridge was ushered into my room, I received him with a certain coldness which he could not fail to perceive. He was a tall, well-dressed, elderly man. He immediately plunged into the object of his visit.

"I hope you do not consider my unexpected presence an intrusion, Mr. Bell," he said. "But I have heard of you from our mutual friends, the Greys of Uplands. You may remember once doing that family a great service."

"I remember perfectly well," I answered more cordially. "Pray tell me what you want; I shall listen with attention."

"I believe you are the one man in London who can help me," he continued. "I refer to a matter especially relating to your own particular study. I need hardly say that whatever you do will not be unrewarded."

"That is neither here nor there," I said; "but before you go any further, allow me to ask one question. Do you want me to leave London at present?"

He raised his eyebrows in dismay.

"I certainly do," he answered.

"Very well; pray proceed with your story."

He looked at me with anxiety.

"In the first place," he began, "I must tell you that I am chairman of the Lytton Vale Railway Company in Wales, and that it is on an important matter connected with our line that I have come to consult you. When I explain to you the nature of the mystery, you will not wonder, I think, at my soliciting your aid."

"I will give you my closest attention," I answered; and then I added, impelled to say the latter words by a certain expression on his face, "if I can see my way to assisting you I shall be ready to do so."

"Pray accept my cordial thanks," he replied. "I have come up from my place at Felwyn to-day on purpose to consult you. It is in that neighbourhood that the affair has occurred. As it is essential that you should be in possession of the facts of the whole matter, I will go over things just as they happened."

I bent forward and listened attentively.

"This day fortnight," continued Mr. Bainbridge, "our quiet little village was horrified by the news that the signalman on duty at the mouth of the Felwyn Tunnel had been found dead under the most mysterious circumstances. The tunnel is at the end of a long cutting between Llanlys and Felwyn stations. It is about a mile long, and the signal-box is on the Felwyn side. The place is extremely lonely, being six miles from the village across the mountains. The name of the poor fellow who met his death in this mysterious fashion was David Pritchard. I have known him from a boy, and he was quite one of the steadiest and most trustworthy men on the line. On Tuesday evening he went on duty at six o'clock; on Wednesday morning the day-man who had come to relieve him was surprised

not to find him in the box. It was just getting daylight, and the
6.30 local was coming down, so he pulled the signals and let her
through. Then he went out, and, looking up the line towards the
tunnel, saw Pritchard lying beside the line close to the mouth of
the tunnel. Roberts, the day-man, ran up to him and found, to his
horror, that he was quite dead. At first Roberts naturally supposed
that he had been cut down by a train, as there was a wound at the
back of the head; but he was not lying on the metals. Roberts ran
back to the box and telegraphed through to Felwyn Station. The
message was sent on to the village, and at half-past seven o'clock
the police inspector came up to my house with the news. He and I,
with the local doctor, went off at once to the tunnel. We found the
dead man lying beside the metals a few yards away from the mouth
of the tunnel, and the doctor immediately gave him a careful examination. There was a depressed fracture at the back of the skull,
which must have caused his death; but how he came by it was not
so clear. On examining the whole place most carefully, we saw,
further, that there were marks on the rocks at the steep side of the
embankment as if some one had tried to scramble up them. Why
the poor fellow had attempted such a climb, God only knows. In
doing so he must have slipped and fallen back on to the line, thus
causing the fracture of the skull. In no case could he have gone up
more than eight or ten feet, as the banks of the cutting run sheer
up, almost perpendicularly, beyond that point for more than a
hundred and fifty feet. There are some sharp boulders beside the
line, and it was possible that he might have fallen on one of these
and so sustained the injury. The affair must have occurred some
time between 11.45 p.m. and 6 a.m., as the engine-driver of the
express at 11.45 p.m. states that the line was signalled clear, and
he also caught sight of Pritchard in his box as he passed."

"This is deeply interesting," I said; "pray proceed."

Bainbridge looked at me earnestly; he then continued:—

"The whole thing is shrouded in mystery. Why should Pritchard
have left his box and gone down to the tunnel? Why, having done
so, should he have made a wild attempt to scale the side of the
cutting, an impossible feat at any time? Had danger threatened,

the ordinary course of things would have been to run up the line towards the signal-box. These points are quite unexplained. Another curious fact is that death appears to have taken place just before the day-man came on duty, as the light at the mouth of the tunnel had been put out, and it was one of the night signalman's duties to do this as soon as daylight appeared; it is possible, therefore, that Pritchard went down to the tunnel for that purpose. Against this theory, however, and an objection that seems to nullify it, is the evidence of Dr. Williams, who states that when he examined the body his opinion was that death had taken place some hours before. An inquest was held on the following day, but before it took place there was a new and most important development. I now come to what I consider the crucial point in the whole story.

"For a long time there had been a feud between Pritchard and another man of the name of Wynne, a platelayer on the line. The object of their quarrel was the blacksmith's daughter in the neighbouring village—a remarkably pretty girl and an arrant flirt. Both men were madly in love with her, and she played them off one against the other. The night but one before his death Pritchard and Wynne had met at the village inn, had quarrelled in the bar— Lucy, of course, being the subject of their difference. Wynne was heard to say (he was a man of powerful build and subject to fits of ungovernable rage) that he would have Pritchard's life. Pritchard swore a great oath that he would get Lucy on the following day to promise to marry him. This oath, it appears, he kept, and on his way to the signal-box on Tuesday evening met Wynne, and triumphantly told him that Lucy had promised to be his wife. The men had a hand-to-hand fight on the spot, several people from the village being witnesses of it. They were separated with difficulty, each vowing vengeance on the other. Pritchard went off to his duty at the signal-box and Wynne returned to the village to drown his sorrows at the public-house.

"Very late that same night Wynne was seen by a villager going in the direction of the tunnel. The man stopped him and questioned him. He explained that he had left some of his tools on the line, and was on his way to fetch them. The villager noticed that he looked queer and excited, but not wishing to pick a quarrel thought it best not to question him further. It has been proved that Wynne never returned home that night, but came back at an early hour on the following morning, looking dazed and stupid. He was arrested on suspicion, and at the inquest the verdict was against him."

"Has he given any explanation of his own movements?" I asked.

"Yes; but nothing that can clear him. As a matter of fact, his tools were nowhere to be seen on the line, nor did he bring them home with him. His own story is that being considerably the worse for drink, he had fallen down in one of the fields and slept there till morning."

"Things look black against him," I said.

"They do; but listen, I have something more to add. Here comes a very queer feature in the affair. Lucy Ray, the girl who had caused the feud between Pritchard and Wynne, after hearing the news of Pritchard's death, completely lost her head, and ran frantically about the village declaring that Wynne was the man she really loved, and that she had only accepted Pritchard in a fit of rage with Wynne for not himself bringing matters to the point. The case looks very bad against Wynne, and yesterday the magistrate committed him for trial at the coming assizes. The unhappy Lucy Ray and the young man's parents are in a state bordering on distraction."

"What is your own opinion with regard to Wynne's guilt?" I asked.

"Before God, Mr. Bell, I believe the poor fellow is innocent, but the evidence against him is very strong. One of the favourite theories is that he went down to the tunnel and extinguished the light, knowing that this would bring Pritchard out of his box to see what was the matter, and that he then attacked him, striking the blow which fractured the skull."

"Has any weapon been found about, with which he could have given such a blow?"

"No; nor has anything of the kind been discovered on Wynne's person; that fact is decidedly in his favour."

"But what about the marks on the rocks?" I asked.

"It is possible that Wynne may have made them in order to divert suspicion by making people think that Pritchard must have fallen, and so killed himself. The holders of this theory base their belief on the absolute want of cause for Pritchard's trying to scale the rock. The whole thing is the most absolute enigma. Some of the country folk have declared that the tunnel is haunted (and there certainly has been such a rumour current among them for years). That Pritchard saw some apparition, and in wild terror sought to escape from it by climbing the rocks, is another theory, but only the most imaginative hold it."

"Well, it is a most extraordinary case," I replied.

"Yes, Mr. Bell, and I should like to get your opinion of it. Do you see your way to elucidate the mystery?"

"Not at present; but I shall be happy to investigate the matter to my utmost ability."

"But you do not wish to leave London at present?"

"That is so; but a matter of such importance cannot be set aside. It appears, from what you say, that Wynne's life hangs more or less on my being able to clear away the mystery?"

"That is indeed the case. There ought not to be a single stone left unturned to get at the truth, for the sake of Wynne. Well, Mr. Bell, what do you propose to do?"

"To see the place without delay," I answered.

"That is right; when can you come?"

"Whenever you please."

"Will you come down to Felwyn with me to-morrow? I shall leave Paddington by the 7.10, and if you will be my guest I shall be only too pleased to put you up."

"That arrangement will suit me admirably," I replied. "I will meet you by the train you mention, and the affair shall have my best attention."

"Thank you," he said, rising. He shook hands with me and took his leave.

The next day I met Bainbridge at Paddington Station, and we were soon flying westward in the luxurious private compartment that had been reserved for him. I could see by his abstracted manner and his long lapses of silence that the mysterious affair at Felwyn Tunnel was occupying all his thoughts.

It was two o'clock in the afternoon when the train slowed down at the little station of Felwyn. The station-master was at the door in an instant to receive us.

"I have some terribly bad news for you, sir," he said, turning to Bainbridge as we alighted; "and yet in one sense it is a relief, for it seems to clear Wynne."

"What do you mean?" cried Bainbridge. "Bad news? Speak out at once!"

"Well, sir, it is this: there has been another death at Felwyn signal-box. John Davidson, who was on duty last night, was found dead at an early hour this morning in the very same place where we found poor Pritchard."

"Good God!" cried Bainbridge, starting back, "what an awful thing! What, in the name of Heaven, does it mean, Mr. Bell? This is too fearful. Thank goodness you have come down with us."

"It is as black a business as I ever heard of, sir," echoed the station-master; "and what we are to do I don't know. Poor Davidson was found dead this morning, and there was neither mark nor sign of what killed him—that is the extraordinary part of it. There's a perfect panic abroad, and not a signalman on the line will take duty to-night. I was quite in despair, and was afraid at one time that the line would have to be closed, but at last it occurred to me to wire to Lytton Vale, and they are sending down an inspector. I expect him by a special every moment. I believe this is he coming now," added the station-master, looking up the line.

There was the sound of a whistle down the valley, and in a few moments a single engine shot into the station, and an official in uniform stepped on to the platform.

"Good-evening, sir," he said, touching his cap to Bainbridge; "I have just been sent down to inquire into this affair at the Felwyn Tunnel, and though it seems more of a matter for a Scotland Yard detective than one of ourselves, there was nothing for it but to

come. All the same, Mr. Bainbridge, I cannot say that I look forward to spending to-night alone at the place."

"You wish for the services of a detective, but you shall have
some one better," said Bainbridge, turning towards me. "This
gentleman, Mr. John Bell, is the man of all others for our business. I have just brought him down from London for the purpose."

An expression of relief flitted across the inspector's face.

"I am very glad to see you, sir," he said to me, "and I hope you
will be able to spend the night with me in the signal-box. I must
say I don't much relish the idea of tackling the thing single-handed;
but with your help, sir, I think we ought to get to the bottom of it
somehow. I am afraid there is not a man on the line who will take
duty until we do. So it is most important that the thing should be
cleared, and without delay."

I readily assented to the inspector's proposition, and Bainbridge and I arranged that we should call for him at four o'clock at
the village inn and drive him to the tunnel.

We then stepped into the wagonette which was waiting for us,
and drove to Bainbridge's house.

Mrs. Bainbridge came out to meet us, and was full of the tragedy. Two pretty girls also ran to greet their father, and to glance
inquisitively at me. I could see that the entire family was in a state
of much excitement.

"Lucy Ray has just left, father," said the elder of the girls. "We
had much trouble to soothe her; she is in a frantic state."

"You have heard, Mr. Bell, all about this dreadful mystery?"
said Mrs. Bainbridge as she led me towards the dining-room.

"Yes," I answered; "your husband has been good enough to give
me every particular."

"And you have really come here to help us?"

"I hope I may be able to discover the cause," I answered.

"It certainly seems most extraordinary," continued Mrs.
Bainbridge. "My dear," she continued, turning to her husband, "you
can easily imagine the state we were all in this morning when the
news of the second death was brought to us."

"For my part," said Ella Bainbridge, "I am sure that Felwyn Tunnel is haunted. The villagers have thought so for a long time, and this second death seems to prove it, does it not?" Here she looked anxiously at me.

"I can offer no opinion," I replied, "until I have sifted the matter thoroughly."

"Come, Ella, don't worry Mr. Bell," said her father; "if he is as hungry as I am, he must want his lunch."

We then seated ourselves at the table and commenced the meal. Bainbridge, although he professed to be hungry, was in such a state of excitement that he could scarcely eat. Immediately after lunch he left me to the care of his family and went into the village.

"It is just like him," said Mrs. Bainbridge; "he takes these sort of things to heart dreadfully. He is terribly upset about Lucy Ray, and also about the poor fellow Wynne. It is certainly a fearful tragedy from first to last."

"Well, at any rate," I said, "this fresh death will upset the evidence against Wynne."

"I hope so, and there is some satisfaction in the fact. Well, Mr. Bell, I see you have finished lunch; will you come into the drawing-room?"

I followed her into a pleasant room overlooking the valley of the Lytton.

By-and-by Bainbridge returned, and soon afterwards the dog-cart came to the door. My host and I mounted, Bainbridge took the reins, and we started off at a brisk pace.

"Matters get worse and worse," he said the moment we were alone. "If you don't clear things up to-night, Bell, I say frankly that I cannot imagine what will happen."

We entered the village, and as we rattled down the ill-paved streets I was greeted with curious glances on all sides. The people were standing about in groups, evidently talking about the tragedy and nothing else. Suddenly, as our trap bumped noisily over the paving-stones, a girl darted out of one of the houses and made frantic motions to Bainbridge to stop the horse. He pulled the mare nearly up on her haunches, and the girl came up to the side of the dog-cart.

"You have heard it?" she said, speaking eagerly and in a gasping voice. "The death which occurred this morning will clear Stephen Wynne, won't it, Mr. Bainbridge?—it will, you are sure, are you not?"

"It looks like it, Lucy, my poor girl," he answered. "But there, the whole thing is so terrible that I scarcely know what to think."

She was a pretty girl with dark eyes, and under ordinary circumstances must have had the vivacious expression of face and the brilliant complexion which so many of her countrywomen possess. But now her eyes were swollen with weeping and her complexion more or less disfigured by the agony she had gone through. She looked piteously at Bainbridge, her lips trembling. The next moment she burst into tears.

"Come away, Lucy," said a woman who had followed her out of the cottage; "Fie—for shame! don't trouble the gentlemen; come back and stay quiet."

"I can't, mother, I can't," said the unfortunate girl. "If they hang him, I'll go clean off my head. Oh, Mr. Bainbridge, do say that the second death has cleared him!"

"I have every hope that it will do so, Lucy," said Bainbridge, "but now don't keep us, there's a good girl; go back into the house. This gentleman has come down from London on purpose to look into the whole matter. I may have good news for you in the morning."

The girl raised her eyes to my face with a look of intense pleading. "Oh, I have been cruel and a fool, and I deserve everything," she gasped; "but, sir, for the love of Heaven, try to clear him."

I promised to do my best.

Bainbridge touched up the mare, she bounded forward, and Lucy disappeared into the cottage with her mother.

The next moment we drew up at the inn where the Inspector was waiting, and soon afterwards were bowling along between the high banks of the country lanes to the tunnel. It was a cold, still afternoon; the air was wonderfully keen, for a sharp frost had held the countryside in its grip for the last two days. The sun was just tipping the hills to westward when the trap pulled up at the top of the cutting. We hastily alighted, and the Inspector and I bade Bainbridge good-bye. He said that he only wished that he could stay with us for the night, assured us that little sleep would visit him, and that he would be back at the cutting at an early hour on the following morning; then the noise of his horse's feet was heard fainter and fainter as he drove back over the frost-bound roads. The Inspector and I ran along the little path to the wicket-gate in the fence, stamping our feet on the hard ground to restore circulation after our cold drive. The next moment we were looking down upon the scene of the mysterious deaths, and a weird and lonely place it looked. The tunnel was at one end of the rock cutting, the sides of which ran sheer down to the line for over a hundred and fifty feet. Above the tunnel's mouth the hills rose one upon the other. A more dreary place it would have been difficult to imagine. From a little clump of pines a delicate film of blue smoke rose straight up on the still air. This came from the chimney of the signal-box.

As we started to descend the precipitous path the Inspector sang out a cheery "Hullo!" The man on duty in the box immediately answered. His voice echoed and reverberated down the cutting, and the next moment he appeared at the door of the box. He told us that he would be with us immediately; but we called back to him to stay where he was, and the next instant the Inspector and I entered the box.

"The first thing to do," said Henderson the Inspector, "is to send a message down the line to announce our arrival."

This he did, and in a few moments a crawling goods train came panting up the cutting. After signalling her through we descended the wooden flight of steps which led from the box down to the line and walked along the metals towards the tunnel till we stood on the spot where poor Davidson had been found dead that morning. I examined the ground and all around it most carefully. Everything tallied exactly with the description I had received. There could be

JOHN BELL: GHOST EXPOSER

no possible way of approaching the spot except by going along the line, as the rocky sides of the cutting were inaccessible.

"It is a most extraordinary thing, sir," said the signalman whom we had come to relieve. "Davidson had neither mark nor sign on him—there he lay stone dead and cold, and not a bruise nowhere; but Pritchard had an awful wound at the back of the head. They said he got it by climbing the rocks—here, you can see the marks for yourself, sir. But now, is it likely that Pritchard would try to climb rocks like these, so steep as they are?"

"Certainly not," I replied.

"Then how do you account for the wound, sir?" asked the man with an anxious face.

"I cannot tell you at present," I answered.

"And you and Inspector Henderson are going to spend the night in the signal-box?"

"Yes."

A horrified expression crept over the signalman's face.

"God preserve you both," he said; "I wouldn't do it—not for fifty pounds. It's not the first time I have heard tell that Felwyn Tunnel is haunted. But, there, I won't say any more about that. It's a black business, and has given trouble enough. There's poor Wynne, the same thing as convicted of the murder of Pritchard; but now they say that Davidson's death will clear him. Davidson was as good a fellow as you would come across this side of the country; but for the matter of that, so was Pritchard. The whole thing is terrible—it upsets one, that it do, sir."

"I don't wonder at your feelings," I answered; "but now, see here, I want to make a most careful examination of everything. One of the theories is that Wynne crept down this rocky side and fractured Pritchard's skull. I believe such a feat to be impossible. On examining these rocks I see that a man might climb up the side of the tunnel as far as from eight to ten feet, utilising the sharp projections of rock for the purpose; but it would be out of the question for any man to come down the cutting. No; the only way Wynne could have approached Pritchard was by the line itself. But, after all, the real thing to discover is this," I continued: "what killed

Davidson? Whatever caused his death is, beyond doubt, equally responsible for Pritchard's. I am now going into the tunnel."

Inspector Henderson went in with me. The place struck damp and chill. The walls were covered with green, evil-smelling fungi, and through the brickwork the moisture was oozing and had trickled down in long lines to the ground. Before us was nothing but dense darkness.

When we re-appeared the signalman was lighting the red lamp on the post, which stood about five feet from the ground just above the entrance to the tunnel.

"Is there plenty of oil?" asked the Inspector.

"Yes, sir, plenty," replied the man. "Is there anything more I can do for either of you gentlemen?" he asked, pausing, and evidently dying to be off.

"Nothing," answered Henderson; "I will wish you good-evening."

"Good-evening to you both," said the man. He made his way quickly up the path and was soon lost to sight.

Henderson and I then returned to the signal-box.

By this time it was nearly dark.

"How many trains pass in the night?" I asked of the Inspector.

"There's the 10.20 down express," he said, "it will pass here at about 10.40; then there's the 11.45 up, and then not another train till the 6.30 local to-morrow morning. We shan't have a very lively time," he added.

I approached the fire and bent over it, holding out my hands to try and get some warmth into them.

"It will take a good deal to persuade me to go down to the tunnel, whatever I may see there," said the man. "I don't think, Mr. Bell, I am a coward in any sense of the word, but there's something very uncanny about this place, right away from the rest of the world. I don't wonder one often hears of signalmen going mad in some of these lonely boxes. Have you any theory to account for these deaths, sir?"

"None at present," I replied.

"This second death puts the idea of Pritchard being murdered quite out of court," he continued.

"I am sure of it," I answered.

"And so am I, and that's one comfort," continued Henderson. "That poor girl, Lucy Ray, although she was to be blamed for her conduct, is much to be pitied now; and as to poor Wynne himself, he protests his innocence through thick and thin. He was a wild fellow, but not the sort to take the life of a fellow-creature. I saw the doctor this afternoon while I was waiting for you at the inn, Mr. Bell, and also the police sergeant. They both say they do not know what Davidson died of. There was not the least sign of violence on the body."

"Well, I am as puzzled as the rest of you," I said. "I have one or two theories in my mind, but none of them will quite fit the situation."

The night was piercingly cold, and, although there was not a breath of wind, the keen and frosty air penetrated into the lonely signal-box. We spoke little, and both of us were doubtless absorbed by our own thoughts and speculations. As to Henderson, he looked distinctly uncomfortable, and I cannot say that my own feelings were too pleasant. Never had I been given a tougher problem to solve, and never had I been so utterly at my wits' end for a solution.

Now and then the Inspector got up and went to the telegraph instrument, which intermittently clicked away in its box. As he did so he made some casual remark and then sat down again. After the 10.40 had gone through, there followed a period of silence which seemed almost oppressive. All at once the stillness was broken by the whirr of the electric bell, which sounded so sharply in our ears that we both started. Henderson rose.

"That's the 11.45 coming," he said, and, going over to the three long levers, he pulled two of them down with a loud clang. The next moment, with a rush and a scream, the express tore down the cutting, the carriage lights streamed past in a rapid flash, the ground trembled, a few sparks from the engine whirled up into the darkness, and the train plunged into the tunnel.

"And now," said Henderson, as he pushed back the levers, "not another train till daylight. My word, it is cold!"

It was intensely so. I piled some more wood on the fire and, turning up the collar of my heavy ulster, sat down at one end of the bench and leant my back against the wall. Henderson did likewise; we were neither of us inclined to speak. As a rule, whenever I have any night work to do, I am never troubled with sleepiness, but on this occasion I felt unaccountably drowsy. I soon perceived that Henderson was in the same condition.

"Are you sleepy?" I asked of him.

"Dead with it, sir," was his answer; "but there's no fear, I won't drop off."

I got up and went to the window of the box. I felt certain that if I sat still any longer I should be in a sound sleep. This would never do. Already it was becoming a matter of torture to keep my eyes open. I began to pace up and down; I opened the door of the box and went out on the little platform.

"What's the matter, sir?" inquired Henderson, jumping up with a start.

"I cannot keep awake," I said.

"Nor can I," he answered, "and yet I have spent nights and nights of my life in signal-boxes and never was the least bit drowsy; perhaps it's the cold."

"Perhaps it is," I said; "but I have been out on as freezing nights before, and—"

The man did not reply; he had sat down again; his head was nodding.

I was just about to go up to him and shake him, when it suddenly occurred to me that I might as well let him have his sleep out. I soon heard him snoring, and he presently fell forward in a heap on the floor. By dint of walking up and down, I managed to keep from dropping off myself, and in torture which I shall never be able to describe, the night wore itself away. At last, towards morning, I awoke Henderson.

"You have had a good nap," I said; "but never mind, I have been on guard and nothing has occurred."

"Good God! have I been asleep?" cried the man.

"Sound," I answered.

"Well, I never felt anything like it," he replied. "Don't you find the air very close, sir?"

"No," I said; "it is as fresh as possible; it must be the cold."

"I'll just go and have a look at the light at the tunnel," said the man; "it will rouse me."

He went on to the little platform, whilst I bent over the fire and began to build it up. Presently he returned with a scared look on his face. I could see by the light of the oil lamp which hung on the wall that he was trembling.

"Mr. Bell," he said, "I believe there is somebody or something down at the mouth of the tunnel now." As he spoke he clutched me by the arm. "Go and look," he said; "whoever it is, it has put out the light."

"Put out the light?" I cried. "Why, what's the time?"

Henderson pulled out his watch.

"Thank goodness, most of the night is gone," he said; "I didn't know it was so late, it is half-past five."

"Then the local is not due for an hour yet?" I said.

"No; but who should put out the light?" cried Henderson.

I went to the door, flung it open, and looked out. The dim outline of the tunnel was just visible looming through the darkness, but the red light was out.

"What the dickens does it mean, sir?" gasped the Inspector. "I know the lamp had plenty of oil in it. Can there be any one standing in front of it, do you think?"

We waited and watched for a few moments, but nothing stirred.

"Come along," I said, "let us go down together and see what it is."

"I don't believe I can do it, sir; I really don't!"

"Nonsense," I cried. "I shall go down alone if you won't accompany me. Just hand me my stick, will you?"

"For God's sake, be careful, Mr. Bell. Don't go down, whatever you do. I expect this is what happened before, and the poor fellows went down to see what it was and died there. There's some devilry at work, that's my belief."

"That is as it may be," I answered shortly; "but we certainly shall not find out by stopping here. My business is to get to the bottom of this, and I am going to do it. That there is danger of some sort, I have very little doubt; but danger or not, I am going down."

"If you'll be warned by me, sir, you'll just stay quietly here."

"I must go down and see the matter out," was my answer. "Now listen to me, Henderson. I see that you are alarmed, and I don't wonder. Just stay quietly where you are and watch, but if I call come at once. Don't delay a single instant. Remember I am putting my life into your hands. If I call 'Come,' just come to me as quick as you can, for I may want help. Give me that lantern."

He unhitched it from the wall, and taking it from him, I walked cautiously down the steps on to the line. I still felt curiously, unaccountably drowsy and heavy. I wondered at this, for the moment was such a critical one as to make almost any man wide awake. Holding the lamp high above my head, I walked rapidly along the line. I hardly knew what I expected to find. Cautiously along the metals I made my way, peering right and left until I was close to the fatal spot where the bodies had been found. An uncontrollable shudder passed over me. The next moment, to my horror, without the slightest warning, the light I was carrying went out, leaving me in total darkness. I started back, and stumbling against one of the loose boulders reeled against the wall and nearly fell. What was the matter with me? I could hardly stand. I felt giddy and faint, and a horrible sensation of great tightness seized me across the chest. A loud ringing noise sounded in my ears. Struggling madly for breath, and with the fear of impending death upon me, I turned and tried to run from a danger I could neither understand nor grapple with. But before I had taken two steps my legs gave way from under me, and uttering a loud cry I fell insensible to the ground.

Out of an oblivion which, for all I knew, might have lasted for moments or centuries, a dawning consciousness came to me. I knew that I was lying on hard ground; that I was absolutely incapable of realising, nor had I the slightest inclination to discover, where I was. All I wanted was to lie quite still and undisturbed. Presently I opened my eyes.

Some one was bending over me and looking into my face.

"Thank God, he is not dead," I heard in whispered tones. Then, with a flash, memory returned to me.

"What has happened?" I asked.

"You may well ask that, sir," said the Inspector gravely. "It has been touch and go with you for the last quarter of an hour; and a near thing for me too."

I sat up and looked around me. Daylight was just beginning to break, and I saw that we were at the bottom of the steps that led up to the signal-box. My teeth were chattering with the cold and I was shivering like a man with ague.

"I am better now," I said; "just give me your hand."

I took his arm, and holding the rail with the other hand staggered up into the box and sat down on the bench.

"Yes, it has been a near shave," I said; "and a big price to pay for solving a mystery."

"Do you mean to say you know what it is?" asked Henderson eagerly.

"Yes," I answered, "I think I know now; but first tell me how long was I unconscious?"

"A good bit over half an hour, sir, I should think. As soon as I heard you call out I ran down as you told me, but before I got to you I nearly fainted. I never had such a horrible sensation in my life. I felt as weak as a baby, but I just managed to seize you by the arms and drag you along the line to the steps, and that was about all I could do."

"Well, I owe you my life," I said; "just hand me that brandy flask, I shall be the better for some of its contents."

I took a long pull. Just as I was laying the flask down Henderson started from my side.

"There," he cried, "the 6.30 is coming." The electric bell at the instrument suddenly began to ring. "Ought I to let her go through, sir?" he inquired.

"Certainly," I answered. "That is exactly what we want. Oh, she will be all right."

"No danger to her, sir?"

"None, none; let her go through."

He pulled the lever and the next moment the train tore through the cutting.

"Now I think it will be safe to go down again," I said. "I believe I shall be able to get to the bottom of this business."

Henderson stared at me aghast.

"Do you mean that you are going down again to the tunnel?" he gasped.

"Yes," I said; "give me those matches. You had better come too. I don't think there will be much danger now; and there is daylight, so we can see what we are about."

The man was very loth to obey me, but at last I managed to persuade him. We went down the line, walking slowly, and at this moment we both felt our courage revived by a broad and cheerful ray of sunshine.

"We must advance cautiously," I said, "and be ready to run back at a moment's notice."

"God knows, sir, I think we are running a great risk," panted poor Henderson; "and if that devil or whatever else it is should happen to be about—why, daylight or no daylight—"

"Nonsense! man," I interrupted; "if we are careful, no harm will happen to us now. Ah! and here we are!" We had reached the spot where I had fallen. "Just give me a match, Henderson."

He did so, and I immediately lit the lamp. Opening the glass of the lamp, I held it close to the ground and passed it to and fro. Suddenly the flame went out.

"Don't you understand now?" I said, looking up at the Inspector.

"No, I don't, sir," he replied with a bewildered expression.

Suddenly, before I could make an explanation, we both heard shouts from the top of the cutting, and looking up I saw Bainbridge hurrying down the path. He had come in the dog-cart to fetch us.

"Here's the mystery," I cried as he rushed up to us, "and a deadlier scheme of Dame Nature's to frighten and murder poor humanity I have never seen."

As I spoke I lit the lamp again and held it just above a tiny fissure in the rock. It was at once extinguished.

"What is it?" said Bainbridge, panting with excitement.

"Something that nearly finished me," I replied. "Why, this is a natural escape of choke damp. Carbonic acid gas—the deadliest gas imaginable, because it gives no warning of its presence, and it has no smell. It must have collected here during the hours of the night when no train was passing, and gradually rising put out the signal light. The constant rushing of the trains through the cutting all day would temporarily disperse it."

As I made this explanation Bainbridge stood like one electrified, while a curious expression of mingled relief and horror swept over Henderson's face.

"An escape of carbonic acid gas is not an uncommon phenomenon in volcanic districts," I continued, "as I take this to be; but it is odd what should have started it. It has sometimes been known to follow earthquake shocks, when there is a profound disturbance of the deep strata."

"It is strange that you should have said that," said Bainbridge, when he could find his voice.

"What do you mean?"

"Why, that about the earthquake. Don't you remember, Henderson," he added, turning to the Inspector, "we had felt a slight shock all over South Wales about three weeks back?"

"Then that, I think, explains it," I said. "It is evident that Pritchard really did climb the rocks in a frantic attempt to escape from the gas and fell back on to these boulders. The other man was cut down at once, before he had time to fly."

"But what is to happen now?" asked Bainbridge. "Will it go on for ever? How are we to stop it?"

"The fissure ought to be drenched with lime water, and then filled up; but all really depends on what is the size of the supply and also the depth. It is an extremely heavy gas, and would lie at the bottom of a cutting like water. I think there is more here just now than is good for us," I added.

"But how," continued Bainbridge, as we moved a few steps from the fatal spot, "do you account for the interval between the first death and the second?"

"The escape must have been intermittent. If wind blew down the cutting, as probably was the case before this frost set in, it would keep the gas so diluted that its effects would not be noticed. There was enough down here this morning, before that train came through, to poison an army. Indeed, if it had not been for Henderson's promptitude, there would have been another inquest—on myself."

I then related my own experience.

"Well, this clears Wynne, without doubt," said Bainbridge; "but alas! for the two poor fellows who were victims. Bell, the Lytton Vale Railway Company owe you unlimited thanks; you have doubtless saved many lives, and also the Company, for the line must have been closed if you had not made your valuable discovery. But now come home with me to breakfast. We can discuss all those matters later on."

THE EIGHT-MILE LOCK

It was in the August of 1889, when I was just arranging my annual holiday, that I received the following letter. I tore it open and read:—

> "Theodora House-boat,
>   Goring.
>
> "Dear Mr. Bell,—
> "Can you come down on Wednesday and stay with us for a week? The weather is glorious and the river looking its best. We are a gay party, and there will be plenty of fun going on.
> "Yours very truly,
> "Helena Ridsdale."

This was exactly what I wanted. I was fond of the river, and scarcely a summer passed that I did not spend at least a fortnight on the Thames. I could go for a week to the Ridsdales, and then start off on my own quiet holiday afterwards. I had known Lady Ridsdale since she was a girl, and I had no doubt my visit would prove a most enjoyable one. I replied immediately, accepting the invitation, and three days later arrived at Goring.

As the well-cushioned little punt, which had been sent to bring me across the river, drew up alongside the Theodora, the Countess came down from the deck to welcome me.

"I am so glad you could come, Mr. Bell," she said. "I was afraid you might be away on some of your extraordinary campaigns against the supernatural. This is Mr. Ralph Vyner; he is also, like yourself, devoted to science. I am sure you will find many interests in common."

A short, thickset, wiry little man, dressed in white flannels, who had been lolling in a deck chair, now came forward and shook hands with me.

"I know of you by reputation, Mr. Bell," he said, "and I have often hoped to have the pleasure of meeting you. I am sure we shall all be anxious to hear of some of your experiences. We are such an excessively frivolous party that we can easily afford to be leavened with a little serious element."

"But I don't mean to be serious in the least," I answered, laughing; "I have come here to enjoy myself, and intend to be as frivolous as the rest of you."

"You will have an opportunity this evening," said the Countess; "we are going to have a special band from town, and intend to have a moonlight dance on deck. Ah! here comes Charlie with the others," she added, shading her eyes and looking down the stream.

In a few moments a perfectly appointed little electric launch shot up, and my host with the rest of the party came on board. We shortly afterwards sat down to lunch, and a gayer and pleasanter set of people I have seldom met. In the afternoon we broke up into detachments, and Vyner and I went for a long pull up stream. I found him a pleasant fellow, ready to talk at any length not only about his own hobbies, but about the world at large. I discovered presently that he was a naval engineer of no small attainments.

When we returned to the house-boat, it was nearly time to prepare for dinner. Most of the ladies had already retired to their cabins. Lady Ridsdale was standing alone on deck. When she saw us both, she called to us to come to her side.

"This quite dazzles me," she said in a low, somewhat mysterious tone, "and I must show it to you. I know you at least, Mr. Vyner, will appreciate it."

As she spoke she took a small leather case out of her pocket—it was ornamented with a monogram, and opened with a catch. She pressed the lid, it flew up, and I saw, resting on a velvet bed, a glittering circlet of enormous diamonds. The Countess lifted them out, and slipped them over her slender wrist.

"They are some of the family diamonds," she said with excitement, "and of great value. Charlie is having all the jewels reset for me, but the rest are not ready yet. He has just brought this down from town. Is it not superb? Did you ever see such beauties?"

The diamonds flashed on her white wrist; she looked up at me with eyes almost as bright.

"I love beautiful stones," she said, "and I feel as if these were alive. Oh, do look at the rays of colour in them, as many as in the rainbow."

I congratulated Lady Ridsdale on possessing such a splendid ornament, and then glanced at Vyner, expecting him to say something.

The expression on his face startled me, and I was destined to remember it by-and-by. The ruddy look had completely left it, his eyes were half starting from his head. He peered close, and suddenly, without the slightest warning, stretched out his hand, and touched the diamonds as they glittered round Lady Ridsdale's wrist. She started back haughtily, then, recovering herself, took the bracelet off and put it into his hand.

"Charlie tells me," she said, "that this bracelet is worth from fifteen to twenty thousand pounds."

"You must take care of it," remarked Vyner; "don't let your maid see it, for instance."

"Oh, nonsense!" laughed Lady Ridsdale. "I would trust Louise as I would trust myself."

Soon afterwards we separated, and I went down to my little cabin to prepare for dinner. When we met in the dining saloon I noticed that Lady Ridsdale was wearing the diamond bracelet. Almost immediately after dinner the band came on board and the dancing began.

We kept up our festivities until two o'clock, and more than once, as she flashed past me, I could not help noticing the glittering circlet round her wrist. I considered myself a fair judge of precious stones, but had never seen any diamonds for size and brilliancy to equal these.

As Vyner and I happened to stand apart from the others he remarked upon them.

"It was imprudent of Ridsdale to bring those diamonds here," he said. "Suppose they are stolen?"

"Scarcely likely," I answered; "there are no thieves on board."

He gave an impatient movement.

"As far as we know there are not," he said slowly, "but one can never tell. The diamonds are of exceptional value, and it is not safe to expose ordinary folk to temptation. That small circlet means a fortune."

He sighed deeply, and when I spoke to him next did not answer me. Not long afterwards our gay party dispersed, and we retired to our respective cabins.

I went to mine and was quickly in bed. As a newly-arrived guest I was given a cabin on board, but several other members of the party were sleeping in tents on the shore. Vyner and Lord Ridsdale were amongst the latter number. Whether it was the narrowness of my bunk or the heat of the night, I cannot tell, but sleep I could not. Suddenly through my open window I heard voices from the shore near by. I could identify the speakers by their tones—one was my host, Lord Ridsdale, the other Ralph Vyner. Whatever formed the subject of discourse it was evidently far from amicable. However much averse I might feel to the situation, I was compelled to be an unwilling eavesdropper, for the voices rose, and I caught the following words from Vyner:

"Can you lend me five thousand pounds till the winter?"

"No, Vyner, I have told you so before, and the reason too. It is your own fault, and you must take the consequences."

"Do you mean that to be final?" asked Vyner.

"Yes."

"Very well, then I shall look after myself. Thank God, I have got brains if I have not money, and I shall not let the means interfere with the end."

"You can go to the devil for all I care," was the angry answer, "and, after what I know, I won't raise a finger to help you."

The speakers had evidently moved further off, for the last words I could not catch. But what little I heard by no means conduced to slumber. So Vyner, for all his jovial and easy manner, was in a fix for money, and Ridsdale knew something about him scarcely to his credit!

I kept thinking over this, and also recalling his words when he spoke of Lady Ridsdale's diamonds as representing a fortune. What did he mean by saying that he would not let the means interfere with the end? That brief sentence sounded very much like the outburst of a desperate man. I could not help heartily wishing that Lady Ridsdale's diamond circlet was back in London, and, just before I dropped to sleep, I made up my mind to speak to Ridsdale on the subject.

Towards morning I did doze off, but I was awakened by hearing my name called, and, starting up, I saw Ridsdale standing by my side. His face looked queer and excited.

"Wake up, Bell," he cried; "a terrible thing has happened."

"What is it?" I asked.

"My wife's bracelet is stolen."

Like a flash I thought of Vyner, and then as quickly I knew that I must be careful to give no voice to hastily-formed suspicions.

"I won't be a moment dressing, and then I'll join you," I said.

Ridsdale nodded and left my cabin.

In five minutes I was with him on deck. He then told me briefly what had happened.

"Helena most imprudently left the case on her dressing-table last night," he said, "and owing to the heat she kept the window open. Some one must have waded into the water in the dark and stolen it. Perhaps one of the bandsmen may have noticed the flashing of the diamonds on her wrist and returned to secure the bracelet—

there's no saying. The only too palpable fact is that it is gone—it was valued at twenty thousand pounds!"

"Have you sent for the police?" I asked.

"Yes, and have also wired to Scotland Yard for one of their best detectives. Vyner took the telegram for me, and was to call at the police station on his way back. He is nearly as much upset as I am. This is a terrible loss. I feel fit to kill myself for my folly in bringing that valuable bracelet on board a house-boat."

"It was a little imprudent," I answered, "but you are sure to get it back."

"I hope so," he replied moodily.

Just then the punt with Vyner and a couple of policemen on board was seen rapidly approaching. Ridsdale went to meet them, and was soon in earnest conversation with the superintendent of police. The moment Vyner leapt on board he came to the part of the deck where I was standing.

"Ah, Bell," he cried, "what about my prognostications of last night?"

"They have been verified too soon," I answered. I gave him a quick glance. His eyes looked straight into mine.

"Have you any theory to account for the theft?" I asked.

"Yes, a very simple one. Owing to the heat of the evening the Countess slept with her window open. It was an easy matter to wade through the water, introduce a hand through the open window and purloin the diamonds."

"Without being seen by any occupants of the tents?" I queried.

"Certainly," he answered, speaking slowly and with thought.

"Then you believe the thief came from without?"

"I do."

"What about your warning to Lady Ridsdale yesterday evening not to trust her maid?"

I saw his eyes flash. It was the briefest of summer lightning that played in their depths. I knew that he longed to adopt the suggestion that I had on purpose thrown out, but dared not. That one look was enough for me. I had guessed his secret.

Before he could reply to my last remark Lord Ridsdale came up.

"What is to be done?" he said; "the police superintendent insists on our all, without respect of persons, being searched."

"There is nothing in that," I said; "it is the usual thing. I will be the first to submit to the examination."

The police went through their work thoroughly, and, of course, came across neither clue nor diamonds. We presently sat down to breakfast, but I don't think we any of us had much appetite. Lady Ridsdale's eyes were red with crying, and I could see that the loss had shaken both her nerve and fortitude. It was more or less of a relief when the post came in. Amongst the letters I found a telegram for myself. I knew what it meant before I opened it. It was from a man in a distant part of the country whom I had promised to assist in a matter of grave importance. I saw that it was necessary for me to return to town without delay. I was very loth to leave my host and hostess in their present dilemma, but there was no help for it, and soon after breakfast I took my leave. Ridsdale promised to write me if there was any news of the diamonds, and soon the circumstance passed more or less into the background of my brain, owing to the intense interest of the other matter which I had taken up. My work in the north was over, and I had returned to town, when I received a letter from Ridsdale.

"We are in a state of despair," he wrote; "we have had two detectives on board, and the police have moved heaven and earth to try and discover the bracelet—all in vain; not the slightest clue has been forthcoming. No one has worked harder for us than Vyner. He has a small place of his own further down the river, and comes up to see us almost daily. He has made all sorts of suggestions for the recovery of the diamonds, but hitherto they have led to nothing. In short, our one hope now turns upon you, Bell; you have done as difficult things as this before. Will you come and see us, and give us the benefit of your advice? If any man can solve this mystery, you are the person."

I wrote immediately to say that I would return to the Theodora on the following evening, and for the remainder of that day tried to the best of my ability to think out this most difficult problem. I felt morally certain that I could put my hand on the thief, but I had no real clue to work upon—nothing beyond a nameless suspicion. Strange as it may seem, I was moved by sentiment. I had spent some pleasant hours in Vyner's society—I had enjoyed his conversation; I had liked the man for himself. He had abilities above the average, of that I was certain—if he were proved guilty, I did not want to be the one to bring his crime home to him. So uncomfortable were my feelings that at last I made up my mind to take a somewhat bold step. This was neither more nor less than to go to see Vyner himself before visiting the house-boat. What I was to do and say when I got to him I was obliged to leave altogether to chance; but I had a feeling almost amounting to a certainty that by means of this visit I should ultimately return the bracelet to my friends the Ridsdales.

The next afternoon I found myself rowing slowly down the river, thinking what the issue of my visit to Vyner would be. It happened to be a perfect evening. The sun had just set. The long reach of river stretched away to the distant bend, where, through the gathering twilight, I could just see the white gates of the Eight-Mile Lock. Raising my voice, I sang out in a long-drawn, sonorous monotone the familiar cry of "Lock! lock! lock!" and, bending to the sculls, sent my little skiff flying down stream. The sturdy figure of old James Pegg, the lock-keeper, whom I had known for many years, instantly appeared on the bridge. One of the great gates slowly swung open, and, shipping my sculls, I shot in, and called out a cheery good-evening to my old friend.

"Mr. Bell!" exclaimed the old fellow, hurrying along the edge of the lock. "Well, I never! I did not see it was you at first, and yet I ought to have known that long, swinging stroke of yours. You are the last person I expected to see. I was half afraid it might be some one else, although I don't know that I was expecting any one in particular. Excuse me, sir, but was it you called out 'Lock' just now?"

"Of course it was," I answered, laughing. "I'm in the deuce of a hurry to-night, Jimmy, as I want to get on to Wotton before dark. Look sharp, will you, and let me down."

"All right, sir—but you did frighten me just now. I wish you hadn't called out like that!"

As I glanced up at him, I was surprised to see that his usually ruddy, round face was as white as a sheet, and he was breathing quickly.

"Why, what on earth is the matter, Jimmy?" I cried; "how can I have frightened you?"

"Oh, it's nothing, sir; I suppose I'm an old fool," he faltered, smiling. "I don't know what's the matter with me, sir—I'm all of a tremble. The fact is, something happened here last night, and I don't seem to have got over it. You know, I am all by myself here now, sir, and a lonely place it is."

"Something happened?" I said; "not an accident, I hope?"

"No, sir, no accident that I know of, and yet I have been half expecting one to occur all day, and I have been that weak I could hardly wind up the sluices. I am getting old now, and I'm not the man I was; but I'm right glad to see you, Mr. Bell, that I am."

He kept pausing as he spoke, and now and then glanced up the river, as if expecting to see a boat coming round the bend every moment. I was much puzzled by his extraordinary manner. I knew him to be a steady man, and one whose services were much valued by the Conservancy; but it needed only a glance now to show that there was something very much amiss with him.

The darkness was increasing every moment, and, being anxious to get on as soon as possible, I was just going to tell him again to hurry up with the sluices, when he bent down close to me, and said,—

"Would you mind stepping out for a moment, sir, if you can spare the time? I wish to speak to you, sir. I'd be most grateful if you would wait a minute or two."

"Certainly, Jimmy," I answered, hauling myself to the side with the boat-hook, and getting out. "Is there anything I can do for you? I am afraid you are not well. I never saw you like this before."

"No, sir; and I never felt like it before, that I can remember. Something happened here last night that has taken all the nerve out of me, and I want to tell you what it was. I know you are so clever, Mr. Bell, and I have heard about your doings up at Wallinghurst last autumn, when you cleared up the Manor House ghost, and got old Monkford six months."

"Well, fire away," I said, filling my pipe, and wondering what was coming.

"It is this way, sir," he began. "Last night after I had had my supper I thought I'd like a stroll and a quiet smoke along the towing path before turning in. I did not expect any more boats, as it was getting on for ten o'clock. I walked about three-quarters of a mile, and was just going to turn round, when I saw a light down on the surface of the water in mid-stream. It was pretty dark, for the moon was not up yet, and there was a thick white mist rising from the water. I thought it must be some one in a canoe at first, so I waited a bit and watched. Then it suddenly disappeared, and the next instant I saw it again about a hundred yards or so higher up the stream, but only for a second, and then it went out. It fairly puzzled me to know what it could be, as I had never seen anything like it before. I felt sure it wasn't any sort of craft, but I had heard of strange lights being seen at times on the water—what they call jack-o'-lanterns, I believe, sir. I reckoned it might be one of them, but I thought I'd get back to the lock, so that, if it was a canoe, I could let it through. However, nothing came of it, and I waited and watched, and worried all the evening about it, but couldn't come to any sort of idea, so I went to bed. Well, about one o'clock this morning I suddenly woke up and thought I could hear some one a long way off calling exactly as you did just now, 'Lock! lock! lock!' but it sounded ever so far away.

"'It's some of those theatre people coming back to the Will-o'-the-Wisp house-boat,' I said to myself, 'and I'm not going to turn out for them.' The lock was full at the time, so I thought I would just let them work it for themselves. I waited a bit, expecting to hear them every minute come up, singing and swearing as they do, but they never came, and I was just dropping off when I heard the call again. It was not an ordinary sort of voice, but a long, wailing cry, just as if some one was in trouble or drowning. 'Hi! hi! Lock! lo-oock!' it went.

"I got up then and went out. The moon was up now and quite bright, and the mist had cleared off, so I went to the bridge on the upper gates and looked up stream. This is where I was standing, sir, just as we are standing now. I could see right up to the bend, and there was not the sign of a boat. I stood straining my eyes, expecting to see a boat come round every moment, when I heard the cry again, and this time it sounded not fifty yards up stream. I could not make it out at all, so I shouted out as loud as I could, 'Who are you? What's the matter?' but there was no answer; and then suddenly, the next instant, close below me, from inside the lock this time, just here, came a shout, piercing, shrill, and loud, 'Open the lock, quick, quick! Open the lock!'

"I tell you, sir, my heart seemed to stand dead still, and I nearly fell back over the bridge. I wheeled round sharp, but there was nothing in the lock, that I'll swear to my dying day—for I could see all over it, and nothing could have got in there without passing me. The moon was quite bright, and I could see all round it. Without knowing what I was doing, I rushed down like mad to the lower gates, and began to wind up one of the sluices, and then I stood there and waited, but nothing came. As the lock emptied I looked down, but there was no sign of anything anywhere, so I let down the sluice without opening the gates, and then filled up the lock again. I stood by the post, hardly daring to move, when, about half-past five, thank God, I heard the whistle of a tug, and, after seeing her through, it was broad daylight.

"That's the whole story, sir, and how I'm going to live through the night again I don't know. It was a spirit if ever there was one in the world. It's a warning to me, sir; and what's going to happen I don't know."

"Well, Jimmy," I answered, "it certainly is a most extraordinary story, and if I didn't know you as well as I do, I should say you had taken something more than a smoke before you turned in last night."

"I never touch a drop, sir, except when I go into Farley and have a glass of beer, but I have not been there for more than a week now."

I confess that Jimmy's story had left a most unpleasant impression on me. I had little doubt that the whole thing was some strange subjective hallucination, but for a weird and ghostly experience it certainly beat most of the tales I had ever heard. I thought for a moment—it was now quite dark, and I felt little inclined to go on to Wotton. My keenest interests were awakened.

"Look here," I said, "what do you say if I stay here to-night? Can you give me a shake-down of any sort?"

"That I will, sir, and right gladly, and thank God if you will but stay with me. If I was alone here again, and heard that voice, I believe it would kill me. I'll tie up your boat outside, and bring your things in, and then we'll have supper. I'll feel a new man with you staying here, sir."

In a few minutes we were both inside old Jimmy's cosy quarters. His whole bearing seemed to have changed suddenly, and he ran about with alacrity, getting supper ready, and seeming quite like himself again. During the whole evening he kept harping at intervals on the subject of the mysterious voice, but we heard no sound whatever, and I felt more and more certain that the whole thing was due to hallucination on the part of the old man. At eleven o'clock a skiff came up through the lock, and almost immediately afterwards I bade Jimmy good-night and went into the little room he had prepared for me.

I went quickly to bed, and, tired after my long pull, despite the originality of the situation, fell fast asleep. Suddenly I awoke—some one was bending over me and calling me by my name. I leapt up, and, not realising where I was for the moment, but with a sort of dim idea that I was engaged in some exposure, instinctively seized the man roughly by the throat. In a moment I remembered everything, and quickly released my grip of poor old Jimmy, who was gurgling and gasping with horror. I burst out laughing at my mistake, and begged his pardon for treating him so roughly.

"It is all right, sir," he panted. "I hope I didn't frighten you, but I have heard it again, not five minutes ago."

"The deuce you have," I said, striking a match and looking at my watch.

It was nearly two o'clock, and before the minute was up I heard distinctly a cry, as if from some great distance, of "Lock, lock, lock!" and then all was silence again.

"Did you hear it, sir?" whispered the old man, clutching me by the arm with a trembling hand.

"Yes, I heard it," I said. "Don't you be frightened, Jimmy; just wait till I get my clothes on; I am going to see this thing through."

"Be careful, sir; for God's sake, be careful," he whispered.

"All right," I said, slipping on some things. "Just get me a good strong boat-hook, and don't make too much noise. If this mystery is flesh and blood I'll get to the bottom of it somehow. You stay here; and if I call, come out."

I took the thick, short boat-hook which he had brought me and, softly unlatching the door, went out.

The moon was now riding high overhead and casting black fantastic shadows across the little white cottage. All my senses were on the keenest alert, my ears were pricked up for the slightest sound. I crept softly to the bridge on the upper gate which was open. I looked up stream and thought I could see some little ripples on the surface of the water as if a swift boat had just passed down, but there was no sign of any craft whatever to be seen. It was intensely still, and no sound broke the silence save the intermittent croaking of some bull-frogs in the dark shadows of the pollards on the further bank. Behind me could also be heard the gurgling twinkle of the overflow through the chinks of the lower gate.

I stood quite still, gripping the boat-hook in my hand, and looking right and left, straining my eyes for the slightest movement of anything around, when suddenly, close below me from the water, inside the lock, came a loud cry—

"Open the lock, for God's sake, open the lock!"

I started back, feeling my hair rise and stiffen. The sound echoed and reverberated through the silent night, and then died away; but before it had done so I had sprung to the great beam and closed the upper gate. As I did so I caught sight of the old man trembling and shaking at the door of the cottage. I called to him to go and watch the upper gate, and, racing down to the lower ones, wound up one of the sluices with a few pulls, so as to let out the water with as little escape room as possible. I knew by this means if there were any creature of tangible form in the water we must find it when the lock was emptied, as its escape was cut off.

Each of the following minutes seemed stretched into a lifetime as, with eyes riveted on the dark water in the lock, I watched its gradual descent. I hardly dared to think of what I expected to see rise to the surface any moment. Would the lock never empty? Down, down sank the level, and still I saw nothing. A long, misshapen arm of black cloud was slowly stretching itself across the moon.

Hark! there was something moving about down in the well of darkness below me, and as I stood and watched I saw that the water was uncovering a long, black mass and that something ran slowly out of the water and began to clamber up the slimy, slippery beams. What in the name of heaven could it be? By the uncertain light I could only see its dim outline; it seemed to have an enormous bulbous head and dripping, glistening body. The sound of a rapid patter up the tow-path told me that the old man had seen it and was running for his life.

I rushed down to where the thing was, and as its great head appeared above the edge, with all my force struck it a terrific blow with the boat-hook. The weapon flew into splinters in my hand, and the next moment the creature had leapt up beside me and dashed me to the ground with almost superhuman force. I was up and on to it again in a second, and as I caught and closed with it saw that I had at least to deal with a human being, and that what he lacked in stature he more than made up for in strength. The struggle that ensued was desperate and furious. The covering to his head that had splintered the boat-hook was, I saw, a sort of helmet, completely protecting the head from any blow, and the body was cased in a slippery, closely fitting garment that kept eluding my grasp. To and fro we swayed and wrestled, and for a moment I thought I had met my match till, suddenly freeing my right arm, I got in a smashing blow in the region of the heart. The creature uttered a cry of pain and fell headlong to the ground.

Old Jimmy Pegg had hurried back as soon as he heard our struggles and knew that he was not dealing with a being of another world. He ran up eagerly to me.

"Here's your ghost, you old coward!" I panted; "he has got the hardest bone and muscle I ever felt in a ghost yet. I am not used to fighting men in helmets, and he is as slippery as an eel, but I hope to goodness I have not done more than knock the wind out of him. He is a specimen I should rather like to take alive. Catch hold of his feet and we'll get him inside and see who he is."

Between us we carried the prostrate figure inside the cottage and laid him down like a log on the floor. He never moved nor uttered a sound, and I was afraid at first that I had finished him for good and all. I next knelt down and proceeded to unfasten the helmet, which, from its appearance, was something like the kind used by divers, while the old man brought the lantern close to his face. At the first glance I knew in an instant that I had seen the face before, and the next second recognised, to my utter astonishment and horror, that it belonged to Ralph Vyner.

For the moment I was completely dumbfounded, and gazed at the man without speaking. It was obvious that he had only fainted from the blow, for I could see that he was breathing, and in a few minutes he opened his eyes and fixed them on me with a dull and vacant stare. Then he seemed to recall the situation, though he evidently did not recognise me.

"Let me go," he cried, making an effort to rise. "My God! you have killed me." He pressed his hand to his side and fell back again: his face was contorted as if in great pain.

There was obviously only one thing to be done, and that was to send for medical assistance at once. It was clear that the man was badly injured, but to what extent I could not determine. It was impossible to extract the slightest further communication from him—he lay quite still, groaning from time to time.

I told Jimmy to go off at once to Farley and bring the doctor. I scribbled a few directions on a piece of paper.

The old man hurried out of the cottage, but in less than a minute he was back again in great excitement.

"Look here, sir, what I have just picked up," he said; "it's something he has dropped, I reckon."

As Jimmy spoke he held out a square leather case: there was a monogram on it. I took it in my hand and pressed the lid; it flew open, and inside, resting on its velvet bed, lay the glittering circlet of diamonds. I held Lady Ridsdale's lost bracelet in my hand. All my suspicions were confirmed: Vyner was the thief.

Without saying a word I shut the box and despatched the old man at once for the doctor, bidding him go as fast as he could. Then I sat down by the prostrate man and waited. I knew that Jimmy could not be back for at least two hours. The grey dawn was beginning to steal in through the little latticed window when Vyner moved, opened his eyes and looked at me. He started as his eyes fell on the case.

"You are Mr. Bell," he said slowly. "Ridsdale told me that you were coming to the Theodora on purpose to discover the mystery of the lost diamonds. You didn't know that I should give you an opportunity of discovering the truth even before you arrived at the house-boat. Bend down close to me—you have injured me; I may not recover; hear what I have to say."

I bent over him, prepared to listen to his words, which came out slowly.

"I am a forger and a desperate man. Three weeks ago I forged one of Ridsdale's cheques and lessened my friend's balance to the tune of five thousand pounds. He and his wife were old friends of mine, but I wanted the money desperately, and was impervious to sentiment or anything else. On that first day when you met me, although I seemed cheery enough, I was fit to kill myself. I had hoped to be able to restore the stolen money long before Ridsdale was likely to miss it. But this hope had failed. I saw no loophole of escape, and the day of reckoning could not be far off. What devil prompted Ridsdale to bring those diamonds on board, Heaven only knows. The moment I saw them they fascinated me and I knew I should have a try for them. All during that evening's festivity I could think of nothing else. I made up my mind to secure them by hook or by crook. Before we retired for the night, however, I thought I would give Ridsdale a chance. I asked him if he would lend me the exact sum I had already stolen from him, five thousand pounds, but he had heard rumours to my discredit and refused point-blank. I hated him for it. I went into my tent under the pretence of lying down, but in reality to concoct and, if possible, carry out my plot. I waited until the quietest hour before dawn, then I slipped out of my tent, waded into the water, approached the open window of the Countess's cabin, thrust in my hand, took out the case, and, going down the river about a quarter of a mile, threw the diamonds into the middle of the stream. I marked well the place where they sank; I then returned to my tent and went to bed.

"You know what occurred the following morning. I neither feared Ridsdale nor his wife, but you, Bell, gave me a considerable amount of uneasiness. I felt certain that in an evil moment on the night before I had given you a clue. To a man of your ability the slightest clue was all-sufficient. I felt that I must take the bull by the horns and find out whether you suspected me or not. I talked to you, and guessed by the tone of your remarks that you had your suspicions. My relief was immense when that telegram arrived which hurried you away from the Theodora. On the following day I returned to my own little place on the banks of the river four miles below this lock. I knew it was necessary for me to remain quiet for a time, but all the same my plans were clearly made, and I only waited until the first excitement of the loss had subsided and the police and detectives were off their guard. In the meantime I went to see Ridsdale almost daily, and suggested many expedients for securing the thief and getting hold of the right clue. If he ever suspected me, which I don't for a moment suppose, I certainly put him off the scent. My intention was to take the diamonds out of the country, sell them for all that I could get, then return the five thousand pounds which I had stolen from his bank, and leave England for ever. As a forger I should be followed to the world's end, but as the possessor of stolen diamonds I felt myself practically safe. My scheme was too cleverly worked out to give the ordinary detective a chance of discovering me.

"Two days ago I had a letter from Ridsdale in which he told me that he intended to put the matter into your hands. Now this was by no means to my mind, for you, Bell, happened to be the one man in the world whom I really dreaded. I saw that I must no longer lose time. Under my little boat-house I had a small submarine boat which I had lately finished, more as a hobby than anything else. I had begun it years ago in my odd moments on a model I had seen of a torpedo used in the American War. My boat is now in the lock outside, and you will see for yourself what ingenuity was needed to construct such a thing. On the night before the one which has just passed, I got it ready, and, as soon as it was dark, started off in it to recover the diamonds. I got through the lock easily by going in under the water with a barge, but when I reached the spot where I had sunk the diamonds, found to my dismay that my electric light would not work. There was no help for it—I could not find the bracelet without the aid of the light, and was bound to return home to repair the lamp. This delay was fraught with danger, but there was no help for it. My difficulty now was to get back through the lock; for though I waited for quite three hours no boats came along. I saw the upper gates were open, but how to get through the lower ones I could not conceive. I felt sure that my only chance was to frighten the lock-keeper, and get him to open the sluices, for I knew I could pass through them unobserved if they were open, as I had done once before.

"In my diver's helmet was a thick glass face-piece. This had an opening, closed by a cap, which could be unscrewed, and through which I could breathe when above water, and also through which my voice would come, causing a peculiar hollowness which I guessed would have a very startling effect, especially as I myself would be quite invisible. I got into the lock, and shouted to Pegg. I succeeded in frightening him; he hurried to do what I ordered. He wound up the lower sluice, I shot through under water, and so got back unseen. All yesterday I hesitated about trying the experiment again, the risk was so great; but I knew that Ridsdale was certain to see his bank-book soon, that my forgery was in imminent danger of being discovered, also that you, Bell, were coming upon the scene.

"Yes, at any risk, I must now go on.

"I repaired my light, and again last night passed through the lock on my way up, by simply waiting for another boat. As a matter of fact, I passed up through this lock under a skiff about eleven o'clock. My light was now all right, I found the diamond case easily, and turned to pass down the stream by the same method as before. If you had not been here I should have succeeded, and should have been safe, but now it is all up."

He paused, and his breath came quickly.

"I doubt if I shall recover," he said in a feeble voice.

"I hope you will," I replied; "and hark! I think I hear the doctor's steps."

I was right, for a moment or two later old Jimmy Pegg and Dr. Simmons entered the cottage. While the doctor was examining the patient and talking to him, I went out with Jimmy to have a look at the submarine boat. By fixing a rope round it we managed to haul it up, and then proceeded to examine it. It certainly was the most wonderful piece of ingenious engineering I had ever seen. The boat was in the shape of an enormous cigar, and was made of aluminium. It was seven feet long, and had a circular beam of sixteen inches. At the pointed end, close to where the occupant's feet would be, was an air chamber capable of being filled or emptied at will by means of a compressed air cylinder, enabling the man to rise or sink whenever he wished to. Inside, the boat was lined with flat chambers of compressed air for breathing purposes, which were governed by a valve. It was also provided with a small accumulator and electric motor which drove the tiny propeller astern. The helmet which the man wore fitted around the opening at the head end.

After examining the boat it was easy to see how Vyner had escaped through the lock the night before I arrived, as this submarine wonder of ingenuity would be able to shoot through the sluice gate under water, when the sluice was raised to empty the lock.

After exchanging a few remarks with Jimmy, I returned to the cottage to learn the doctor's verdict.

It was grave, but not despairing. The patient could not be moved for a day or two. He was, in Dr. Simmons's opinion, suffering more from shock than anything else. If he remained perfectly quiet, he would in all probability recover; if he were disturbed, the consequences might be serious.

An hour afterwards I found myself on my way up stream sculling as fast as I could in the direction of the Theodora. I arrived there at an early hour, and put the case which contained the diamonds into Lady Ridsdale's hands.

I shall never forget the astonishment of Ridsdale and his wife when I told my strange tale. The Countess burst into tears, and Ridsdale was terribly agitated.

"I have known Vyner from a boy, and so has my wife," he exclaimed. "Of course, this proves him to be an unmitigated scoundrel, but I cannot be the one to bring him to justice."

"Oh, no, Charlie, whatever happens we must forgive him," said Lady Ridsdale, looking up with a white face.

I had nothing to say to this, it was not my affair. Unwittingly I had been the means of restoring to the Ridsdales their lost bracelet; they must act as they thought well with regard to the thief.

As a matter of fact, Vyner did escape the full penalty of his crime. Having got back the diamonds Lord Ridsdale would not prosecute. On the contrary, he helped the broken-down man to leave the country. From the view of pure justice he was, of course, wrong, but I could not help being glad.

As an example of what a desperate man will do, I think it would be difficult to beat Vyner's story. The originality and magnitude of the conception, the daring which enabled the man, single-handed, to do his own dredging in a submarine boat in one of the reaches of the Thames have seldom been equalled.

As I thought over the whole scheme, my only regret was that such ability should not have been devoted to nobler ends.

HOW SIVA SPOKE

During the summer of the past year a medical friend of mine sent me an invitation to dine with him and two of his fellow-craftsmen at the Welcome Club at the Earl's Court Exhibition. One of our party was a certain Dr. Laurier, a young man of considerable ability, whose special attention had been directed to mental diseases. He was, indeed, a noted authority on this subject, and had just completed an appointment at one of the large London asylums. During dinner he entertained us with a few of his late experiences—

"I assure you, Mr. Bell," he said, "there is absolutely no limit to the vagaries of the human mind. At the present moment a most grotesque and painful form of mental disease has come under my notice. The patient is not a pauper, but a gentleman of good standing and means. He is unmarried, and owns a lovely place in the country. He spent the early years of his life in India, and when there the craze began which now assumes the magnitude of a monomania."

"Pray let me hear about him, if your professional etiquette allows you to talk on the subject," I answered.

"I will certainly tell you what I can," he replied. "I have known the man for years, having met him in town on several occasions. Last week his nephew came to see me, and spoke seriously with regard to his uncle's state of mind. His great craze for years has been spiritualism, theosophy, and mahatmas, with all their attendant hocus-pocus. He firmly believes in his power to call up spirits from the vasty deep, and holds many extraordinary séances."

"But surely such a craze is not sufficient to prove insanity!" I said. "Hundreds of people believe in such manifestations at the present day."

"I know that well, and perfectly harmless such crazes are so long as the victims confine their beliefs to spirit-rapping, table-turning, and humbug of that sort; but when their convictions lead them to commit actions which compromise serious interests, and when, as in this case, there is a possibility of life itself being in danger, it is time they should be looked after."

"What is the particular nature of your friend's delusion?" I asked.

"This. He is practically a Brahmin, having been deeply imbued with the peculiar doctrines of Brahminism when in India. Amongst his friends in the East was a Brahmin of high degree in whose house were three idols, representing the Hindu Trinity—Vishnu, Brahma, and Siva. By some means which have never been explained to me, my friend managed to get possession of Siva, and brought the idol home. He placed it in a gallery which he has in his house, believing from the first that it possessed mystical properties which it was his duty to fathom. The nephew now tells me that he has brought his craze to such a pass that he firmly believes that Siva speaks to him in Hindustanee. The unhappy man kneels nightly at the altar in front of the idol, receiving, as he imagines, directions from him. The consequence is that he does all sorts of mad and extraordinary things, spending his large fortune lavishly in the decoration of this hideous monster, buying pearls, rubies, and even diamonds for the purpose, and really being, as he imagines, guided by it in the disposition of his life and property. He has a young niece residing with him, to whom he has always been very much attached; but of late he has been cruel to her, banishing her from his presence, refusing her his sympathy, and has even gone to the length of threatening to take her life, saying quite openly that Siva informs him night after night of her treachery towards him. Now the nephew is engaged to this girl, and is naturally anxious about her; but, say what he will, nothing will induce her to turn against her uncle, to whom she is deeply attached. She denies that he threatens her life, although the nephew declares that he did so in his own presence. Under such circumstances, her friends are, naturally, most anxious about her, and feel it their duty to get a medical opinion with regard to the uncle. I am going down to his place to-morrow, and shall there meet his regular medical attendant in consultation."

"And then, I suppose, certify as to his insanity?" I answered.

"Doubtless; that is, if we come to the conclusion that the man is really insane."

"What an awful responsibility is reposed in you doctors!" I said. "Think what it means to condemn a man to a lunatic asylum. In the hands of the unscrupulous such a power is terrible."

Dr. Laurier knitted his brows, and looked keenly at me.

"What do you mean?" he said in a curious tone. "Of course mistakes are made now and then, but not, I believe, often. To act in good faith and exercise reasonable care are the two requisites of the law."

"Of course," I replied, "there are great difficulties on both sides of this momentous question; but if I belonged to the profession, I can frankly say that nothing would induce me to sign a certificate of lunacy."

A few moments afterwards we all rose and strolled about the grounds. As we were parting at the exit gates I called Dr. Laurier aside.

"The love of mystery is to me a ruling passion," I said. "Will you excuse the great liberty I take when I ask you to let me know the result of your visit of to-morrow? I am immensely interested in your spiritualist patient."

As I spoke I scribbled my address on a card and handed it to him, half expecting that he would resent my intrusiveness. A smile flitted across his clever face, and he stood looking at me for a moment under the glare of the great arc lights.

"I will certainly give you the result of my visit, as you are so much interested," he replied. "Good-night."

We got into our respective hansoms, and drove off in different directions.

I had much to do, and soon forgot both Dr. Laurier and his patient; therefore, on the following Monday, when he was ushered into my presence, my surprise was great.

"I have come to fulfil my promise," he began. "I am here not only to satisfy your curiosity about my patient, but also to ask your advice. The fact is the matter has, I think, now merged more into your domain than mine."

"Pray tell me what has happened," I asked.

"That is what I am about to do; but first I must ensure your absolute confidence and secrecy, for my professional reputation may be seriously compromised if it is known that I consulted you."

I gave him the assurance, and he proceeded:—

"My patient's name is Edward Thesiger; he lives in a place called The Hynde, in Somersetshire. I went down as I had arranged, and was met at the station by his nephew, Jasper Bagwell. Bagwell is a thin, anxious-looking man of about five-and-thirty. He drove me over to The Hynde, and I was there met by Thesiger's own physician, Dr. Dalton. Dalton and I each made a separate examination of the patient, and came to the conclusion that he was undoubtedly queer.

"In the course of the afternoon we were all wandering round the grounds, when we were joined by the young girl to whom Bagwell is engaged. When she saw me she gave me a very eager glance, and soon attached herself to my side.

"'I want to speak to you, Dr. Laurier,' she said in a low voice.

"I managed to drop behind in order to give her an opportunity.

"'I know what you have come about,' she said. 'What do you think of my uncle's case?'

"'I am not prepared to hazard an opinion,' I replied.

"'Well, please listen to something I have got to say. Jasper Bagwell has his own reasons for what he tells you. You do very wrong to listen to him. Uncle Edward is queer, I grant, with regard to the idol Siva, that is because he is in reality a Brahmin; but if you sign a certificate to the effect that he is mad, you will be making a very terrible mistake.'

"As she spoke her lips trembled, and tears filled her eyes.

"'I am terribly unhappy about it all,' she continued.

"I looked at her earnestly, then I said in a low voice:

"'Forgive me if I reply to you as plainly as you have just spoken to me. You arouse my surprise when you speak as you do of Mr. Bagwell. Is it not the case that you are engaged to marry him?'

"She gave a visible start.

"'It is the case,' she answered slowly. Then she continued, speaking with great emphasis, 'I only marry my cousin because it is the one—the one chance of saving Uncle Edward.'

"'What do you mean?' I asked in astonishment.

"'I wish I could tell you, but I dare not. I am a very miserable girl. There is foul play somewhere, of that I am convinced. Oh, believe me! won't you believe me?'

"To these extraordinary words I made a somewhat dubious reply, and she soon left me, to walk by her uncle's side.

"Late that evening I was alone with the patient, and he then confided to me much which he had withheld at first. He spoke about the years he had spent in India, and in especial alluded to the Brahmin religion. He told me also that he now possesses the idol Siva, and has set it up in a marble gallery where he can hold his spiritualistic séances. Bending forward as he spoke, and fixing me with his intelligent and yet strange glance, he said solemnly, and with an appearance of perfect truth on his face, that by certain incenses and secret incantations he could make the idol speak to him in Hindustanee. He said further that he felt himself completely dominated by it, and was bound to obey all its dictates. As he said the latter words his face grew white to the lips.

"'Siva is exigent in his demands,' he said slowly— 'exigent and terrible. But come, I will take you into the gallery, and you shall see him for yourself.'

"I went gladly. We had to go through a long conservatory which opened out of the dining-room; from there we entered an oval-shaped room. Thesiger brought me straight up to the idol. It was placed upon a pedestal. It is a hideous monster made of wood, and has five heads; in its hand it holds a trident. I could hardly refrain from smiling when I first saw it. It was difficult to believe that any man, sane or insane, could hold faith in such a monstrosity. My object, however, was to draw the poor mad fellow out, and I begged of him to take what steps he considered necessary in order to induce the creature to speak. He willingly obeyed my desire, and with great solemnity went through elaborate operations; then, turning the lamp very low, knelt at the altar in front of the idol and began to address it. He waited for its replies, which were, of course, inaudible, and then continued speaking again. After some moments spent in this way he declared solemnly that it had replied to him, and practically called me a liar when I said I had not heard it.

"When he turned up the lamp at the end of this strange scene, I noticed for the first time that the idol was decorated with precious stones of extraordinary value. To leave such valuables in a room with an unlocked door was in itself a symptom of insanity, and when I parted with Thesiger for the night I had not the least doubt that my unfortunate host was really insane. All the same, I had a curious unwillingness with regard to signing the certificate. Bagwell eagerly asked me if I did not intend to sign. To his astonishment, I replied in the negative. I said that the case was a very peculiar one, and that it would be necessary for me to pay a second visit to the patient before I could take this extreme step. He was, I could see, intensely annoyed, but I remained firm."

Laurier stopped speaking and looked me full in the face.

"Well?" I asked.

"I have come to consult with you over the matter. You remember what you said about the responsibility of signing such certificates! It is on account of those words I have come to you."

"Well, Dr. Laurier," I answered, "I shall of course be happy to do anything I can to help you, but I must frankly confess that I fail to see exactly on what point I can be of service. I know little about disease in general, and nothing about mental diseases in particular. Miss Thesiger seems to think that there is foul play; but have you any suspicions on your own account?"

"I have no proofs, but, all the same, I do suspect foul play, although, perhaps, I have no right to say so."

"Then what do you want me to do?" I asked.

"This," he answered. "Will you come down with me to Somersetshire as my friend, and in the role of a great spiritualist? Thesiger will be only too delighted to meet some one of his own way of thinking. Will you come?"

I thought for a moment—it was not a role I cared to assume, but the case was peculiar, and might possibly lie within my province. I eventually agreed to accompany Laurier into Somersetshire, and, as a matter of fact, went down with him the next day. He had telegraphed our arrival to The Hynde, and a hearty invitation was accorded to me.

As we were driving through the grounds late the following afternoon we were met by a tall girl, who was accompanied by two thoroughbred retrievers.

"Here is Miss Thesiger," said Laurier. He called to the driver to stop, and jumping down, went to her side. I accompanied him.

"Miss Thesiger," said Laurier, "let me introduce my friend, Mr. John Bell."

She looked me full in the face, then her grey eyes seemed to lighten with momentary pleasure, and she held out her hand.

"What have you come back for?" she asked the next moment, turning to Laurier.

"To see your uncle."

"Are you to meet Dr. Dalton?" her lips trembled.

"I believe so. I assure you, Miss Thesiger, I have come with no sinister design." Laurier smiled as he spoke. "On the contrary, I am here to-day in order, if possible, to get at the truth. There is no one who can help me better than this gentleman."

"Then you do suspect foul play?" she said, her eyes lighting up with sudden hope.

"I have no reason to do so," he answered.

"It exists," she replied. "I know what I am saying; will you not believe me?" As she spoke she glanced hurriedly behind her—footsteps were heard rapidly approaching.

"There is my cousin," she said; "he follows me like a shadow. Dr. Laurier and Mr. Bell, I must see you both, or one of you, in private. I have something of great importance which you ought to know."

Before either of us could answer her, Jasper Bagwell came up. He gave us a polite welcome, and glanced keenly at his cousin, who took no notice of him, but continued her walk.

"Poor girl!" he said with a deep sigh, as we three walked slowly to the house.

"Why do you pity her?" I could not help asking.

"Because she is nearly as much under a delusion as my uncle himself. The fact is she is in the utmost danger, and yet refuses absolutely to believe it. The more eccentric my unfortunate uncle grows, the more she clings to him; she scarcely leaves his side, although it is most unsafe for her to be with him. I think it my absolute duty to watch her day and night, and am really almost worn out with anxiety. The whole of last night I spent in the corridor which divides her room from Mr. Thesiger's. Three times in the course of the night I saw the unfortunate madman gliding down this corridor, and but for my timely appearance on the scene I have not the slightest doubt that he would have entered Helen's room with the most fell design. I see the madness in his eye when he even glances at her. He told me solemnly not later than yesterday that Siva had laid it upon him to take her life, as she was opposed heart and soul to the doctrines of Brahminism, and was a serious obstacle in the way of the great work which my uncle was meant by the idol to undertake. I told Helen exactly what he said, but she goes on as if nothing were wrong. The fact is this, Laurier, if you don't sign that certificate I must get another doctor who will."

Bagwell's communications were certainly alarming, but we had scarcely time to reply to them before we reached the house. When we entered the hall the frown departed from his face like magic, he assumed a thoroughly pleasant manner, and conducted us quickly into the presence of the owner of the house.

Edward Thesiger was a handsome old man, tall and dignified in appearance. He possessed a particularly lofty and intelligent cast of face, aquiline features, and silver hair which flowed down over his shoulders. His face was clean shaven, which allowed the handsome curves of his mobile mouth to be plainly seen. His conversation betokened the man of learning, his words were well chosen, his manner was extremely calm and quiet. At a first glance no one could look more thoroughly sane.

During dinner that night I happened to be seated opposite Miss Thesiger. She was very silent, and seemed terribly depressed. I noticed that she often glanced at her uncle, and further observed that he carefully avoided meeting her eyes. When she came into the room he manifested distinct uneasiness, and when she retired to the drawing-room after dinner a look of relief filled his fine face. He drew up his chair near mine and began to talk.

"I am glad you were able to come," he said. "It is not often one has the privilege of meeting a thoroughly kindred spirit. Now, tell me, have you carefully studied Brahminism?"

"I have done so cursorily," I replied, "and have had from time to time curious dealings with the supernatural." I then added abruptly, "I am much interested to hear from Laurier that you, Mr. Thesiger, possess the idol Siva in this house."

"Hush!" he said, starting and turning very pale. "Do not say the name in such a loud and reckless tone." As he spoke he bent towards me, and his voice dropped. "Mr. Bell, I have extraordinary confidences which I can make to you by-and-by."

"I shall be happy to hear them," I answered.

"Have you had wine enough? Shall we go into the gallery now?"

I rose immediately. My host led me into a conservatory, and from there straight into a marble gallery. It was a curious-looking place, being a large oval chamber forty feet long, the walls were faced with marble, and a dado painted in Egyptian style ran round the room. Half way between the middle of the room and the end stood a fountain of curious design. It consisted of the bronze figure of a swan with wings outspread. From its bill the water issued and fell into a circular basin. Facing this fountain, twenty feet away, stood the idol, with its little altar in front of it. I went up and examined it with intense interest. The pedestal on which it rested was about three feet high—the idol itself was the same height, so that its five heads were almost on a level with my face. Round the neck, and decorating each of the heads, were jewels of extraordinary magnificence; the hand which held the trident was loaded with diamond rings. It is almost impossible to describe the sinister effect of this grotesque and horrible monster; and when I saw Mr. Thesiger gazing at it with a peculiar expression of reverence not unmixed with fear, I felt certain that Bagwell was right, and that the man was dangerously insane.

As I was thinking these thoughts my host groaned quite audibly, and then looked steadily at me.

"I am living through a very terrible time," he said in a low voice. "I am the victim of a strange and awful power." Here his words dropped to an intense whisper. "Years ago, when I became a Brahmin," he continued, "voluntarily giving up the faith in which I was born, I little knew to what such a step would lead. I stole Siva from the house of my Indian friend and brought the idol home. From the first it began to exercise a marvellous power over me. I had made a large fortune in India; and when I came to England, bought this place, and finding this curious gallery already in existence, had it lined with marble, and set up Siva in its midst. The study of the faith which I had adopted, the holding of spiritualistic séances and matters of that sort, occupied my time, and I became more and more imbued with the strange mysticism of my belief. As the years flew by I was more and more firmly convinced that what looks like mere wood is in reality imbued with strange and awful qualities. I shall never forget that terrible evening when Siva first spoke to me."

"How long ago was that?" I interrupted.

"Some months ago now. I was kneeling by the altar, and was speaking to him as usual, when I heard words uttered in Hindustanee. At first I could scarcely credit my own ears, but soon I grew accustomed to the fact that Siva wished to hold communication with me, and listened to him nightly. At the beginning of our remarkable intercourse he laid certain mandates upon me which resulted, as you see, in my decorating him with these precious stones. I felt bound to obey him, whatever he dictated; but of late he has told me—he has told me—" The old man began to shudder and tremble.

While he had been speaking to me he had been gazing at the idol; now he walked a few steps away and turned his back on it.

"Sooner or later I must obey him," he said in a feeble voice; "but the thing is driving me crazed—*crazed*."

"What is it?" I asked; "tell me, I beseech you."

"I cannot; it is too awful—it relates to the one I love best in the world. The sacrifice is too horrible, and yet I am drawn to it—I am drawn to the performing of an awful deed by a terrific power. Ask me no more, Mr. Bell; I see by your face that I have your pity."

"You have, truly," I answered.

I had scarcely said the last words before the door of the gallery was opened, and Miss Thesiger, Bagwell, and Laurier appeared. Miss Thesiger went straight to her uncle's side, and laid her hand on his shoulder.

"Must you stay up any longer?" she asked in a gentle voice. "I heard you walking about last night; you were restless and did not sleep. Do go to bed now; you seem so tired. I know these gentlemen will excuse you," she added, glancing from Laurier to me.

"Certainly," said Laurier. "I should recommend Mr. Thesiger to retire at once; he looks quite worn out."

"I shall go presently—presently," said Thesiger, in a somewhat curt voice. "Leave us, Helen; there's a good child; go, my dear."

"Go, Helen; don't irritate him," I heard Bagwell say.

She gave a quick, despairing glance from one man to the other; then, turning, left the room.

"And now, Mr. Thesiger," I said, "will you not grant me the favour of a séance?"

Mr. Thesiger remained gravely silent for a moment; then he said:

"By virtue of your power as a medium, you may be able to hear the voice, and so convince Dr. Laurier of its reality."

He then proceeded to go through some elaborate operations, and finally kneeling at the altar, began to speak Hindustanee.

It was about the strangest scene I had ever witnessed; and though I stood almost at his elbow, I could hear no sound whatever but his own voice.

"Siva will not speak to-night," he said, rising; "there must be some one here whose influence is adverse. I cannot hear him. It is strange!"

He looked puzzled, and more relieved than otherwise.

"You will go to bed now, sir," said Bagwell; "you look very tired."

"I am," he replied. "I will leave my friends with you, Jasper. You will see that they have all they want." He bade Laurier and me a courteous good-night, nodded to his nephew, and left the room.

"This is the most extraordinary phase of mental delusion I ever heard of," I said. "If you will permit me, Mr. Bagwell, I will examine this idol more particularly."

"You can do so if you please," he said, but he did not speak in a cordial tone.

"Examine it to your heart's content," he continued a moment later; "only pray don't disarrange it—he seems to know by instinct if it is touched. Bah! it is sickening. Shall we go into another room, gentlemen?"

Watching his face carefully, I resolved to make my examination in private, and now followed him into the smoking-room. We stayed there for a short time, talking in a desultory manner, and soon afterwards retired for the night.

On my dressing-table a note awaited me. I opened it hastily, and saw to my surprise that it was from Miss Thesiger.

"I could not get the opportunity I needed to-night," she wrote, "but will you meet me in the Laurel Walk to-morrow morning at five o'clock?"

I tore up the letter after reading it, and soon afterwards got into bed. I must confess that I slept badly that night; I felt worried and anxious. There was not the least doubt that Thesiger was mad; it was all too apparent that his madness was daily and hourly assuming a more and more dangerous form. The affectionate girl who clung to him ought undoubtedly to be removed from his neighbourhood.

At the hour named by Miss Thesiger, I rose, dressed, and stole downstairs through the silent house. I found her as she had indicated in the Laurel Walk.

"How good of you to come!" she said. "But we must not talk here; it would not be safe."

"What do you mean?" I answered. "No one can possibly watch us at this hour."

"Jasper may be about," she said; "as far as I can tell he seems never to sleep. I believe he paces outside my room the greater part of the night."

"You can scarcely blame him for that," I said; "he does it in order to ensure your safety."

She gave me an impatient glance.

"I see he has been talking to you," she replied; "but now it is necessary for you to hear my side of the story. Come into this summer-house; he will never guess that we are here."

Turning abruptly, she led the way into a small, tastefully arranged summer-house. Shutting the door behind her, she turned at once and faced me.

"Now," she said in an eager voice, "I will tell you everything. There is an unexplained mystery about all this, and I am convinced that Jasper is at the bottom of it."

"What do you mean?" I asked.

"I have nothing whatever but a woman's intuition to guide me, but, all the same, I am convinced of what I am saying. Before Jasper came home Uncle Edward was a Brahmin beyond doubt. His séances were intensely disagreeable to me, and I took care never to witness them nor to speak to him on the terrible subject of Siva; but, beyond the fact that he was a Brahmin deeply imbued with the mysteries of his so-called religion, he was a perfectly sane, happy, intelligent, and affectionate man. He loved me devotedly, as I am the child of his favourite brother, and told me just before Jasper's arrival that he had made me his heiress, leaving me all that he possessed in the world. He had never liked Jasper, and was annoyed when he came here and made this house his headquarters. I had not met my cousin since I was a little child, and when he arrived on the scene took a great dislike to him. He began at once to pay me hateful attentions, and to question me eagerly with regard to Uncle Edward and his ways. By a curious coincidence, he had known this house before he went to India, having stayed here as a boy. He showed particular interest in the oval gallery, and encouraged Uncle Edward to talk of Siva, although he saw that the subject excited him considerably.

"Jasper had been about a fortnight in the house when my poor uncle made, as he considered, the astounding discovery that Siva could speak to him. I shall never forget the first day when he told me of this, the sparkle in his eyes, the tremble of his hands, the nervous energy which seemed to animate him. From that hour day by day came the gradual diminution of strength both of mind and body, the loss of appetite, the feverish touch. All these things puzzled and distressed me, but I could not bear to confide my fears to Jasper.

"These things went on for over a month, and Uncle Edward certainly deteriorated in every way. He spent the greater part of both day and night in the gallery, begging of me to come with him, imploring me to listen for the voice. During that month he spent a large fortune in precious stones for Siva, showing them to me first before he decorated the hideous thing with them. I felt wild with misery, and all the time Jasper was here watching and watching. At the end of the first month there came a distinct change. Uncle Edward, who had been devoted to me up to then, began to show a new attitude. He now began to dislike to have me in his presence, often asking me as a special favour to leave the room. One day he said to me:

"'Do you keep your door locked at night?'

"I laughed when he spoke.

"'Certainly not,' I answered.

"'I wish you would do so,' he said very earnestly; 'will you, as a personal favour to me?'

"Jasper was in the room when he spoke. I saw a queer light flashing through his eyes, and then he bent over his book as if he had not heard.

"'As a special favour to me, keep your door locked, Helen,' said Uncle Edward.

"I made him a soothing answer, and pretended to assent. Of course I never locked my door. Then Jasper began to talk to me.

He said that Uncle Edward was not only mad, but that his mania was assuming a terrible form, and against me. He said that my life was in danger—he thought to frighten me—little he knew!"

Here the brave girl drew herself up, indignation sweeping over her face and filling her eyes.

"I told him I did not believe a word of what he said; I declared that Uncle Edward could not hate me—is he not the one I love best in the world? Jasper grew very angry.

"'Look here, Helen,' he said, 'I know enough to lock him up.'

"'To lock him up in a lunatic asylum?' I cried.

"'Yes,' he answered. 'I have only to get two doctors to certify to the fact of his insanity, and the deed is done. I have made up my mind to do it.'

"'You could never be so cruel,' I replied. 'Think of his grey hairs, Jasper,' I pleaded. 'He is the dearest to me in all the world; you could not take his liberty away. Do just respect his one little craze; believe me, he is not really mad. Go away if you are afraid of him; I am not. Oh, why don't you leave us both in peace?'

"'I dare not,' he answered. 'I love you, and I am determined you shall marry me. Engage yourself to me at once, and I will do nothing to take away Uncle Edward's liberty for at least a month.'

"I struggled against this horrible wish of my cousin's, but in the end I yielded to it. I became engaged to him secretly, for he did not wish Uncle Edward to know. I knew, of course, why he wished to marry me; he had heard that I am some day to inherit my uncle's wealth. Jasper himself is a very poor man. Now, Mr. Bell, you know everything. Things get worse and worse, and at times I am almost inclined to believe that my life is in some danger. A fiend has taken possession of the uncle whose heart was so warm and loving. Ah, it is fearful! I do not believe a bitterer trial could be given to any girl—it is too awful to feel that the one she loves best in all the world has changed in his feelings towards her. It is not so much the sacrifice of my poor life I mind as the feeling that things are so bitterly altered with him. Jasper put an alternative to me last night. Either I am to marry him within a week, or I am to use my influence to induce Dr. Laurier to sign the certificate. If I accept neither proposal, he will get down two other doctors from London for the purpose."

"What have you decided to do?" I asked.

"I will marry Jasper; yes, within a week I shall be his wife, unless something happens to show us what is the meaning of this fearful mystery, for I cannot—never, never can I deprive Uncle Edward of his liberty."

"I am glad you have confided in me," I said after a pause, "and I will do my utmost for you. When did you say that your uncle first heard the idol speak?"

"Two or three months ago now, soon after Jasper came home. Mr. Bell, is there any chance of your being able to help me?"

"I will promise to do my utmost, but just at present I can see no special light. By the way, would it not be well for you to leave The Hynde for a short time?"

"No, I am not at all afraid; I can take care of myself. It is not my dear uncle whom I fear; it is Jasper."

Soon afterwards she left me, and as it was still quite early, and the servants were not yet even up, I considered that an excellent opportunity had occurred for examining the idol.

I made my way to the gallery, and softly opening the door, stole in. The bright sunlight which was now flooding the chamber seemed to rob the grotesque old idol of half its terrors, and I made up my mind not to leave a stone unturned to discover if any foul play in connection with it could possibly be perpetrated. But the impossibility of such being the case seemed more and more evident as I went on with my search. Only a pigmy could be secreted inside the idol. There was no vulgar form of deception possible on the lines, for instance, of the ancient priests of Pompeii who conducted a speaking-tube to an idol's mouth. Siva was not even standing by the wall, thus precluding the possibility of the sounds being conducted on the plan of a whispering gallery. No—I was, against my own will, forced to the absolute conviction that the voice was an hallucination of the diseased mind of Edward Thesiger.

I was just going to abandon my investigations and return to my own room, when, more by chance than design, I knelt down for a moment at the little altar. As I was about to rise I noticed something rather odd. I listened attentively. It was certainly remarkable. As I knelt I could just hear a low, continuous hissing sound. Directly I moved away it ceased. As I tried it several times with the same invariable result, I became seriously puzzled to account for it. What devilry could be at work to produce this? Was it possible that some one was playing a trick on me?—and if so, by what means?

I glanced rapidly round, and as I did so a mad thought struck me. I hurried across to the fountain and put my ear close to the swan's mouth, from which a tiny jet of water was issuing. The low, scarcely audible noise that the water made as it flowed out through the swan's bill was exactly the same sound I had heard nearly twenty feet away at the altar. The enormity of the situation stunned me for a moment, then gradually, piece by piece, the plot revealed itself.

The shape of the gallery was a true oval, a geometrical ellipse, the extraordinary acoustic properties of which I knew well. This peculiarly shaped gallery contained two foci—one towards each end—and the nature of the curve of the walls was such that sound issuing from either focus was directed by reflection at various points to the other focus, and to the other focus alone. Even across an enormous distance between such would be the case. The swan's mouth was evidently at one focus; the position of a man's head as he knelt at the altar would be without the slightest doubt at the other. Could the pipe be used as a speaking-tube when the water was turned off?

I felt so excited by this extraordinary discovery that it was only with an effort that I maintained my self-control. I knew that presence of mind was absolutely necessary in order to expose this horrible scheme. I left the gallery and passed through the conservatory. Here I found the gardener arranging some pots. I chatted to him for a few moments. He looked surprised at seeing me up at such an unusual hour.

"Can you tell me how the fountain in the gallery is turned on or off?" I asked.

"Yes, I can, sir," he replied; "the pipe runs along outside this stand, and here's the tap."

I went across and looked at it. In the leaden pipe that was fastened to the wall were two nuts, which could be turned by a small spanner, and between them was a brass cap, which fitted on to a circular outlet from the pipe.

"What is this used for?" I asked, pointing to the little outlet which was closed by the cap.

"We screw the hose on there, sir, to water the flowers."

"I see," I answered; "so when you use the hose you shut off the water from the fountain in the gallery."

"That's it, sir, and a wonderful deal of trouble it saves. Why it was never done before I can't think."

"When was it done, then?" I asked. My heart was beating fast.

"It was Mr. Bagwell's thought, sir; he had it fixed on soon after he came. He wanted to have plenty of water handy in order to water the plants he brought back from India; but, lor! sir, they'll never live through the winter, even under glass."

I waited to hear no more—the whole infernal plot was laid bare. The second tap, which shut off the water both from the fountain and the hose pipe, was, of course, quite useless, except for Bagwell's evil purpose.

I hurried straight up to Laurier's room. He was just preparing to rise. His astonishment when I told him of my discovery was beyond words.

"Then, by shutting off the water, and applying his mouth to the place where the hose is fixed on, he could convey his voice to the swan's mouth like an ordinary speaking-tube, which, owing to the peculiar construction of the gallery, would be carried across to the other focus at the altar?" he said.

"Exactly," I replied. "And now, Dr. Laurier, you must please allow me to regulate our future plans. They're simply these. You must tell Bagwell that you absolutely refuse to sign the certificate unless Thesiger declares that he hears the voice again in your presence, and arrange that the séance takes place at nine o'clock tonight. I in the meantime shall ostensibly take my departure, and so leave the ground clear for Bagwell. He is evidently rather afraid of me. My going will throw him completely off his guard; but I shall in reality only leave the train at the next station and return here after dark. You will have to see that the conservatory door leading on to the terrace is left unlocked. I shall steal in, and, hiding myself in the conservatory, shall await Bagwell. You in the meantime will be in the gallery with Thesiger. When you hear me call out, come in at once. Our only hope is to take that wretch red-handed."

To this hastily constructed scheme Laurier instantly agreed, and at four o'clock that afternoon I took my leave, Miss Thesiger, looking white and miserable, standing on the steps to see me off. Bagwell drove me himself to the station, and bade me good-bye with a heartiness which was at least sincere.

I was back again at The Hynde at half-past eight that evening. Laurier had left the conservatory door unlocked, and, slipping in, it being now quite dark, I hid myself behind some large flowering shrubs and waited. Presently I heard the door of the conservatory open, and in stole Bagwell. I saw him approach the pipe, turn the spanner which shut off the water from the fountain and also from the hose pipe, and then proceed to unscrew the brass cap. I waited till I saw him place his mouth to the opening and begin to speak, and then I dashed out upon him and called loudly for Laurier. Bagwell's surprise and terror at my unexpected attack absolutely bereft him of speech, and he stood gazing at me with a mixed expression of fury and fear. The next minute Laurier and Thesiger both burst in from the gallery. I still retained my hold of Bagwell. The moment I saw Thesiger, I went up to him, and in a few words explained the whole fraud. But it was not until I had demonstrated the trick in the oval gallery that he became convinced; then the relief on his face was marvellous.

"You leave my house at once," he said to Bagwell; "go, sir, if you do not wish to be in the hands of the police. Where is Helen? where is my child?"

He had scarcely said the words, and Bagwell was just slinking off with a white face like a whipped cur towards the door, when Helen appeared upon the scene.

"What is it?" she cried. "Is anything the matter?"

The old man strode up to her; he took her in his arms.

"It is all right, Helen," he said, "all right. I can never explain; but, take my word, it is all right. I was a fool, and worse—nay, I was mad—but I am sane now. Mr. Bell, I can never express my obligations to you. But now, will you do one thing more?"

"What is that? Be assured I will do anything in my power," I answered.

"Then return here to-night and destroy Siva. How I could have been infatuated enough to believe in that senseless piece of wood is beyond my power to understand. But destroy it, sir; take it away; let me never lay eyes on it again."

Early on the following morning, when I was leaving the house, Bagwell, who must have been waiting for the purpose, suddenly stepped across my path.

"I have a word of explanation to give," he said. "You, Mr. Bell, have won, and I have lost. I played a deep game and for a large cause. It did not occur to me as possible that any one could discover the means by which I made Siva speak. I am now about to leave England for ever, but before I do so, it may interest you to know that the temptation offered to me was a very peculiar and strong one. I had not been an hour at the Hynde before I suddenly remembered having spent some months in the old house when a boy. I recollected the oval gallery. Its peculiar acoustic qualities had been pointed out to me by a scientist who happened to live there at the time. The desire to win, not Helen, but my uncle's property, was too strong to be resisted by a penniless man. My object was to terrify Thesiger, whose brain was already nearly overbalanced, into complete insanity, get him locked up, and marry Helen. How I succeeded, and in the end failed, you know well!"

TO PROVE AN ALIBI

I first met Arthur Cressley in the late spring of 1892. I had been spending the winter in Egypt, and was returning to Liverpool. One calm evening, about eleven o'clock, while we were still in the Mediterranean, I went on deck to smoke a final cigar before turning in. After pacing up and down for a time I leant over the taff-rail and began idly watching the tiny wavelets with their crests of white fire as they rippled away from the vessel's side. Presently I became aware of some one standing near me, and, turning, saw that it was one of my fellow-passengers, a young man whose name I knew but whose acquaintance I had not yet made. He was entered in the passenger list as Arthur Cressley, belonged to an old family in Derbyshire, and was returning home from Western Australia, where he had made a lot of money. I offered him a light, and after a few preliminary remarks we drifted into a desultory conversation. He told me that he had been in Australia for fifteen years, and having done well was now returning to settle in his native land.

"Then you do not intend going out again?" I asked.

"No," he replied; "I would not go through the last fifteen years for double the money I have made."

"I suppose you will make London your headquarters?"

"Not altogether; but I shall have to spend a good deal of time there. My wish is for a quiet country life, and I intend to take over the old family property. We have a place called Cressley Hall, in Derbyshire, which has belonged to us for centuries. It would be a sort of white elephant, for it has fallen into pitiable decay; but, luckily, I am now in a position to restore it and set it going again in renewed prosperity."

"You are a fortunate man," I answered.

"Perhaps I am," he replied. "Yes, as far as this world's goods go I suppose I am lucky, considering that I arrived in Australia fifteen years ago with practically no money in my pocket. I shall be glad to be home again for many reasons, chiefly because I can save the old property from being sold."

"It is always a pity when a fine old family seat has to go to the hammer for want of funds," I remarked.

"That is true, and Cressley Hall is a superb old place. There is only one drawback to it; but I don't believe there is anything in that," added Cressley in a musing tone.

Knowing him so little I did not feel justified in asking for an explanation. I waited, therefore, without speaking. He soon proceeded:

"I suppose I am rather foolish about it," he continued; "but if I am superstitious, I have abundant reason. For more than a century and a half there has been a strange fatality about any Cressley occupying the Hall. This fatality was first exhibited in 1700, when Barrington Cressley, one of the most abandoned libertines of that time, led his infamous orgies there—of these even history takes note. There are endless legends as to their nature, one of which is that he had personal dealings with the devil in the large turret room, the principal bedroom at the Hall, and was found dead there on the following morning. Certainly since that date a curious doom has hung over the family, and this doom shows itself in a strange way, only attacking those victims who are so unfortunate as to sleep in the turret room. Gilbert Cressley, the young Court favourite of George the Third, was found mysteriously murdered there, and my own great-grandfather paid the penalty by losing his reason within those gloomy walls."

"If the room has such an evil reputation, I wonder that it is occupied," I replied.

"It happens to be far and away the best bedroom in the house, and people always laugh at that sort of thing until they are brought face to face with it. The owner of the property is not only born there, as a rule, but also breathes his last in the old four-poster, the most extraordinary, wonderful old bedstead you ever laid eyes on. Of course I do not believe in any malevolent influences from the unseen world, but the record of disastrous coincidences in that one room is, to say the least of it, curious. Not that this sort of thing will deter me from going into possession, and I intend to put a lot of money into Cressley Hall."

"Has no one been occupying it lately?" I asked.

"Not recently. An old housekeeper has had charge of the place for the last few years. The agent had orders to sell the Hall long ago, but though it has been in the market for a long time I do not believe there was a single offer. Just before I left Australia I wired to Murdock, my agent, that I intended taking over the place, and authorised its withdrawal from the market."

"Have you no relations?" I inquired.

"None at all. Since I have been away my only brother died. It is curious to call it going home when one has no relatives and only friends who have probably forgotten one."

I could not help feeling sorry for Cressley as he described the lonely outlook. Of course, with heaps of money and an old family place he would soon make new friends; but he looked the sort of chap who might be imposed upon, and although he was as nice a fellow as I had ever met, I could not help coming to the conclusion that he was not specially strong, either mentally or physically. He was essentially good-looking, however, and had the indescribable bearing of a man of old family. I wondered how he had managed to make his money. What he told me about his old Hall also excited my interest, and as we talked I managed to allude to my own peculiar hobby, and the delight I took in such old legends.

As the voyage flew by our acquaintance grew apace, ripening into a warm friendship. Cressley told me much of his past life, and finally confided to me one of his real objects in returning to England.

While prospecting up country he had come across some rich veins of gold, and now his intention was to bring out a large syndicate in order to acquire the whole property, which, he anticipated, was worth at least a million. He spoke confidently of this great scheme, but always wound up by informing me that the money which he hoped to make was only of interest to him for the purpose of re-establishing Cressley Hall in its ancient splendour.

As we talked I noticed once or twice that a man stood near us who seemed to take an interest in our conversation. He was a thickly set individual with a florid complexion and a broad Ger-man cast of face. He was an inveterate smoker, and when he stood near us with a pipe in his mouth the expression of his face was almost a blank; but watching him closely I saw a look in his eyes which betokened the shrewd man of business, and I could scarcely tell why, but I felt uncomfortable in his presence. This man, Wickham by name, managed to pick up an acquaintance with Cressley, and soon they spent a good deal of time together. They made a contrast as they paced up and down on deck, or played cards in the evening; the Englishman being slight and almost frag-ile in build, the German of the bulldog order, with a manner at once curt and overbearing. I took a dislike to Wickham, and won-dered what Cressley could see in him.

"Who is the fellow?" I asked on one occasion, linking my hand in Cressley's arm and drawing him aside as I spoke.

"Do you mean Wickham?" he answered. "I am sure I cannot tell you. I never met the chap before this voyage. He came on board at King George's Sound, where I also embarked; but he never spoke to me until we were in the Mediterranean. On the whole, Bell, I am inclined to like him; he seems to be downright and honest. He knows a great deal about the bush, too, as he has spent several years there."

"And he gives you the benefit of his information?" I asked.

"I don't suppose he knows more than I do, and it is doubtful whether he has had so rough a time."

"Then in that case he picks your brains."

"What do you mean?"

The young fellow looked at me with those clear grey eyes which were his most attractive feature.

"Nothing," I answered, "nothing; only if you will be guided by a man nearly double your age, I would take care to tell Wickham as little as possible. Have you ever observed that he happens to be about when you and I are engaged in serious conversation?"

"I can't say that I have."

"Well, keep your eyes open and you'll see what I mean. Be as friendly as you like, but don't give him your confidence—that is all."

"You are rather late in advising me on that score," said Cressley, with a somewhat nervous laugh. "Wickham knows all about the old Hall by this time."

"And your superstitious fears with regard to the turret room?" I queried.

"Well, I have hinted at them. You will be surprised, but he is full of sympathy."

"Tell him no more," I said in conclusion.

Cressley made a sort of half-promise, but looked as if he rather resented my interference.

A day or two later we reached Liverpool; I was engaged long ago to stay with some friends in the suburbs, and Cressley took up his abode at the Prince's Hotel. His property was some sixty miles away, and when we parted he insisted on my agreeing to come down and see his place as soon as he had put things a little straight.

I readily promised to do so, provided we could arrange a visit before my return to London.

Nearly a week went by and I saw nothing of Cressley; then, on a certain morning, he called to see me.

"How are you getting on?" I asked.

"Capitally," he replied. "I have been down to the Hall several times with my agent, Murdock, and though the place is in the most shocking condition I shall soon put things in order. But what I have come specially to ask you now is whether you can get away to-day and come with me to the Hall for a couple of nights. I had arranged with the agent to go down this afternoon in his company, but he has been suddenly taken ill—he is rather bad, I believe—and cannot possibly come with me. He has ordered the housekeeper to get a couple of rooms ready, and though I am afraid it will be rather roughing it, I shall be awfully glad if you can come."

I had arranged to meet a man in London on special business that very evening, and could not put him off; but my irresistible desire to see the old place from the description I had heard of it decided me to make an effort to fall in as well as I could with Cressley's plans.

"I wish I could go with you to-day," I said; "but that, as it happens, is out of the question. I must run up to town on some pressing business; but if you will allow me I can easily come back again to-morrow. Can you not put off your visit until to-morrow evening?"

"No, I am afraid I cannot do that. I have to meet several of the tenants, and have made all arrangements to go by the five o'clock train this afternoon."

He looked depressed at my refusal, and after a moment said thoughtfully:

"I wish you could have come with me to-day. When Murdock could not come I thought of you at once—it would have made all the difference."

"I am sorry," I replied; "but I can promise faithfully to be with you to-morrow. I shall enjoy seeing your wonderful old Hall beyond anything; and as to roughing it, I am used to that. You will not mind spending one night there by yourself?"

He looked at me as if he were about to speak, but no words came from his lips.

"What is the matter?" I said, giving him an earnest glance. "By the way, are you going to sleep in the turret room?"

"I am afraid there is no help for it; the housekeeper is certain to get it ready for me. The owner of the property always sleeps there, and it would look like a confession of weakness to ask to be put into another bedroom."

"Nevertheless, if you are nervous, I should not mind that," I said.

"Oh, I don't know that I am absolutely nervous, Bell, but all the same I have a superstition. At the present moment I have the queerest sensation; I feel as if I ought not to pay this visit to the Hall."

"If you intend to live there by-and-by, you must get over this sort of thing," I remarked.

"Oh yes, I must, and I would not yield to it on any account whatever. I am sorry I even mentioned it to you. It is good of you to promise to come to-morrow, and I shall look forward to seeing you. By what train will you come?"

We looked up the local time-table, and I decided on a train which would leave Liverpool about five o'clock.

"The very one that I shall go down by to-day," said Cressley; "that's capital, I'll meet you with a conveyance of some sort and drive you over. The house is a good two hours' drive from the station, and you cannot get a trap there for love or money."

"By the way," I said, "is there much the matter with your agent?"

"I cannot tell you; he seems bad enough. I went up to his house this morning and saw the wife. It appears that he was suddenly taken ill with a sort of asthmatic attack to which he is subject. While I was talking to Mrs. Murdock, a messenger came down to say that her husband specially wished to see me, so we both went to his room, but he had dozed off into a queer restless sleep before we arrived. The wife said he must not be awakened on any account, but I caught a glimpse of him and he certainly looked bad, and was moaning as if in a good deal of pain. She gave me the keys of a bureau in his room, and I took out some estimates, and left a note for him telling him to come on as soon as he was well enough."

"And your visit to his room never roused him?" I said.

"No, although Mrs. Murdock and I made a pretty good bit of noise moving about and opening and shutting drawers. His moans were quite heartrending—he was evidently in considerable pain; and I was glad to get away, as that sort of thing always upsets me."

"Who is this Murdock?" I asked.

"Oh, the man who has looked after the place for years. I was referred to him by my solicitors. He seems a most capable person, and I hope to goodness he won't be ill long. If he is I shall find myself in rather a fix."

I made no reply to this, and soon afterwards Cressley shook hands with me and departed on his way. I went to my room, packed my belongings, and took the next train to town. The business which I had to get through occupied the whole of that evening and also some hours of the following day. I found I was not able to start for Liverpool before the 12.10 train at Euston, and should not therefore arrive at Lime Street before five o'clock—too late to catch the train for Brent, the nearest station to Cressley's place. Another train left Central Station for Brent, however, at seven o'clock, and I determined to wire to Cressley to tell him to meet me by the latter train. This was the last train in the day, but there was no fear of my missing it.

I arrived at Lime Street almost to the moment and drove straight to the Prince's Hotel, where I had left my bag the day before. Here a telegram awaited me; it was from Cressley, and ran as follows:—

"Hope this will reach you time; if so, call at Murdock's house, No. 12, Melville Gardens. If possible see him and get the documents referred to in Schedule A—he will know what you mean. Most important.
"Cressley"

I glanced at the clock in the hall; it was now a quarter past five—my train would leave at seven. I had plenty of time to get something to eat and then go to Murdock's.

Having despatched my telegram to Cressley, telling him to look out for me by the train which arrived at Brent at nine o'clock, I ordered a meal, ate it, and then hailing a cab, gave the driver the number of Murdock's house. Melville Gardens was situated somewhat in the suburbs, and it was twenty minutes' drive from my hotel. When we drew up at Murdock's door I told the cabman to wait, and, getting out, rang the bell. The servant who answered my summons told me that the agent was still very ill and could not be seen by any one. I then inquired for the wife. I was informed that she was out, but would be back soon. I looked at my watch. It was just six o'clock. I determined to wait to see Mrs. Murdock if possible.

Having paid and dismissed my cab, I was shown into a small, untidily kept parlour, where I was left to my own meditations. The weather was hot and the room close. I paced up and down restlessly. The minutes flew by and Mrs. Murdock did not put in an appearance. I looked at my watch, which now pointed to twenty minutes past six. It would take me, in an ordinary cab, nearly twenty minutes to reach the station. In order to make all safe I ought to leave Murdock's house in ten minutes from now at the latest.

I went and stood by the window watching anxiously for Mrs. Murdock to put in an appearance. Melville Gardens was a somewhat lonely place, and few people passed the house, which was old and shabby; it had evidently not been done up for years. I was just turning round in order to ring the bell to leave a message with the servant, when the room door was opened and, to my astonishment, in walked Wickham, the man I had last seen on board the *Euphrates*. He came up to me at once and held out his hand.

"No doubt you are surprised at seeing me here, Mr. Bell," he exclaimed.

"I certainly was for a moment," I answered; but then I added, "The world is a small place, and one soon gets accustomed to acquaintances cropping up in all sorts of unlikely quarters."

"Why unlikely?" said Wickham. "Why should I not know Murdock, who happens to be a very special and very old friend of mine? I might as well ask you why you are interested in him."

"Because I happen to be a friend of Arthur Cressley's," I answered, "and have come here on his business."

"And so am I also a friend of Cressley's. He has asked me to go and see him at Cressley Hall some day, and I hope to avail myself of his invitation. The servant told me that you were waiting for Mrs. Murdock—can I give her any message from you?"

"I want to see Murdock himself," I said, after a pause. "Do you think that it is possible for me to have an interview with him?"

"I left him just now and he was asleep," said Wickham. "He is still very ill, and I think the doctor is a little anxious about him. It would not do to disturb him on any account. Of course, if he happens to awake he might be able to tell you what you want to know. By the way, has it anything to do with Cressley Hall?"

"Yes; I have just had a telegram from Cressley, and the message is somewhat important. You are quite sure that Murdock is asleep?"

"He was when I left the room, but I will go up again and see. Are you going to London to-night, Mr. Bell?"

"No; I am going down to Cressley Hall, and must catch the seven o'clock train. I have not a moment to wait." As I spoke I took out my watch.

"It only wants five-and-twenty minutes to seven," I said, "and I never care to run a train to the last moment. There is no help for it, I suppose I must go without seeing Murdock. Cressley will in all probability send down a message to-morrow for the papers he requires."

"Just stay a moment," said Wickham, putting on an anxious expression; "it is a great pity that you should not see Cressley's agent if it is as vital as all that. Ah! and here comes Mrs. Murdock; wait one moment, I'll go and speak to her."

He went out of the room, and I heard him say something in a low voice in the passage—a woman's voice replied, and the next instant Mrs. Murdock stood before me. She was a tall woman with a sallow face and sandy hair; she had a blank sort of stare about her, and scarcely any expression. Now she fixed her dull, light-blue eyes on my face and held out her hand.

"You are Mr. Bell?" she said. "I have heard of you, of course, from Mr. Cressley. So you are going to spend to-night with him at Cressley Hall. I am glad, for it is a lonely place—the most lonely place I know."

"Pardon me," I interrupted, "I cannot stay to talk to you now or I shall miss my train. Can I see your husband or can I not?"

She glanced at Wickham, then she said with hesitation,—

"If he is asleep it would not do to disturb him, but there is a chance of his being awake now. I don't quite understand about the papers, I wish I did. It would be best for you to see him certainly; follow me upstairs."

"And I tell you what," called Wickham after us, "I'll go and engage a cab, so that you shall lose as short a time as possible, Mr. Bell."

I thanked him and followed the wife upstairs. The stairs were narrow and steep, and we soon reached the small landing at the top. Four bedrooms opened into it. Mrs. Murdock turned the handle of the one which exactly faced the stairs, and we both entered. Here the blinds were down, and the chamber was considerably darkened. The room was a small one, and the greater part of the space was occupied by an old-fashioned Albert bedstead with the curtains pulled forward. Within I could just see the shadowy outline of a figure, and I distinctly heard the feeble groans of the sick man.

"Ah! what a pity, my husband is still asleep," said Mrs. Murdock, as she turned softly round to me and put her finger to her lips. "It would injure him very much to awaken him," she said. "You can go and look at him if you like; you will see how very ill he is. I wonder if I could help you with regard to the papers you want, Mr. Bell?"

"I want the documents referred to in Schedule A," I answered.

"Schedule A?" she repeated, speaking under her breath. "I remember that name. Surely all the papers relating to it are in this drawer. I think I can get them for you."

She crossed the room as she spoke, and standing with her back to the bedstead, took a bunch of keys from a table which stood near and fitted one into the lock of a high bureau made of mahogany. She pulled open a drawer and began to examine its contents.

While she was so occupied I approached the bed, and bending slightly forward, took a good stare at the sick man. I had never seen Murdock before. There was little doubt that he was ill—he looked very ill, indeed. His face was long and cadaverous, the cheek bones were high, and the cheeks below were much sunken in; the lips, which were clean-shaven, were slightly drawn apart, and some broken irregular teeth were visible. The eyebrows were scanty, and the hair was much worn away from the high and hollow forehead. The man looked sick unto death. I had seldom seen any one with an expression like his—the closed eyes were much sunken, and the moaning which came from the livid lips was horrible to listen to.

After giving Murdock a long and earnest stare, I stepped back from the bed, and was just about to speak to Mrs. Murdock, who was rustling papers in the drawer, when the most strong and irresistible curiosity assailed me. I could not account for it, but I felt bound to yield to its suggestions. I turned again and bent close over the sick man. Surely there was something monotonous about that deep-drawn breath; those moans, too, came at wonderfully regular intervals. Scarcely knowing why I did it, I stretched out my hand and laid it on the forehead. Good God! what was the matter? I felt myself turning cold; the perspiration stood out on my own brow. I had not touched a living forehead at all. Flesh was flesh, it was impossible to mistake the feel, but there was no flesh here. The figure in the bed was neither a living nor a dead man, it was a wax representation of one; but why did it moan, and how was it possible for it not to breathe?

Making the greatest effort of my life, I repressed an exclamation, and when Mrs. Murdock approached me with the necessary papers in her hand, took them from her in my usual manner.

"These all relate to Schedule A," she said. "I hope I am not doing wrong in giving them to you without my husband's leave. He looks very ill, does he not?"

"He looks as bad as he can look," I answered. I moved towards the door. Something in my tone must have alarmed her, for a curious expression of fear dilated the pupils of her light blue eyes. She followed me downstairs. A hansom was waiting for me. I nodded to Wickham, did not even wait to shake hands with Mrs. Murdock, and sprang into the cab.

"Central Station!" I shouted to the man; and then as he whipped up his horse and flew down the street, "A sovereign if you get there before seven o'clock."

We were soon dashing quickly along the streets. I did not know Liverpool well, and consequently could not exactly tell where the man was going. When I got into the hansom it wanted twelve minutes to seven o'clock; these minutes were quickly flying, and still no station.

"Are you sure you are going right?" I shouted through the hole in the roof.

"You'll be there in a minute, sir," he answered. "It's Lime Street Station you want, isn't it?"

"No; Central Station," I answered. "I told you Central Station; drive there at once like the very devil. I must catch that train, for it is the last one to-night."

"All right, sir; I can do it," he cried, whipping up his horse again.

Once more I pulled out my watch; the hands pointed to three minutes to seven.

At ten minutes past we were driving into the station. I flung the man half a sovereign, and darted into the booking-office.

"To Brent, sir? The last train has just gone," said the clerk, with an impassive stare at me through the little window.

I flung my bag down in disgust and swore a great oath. But for that idiot of a driver I should have just caught the train. All of a sudden a horrible thought flashed through my brain. Had the cabman been bribed by Wickham? No directions could have been plainer than mine. I had told the man to drive to Central Station. Central Station did not sound the least like Lime Street Station. How was it possible for him to make so grave a mistake?

The more I considered the matter the more certain I was that a black plot was brewing, and that Wickham was in the thick of it. My brain began to whirl with excitement. What was the matter? Why was a lay figure in Murdock's bed? Why had I been taken upstairs to see it? Without any doubt both Mrs. Murdock and Wickham wished me to see what was such an admirable imitation of a sick man—an imitation so good, with those ghastly moans coming from the lips, that it would have taken in the sharpest detective in Scotland Yard. I myself was deceived until I touched the forehead. This state of things had not been brought to pass without a reason. What was the reason? Could it be possible that Murdock was wanted elsewhere, and it was thought well that I should see him in order to prove an alibi, should he be suspected of a ghastly crime? My God! what could this mean? From the first I had mistrusted Wickham. What was he doing in Murdock's house? For what purpose had he bribed the driver of the cab in order to make me lose my train?

The more I thought, the more certain I was that Cressley was in grave danger; and I now determined, cost what it might, to get to him that night.

I left the station, took a cab, and drove back to my hotel. I asked to see the manager. A tall, dark man in a frock-coat emerged from a door at the back of the office and inquired what he could do for me. I begged permission to speak to him alone, and we passed into his private room.

"I am in an extraordinary position," I began. "Circumstances of a private nature make it absolutely necessary that I should go to a place called Cressley Hall, about fourteen miles from Brent. Brent is sixty miles down the line, and the last train has gone. I could take a 'special,' but there might be an interminable delay at Brent, and I prefer to drive straight to Cressley Hall across country. Can you assist me by directing me to some good jobmaster from whom I can hire a carriage and horses?"

The man looked at me with raised eyebrows. He evidently thought I was mad.

"I mean what I say," I added, "and am prepared to back my words with a substantial sum. Can you help me?"

"I dare say you might get a carriage and horses to do it," he replied; "but it is a very long way, and over a hilly country. No two horses could go such a distance without rest. You would have to change from time to time as you went. I will send across to the hotel stables for my man, and you can see him about it."

He rang the bell and gave his orders. In a few moments the jobmaster came in. I hurriedly explained to him what I wanted. At first he said it was impossible, that his best horses were out, and that those he had in his stables could not possibly attempt such a journey; but when I brought out my cheque-book and offered to advance any sum in reason, he hesitated.

"Of course there is one way in which it might be managed, sir. I would take you myself as far as Ovenden, which is five-and-twenty miles from here. There, I know, we could get a pair of fresh horses from the Swan; and if we wired at once from here, horses might be ready at Carlton, which is another twenty miles on the road. But, at our best, sir, it will be between two and three in the morning before we get to Brent."

"I am sorry to hear you say so," I answered; "but it is better to arrive then than to wait until to-morrow. Please send the necessary telegram off without a moment's delay, and get the carriage ready."

"Put the horses in at once, John," said the manager. "You had better take the light wagonette. You ought to get there between one and two in the morning with that."

Then he added, as the man left the room,—

"I suppose, sir, your business is very urgent?"

"It is," I replied shortly.

He looked as if he would like to question me further, but refrained.

A few moments later I had taken my seat beside the driver, and we were speeding at a good round pace through the streets of Liverpool. We passed quickly through the suburbs, and out into the open country. The evening was a lovely one, and the country looked its best. It was difficult to believe, as I drove through the peaceful landscape, that in all probability a dark deed was in contemplation, and that the young man to whom I had taken a most sincere liking was in danger of his life.

As I drove silently by my companion's side I reviewed the whole situation. The more I thought of it the less I liked it. On board the *Euphrates* Wickham had been abnormally interested in Cressley. Cressley had himself confided to him his superstitious dread with regard to the turret room. Cressley had come home with a fortune; and if he floated his syndicate he would be a millionaire. Wickham scarcely looked like a rich man. Then why should he know Murdock, and why should a lay figure be put in Murdock's bed? Why, also, through a most unnatural accident, should I have lost my train?

The more I thought, the graver and graver became my fears. Gradually darkness settled over the land, and then a rising moon flooded the country in its weird light. I had been on many a wild expedition before, but in some ways never a wilder than this. Its very uncertainty, wrapped as it was in unformed suspicions, gave it an air of inexpressible mystery.

On and on we went, reaching Ovenden between nine and ten at night. Here horses were ready for us, and we again started on our way. When we got to Carlton, however, there came a hitch in my well-formed arrangements. We drew up at the little inn, to find the place in total darkness, and all the inhabitants evidently in bed and asleep. With some difficulty we roused the landlord, and asked why the horses which had been telegraphed for had not been got ready.

"We did not get them when the second telegram arrived," was the reply.

"The second telegram!" I cried, my heart beating fast. "What do you mean?"

"There were two, sir, both coming from the same stables. The first was written desiring us to have the horses ready at any cost. The second contradicted the first, and said that the gentleman had changed his mind, and was not going. On receipt of that, sir, I shut up the house as usual, and we all went to bed. I am very sorry if there has been any mistake."

"There has, and a terrible one," I could not help muttering under my breath. My fears were getting graver than ever. Who had sent the second telegram? Was it possible that I had been followed by Wickham, who took these means of circumventing me?

"We must get horses, and at once," I said. "Never mind about the second telegram; it was a mistake."

Peach, the jobmaster, muttered an oath.

"I can't understand what is up," he said. He looked mystified and not too well pleased. Then he added,—

"These horses can't go another step, sir."

"They must if we can get no others," I said. I went up to him, and began to whisper in his ear.

"This is a matter of life and death, my good friend. Only the direst necessity takes me on this journey. The second telegram without doubt was sent by a man whom I am trying to circumvent. I know what I am saying. We must get horses, or these must go on. We have not an instant to lose. There is a conspiracy afoot to do serious injury to the owner of Cressley Hall."

"What! the young gentleman who has just come from Australia? You don't mean to say he is in danger?" said Peach.

"He is in the gravest danger. I don't mind who knows. I have reason for my fears."

While I was speaking the landlord drew near. He overheard some of my last words. The landlord and Peach now exchanged glances. After a moment the landlord spoke,—

"A neighbour of ours, sir, has got two good horses," he said. "He is the doctor in this village. I believe he'll lend them if the case is as urgent as you say."

"Go and ask him," I cried. "You shall have ten pounds if we are on the road in five minutes from the present moment."

At this hint the landlord flew. He came back in an incredibly short space of time, accompanied by the doctor's coachman leading the horses. They were quickly harnessed to the wagonette, and once more we started on our way.

"Now drive as you never drove before in the whole course of your life," I said to Peach. "Money is no object. We have still fifteen miles to go, and over a rough country. You can claim any reward in reason if you get to Cressley Hall within an hour."

"It cannot be done, sir," he replied; but then he glanced at me, and some of the determination in my face was reflected in his. He whipped up the horses. They were thoroughbred animals, and worked well under pressure.

We reached the gates of Cressley Hall between two and three in the morning. Here I thought it best to draw up, and told my coachman that I should not need his services any longer.

"If you are afraid of mischief, sir, would it not be best for me to lie about here?" he asked. "I'd rather be in the neighbourhood in case you want me. I am interested in this here job, sir."

"You may well be, my man. God grant it is not a black business. Well, walk the horses up and down, if you like. If you see nothing of me within the next couple of hours, judge that matters are all right, and return with the horses to Carlton."

This being arranged, I turned from Peach and entered the lodge gates. Just inside was a low cottage surrounded by trees. I paused for a moment to consider what I had better do. My difficulty now was how to obtain admittance to the Hall, for of course it would be shut up and all its inhabitants asleep at this hour. Suddenly an idea struck me. I determined to knock up the lodge-keeper, and to enlist her assistance. I went across to the door, and presently succeeded in rousing the inmates. A woman of about fifty appeared. I explained to her my position, and begged of her to give me her help. She hesitated at first in unutterable astonishment; but then, seeing something in my face which convinced her, I suppose, of the truth of my story, for it was necessary to alarm her in order to induce her to do anything, she said she would do what I wished.

"I know the room where Mitchell, the old housekeeper, sleeps," she said, "and we can easily wake him by throwing stones up at his window. If you'll just wait a minute I'll put a shawl over my head and go with you."

She ran into an inner room and quickly re-appeared. Together we made our way along the drive which, far as I could see, ran through a park studded with old timber. We went round the house to the back entrance, and the woman, after a delay of two or three moments, during which I was on thorns, managed to wake up Mitchell the housekeeper. He came to his window, threw it open, and poked out his head.

"What can be wrong?" he said.

"It is Mr. Bell, James," was the reply, "the gentleman who has been expected at the Hall all the evening; he has come now, and wants you to admit him."

The old man said that he would come downstairs. He did so, and opening a door, stood in front of it, barring my entrance.

"Are you really the gentleman Mr. Cressley has been expecting?" he said.

"I am," I replied; "I missed my train, and was obliged to drive out. There is urgent need why I should see your master immediately; where is he?"

"I hope in bed, sir, and asleep; it is nearly three o'clock in the morning."

"Never mind the hour," I said; "I must see Mr. Cressley immediately. Can you take me to his room?"

"If I am sure that you are Mr. John Bell," said the old man, glancing at me with not unnatural suspicion.

"Rest assured on that point. Here, this is my card, and here is a telegram which I received to-day from your master."

"But master sent no telegram to-day."

"You must be mistaken, this is from him."

"I don't understand it, sir, but you look honest, and I suppose I must trust you."

"You will do well to do so," I said.

He moved back and I entered the house. He took me down a passage, and then into a lofty chamber, which probably was the old banqueting-hall. As well as I could see by the light of the candle, it was floored, and panelled with black oak. Round the walls stood figures of knights in armour, with flags and banners hanging from the panels above. I followed the old man up a broad staircase and along endless corridors to a more distant part of the building. We turned now abruptly to our right, and soon began to ascend some turret stairs.

"In which room is your master?" I asked.

"This is his room, sir," said the man. He stood still and pointed to a door.

"Stay where you are; I may want you," I said.

I seized his candle, and holding it above my head, opened the door. The room was a large one, and when I entered was in total darkness. I fancied I heard a rustling in the distance, but could see no one. Then, as my eyes got accustomed to the faint light caused by the candle, I observed at the further end of the chamber a large four-poster bedstead. I immediately noticed something very curious about it. I turned round to the old housekeeper.

"Did you really say that Mr. Cressley was sleeping in this room?" I asked.

"Yes, sir; he must be in bed some hours ago. I left him in the library hunting up old papers, and he told me he was tired and was going to rest early."

"He is not in the bed," I said.

"Not in the bed, sir! Good God!" a note of horror came into the man's voice. "What in the name of fortune is the matter with the bed?"

As the man spoke I rushed forward. Was it really a bed at all? If it was, I had never seen a stranger one. Upon it, covering it from head to foot, was a thick mattress, from the sides of which tassels were hanging. There was no human being lying on the mattress, nor was it made up with sheets and blankets like an ordinary bed. I glanced above me. The posts at the four corners of the bedstead stood like masts. I saw at once what had happened. The canopy had descended upon the bed. Was Cressley beneath? With a shout I desired the old man to come forward, and between us we seized the mattress, and exerting all our force, tried to drag it from the bed. In a moment I saw it was fixed by cords that held it tightly in its place. Whipping out my knife, I severed these, and then hurled the heavy weight from the bed. Beneath lay Cressley, still as death. I put my hand on his heart and uttered a thankful exclamation. It was still beating. I was in time; I had saved him. After all, nothing else mattered during that supreme moment of thankfulness. A few seconds longer beneath that smothering mass and he would have been dead. By what a strange sequence of events had I come to his side just in the nick of time!

"We must take him from this room before he recovers consciousness," I said to the old man, who was surprised and horror-stricken.

"But, sir, in the name of Heaven, what has happened?"

"Let us examine the bed, and I will tell you," I said. I held up the candle as I spoke. A glance at the posts was all-sufficient to show me how the deed had been done. The canopy above, on which the heavy mattress had been placed, was held in position by strong cords which ran through pulleys at the top of the posts. These were thick and heavy enough to withstand the strain. When the cords were released, the canopy, with its heavy weight, must quickly descend upon the unfortunate sleeper, who would be smothered beneath it in a few seconds. Who had planned and executed this murderous device?

There was not a soul to be seen.

"We will take Mr. Cressley into another room and then come back," I said to the housekeeper. "Is there one where we can place him?"

"Yes, sir," was the instant reply; "there's a room on the next floor which was got ready for you."

"Capital," I answered; "we will convey him there at once."

We did so, and after using some restoratives, he came to himself. When he saw me he gazed at me with an expression of horror on his face.

"Am I alive, or is it a dream?" he said.

"You are alive, but you have had a narrow escape of your life," I answered. I then told him how I had found him.

He sat up as I began to speak, and as I continued my narrative his eyes dilated with an expression of terror which I have seldom seen equalled.

"You do not know what I have lived through," he said at last. "I only wonder I retain my reason. Oh, that awful room! no wonder men died and went mad there!"

"Well, speak, Cressley; I am all attention," I said; "you will be the better when you have unburdened yourself."

"I can tell you what happened in a few words," he answered. "You know I mentioned the horrid sort of presentiment I had about coming here at all. That first night I could not make up my mind to sleep in the house, so I went to the little inn at Brent. I received your telegram yesterday, and went to meet you by the last train. When you did not come, I had a tussle with myself; but I could think of no decent excuse for deserting the old place, and so came back. My intention was to sit up the greater part of the night arranging papers in the library. The days are long now, and I thought I might go to bed when morning broke. I was irresistibly sleepy, however, and went up to my room soon after one o'clock. I was determined to think of nothing unpleasant, and got quickly into bed, taking the precaution first to lock the door. I placed the key under my pillow, and, being very tired, soon fell into a heavy sleep. I awoke suddenly, after what seemed but a few minutes, to find the room dark, for the moon must just have set. I was very sleepy, and I wondered vaguely why I had awakened; and then suddenly, without warning, and without cause, a monstrous, unreasonable fear seized me. An indefinable intuition told me that I was not alone—that some horrible presence was near. I do not think the certainty of immediate death could have inspired me with a greater dread than that which suddenly came upon me. I dared not stir hand nor foot. My powers of reason and resistance were paralysed. At last, by an immense effort, I nerved myself to see the worst. Slowly, very slowly, I turned my head and opened my eyes. Against the tapestry at the further corner of the room, in the dark shadow, stood a figure. It stood out quite boldly, emanating from itself a curious light. I had no time to think of phosphorus. It never occurred to me that any trick was being played upon me. I felt certain that I was looking at my ancestor, Barrington Cressley, who had come back to torture me in order to make me give up possession. The figure was that of a man six feet high, and broad in proportion. The face was bent forward and turned toward me, but in the uncertain light I could neither see the features nor the expression. The figure stood as still as a statue, and was evidently watching me. At the end of a moment, which seemed to me an eternity, it began to move, and, with a slow and silent step, approached me. I lay perfectly still, every muscle braced, and watched the figure between half-closed eyelids. It was now within a foot or two of me, and I could distinctly see the face. What was my horror to observe that it wore the features of my agent Murdock.

"'Murdock!' I cried, the word coming in a strangled sound from my throat. The next instant he had sprung upon me. I heard a noise of something rattling above, and saw a huge shadow descending upon me. I did not know what it was, and I felt certain that I was being murdered. The next moment all was lost in unconsciousness. Bell, how queer you look! Was it—was it Murdock? But it could not have been; he was very ill in bed at Liverpool. What in the name of goodness was the awful horror through which I had lived?"

"I can assure you on one point," I answered; "it was no ghost. And as to Murdock, it is more than likely that you did see him."

I then told the poor fellow what I had discovered with regard to the agent, and also my firm conviction that Wickham was at the bottom of it.

Cressley's astonishment was beyond bounds, and I saw at first that he scarcely believed me; but when I said that it was my intention to search the house, he accompanied me.

We both, followed by Mitchell, returned to the ill-fated room; but, though we examined the tapestry and panelling, we could not find the secret means by which the villain had obtained access to the chamber.

"The carriage which brought me here is still waiting just outside the lodge gates," I said. "What do you say to leaving this place at once, and returning, at least, as far as Carlton? We might spend the remainder of the night there, and take the very first train to Liverpool."

"Anything to get away," said Cressley. "I do not feel that I can ever come back to Cressley Hall again."

"You feel that now, but by-and-by your sensations will be different," I answered. As I spoke I called Mitchell to me. I desired him to go at once to the lodge gates and ask the driver of the wagonette to come down to the Hall.

This was done, and half an hour afterwards Cressley and I were on our way back to Carlton. Early the next morning we went to

Liverpool. There we visited the police, and I asked to have a war-
rant taken out for the apprehension of Murdock.

The superintendent, on hearing my tale, suggested that we
should go at once to Murdock's house in Melville Gardens. We did
so, but it was empty, Murdock, his wife, and Wickham having
thought it best to decamp. The superintendent insisted, however,
on having the house searched, and in a dark closet at the top we
came upon a most extraordinary contrivance. This was no less than
an exact representation of the agent's head and neck in wax. In it
was a wonderfully skilful imitation of a human larynx, which, by a
cunning mechanism of clockwork, could be made exactly to simu-
late the breathing and low moaning of a human being. This the
man had, of course, utilized with the connivance of his wife and
Wickham in order to prove an alibi, and the deception was so complete that only my own irresistible curiosity could have enabled
me to discover the secret. That night the police were fortunate
enough to capture both Murdock and Wickham in a Liverpool slum.
Seeing that all was up, the villains made complete confession,
and the whole of the black plot was revealed. It appeared that two
adventurers, the worst form of scoundrels, knew of Cressley's great
discovery in Western Australia, and had made up their minds to
forestall him in his claim. One of these men had come some months
ago to England, and while in Liverpool had made the acquaintance
of Murdock. The other man, Wickham, accompanied Cressley on
the voyage in order to keep him in view, and worm as many secrets
as possible from him. When Cressley spoke of his superstition with
regard to the turret room, it immediately occurred to Wickham to
utilize the room for his destruction. Murdock proved a ready tool
in the hands of the rogues. They offered him an enormous bribe.
And then the three between them evolved the intricate and subtle
details of the crime. It was arranged that Murdock was to commit
the ghastly deed, and for this purpose he was sent down quietly to
Brent disguised as a journeyman the day before Cressley went to
the Hall. The men had thought that Cressley would prove an easy
prey, but they distrusted me from the first. Their relief was great
when they discovered that I could not accompany Cressley to the

Hall. And had he spent the first night there, the murder would have been committed; but his nervous terrors inducing him to spend the night at Brent foiled this attempt. Seeing that I was returning to Liverpool, the men now thought that they would use me for their own devices, and made up their minds to decoy me into Murdock's bedroom in order that I might see the wax figure, their object, of course, being that I should be forced to prove an alibi in case Murdock was suspected of the crime. The telegram which reached me at Prince's Hotel on my return from London was sent by one of the ruffians, who was lying in ambush at Brent. When I left Murdock's house, the wife informed Wickham that she thought from my manner I suspected something. He had already taken steps to induce the cab-driver to take me in a wrong direction, in order that I should miss my train, and it was not until he visited the stables outside the Prince's Hotel that he found that I intended to go by road. He then played his last card, when he telegraphed to the inn at Carlton to stop the horses. By Murdock's means Wickham and his confederate had the run of the rooms at the Hall ever since the arrival of Wickham from Australia, and they had rigged up the top of the old bedstead in the way I have described. There was, needless to say, a secret passage at the back of the tapestry, which was so cunningly hidden in the panelling as to baffle all ordinary means of discovery.

THE SECRET OF EMU PLAIN

It so happened that business called me to Queensland in the late October of 1894, and hearing that my old friend, Rosamund Dale, was about to be married, I determined to present myself at Jim Macdonald's station on the Barcoo District in December, in order to be present at the ceremony. I had seen a good deal of Rosamund when she was a child, and it was an old promise of mine that, if possible, I was to be one of the guests at her wedding.

I arrived at Macdonald's a week before Christmas, and when a hot wind, or sirocco, was blowing in from the west. I little thought, as I did so, that the strangest, and most terrible adventure of my life was about to take place in the Queensland bush. But so it was, and this is the story just as it happened.

I had been delayed on my journey, and on the evening of my arrival the wedding was to take place. Macdonald's property was about seven hundred and fifty square miles in extent, and was in the heart of the hills, which are the fountain-head of the countless creeks that run south, and join to form the Warrego, and eventually the Great Darling River, some four hundred miles away. It was good grazing country on the whole, but contained one enormous tract of arid sand, some forty square miles in extent, which went by the name of Emu Plain. Skirting one corner of this plain ran the coach road from Blackall to Charleville, along which ran Cobb & Co.'s coach once a fortnight. Almost in the middle of the plain stood in solitary grandeur the great Emu Rock, a grotesque, bare, perpendicular crag of limestone, rising a sheer three hundred feet from the ground.

Leaving my heavy luggage at Blackall, I had come with a valise by Cobb & Co.'s coach to the cross roads, and had then ridden over to Macdonald's house, a low wooden homestead of one storey, with a verandah running all round it. The sitting-rooms opened into the verandah. There was a garden at the back, enclosed by a fence. Macdonald met me with words of hearty welcome.

"But you are late, Bell," he exclaimed, "Rosamund has been waiting impatiently for your arrival all day. She never forgets how good you were to her when she was a child, and all alone in the old country. But let me take you to your room for a tub and brush up, for she would like to see you for a moment or two before the wedding."

Jim took me to my apartment in the left wing of the house, and half an hour later I joined Rosamund Dale on the balcony. She was a handsome dark-eyed girl, with a bright vivacious face and sparkling eyes. She had changed much in appearance since I had last seen her, as a small and somewhat awkward schoolgirl, but her affectionate heart and frank manners were still abundantly manifest. She made me seat myself in a deck chair, and began at once to talk about her bridegroom. Goodwin was the best man in the world, she loved him with all her heart and soul; she liked the life in the bush, too. Notwithstanding its loneliness there was an element of excitement about it which quite suited her nature.

As she spoke to me I noticed that she looked anxiously out, and shading her eyes with her hand I saw them travel across the paddock, and up the road.

"What is the matter, Rosamund," I said at last; "and, by the way," I added, "won't you introduce me to Mr. Goodwin?"

"He has not come yet, and I cannot understand it," replied the girl; "he ought to have been here an hour ago. His station is about thirty miles from here, just across Emu Plain."

"What a hideous piece of desolation that Emu Plain is," I answered. "I skirted it on the coach, and never saw anything so repulsive in my life."

I noticed that Rosamund shuddered, and her face turned pale.

"It is an ugly place," she said at last, "and bears a bad name."

"What do you mean by that?" I interrupted.

"You will laugh at me, Mr. Bell," was her reply, "but people say the plain is haunted. Some most extraordinary disappearances have taken place there from time to time. If Frank came across the plain there is no saying, but"—she looked me full in the face.

"I am surely frightening myself about nothing," she said. "Will you excuse me a moment? I must just go into the drawing-room and ask if there is any news of Frank."

She rose, and I followed her into the room behind the verandah. I there, for the first time, made Mrs. Macdonald's acquaintance. She was a hearty, good-natured looking woman, with eyes like Rosamund's. She seemed devotedly attached to her niece, and now went up to the girl, and kissed her affectionately.

"Your uncle has just gone off to meet Frank," she said; "they are sure to be here in a few moments."

She spoke cheerfully, but I felt certain that I noticed a veiled anxiety in her eyes.

At that moment a man crossed the room, came up to Rosamund, and held out his hand.

"How do you do, Mr. Corry?" said the girl gravely. She had beautiful dark eyes, with magnificent lashes, and I observed, as Corry spoke to her, that she lowered them, and avoided looking at him. He was a thin, tall man, with red hair, and a slight cast in one eye. His lips were thin, the thinnest I had ever seen, and their expression, joined to the cast in the eye, gave him a sinister look. He was on good terms, however, with all the guests, and had the manners of a gentleman. Rosamund returned to the verandah, and I followed her.

"Are you really nervous about anything?" I said. "Is it possible that you apprehend that an accident has happened to Goodwin?"

"How can I tell?" she answered, and now a look of agony crossed her strong face. "He ought to be here before now; he has never failed before, and on his wedding evening, too! The Plain is haunted, you know, Mr. Bell. Don't laugh at me when I say that I— I believe in the ghost of Emu Plain."

"You must tell me more," I answered. "You know," I continued with a smile, "that I am interested in ghosts."

She could not return my smile; her face grew whiter and whiter.

"Who is that man Corry?" I said, after a pause.

"Oh, never mind about him," she answered impatiently. "He has a selection about twenty miles from here, and is, I believe, an Englishman. I cannot think what is keeping Frank," she added. "Ah! thank God! I hear horses' hoofs at last."

She ran to the farther end of the verandah, and stood there, gazing up the road with the most longing, perplexed expression I had ever seen on human face. Alas! only one rider was returning, and that was Macdonald himself. He came in cheerfully, said that Frank might appear at any moment, and suggested we should all go to supper.

At that meal I noticed that Rosamund only played with her food. She was seated near Mr. Lee, the clergyman from the nearest township, who had come over to marry her. He talked to her in low tones, and she replied listlessly. It was evident that her thoughts were with her absent lover, and that she could think of nothing else. At last the miserable meal had dragged to an end, the evening passed away somehow, and the different guests retired to their rooms. By and by Macdonald and I found ourselves alone.

"Now, what is up?" I said, going up to him at once; "Jim, what is the meaning of this?"

"God only knows," was his reply; "I don't like it, Bell, and that's a fact. You noticed that big plain as you came along by the coach?"

"Emu Plain?" I replied.

Jim nodded.

"It bears an ugly reputation," he said. "There have been the most extraordinary disappearances there from time to time. The blacks say that the place is haunted by a ghost, which they call the Bunyip. Of course, I don't believe in anything of that sort; but it is a fact that you will scarcely get a black man to cross the plain after dark, and two or three of our settlers have entered that plain alone and never been heard of since. Whether the agency which causes them to disappear is ghostly or otherwise it is impossible for me to say."

"You surely do not believe in the Bunyip?" I said, with a slight laugh.

"Hush!" he answered. "The fact is this, Bell, old man; I cannot laugh over the matter. If anything has happened to Goodwin I believe he—hollo! who can this be? Lie down, boy," added Jim to Help, his big collie.

We went out into the paddock. As we did so a man rode quickly up, whom Jim recognised at once as one of the mounted police.

"What's up, Jack?" said Jim.

"A traveller riding alone from Blackall has got bushed on the ranges," was the man's reply. "I heard that Frank Goodwin had not turned up here, and it occurred to me that you ought to know at once. The man's horse, with an empty saddle, was found on your boundary fence. It is possible that he had an accident. Could you let me have Billy, your black tracker? The poor chap may be lying crippled and cannot move on some of the ranges. There is not a moment to lose."

"Good God! Then it must be Goodwin," exclaimed Jim. "We won't tell Rosamund yet. We will bring Billy and go with you at once, Jack," he continued. "You will come along, too, won't you, Bell?" he added briskly. "Anything is better than suspense. I'll get the horses up and we'll start in a moment, though we won't be able to do much before daylight."

In less than a quarter of an hour we set out. Billy, the black tracker, looked sulky, and also considerably alarmed, and Jim whispered to me that he had great difficulty in making him come at all.

"He believes in that Bunyip," he added, dropping his voice to a hoarse whisper.

Billy himself was an ill-favoured looking creature, but as a tracker he was possessed of almost superhuman powers, and was noted in all the district as one who could follow tracks of almost any kind. He had only one eye, the other having been knocked out in a scrimmage, but with that eye he could read the ground as a civilised man reads a book.

We started off slowly. Billy was presently induced to ride ahead. He sucked his pipe as if he took no interest in the affair.

"Goodwin must be somewhere on the ranges," said Macdonald emphatically. "But how he got off the track beats me, as he knows every yard of the place. There is foul play somewhere."

Just as he said the last words Billy turned in his saddle, and cocking his one eye round, said slowly:

"Baal boodgeree Emu Plain night time. Bunyip there."

"Nonsense, Billy," replied Macdonald almost angrily. "There is no such thing as the Bunyip, and you know that as well as I do."

"I see Bunyip once in Emu Plain, along rock," the black went on. "I make tracks, my word!"

Just as the day broke, our way led us out of the scrub, and the trees began to get more sparsely scattered, till we suddenly burst upon the borders of the great plain itself. A few moments afterwards Billy uttered a cry and picked up the tracks. With his one eye fixed on the ground he dismounted, and began to examine some bent grass and disturbed stones. To my unaccustomed vision the signs that guided him were absolutely invisible. It was an exhibition of instinct that no one would believe without seeing it.

On and on we went through the heat, silent and expectant; now up, now down, over ridge and gully. Suddenly Billy uttered a sharp cry, and leaping from his horse gave me the reins, and walked round and round, peering about and grunting to himself. At last, looking up, he exclaimed "Man meet someone here."

"Meet someone," cried Macdonald. "Are you sure, Billy?"

"Quite sure," was the answer. He took his tomahawk and cut a notch in one of the trees in order to mark the spot. We then remounted and rode on. In a moment Billy spoke again. "More horses! my word!" he said. "Look! "

The marks were clear enough now, even to us. In a piece of soft ground were the hoof-marks of three horses. Billy said no more, but put his horse in a canter. We followed him. About a mile farther we pulled up at the edge of the scrub. We were now close to the great Emu Rock. I noticed at once that a number of crows were wheeling round its summit.

"It is strange," said Jim, speaking in a hoarse voice, "but I never come near this great rock that I don't see the crows whirling round the top. Ay, there they go, as usual," he added, clutching my arm. "My God! whenever a man disappears there are marks of a struggle at the foot of the rock. Watch Billy now, he will know in a moment. Oh! merciful heaven! it is true then, and something has happened to Goodwin. Poor Rosamund; this will break her heart. Yes, there are the marks, Billy notices them. Now, Bell, you never had a greater mystery than this to solve. Marks at the foot of the rock, a man disappears, never found again. What does it mean, Bell? Where does he go? There must be devilry in the matter."

Billy had dismounted and was bending over the ground. Suddenly he uttered a sharp shrill cry.

"The marks! the marks!" he gasped. "Bunyip here, man here. Debil, debil take him. See! see! see!"

His intense excitement communicated itself to us. He began to run about, peering down low over the ground.

"See! see!" he repeated. "They get off here. Go this way, that way. Ah! a spur come off." His quick eye had caught the glitter. He picked up a long spur. "Yes, yes; it is as it always is: three men fight, two men go away; one man—where he go? Debil take him." He pointed to the sky, gazing up and showing his white teeth in horror.

"Nonsense, Billy!" said Macdonald, in a voice which he tried to render commonplace and assured.

I looked at him and saw that he was shaking from head to foot.

"Come away," he said to me. "Poor girl, poor Rosamund. Billy," he added abruptly, turning to the tracker, "we must pick up the tracks of these horses."

We mounted and followed the horse tracks again. We ran the tracks back to the coach road, and then lost them in the confusion of a mob of cattle that had passed during the morning.

"Well, this is a bad business," said Macdonald. "Goodwin is missing, and what took place on the plain by the rock, and how he has disappeared from the face of the earth, and who are the men who had a hand in it, are insoluble problems. It is not the first time, Bell, and that's the horror of the thing. I tell you, I don't like the business at all. It looks uncommonly like another of those queer disappearances."

"Tell me about them," I said suddenly.

He began to talk, lowering his voice to a whisper.

"A year ago a man was lost on Emu Plain; he was a young fellow, an Englishman, and the heir to a big property. He was seen to cross the plain on horseback one afternoon, and was never heard of or seen again, and there were the marks of a struggle by the great rock, just as we saw them to-day, Bell. His people have spent thousands trying to discover the mystery, but all in vain. Since then the neighbourhood of the rock has been avoided, and the horror of the plain has grown in the minds of everybody. For this disappearance was not the first, others had preceded it. From time to time, at longer or shorter intervals, a man entered that desolate plain, and never, as far as human being could tell, left it again. What does the thing portend?"

Billy kept on croaking "Bunyip! Bunyip!" At last Macdonald shouted to him that he would break his head if he said the word any more.

We returned to the station. Rosamund, with a face like death, came out to meet us.

"You must bear up, my dear," said her uncle.

"Any news?" she asked.

"Well, there are tracks of a struggle on the plain," he said, with evident reluctance, "but we cannot follow them. A mob of cattle passed up the road this morning and have confused the tracks."

"Where was the struggle?" she said in a low voice.

Macdonald avoided her eyes. She gave him a direct and piercing glance.

"Come on to the verandah, Uncle Jim, and you too, Mr. Bell, and tell me everything," said the girl. Her voice was quiet and had a strange stillness about it. We followed her without a word. She drew deck chairs forward as we entered the cool verandah, and then kneeling by my side, laid her hand on my shoulder.

"Now," she said, facing Macdonald, "tell me all. Where was the struggle?"

"Rosamund, you must bear up; it was in the old spot, at the foot of the great rock. There, my girl," he added hastily, rising as he spoke, "I don't give up hope yet. I will send off Jack immediately, and have the affair telegraphed all round the country."

He left the verandah, walking slowly. Rosamund turned to me.

"My fears are certainties," she said; "and Frank has disappeared just as the other men have disappeared; but oh, my God," she added, rising hastily to her feet, "I will find him, I will. If he is alive I will find him, and you, Mr. Bell, must help me. You have solved mysteries before, but never so great a one as this. You will help me, will you not?"

"With all my heart, my child," I answered.

"Then there is not a moment to lose, let us go at once."

"No, no, Rosamund, that would be madness," I said. "If Goodwin is alive the police will get tidings of him, and if not—" my voice fell; Rosamund looked at me intently.

"Do you think I can rest so?" she said. "If you do not want to drive me mad, something must be done immediately."

"Then what do you propose?" I asked, looking at her.

"To go back with you to the plain, to examine those marks myself, to bring my woman's wit and intuition to bear on the matter. Where man may fail to discover any cause a woman may succeed; you know I am right."

"And I would take you with me gladly if it were possible, but it is not."

"Do you think anything that is possible for a man is impossible for a woman?" she said. "We can take some food with us, and start at once. We won't consult anyone. If we are quick, we can reach the rock an hour or two before sunset, and I know the whole of the ghastly place so well that we can return in the moonlight. Oh, don't oppose me," she added, "for if you do I will start alone. Anything is better than inaction."

I did not say a word. She gave me a quick, grateful glance, and left the verandah. Half-an-hour later she appeared in the paddock, equipped in a stout habit, and mounted on a splendid black horse; she led another by the bridle for me. We started off at once, and reached the great rock by daylight. The sweltering sun beat down upon our heads, and the arid sand rose in clouds around us, but Rosamund neither faltered nor complained—a spirit burned within her which no obstacle could daunt. There were the marks of the struggle plainly visible. Rosamund knelt on the ground and examined them with as close and keen an eye as even Billy the black tracker himself. We walked round and round the rock, the crows whirled in circles over our heads, making hideous noises as they did so. But, search as we would, we could find no clue beyond the very manifest one, that where three had fought and struggled only two had gone away. What—what in the name of heaven had become of the third?

Before sunset Rosamund put her hand in mine. "Take me home," she said faintly. I did so. We neither of us spoke on that desolate return journey.

Again the next day we visited the rock, and made a careful search, and the next day and the next, and meanwhile the country rang with the disappearance of Frank Goodwin, and with news of Rosamund's grief. But no clue could we obtain anywhere. We could not get the faintest tidings of the missing man. That it was Goodwin's horse which was found by the boundary fence was beyond doubt. He had started from his station in good time on that fatal morning, and in the best of health and spirits, but from that moment he had never been seen.

I stayed with the Macdonalds for over a fortnight, and then, loth as I was to leave Rosamund in her trouble, I had to take my departure, owing to some pressing business in Brisbane, but I promised to return again as soon as I could. My plan was to ride for my first stage to Corry's selection. Billy would come with me, and bring back the horse I was riding. I would then wait for the coach to pick me up.

I arrived at Corry's in good time, sent Billy back with my horse, and as there were still some hours before Cobb's coach would pass it suddenly occurred to me that I would go once again to the Emu Rock, and exert every faculty I possessed to discover the mystery. Corry and the two friends who lived with him, Englishmen of much his own build and make, were out. I told Corry's black servant that I was going to try and bag a plain turkey, and borrowed one of his guns for the purpose.

In about half an hour I reached the rock. The sun was already dipping low over the hills. Across the summit of the rock, crows and eagle-hawks wheeled to and fro. I walked round and round it in despair. I longed to tear its ghastly secret out of the silent rock. What strange scene had it not, in all probability, recently witnessed?

By-and-by I sat down at the base of the rock, and watched the shadow creeping across the plain as the sun sank lower and lower. I was just making up my mind to return to Corry's when suddenly, within a few yards of me, I saw something drop on the sand. It made no noise, but as it fell it caught my eye. Wondering vaguely what it might be I got up, and sauntered across to the place. I saw something on the ground, an odd-looking thing. I bent down to see what it was. As I did so my heart stood still. I was looking at a human finger. The flesh was nearly all picked from the bone. I took it in my hand and gazed at it—my pulses were throbbing, and a deadly fear seized me. Where had it come from? What did it mean? Then in an instant a wild thought struck me. I looked up. Still flying to and fro noisily were the crows and hawks. Could one of them have dropped the finger? Was the body of Frank Goodwin at the top of the Emu Rock? The idea was monstrous, and yet there was the finger, and the crows wheeling round and round above me. But how could I prove my ghastly suspicion? By no earthly means would it be possible to scale three hundred feet of perpendicular rock. If the body of poor Goodwin was there, how in the name of all that was mysterious had it been put there? One thing, at least, was certain, I must go back at once to Macdonald's station and report the horrible discovery I had made, and arrange for an investigation of the summit of the rock to take place immediately.

The sirocco was still blowing hard, and great eddies of sand were circling in the air. A sand-storm was evidently coming on, and there was nothing for me to do but to lie down and bury my face in the ground until it passed by. I did so, my pulses throbbing, the most nameless fear and depression stealing over me. The storm grew greater, it was upon me. I kept my eyes shut, and my face buried. All of a sudden, from what quarter I knew not, there came a dizzy pain; lights danced before my eyes. I seemed to sink into nothingness, my terrors were lifted from me, I was enshadowed in an impregnable darkness, and remembered no more.

When I came to myself I was lying on my back, and gazing up at the stars. Everything around me was silent as the grave, except the noise of the wind through the scrub which, curiously enough, now sounded far below me. I was lying on hard rock, and every bone in my body ached. I managed to turn myself slowly round, and then gazed about me. Where in the name of heaven was I? I saw that I was lying in a sort of basin of rock, the edge of which was some ten feet above me, but what was this dark mass lying a little to my left? I managed to crawl towards it. Great Heavens! it was a human body. The moment I saw it memory returned. I knew what my last conscious thoughts had been. I was in the midst of a sand-storm at the foot of the great Emu Rock. Darkness, joined to heavy pain, had overtaken me. When I came to myself I was at the top of the Emu Rock, and the body beside me was, doubtless, that of Frank Goodwin. By what supernatural agency had I been transported here? For a moment my brain reeled, and I thought that I must be the victim of some hideous nightmare.

The moon was riding high in the heavens; the sand-storm had completely passed; the stars were bright. In this subdued light I could see every object around me almost as vividly as if it were day. I gazed once again at the body of the man by my side. Suddenly my heart leapt with fresh fear, and I raised myself on my elbow. I thought I saw the body stir. Could it be still alive? No. Yet, as if poised above the shoulder, something was moving—a black, smooth object, which swayed gently to and fro with a horrible and perfect regularity. The silence was suddenly broken by a long low hiss, and I now perceived that the coils of an enormous snake heaved and rolled, as the loathsome creature slowly unwound itself, and glided noiselessly up the side of the rock. Drops of sweat broke out upon my forehead, and for fully an hour I lay still, literally paralysed with fear. Then the mad courage of desperation seized me, and with a reckless disregard of danger from the reptile I sprang back to the edge of the rock; but as I did so I knew all the time that a pair of glittering eyes was fixed upon me. Never for a moment did they blink, or withdraw their gaze. Single-handed and unarmed, in a prison from which escape was impossible, I was face to face with this deadly reptile. For all I knew there might be many others close beside me among the rocks.

The dawn began slowly to break. The light grew stronger every moment, as I crouched on one side of my prison, tense and motionless. I knew that if I stirred, the reptile would spring upon me. It was coiled up now on the rock exactly opposite the spot where the body of Frank Goodwin lay. Once I ventured to turn my eyes and look round. Three hundred feet below stretched the plain. Yes, escape was impossible. Now I had to face either a quick death from the bite of this huge brown snake, or a lingering death from thirst and starvation. Just for a moment I nearly yielded to a sudden impulse that assailed me, to take one step back over the edge of the basin and end my sufferings instantaneously. But, sick and faint as I still was, I determined to have one last fight before I destroyed myself. Cautiously, and still keeping my eyes upon the brute, I loosened a large flat stone, weighing nearly a couple of pounds; and; gently and slowly—for all the while those eyes, which never blinked, were fixed upon me—I unfastened my leather belt and made a loop with one end through the buckle. Then slipping in the stone, I drew the strap tightly round the stone. Here was an improvised weapon, a good one if I chanced to have the first blow. Wrapping the end of the belt twice round my hand, I crept slowly forward, across the body of the dead man. As I did so, the great snake moved to and fro, and, opening its jaws, hissed at me in fury. I knew now that in a moment he would spring. I held out my hand, keeping the strap with the stone at the end well behind me, and then with all my force swung it round over my shoulder at the brute. At the same instant, with incredible swiftness, it struck out sideways at me. The huge stone met it halfway, and it fell, with its back broken, at my feet, hissing and wriggling in hideous contortions. I sprang back and, once more swinging round the stone with all my force, crushed its head against the rock. In another moment I had flung it over, and was watching its great body whirling down through the air to the plain below.

This immediate danger passed, I now began as coolly as I could to calculate my own chances. It was impossible to say when the news of my disappearance might reach Jim Macdonald's station. Perhaps not for weeks. Meanwhile, what was to become of me? If there were no more brown snakes lurking between the crevices of the rock, I must, at best, slowly die from thirst and starvation. Surely by superhuman agency had I been transported to this giddy eminence. But escape was absolutely impossible. Poor Rosamund! I had at last succeeded in my quest, and Goodwin's mangled body lay close to me. Was I to share a similar fate?

As the hopelessness of the situation came upon me I trembled. The sun was now well up, and I knew that my sufferings from heat and thirst were all too soon to begin. I removed my shirt, and tearing it into strips fastened them together and then attached the free end to a projection of rock. I then flung the body of poor Goodwin on to the plain below. As I did so the grim idea of ending my sufferings by suicide recurred to me once more. If no help came I would, when my pains became intolerable, fling myself also from the dizzy height. I sat down on a huge stone and looked out towards the coach road. The hours dragged wearily on, but no sign of human life did I see.

The blazing sun beat mercilessly upon my head, and by midday the pangs of thirst had almost arisen to torture, and hunger also now assailed me. I was faint and giddy too, and discovered that I was suffering from a severe blow on the head. Doubtless I had received this blow at the foot of the rock; it had rendered me unconscious, and the mysterious agency which had lifted me to the height above was then brought into requisition. Were they indeed ghostly hands which had dealt me this blow? Was the Bunyip a real devil? Was Emu Plain haunted by a horror which admitted of no solution?

From time to time I shouted insanely, in order to keep off the eagle-hawks and crows which swooped down and wheeled round me. More than once I rose and peered down over the edge of my awful prison. There was not the slightest ledge or projection from the smooth sides for more than a hundred feet. Escape was out of the question.

My weakness was increasing hour by hour, and I resolved that if relief did not come before the sun set to-morrow, I would take that desperate leap and end my sufferings. I dared not sleep lest I might miss the frail chance of anyone coming, and the whole long night I paced around, shouting at intervals, though my voice came hoarse and thick from my parched lips. As morning broke once more I was utterly exhausted, and lay down, now half delirious from raging fever. My head felt as if it would burst, and the great rock seemed to reel and totter beneath me. The hours went by I know not how; time seemed nowhere; reality had merged into a ghostly phantasmagoria, hunger and thirst grew greater and greater. Insensibly, and scarcely knowing why I did it, I crept to the edge of that terrible cup in the rock. I could stand my tortures no longer. Instantaneous death should end my sufferings. I gazed round with haggard eyes for my last look at earth. Suddenly a shrill shout rent the air. I reeled back and clung to the corner of the rock for support. Once again came the noise. I heard my name, followed immediately by the report of a gun. The next instant I saw lying across the cup of rock close beside me a thin piece of cord.

"Catch it and haul in," I heard in a drawling voice as through a telephone from below.

I leapt up, hope had returned. My delirium fell from me like a mantle. For the time I was myself once more. I obeyed the words from below, and began frantically to haul in the rope. Coil after coil came up thicker and thicker till presently I held in my hands a stout rope. I now mustered all my remaining strength and fastened the rope tightly round the neck of a piece of solid rock. After doing this I remembered nothing more.

They told me afterwards, long weeks afterwards, when my fever had left me, and weak as a child I submitted to Rosamund's ministrations—they told me then, in my room at Jim Macdonald's station, what had really occurred.

Rosamund had dreamt the strangest dream of her life. She had gone through overmastering terror; horror beyond description had visited her. She had dreamt that I was on the top of the Emu Rock, and insisted on going there, accompanied by Jim and Billy, the black tracker. At the base of this mighty rock evidence of the most terrible character met her eyes, but, brave girl that she was, she turned her attention to the rescue of the living. A cord was sent up to my dizzy eminence by means of a rocket gun, and when I had fastened the rope to the rock Billy himself had come up and brought me down.

Thus I was saved from the very jaws of death. But what the mystery was, and how Frank Goodwin's body had been hauled up to the top of the Emu Rock, and how I myself had got there, are insoluble mysteries. I have unearthed more than one ghost in my day, but the great Bunyip of Emu Plain has baffled my ingenuity. He has won in the fight, and I bow my head in silence, owning that he, in his unfathomable mystery, is stronger than I.

[This story was published in *Cassell's Magazine*, and readers were given opportunity to submit their own answers to the mystery. In a following issue, the authors then provided their own solution, which follows here.]

Before leaving the old country for Australia, Corry, who was a clever mechanician, had been engaged for a long time in investigating the possible uses of kites for military operations, and had made a large number of very interesting experiments as to their lifting power. He found (and his results corresponded with those of other investigators) that in a fairly strong wind one square foot of kite surface would raise half a pound. He found, also, that to obviate the inconvenience of using a large and unwieldy kite for raising heavy weights, a series of small kites attached vertically one above the other answered the purpose equally well. And by this means he succeeded in raising weights up to 200 lb. by attaching them to the ground-rope about six feet from the lowest of the kites and employing a horse to draw the rope.

By means of a slip-rope arrangement an enormous explosive charge could be raised and dropped over an enemy's fortification with considerable accuracy, three kites, each ten feet square, raising eleven stone.

Hereditarily tainted with criminal instincts, coupled with a fantastic imagination, the peculiar construction of the Emu Rock suggested to him that by means of kites the body of a man could be raised and deposited upon the top where it could never by any possibility be discovered. An opportunity for practically putting this diabolical scheme to the test soon occurred. So long as the sirocco was blowing, the feat was comparatively easy. The manner in which John Bell became one of his victims is already known.

Coachwhip Publications

CoachwhipBooks.com

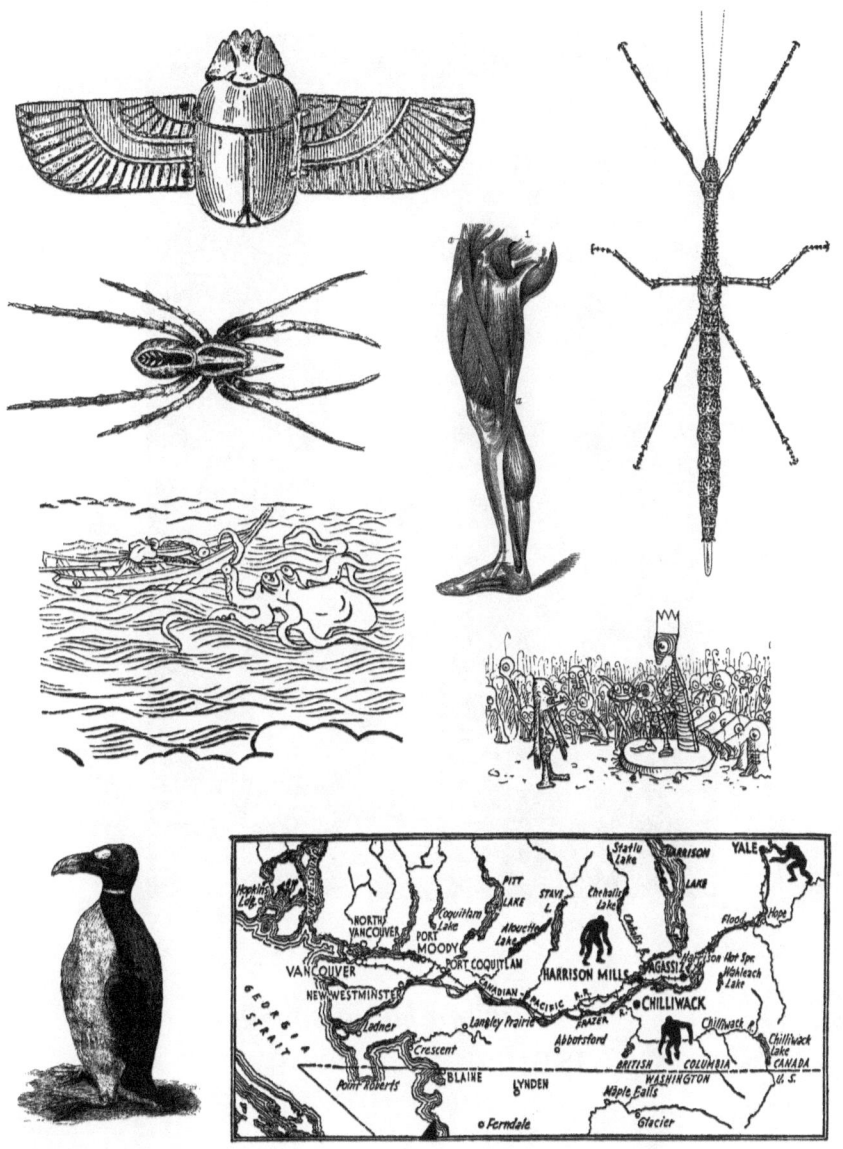

Ancient Haunts
ISBN 1-61646-005-9

THE
SPECULATIVE
CONAN DOYLE

TALES OF TERROR, FANTASY,
AND SCIENCE FICTION BY
SIR ARTHUR CONAN DOYLE

The Speculative Conan Doyle
ISBN 1-61646-024-5

John Silence: The Complete Adventures
ISBN 1-930585-90-X

www.ingramcontent.com/pod-product-compliance
Lightning Source LLC
Chambersburg PA
CBHW030557020726
47494CB00005B/1648